Immortal predators and misunderstood monsters, the entities featured in these twenty-five stories represent humanity's fears of the bestial nature within and of what lies beyond death. Intrigued by the unknown, these visionary storytellers have cast a light into the shadows and brought these fears to life. From Gothic European villages of centuries past to the American suburbs of modern times, Vampires, Zombies, Werewolves, and Ghosts have always come out after dark to frighten—or enlighten.

Barbara H. Solomon is a professor of English and women's studies at Iona College. Her academic interests include twentieth-century and contemporary American and non-Western fiction. Among the anthologies she's edited are *The Awakening and Selected Stories of Kate Chopin*, *Other Voices, Other Vistas*, *Herland and Selected Stories of Charlotte Perkins Gilman*, *The Haves and Have-Nots*, and *Passages: 24 Modern Indian Stories*.

Eileen Panetta is an associate professor of English at Iona College. Her teaching focuses on the modern British novel, the American short story, and young adult literature. With Barbara Solomon she is the editor of *Passages*, *Once Upon a Childhood*, and *Miss Lulu Bett and Selected Stories of Zona Gale*.

VAMPIRES, ZOMBIES, WEREWOLVES, AND GHOSTS

25 Classic Stories of the Supernatural

Edited and with an Introduction by
Barbara H. Solomon and Eileen Panetta

SIGNET CLASSICS

SIGNET CLASSICS
Published by New American Library, a division of
Penguin Group (USA) Inc., 375 Hudson Street,
New York, New York 10014, USA
Penguin Group (Canada), 90 Eglinton Avenue East, Suite 700, Toronto,
Ontario M4P 2Y3, Canada (a division of Pearson Penguin Canada Inc.)
Penguin Books Ltd., 80 Strand, London WC2R 0RL, England
Penguin Ireland, 25 St. Stephen's Green, Dublin 2,
Ireland (a division of Penguin Books Ltd.)
Penguin Group (Australia), 250 Camberwell Road, Camberwell, Victoria 3124,
Australia (a division of Pearson Australia Group Pty. Ltd.)
Penguin Books India Pvt. Ltd., 11 Community Centre, Panchsheel Park,
New Delhi - 110 017, India
Penguin Group (NZ), 67 Apollo Drive, Rosedale, Auckland 0632,
New Zealand (a division of Pearson New Zealand Ltd.)
Penguin Books (South Africa) (Pty.) Ltd., 24 Sturdee Avenue,
Rosebank, Johannesburg 2196, South Africa

Penguin Books Ltd., Registered Offices:
80 Strand, London WC2R 0RL, England

Published by Signet Classics, an imprint of New American Library,
a division of Penguin Group (USA) Inc.

First Signet Classics Printing, September 2011
10 9 8 7 6 5 4 3 2 1

For our daughters:

Jennifer and Nancy

and

Claire and Jane

Acknowledgments

We wish to express our continuing gratitude to Tracy Bernstein, our editor at NAL, for her enthusiastic support and helpful guidance with this project; to Florence B. Eichin of Penguin's Permissions Department for her valuable aid in locating authors and literary agents; and to Dorothy Lumley of the Dorian Literary Agency of Torquay, England.

At Iona College, a great deal of assistance was provided by Edward L. Helmrich of Ryan Library's Interlibrary Loan Program as well as by the Department of English student assistants Shannon Donlon, Emily E. Ramos, and Emily Morris.

Contents

Introduction

The infamous Capuchin Catacombs are located beneath a quite ordinary convent church in Palermo, Italy. Wandering around the catacombs, the visitor is confronted with a sad overreaching into the realm of the "undead." In vaulted chamber after chamber, the walls are hung with as many as eight thousand decomposing and skeletal remains of mostly eighteenth- and nineteenth-century citizens of the area. Various groups are "hung" together: monks, priests, professionals, virgins, children. Others lie in coffins open at the side for viewing. These individuals often left instructions regarding their final outfits, even that they be redressed after a period of time in fresh clothes. Much of the clothing has survived; alas, the human flesh, the focus of the monks' perhaps overrated embalming skills, has fared much less well. The hoped-for preservation of the body has not been realized and, with the exception of an almost completely preserved two-year-old from the 1920s, the overall effect is a gruesome study in the decomposition of the human body. The Catacombs have become a year-round Halloween setting, a place of horror, pathos and finally a sort of bemused curiosity—a place to exercise and exorcise our fear and curiosity about what death looks like. No protocols of the deathbed or funeral parlor need be observed here—one can stare to one's heart's content.

Not surprisingly, the Catacombs are Palermo's most popular tourist attraction. What is the visitor seeking? At first the sight may inspire awe, may provide a creepy thrill, but not for long. So much dressed-up death appears futile—a little silly even: so much immortal longing has come to this sad end.

For just a little while the sheer numbers can be daunting. Ambling around, one feels small in the presence of room after room of the dead. The thought occurs, too: what if these thousands of skeletal forms deeply resented being gawked at, hanging execution-style, their flesh shorn and shrunken, most with gaping holes for eyes, all teeth and clawlike hands in sharp contrast to their fashionable bonnets and cravats and priestly vestments, lost to the dignity to which they aspired? And what if they could avenge themselves on our tourist curiosity? We have, after all, what they could not manage to hold on to: life. But that chill quickly passes. They are so very dead, empty sad bodies defying the imagination to revivify them. The spark is out. From this place of bones, terror and transcendence have vanished together.

As if to compensate for such emptiness, we have to have monsters. We need them to reanimate the shadow realms where our deepest fears and hopes are intermingled. The imagination expresses its terrors and uneasiness and its fascination with the mysteries of the borderland where life and death converge, in listening for the rap at the window, the howl in the dark, the movement in the grave mound, any stirring of the return, the breaking of the bonds that separate our mortal realm from some dreaded—or hoped-for—elsewhere.

The horror figures encountered in the pages of this anthology—vampires, zombies, werewolves, ghosts, and some who won't lie still in any precise classification—have some interesting and overlapping characteristics. For example, modern accounts of vampires, werewolves, and zombies almost always involve the biting of the innocent, which infects these victims and draws them into the realm of the unholy. Ghosts, traditionally, have not been interested in this active infection of the living, except perhaps with such slower-acting toxins as fear and remorse. Werewolves require a silver bullet, vampires a stake through the heart, and zombies the separation of head from body or destruction of the brain to be stopped, but ghosts must frequently be brought to rest by subtler, more individual means. They must be *appeased.*

On the other hand, ghosts, vampires, and zombies all belong to the ranks of the "undead." That term, originally used by Bram Stoker to designate vampires, is now even more readily associated with zombies, who burst out of their apparently ill-fitting resting places to stagger about in packs, bashing down the equally inadequate hiding places of the living in search of flesh to devour. Vampires, from their earliest literary representation, have generally been subtle, seductive creatures, with a sleek appearance. They have presented themselves as swift, agile, plan-ahead types, calculating in their approach to their prey. Ghosts are often disembodied spirits—the word "ghost" is, of course, a long-standing synonym for "spirit"—while zombies are (much more dreadfully, if one has a preference for spirit over matter) the opposite; they are "disenspirited" bodies, unhooked from what might make them sentimental or nostalgic or even marginally reasonable. Most often they are without name or trace of former identity.

As monsters go, vampires have a decided stylistic edge. Associated with an urban Gothic style, they are nocturnal, dangerously alluring, carefully costumed, anguished, and tragically yet enticingly cut off from daylight reality. They may represent a range of things from the intoxicating, glittering underside of life to the empty craving of the addict. So they appeal to us as fascinating and forlorn.

But it isn't all "night on the town" being a vampire. As a character in the 1979 film *Love at First Bite* sums it up: "Happy? How would you like to dine on nothing but a warm liquid-protein diet while all around you, people are eating lamb chops, potato chips, Mallomars . . . Chivas Regal on the rocks with a twist?"*

We know the type: comes from Transylvania, sleeps all day in a coffin in a crypt (if available), hates garlic, holy water, and crosses, really hates sunlight, has sleek hair, elegant evening dress with a cape, no use for a mirror, is a smooth talker, prefers young females, flashes concealed fangs at the unsuspecting, feeds on fresh blood, leaves two holes in the neck; bite is transformative though sometimes reversible; can be killed with a wooden stake through the heart; beheading and burning to a crisp are also helpful.

*Robert Arp, "Damned if You Do, Damned if You Don't" in *Zombies, Vampires, and Philosophy* (Chicago: Open Court Press, 2010), 146–47.

One or two of these tropes of the trade are enough to signal the condition, especially with appropriate music and atmospheric lighting.

It's all become so familiar and pedestrian; this is the stuff of Muppetry (the long-abandoned Count von Count puppet) and uninspired Halloween costumes. It should have passed into trivia. But we are, after all, talking about the undead.

Vampires have the purest literary pedigree among the monsters represented here, and their evolution through the nineteenth century is familiar territory. The famous contest among the guests at the Villa Diodati on Lake Geneva, in which Lord Byron invited each of his guests to write a ghost story, produced two of the most enduring myths of the past two centuries, Mary Shelley's *Frankenstein* and *The Vampyre*, which eventually came to be credited to John Polidori, and not to Byron himself, to whom Polidori was physician. The vampire of the tale, a long short story really, is called Lord Ruthven, and he is imperious, ruthless, fatal to women and intimidating to the men who should protect them—generally acknowledged to be a fawning and resentful representation of Byron on Polidori's part. While perhaps short on literary merit, *The Vampyre* consolidated the modern fascination with that dangerous type, the Byronic hero.

Varney the Vampire by James Malcolm Rymer followed in 1847, adding fangs and the requisite holes in the neck to the legend, as well as the notion that the vampire is in reality an afflicted individual who hates what he has become. Varney was the first and probably last vampire to end it all by jumping into a volcano.

The Irish ghost story writer Joseph Sheridan Le Fanu added the most far-reaching complexity to the portrait of the vampire that began to emerge. His 1871 *Carmilla* not only established the female vampire but added the elements of mutual attraction and even fierce tenderness. At the end, the rescued innocent heroine acknowledges a longing for her dangerous companion. And the confusion and allure of forbidden love, rather than a feeling of narrow escape, is what lingers in the imagination. Carmilla herself undoubtedly is something of a spiritual sister to the later Lucy Westenra in *Dracula*. (Roger Vadim's 1961 *Blood and Roses*, a film version of *Carmilla*, will belatedly exploit the lesbian connection.)

Bram Stoker's *Dracula* (1897) is the culmination of these earlier works, which Stoker is thought to have studied. Le Fanu was Stoker's editor for a brief period. Count Dracula, the paradigm of vampire representations, is given the fullest, most recognizable treatment in the novel, and the Transylvanian hideaway, the cape and evening dress, the transit to England in a coffin, the dog and bat avatars all begin here. Garlic is effective against the undead, and a stake through the heart and beheading are the methods of choice for destruction. Standard characters are introduced: the female victims Lucy, who becomes a vampire, and Mina, rescued in the nick of time, and the somewhat ineffectual male protectors, eventually galvanized by Professor Van Helsing.

But Stoker's undead dead is unequivocally evil, suave and ingratiating though he be, without some of the complicating ambiguity of the earlier incarnations. The compelling attractiveness, the remorsefulness and the ability to evoke erotic responses become the stuff of later reinventions of the vampire figure.

The first significant silent film version, the brilliant work of F. W. Murnau, *Nosferatu* (1922) was loosely based on Stoker's novel, but the ghoulish Nosferatu, memorably played by Max Schreck, was a far cry from Stoker's creepy but recognizably human Count. The reed-thin body, bony head, black-ringed eyes, and elongated fingers form one of the most memorable images in horror-film history. The film is the first work to introduce the element of sunlight as fatal to the vampire. The final scene, in which Nosferatu is unable to release the yielded body of the heroine and remains too long into the dawn, is still capable of creating erotic unease.

Undoubtedly, the strongest confirmation of Bram Stoker's version of the myth came in the 1931 Universal Studios film version directed by Tod Browning. Despite the fact that Bela Lugosi only played the Count twice on screen, he has inhabited the role of Count Dracula for close to a century. For many he is the definitive vampire, and his heavily accented manner of speaking, not to mention his famously delivered "Good evening" and "I never drink . . . wine," is signature.

London's Hammer Studios took over the Dracula brand

in the postwar period. With Christopher Lee as Dracula—he declined to appear in the second film in the series, so it became *The Brides of Dracula*—Hammer Studios' Dracula became a more overtly sexual predator, and lots of liberties were taken with the original. But Van Helsing, the stake-wielding scientist introduced by Stoker and granddaddy of all vampire hunters, was still around to clamp things down.

Since then, if Dracula has become the stuff of camp, vampires have flooded the imagination—and the bookshelf and the TV screen and the cinema. Here are a few of the more influential representations.

Richard Matheson's novel *I Am Legend* (1954) was made into the film *The Last Man on Earth* (1964) and then twice remade as *The Omega Man* (1971) and *I Am Legend* (2007). The undead characters have vampirelike symptoms, but they behave like zombies. The novel, with its implications of viral infection and apocalypse, was in fact cited by George Romero as an inspiration for his zombie films.

Stephen King's *'Salem's Lot* (1975), a novel that never quite made it as a film but that has been the subject of two TV miniseries, brings an expanding brood of vampires to small-town America and ends in a complete conflagration, a finale we have come to expect, thanks to King.

Dark Shadows (1966–71) was rescued from cancellation and became a wildly popular Gothic soap opera with the introduction of the vampire Barnabas Collins. Collins, chained in his coffin for two hundred years, is released by a foolish character looking for treasure, and he becomes the show's driving force. Though deadly to the folks at Collingswood, he is really just a hopeless romantic yearning for his lost love, Josette. *Dark Shadows* was one of the first soaps to resort to the supernatural. Eventually, a wide variety of figures from various horror genres made an appearance in the series; time travel and parallel universes were employed, and there were borrowings by the scriptwriters from every sort of classic and contemporary horror fiction.

In *Buffy the Vampire Slayer*, both the movie and the TV series that ran from 1997 to 2003, vampires continue to be at once deadly and fatally attractive. *Buffy* spawned a host of games, songs, and comics as well as a variety of academic courses called Buffy Studies at colleges and universities. Out of these came the publication of more than twenty books and scores of articles examining the themes of the show from a wide range of disciplinary perspectives.

A major literary influence on the Gothic scene in the 1980s and '90s was Anne Rice's reimagining of the idea of the vampire. Beginning with *Interview with the Vampire* (1976) and continuing for ten more novels, Rice's characters, most famously Lestat, were depicted as struggling with a kind of existential isolation; this along with their ambivalent or tragic sexuality was instrumental in casting the vampire image as a popular cultural representation of human isolation.

Stephanie Meyer's *Twilight* saga, begun in 2005, is a series of novels and films very popular with teenage readers. The series features a struggle between werewolves and vampires and treats both kinds of characters as misunderstood romantic heroes.

Along the way, we've had responsible vampires who feed without killing, blood banks for vampires, righteous versus unrighteous vampires, and vampire rights movements; moreover, issues like HIV and drug addiction have found analogies in vampirism. The latest TV vampire hit, *True Blood* (based on a series of novels by Charlaine Harris), is southern gothic with a wide-ranging cast of mythic subtypes, including werewolves, maenads, fairies, shapeshifters, and, of course, star-crossed lovers. The central axis of the plot is the effort of the vampire community to "come out of the coffin" and go mainstream—an effort made possible by the invention of a synthetic blood available in bars and convenience stores. Mainstreaming is opposed by some vampires and many humans, prominent among them an intolerant religious organization (analogies to the gay rights movement are not subtle).

There are those who think the vampire needs to be rescued from this existential earnestness and restored to its rightful and villainous place in the dark, free to run wild and dangerous. And it's not all fiction.

The Highgate Vampire is the resident vampire in Highgate Cemetery, in northern London, one of seven private cemeteries established in the Victorian period when the churchyards in the city were too full to accept more bodies.

Beginning in the late 1960s, there have been "sightings," which, despite their original very disparate descriptions, quickly settled on the presence of vampires. (This is not surprising. Anyone who has ever walked Highgate's atmospheric overgrown paths and mused on its ornate Victorian graves in various states of decay and collapse readily senses that this is a site waiting for an urban ghoul.) The manic vampire hunting that followed coincided with the decade's increasing flirtation with the Gothic and the occult. Hammer Studios was quick to use the cemetery as the backdrop for *Dracula A.D. 1972*—a film devoid of merit except for its setting. Of course the place has an older association. In Bram Stoker's *Dracula*, Lucy Westenra, who succumbs to Dracula and becomes a vampire herself, is buried there (though the cemetery is renamed Kingstead by Stoker). So it is to be expected that a vampire would show up in Highgate, inspiring late-night chases, grave desecrations, a possible staking or two, and a vampire-hunting frenzy that is still sorting itself out in the writings of two rival vampire slayers named Manchester and Farrant. The process of enacting the rituals from stories seems to be urban legend in the making; what is the point of the lushly gloomy Victorian cemetery without a specter? Moreover, with so many graves to sleep in during the daylight hours, a vampire could hardly do better than Highgate.

As legend has always warned, vampires plan to be around for a long time.

By comparison with vampires, zombies would seem to be a hard sell. Less literary in origin than the other species of revenant, who generally return as specific individuals with names and stories to tell, the zombie does have an ancestor of a sort. Mary Shelley's *Frankenstein* monster is not technically a zombie but is considered a forerunner. Shelley's creature is a revivified collection of dead body parts, but it possesses superior intelligence, considerable eloquence, and arguably greater moral awareness than its creator, who abandons it in disgust at the very moment of its creation. The creature craves human companionship and is murderous only in proportion to its being deprived of that desired object. In James Whale's 1931 film, Boris Karloff's creature physically resembles the modern zombie with its stiff gait, grunting speech, and hooded eyes. Yet like its literary ancestor it is more sinned against than sinning.

Your more typical zombie is not looking for love, only for flesh to feed upon. Modern zombies are thought to have arisen in response to three types of stimuli: sorcery (black magic), scientific experiment, and, more recently, atomic or biological accident.

William Seabrook's *The Magic Island,* a 1929 self-described travelogue set in American-occupied Haiti, was one of the earliest representations of the zombie. In it, former slaves are regenerated by supernatural means, specifically voodoo ritual. Though only one chapter dealt with zombies, the book appeared during the monster craze and had wide-ranging influence. Seabrook attempted a precise definition of the Haitian zombie as he understood it:

> It seemed that while the zombie came from the grave, it was neither a ghost, nor yet a person who had been raised like Lazarus from the dead. The zombie, they say, is a soulless human corpse, still dead, but taken from the grave and endowed by sorcery with a mechanical semblance of life—it is a dead body which is made to walk and act and move as if it were alive. People who have the power to do this go to a fresh grave, dig up the body before it has had time to rot, galvanize it into movement, and then make of it a servant or slave, occasionally for the commission of some crime, more often simply as a drudge around the habitation or the farm, setting it dull heavy tasks, and beating it like a dumb beast if it slackens.*

Resurrected from the dead to work in the sugar cane plantations, these zombies represent colonial exploitation of a racial underclass. Their role as horror creatures is very much underplayed. Here the zombie's distinguishing characteristic—its mindlessness—is an aspect of its helplessness and its vulnerability to manipulation by self-serving

*William Seabrook, *The Magic Island* (New York: Harcourt, Brace and Co., Inc., 1929), Part II, Chapter 2, "... Dead Men Working in the Cane Fields," 93.

forces. A film version of the book played a major role in shaping the physical image of the zombie.

White Zombie (1932) and *I Walked with a Zombie* (1943) confirmed this identification with voodoo practices; both films feature the transformation of a white woman into a zombie by black magic. Both films also continue the implicitly racist use of the zombie figure, associating it with historical slavery in the Caribbean. Decades later, even after mainstream zombie film and literature had taken a different direction, an ethnobotanist named Wade Davis wrote *The Serpent and the Rainbow* (1987), in which he claimed to have found a "scientific" connection between Haitian zombies and the administration of a toxic drug called tetrodotoxin. While his science was quickly discredited, the association of zombies with scientific experiment has persisted, thanks, in part, to the book's rapid repackaging as a horror film.

However, it has been the films of George Romero that have made the deepest mark on the rehabilitation of this seemingly unsympathetic figure. *Night of the Living Dead* (1968), *Dawn of the Dead* (1978), *Day of the Dead* (1985), *Land of the Dead* (2005), *Diary of the Dead* (2007), and *Survival of the Dead* (2010), along with their various remakes, portray a progressively darkening picture of human civilization and perhaps even a gradual shift in sympathy toward zombie "culture." The films are also the source of the familiar images of shambling hordes of nameless, flesh-eating undead assailing the farmhouses and shopping malls and bunkers—where civilized humans make a last stand.

Today zombies seem to be getting faster, smarter, and more organized. The work of Max Brooks, such as *Zombie Survival Guide* (2003) and *World War Z* (2006), has explored the apocalyptic connotations as well as the spread of zombieism by infection rather than as the result of voodoo or other forms of sorcery. Using a documentary style, Brooks takes aim at the widespread fearfulness on the planet, the bumbling and corruption involved in government attempts to counter disasters, and the global nature of the human predicament.

Milestones in the zombie craze must include Michael Jackson's music video "Thriller"(1983), which features the morphing of shy "boyfriend" Michael into a hugely appealing zombie version of himself. He is joined by a group of the undead from the local graveyard, who twirl, stagger, and slide with a finesse any self-respecting zombie might long to emulate.

Another notable literary take is 2009's *Pride and Prejudice and Zombies* by Jane Austen and Seth Grahame-Smith, a comic attempt to explore the violence seething below the surface of a tightly reined-in society (Regency England) and the concomitant violence, verbal and otherwise, used to combat it. Elizabeth Bennet becomes a particularly accomplished zombie destroyer. Not surprisingly this talent is the chief component in Mr. Darcy's attraction to her, and their side-by-side battles are a wry form of foreplay. Other invasions of the literary canon by zombies are anticipated.

What is the perennial fascination with this rather blank monster, who hangs around in groups and says almost nothing? For starters, the zombie is an avenging *corpse*, and thus a trope for our fear of and curiosity about death. In addition, zombie flesh is available to take the form of all downtrodden, marginalized, exploited subjects, who may at any time enact a faceless march against their oppressors (and maybe even their supporters—remember, they're mindless), threatening the civilized order within which we desperately if futilely take refuge.

Clive Barker, filmmaker and scriptwriter, sums up the warring emotions of sympathy and fear:

> Zombies are the liberal nightmare. Here you have the masses, whom you would love to love, appearing at your front door with their faces falling off; and you're trying to be as humane as you possibly can, but they are, after all, eating the cat. And the fear of mass activity, of mindlessness on a national scale, underlies my fear of zombies.*

The term werewolf literally means "wolf-man." Except in certain rare versions of the myth (the 1943 film *Frankenstein Meets the Wolf Man* is one), werewolves are not the "undead." Instead, they seem a response to other kinds of

*Quoted in John Scipp and Craig Spector, eds., "Introduction" to *Book of the Dead* (New York: Bantam Books, 1989), 7.

anxiety—about the instability of what we call human nature and the animism of the natural world.

References to werewolves in Western culture go back at least as far as Patronius and Ovid. The wolf makes regular, villainous appearances in the tales of Aesop, Grimm, and Perrault. Anxiety about wolves is encoded in the earliest stories we tell our children: "The Three Little Pigs," "Peter and the Wolf," "The Boy Who Cried Wolf," "Little Red Riding Hood," "The Wolf and the Seven Kids." Wolf anxiety understandably derived from a well-deserved fear of forests and other wild places, especially in the northern hemisphere, on the part of those who lived adjacent to such places or whose business took them into the woods. Wolves, usually the dominant predator in their habitats, show up most often in the myths and folk beliefs of human cultures who share habitats with them. Warriors who covered themselves in animal hides (typically bear hides, though wolf pelts were also used) were called berserkers, and their ferocious, seemingly uncontrolled fighting led to the English word "berserk." Wolves appear as the consorts of witches and as potent figures in animal rituals. Britain, which exterminated wolves in the early modern period, has fewer tales to tell, and these are more likely to be stories of hellhounds.

Werewolves are also called lycanthropes, and "lycanthropy" means the transformation of human into wolf, but it is also a clinical term for a mental illness in which the patient believes he has been turned into an animal of some kind. Undoubtedly the fact that there are documented cases of lycanthropy has served to weaken the boundary between science and superstition for some. But it is probably historical events such as the eighteenth-century "beast of Gevaudan" attacks in southwestern France that helped to solidify the myth of the preternatural werewolf. In a short time, almost one hundred people were killed, mostly women and children, and the elusive beast attained mythic size and ferocity, until a smaller animal or perhaps a number of ordinary animals were killed and wolf attacks resumed their normal rate of frequency.

Early legend attributed lycanthropy to a variety of causes: a pact with the devil, an accident of birth, a curse put upon the victim. Only recently has the most recognizable method of contagion, the bite of a werewolf, become dominant. Other elements like the full moon and the silver bullet are also recent additions to the myth.

Though there were werewolf films that preceded it, *The Wolf Man* (1941) with Lon Chaney Jr. gave this creature a Hollywood face, the equivalent of Boris Karloff's Frankenstein monster and Bela Lugosi's Dracula. Perhaps because it had no single literary source, the film was able to carve the fable somewhat definitively into the imagination of popular culture. It enshrined the sympathetic, victimized wolfman, who hates and fears his own condition and who, in the end, seeks death to escape the danger of harming the woman he loves. The film also showcased the transformation process—roughly six hours were required to apply Chaney's makeup—so that the fearsome look of the human as his lycanthropy comes over him became the dominant motif of werewolf films.

The werewolf speaks to our fear of "the animal inside us," that uncivilized remnant that we try to suppress, so memorably metaphorized in Robert Louis Stevenson's *Dr. Jekyll and Mr. Hyde*. In many cases that inner animal is specifically identified with unbridled sexuality; in *The Company of Wolves* (1979), Angela Carter, revisiting the fairy-tale connection, has the heroine Little Red conquering the male beast by meeting him more than halfway and dominating him sexually.

Ultimately, the werewolf evokes mixed emotions about the repressed self, capable when released of uninhibited aggression.

According to the vampire novelist Anne Rice:

> . . . the werewolf in many instances embodies a potent blending of masochistic and sadistic elements. On the one hand man is degraded as he is forced to submit to the bestial metamorphosis; on the other hand he emerges as a powerful sadistic predator who can, without regret, destroy other men. The werewolf as both victim and victimizer, wrapped in magic, may arouse emotions in us that are hard to define.*

*Charlotte F. Otten, ed., *The Literary Werewolf* (New York: Syracuse University Press, 2002), xxvii.

It is that hard-to-define emotion, call it wildness or elation, running alongside horror and fear, that is so very intriguing.

Ghosts are certainly the most amorphous and ubiquitous class of the undead; one can be sure of finding ghost stories in every culture. Earlier ghosts were most often represented as possessed of a corporeal body, attired in the clothes they wore in life, and capable of physical interactions with the living. More recent emanations tend toward the spectral and ethereal.

The existence of ghosts is associated with ancestor worship, the need to honor and appease (really reverse sides of the same impulse) the dead of one's clan and the expectation that the dead could and did interfere in the affairs of the living. Of course the hope was always to turn that interference into an advantage for one's self and a problem for one's enemies. Though ancestor worship was more commonly practiced in Asia and Africa, Western vestiges are found in such festivals as the Day of the Dead and All Souls' Day in early November.

Ghosts appear to have played a fairly limited role in Greek and Roman religion, where rationality among the Greeks and religious formalism among the Romans did not lend themselves to excessive anxiety about the supernatural. There are references to ghosts in both *The Iliad* and *The Odyssey*, but these appearances are important only as they convey information to the living. The returning dead are not objects of fear or even surprise. They are an accepted part of the natural world.

Today ghosts are most readily associated with "unfinished business," remorse, or warnings, or vengeance, unpaid debts and purloined property, or seeking release from some betrayal on their part or by another, before they can achieve a final resting place. Improper burial also lends itself to unrest. While zombies may roam, werewolves run wild, and vampires fly, ghosts are typically associated with a particular space, whether castle, house, or hollow, where they might be seen peering from windows and parapets, or glimpsed in solitary walks, accosting the living who venture near. The locale seems to afford some residual energy that animates the ghost—this is where something important happened in the individual's earthly life. But though they may look hungrily on, no flesh or blood or fur or fangs are involved. They are not biters. While they can be angry and destructive, it is relatively rare for a ghost to physically assault the living. Why then is their power so frightening?

Although the ancients may have regarded them with little alarm, ghostly appearances in later times are more likely to be experienced as transgressive and, even in their milder emanations, disturbing. The softening of the boundaries between the solidity of life and the unknowability of death can only create unease. Not that the presence is always undesirable; in Emily Brontë's *Wuthering Heights*, Heathcliff begs the dying Cathy to haunt him—but the rest of the community is not so pleased when she does.

Ghost, like all other supernatural phenomena, are captured earliest in folktales, myths, and religious traditions. In medieval religious practice, it was accepted that ghosts could be condemned to unrest as part of their punishment, but conjuring ghosts was considered a sinful practice akin to devil worship.

The most recognizable versions of the modern ghost story flourished in the Victorian and Edwardian periods and through the end of World War I (1840–1920). The genre was probably energized by the fashion of lavish funerals, ornate cemeteries, and elaborate mourning rituals, all of which favored the dramatization of the emotions surrounding death over sublimation. In conjunction with this expansion of the rituals of death, the vogue for spiritualism, necromancy, and mesmerism in the midnineteenth century created a rich medium in which the castles, monasteries, and subterranean crypts, the habitats of the Gothic ghost, gave way to the chambers and laboratories where paranormal activity could flourish.

Supernatural fiction is sometimes described as the special province of women writers, as there have been a number of highly effective and successful female practitioners in the Victorian and modern periods. But this may reflect an economic reality rather than any greater psychic susceptibility on the part of women. Ghost stories were eagerly sought by magazines, and women writers found that even a relative unknown could enter the market.

But the substantial representation of women writers and

a high demand among middle-class readers no doubt accounted for the relative domestication of the ghost story. City flats and country houses located at the end of long roads leased by thoroughly modern couples became choice locations, the ghosts having followed their readership to the world of the middle class. A solid realistic setting often worked best, pitting a stubbornly intrusive spirit against the modern skepticism of daylight and common sense.

Modern ghost stories have also turned more frequently to the haunting of the human mind. Henry James, in some of the most enduring ghostly writing of the early-modern period, focuses on the unreliable perceptions of the living, as in *The Turn of the Screw* or "The Jolly Corner," where the ghosts play a somewhat secondary role and the haunted minds of the governess or the returned exile Spencer Brydon are in the foreground.

The twentieth and twenty-first centuries have continued a kind of open-eyed interest in the paranormal, often employing a new type of professional either to mediate or to "ghost bust." In films like *The Sixth Sense* and *The Others*, the ghosts are at the center of the narrative and have a dramatic arc. Joyce Carol Oates, in a story collected here, gives James's *Turn of the Screw* a further twist, telling the story from the point of view of the ghosts of the dead servants Quint and Jessel.

Yet another variation on the ghostly worth noting is the haunting of places and even objects not by the spirits of the dead, but by another sort of indwelling spirit. Examples can be found in the fiction of Algernon Blackwood, whose specialty is the dangerous spirits who inhabit woods and forests. A common device for the horror writer M. R. James involves a scholar who unearths an ancient object and unwittingly unleashes its inner spirit, as in the famous "Oh, Whistle, and I'll Come to You, My Lad." Cabinets, clothing, mirrors and statues have had dangerous and even murderous resident spirits.

One of the best known is found in the opening of Shirley Jackson's *The Haunting of Hill House* (1959), much admired by Stephen King and Joyce Carol Oates:

> No live organism can continue for long to exist sanely under conditions of absolute reality; even larks and

> katydids are supposed, by some, to dream. Hill House, not sane, stood by itself against its hills, holding darkness within; it had stood so for eighty years and might stand for eighty more. Within, walls continued upright, bricks met neatly, floors were firm, and doors were sensibly shut; silence lay steadily against the wood and stone of Hill House, and whatever walked there walked alone.*

Freud's term "return of the repressed" has been applied to zombies, because of their relentless attack on civilization, which seeks to suppress them; the tearing and consuming of flesh is the id rampage of self-satisfaction against that which seeks to repress raw gratification in the name of progress.† In truth, all of these dark others—vampires, werewolves, ghosts, as well as zombies—are manifestations of the "returned repressed," taking their revenge on the human mind filled with dread and guilty desire.

The threatening undead continue to appear; there are frequent calls for an end to the soft side of horror. Let's kill and be killed. In spite of this, the tendency is toward the more human, more complex. We want to tame these revenants, see them as aspects of, or analogies for, our own repressed selves, to commune with them, and ultimately "mate" with them in a psychic and even physical sense. They make our world richer, more dimensioned. In taming them, we may be trying to understand and forgive ourselves.

If the shape-shifting werewolf and the others—the ranks of the undead—can continue to be imagined as analogues of our isolation, our repressed longings, and our murderous impulses, if they can be made into playfellows and foolish entertainments, then perhaps we can hold on to those echoes of other dimensions that we want desperately not to lose. Then perhaps the skeletal ladies and gentlemen of the Capuchin Catacombs won't remain forever as lifeless and

*Shirley Jackson, *The Haunting of Hill House* (New York: Penguin Books, 1959), 1. These are also the last lines of the novel.

† Simon Clark, "The Undead Martyr" in *Vampires, Zombies, and Philosophy*, 198.

empty as they seem; maybe they will yet kick up their bony heels and dance.

These stories are, in their various ways, a testament to such "immortal longings." In the words of two contemporary filmmakers, "Monsters will always provide the possibility of mystery in our mundane 'reality show' lives, hinting at a larger spiritual world; for if there are demons in our midst, there surely must be angels lurking nearby."*

May it be so.

*Guillermo del Toro and Chuck Hogan, "Why Vampires Never Die," *New York Times* op-ed, July 31, 2009.

VAMPIRES, ZOMBIES
WEREWOLVES, AND GHOSTS

Woody Allen

(1935–)

Best known as a filmmaker and actor, Allan Stewart Konigsberg was born in Brooklyn, New York. After studying at New York University and the City College of New York, he quickly became a comedy writer for popular television programs such as *The Ed Sullivan Show*, *The Tonight Show*, Sid Caesar specials, and *Candid Camera*. A successful Broadway playwright and screenwriter, he is the author of four volumes of essays, stories, and one-act plays: *Getting Even* (1971), *Without Feathers* (1975), *Side Effects* (1980), and *Mere Anarchy* (2007). Among his well-known films are *Annie Hall* (1977), *Manhattan* (1979), *Hannah and Her Sisters* (1986), *Crimes and Misdemeanors* (1989), and *Vicky Cristina Barcelona* (2008). Allen has won three Academy Awards, an O. Henry Award, Golden Globe Awards for both Best Screenplay and Best Motion Picture, a Career Golden Lion at the Venice Film Festival, and the Palme des Palmes Lifetime Achievement Award at the Cannes Festival.

Count Dracula

(1966)

Somewhere in Transylvania, Dracula the monster lies sleeping in his coffin, waiting for night to fall. As exposure to the sun's rays would surely cause him to perish, he stays protected in the satin-lined chamber bearing his family name in silver. Then the moment of darkness comes, and through some miraculous instinct the fiend emerges from the safety of his hiding place and, assuming the hideous forms of the bat or the wolf, he prowls the countryside, drinking the blood of his victims. Finally, before the first rays of his archenemy, the sun, announce a new day, he hurries back to the safety of his hidden coffin and sleeps, as the cycle begins anew.

Now he starts to stir. The fluttering of his eyelids are a response to some age-old, unexplainable instinct that the sun is nearly down and his time is near. Tonight, he is particularly hungry and as he lies there, fully awake now, in red lined Inverness cape and tails, waiting to feel with uncanny perception the precise moment of darkness before opening the lid and emerging, he decides who this evening's victims will be. The baker and his wife, he thinks to himself. Succulent, available, and unsuspecting. The thought of the unwary couple whose trust he has carefully cultivated excites his bloodlust to a fever pitch, and he can barely hold back these last seconds before climbing out of the coffin to seek his prey.

Suddenly he knows the sun is down. Like an angel of hell, he rises swiftly, and changing into a bat, flies pell-mell to the cottage of his tantalizing victims.

"Why, Count Dracula, what a nice surprise," the baker's wife says, opening the door to admit him. (He has once again assumed human form, as he enters their home, charmingly concealing his rapacious goal.)

"What brings you here so early?" the baker asks.

"Our dinner date," the Count answers. "I hope I haven't made an error. You did invite me for tonight, didn't you?"

"Yes, tonight, but that's not for seven hours."

"Pardon me?" Dracula queries, looking around the room puzzled.

"Or did you come by to watch the eclipse with us?"

"Eclipse?"

"Yes. Today's the total eclipse."

"What?"

"A few moments of darkness from noon until two minutes after. Look out the window."

"Uh-oh—I'm in big trouble."

"Eh?"

"And now if you'll excuse me . . ."

"What, Count Dracula?"

"Must be going—aha—oh, god . . ." Frantically he fumbles for the doorknob.

"Going? You just came."

"Yes—but—I think I blew it very badly . . ."

"Count Dracula, you're pale."

"Am I? I need a little fresh air. It was nice seeing you . . ."

"Come. Sit down. We'll have a drink."

"Drink? No, I must run. Er—you're stepping on my cape."

"Sure. Relax. Some wine."

"Wine? Oh no, gave it up—liver and all that, you know. And now I really must buzz off. I just remembered. I left the lights on at my castle—bills'll be enormous . . ."

"Please," the baker says, his arm around the Count in firm friendship. "You're not intruding. Don't be so polite. So you're early."

"Really, I'd like to stay but there's a meeting of old Roumanian Counts across town and I'm responsible for the cold cuts."

"Rush, rush, rush. It's a wonder you don't get a heart attack."

"Yes, right—and now—"

"I'm making Chicken Pilaf tonight," the baker's wife chimes in. "I hope you like it."

"Wonderful, wonderful," the Count says, with a smile, as he pushes her aside into some laundry. Then, opening a closet door by mistake, he walks in. "Christ, where's the goddamn front door?"

"Ach," laughs the baker's wife, "such a funny man, the Count."

"I knew you'd like that," Dracula says, forcing a chuckle. "Now get out of my way." At last he opens the front door but time has run out on him.

"Oh, look, Mama," says the baker, "the eclipse must be over. The sun is coming out again."

"Right," says Dracula, slamming the front door. "I've decided to stay. Pull down the window shades quickly—*quickly!* Let's move it!"

"What window shades?" asks the baker.

"There are none, right? Figures. You got a basement in this joint?"

"No," says the wife affably, "I'm always telling Jarslov to build one but he never listens. That's some Jarslov, my husband."

"I'm all choked up. Where's the closet?"

"You did that one already, Count Dracula. Unt Mama and I laughed at it."

"Ach—such a funny man, the Count."

"Look, I'll be in the closet. Knock at seven-thirty." And with that, the Count steps inside the closet and slams the door.

"Hee-hee—he is so funny, Jarslov."

"Oh, Count. Come out of the closet. Stop being a big silly." From inside the closet comes the muffled voice of Dracula.

"Can't—please—take my word for it. Just let me stay here. I'm fine. Really."

"Count Dracula, stop the fooling. We're already helpless with laughter."

"Can I tell you, I love this closet."

"Yes, but . . ."

"I know, I know . . . it seems strange, and yet here I am, having a ball. I was just saying to Mrs. Hess the other day, give me a good closet and I can stand in it for hours. Sweet woman, Mrs. Hess. Fat but sweet . . . Now, why don't you run along and check back with me at sunset. Oh, Ramona, la da da de da da de, Ramona . . ."

Now the Mayor and his wife, Katia, arrive. They are passing by and have decided to pay a call on their good friends, the baker and his wife.

"Hello, Jarslov. I hope Katia and I are not intruding?"

"Of course not, Mr. Mayor. Come out, Count Dracula! We have company!"

"Is the Count here?" asks the Mayor surprised.

"Yes, and you'll never guess where," says the baker's wife.

"It's so rare to see him around this early. In fact I can't ever remember seeing him around in the daytime."

"Well, he's here. Come out, Count Dracula!"

"Where is he?" Katia asks, not knowing whether to laugh or not.

"Come on out now! Let's go!" The baker's wife is getting impatient.

"He's in the closet," says the baker, apologetically.

"Really?" asks the Mayor.

"Let's go," says the baker with mock good humor as he

knocks on the closet door. "Enough is enough. The Mayor's here."

"Come on out, Dracula," His Honor shouts, "let's have a drink."

"No, go ahead. I've got some business in here."

"In the closet?"

"Yes, don't let me spoil your day. I can hear what you're saying. I'll join in if I have anything to add."

Everyone looks at one another and shrugs. Wine is poured and they all drink.

"Some eclipse today," the Mayor says, sipping from his glass.

"Yes," the baker agrees. "Incredible."

"Yeah. Thrilling," says a voice from the closet.

"What, Dracula?"

"Nothing, nothing. Let it go."

And so the time passes, until the Mayor can stand it no longer and forcing open the door to the closet, he shouts, "Come on, Dracula. I always thought you were a mature man. Stop this craziness."

The daylight streams in, causing the evil monster to shriek and slowly dissolve to a skeleton and then to dust before the eyes of the four people present. Leaning down to the pile of white ash on the closet floor, the baker's wife shouts, "Does this mean dinner's off tonight?"

E. F. Benson

(1867–1940)

Edward Frederic Benson was one of six children born into the distinguished household of Edward White Benson, who was to become the Archbishop of Canterbury. In Greece and Egypt, he embarked on a career in archaeology for several years. The immense popularity of his first novel, *Dodo* (1893), published when he was twenty-six, demonstrated that he would be well able to support himself as a writer. A master of several genres, he published horror and supernatural novels such as *The Judgment Books* (1895), *The Angel of Pain* (1905), *Across the Stream* (1919), *The Inheritor* (1930), and *Raven's Brood* (1934), as well as the Mapp and Lucia social satires (six novels and two stories), which became a highly successful television series. Among the volumes of his stories are *Caterpillars* (1912), *The Room in the Tower and Other Stories* (1912), *Visible and Invisible* (1923), *Spook Stories* (1928), and *More Spook Stories* (1934).

The Room in the Tower

(1912)

It is probable that everybody who is at all a constant dreamer has had at least one experience of an event or a sequence of circumstances which have come to his mind in sleep being subsequently realized in the material world. But, in my opinion, so far from this being a strange thing, it would be far odder if this fulfilment did not occasionally happen, since our dreams are, as a rule, concerned with people whom we know and places with which we are familiar, such as might very naturally occur in the awake and daylit world. True, these dreams are often broken into by some absurd and fantastic incident, which puts them out of court in regard to their subsequent fulfilment, but on the mere calculation of chances, it does not appear in the least unlikely that a dream imagined by anyone who dreams constantly should occasionally come true. Not long ago, for instance, I experienced such a fulfilment of a dream which seems to me in no way remarkable and to have no kind of psychical significance. The manner of it was as follows.

A certain friend of mine, living abroad, is amiable enough to write to me about once in a fortnight. Thus, when fourteen days or thereabouts have elapsed since I last heard from him, my mind, probably, either consciously or subconsciously, is expectant of a letter from him. One night last week I dreamed that as I was going upstairs to dress for dinner I heard, as I often heard, the sound of the postman's knock on my front door, and diverted my direction downstairs instead. There, among other correspondence, was a letter from him. Thereafter the fantastic entered, for on opening it I found inside the ace of diamonds, and scribbled across it in his well-known handwriting, "I am sending you this for safe custody, as you know it is running an unreasonable risk to keep aces in Italy." The next evening I was just preparing to go upstairs to dress when I heard the postman's knock, and did precisely as I had done in my dream. There, among other letters, was one from my friend. Only it did not contain the ace of diamonds. Had it done so, I should have attached more weight to the matter, which, as it stands, seems to me a perfectly ordinary coincidence. No doubt I consciously or subconsciously expected a letter from him, and this suggested to me my dream. Similarly, the fact that my friend had not written to me for a fortnight suggested to him that he should do so. But occasionally it is not so easy to find such an explanation, and for the following story I can find no explanation at all. It came out of the dark, and into the dark it has gone again.

All my life I have been a habitual dreamer: the nights are few, that is to say, when I do not find on awaking in the morning that some mental experience has been mine, and sometimes, all night long, apparently, a series of the most dazzling adventures befall me. Almost without exception these adventures are pleasant, though often merely trivial. It is of an exception that I am going to speak.

It was when I was about sixteen that a certain dream first came to me, and this is how it befell. It opened with my being set down at the door of a big red-brick house, where, I understood, I was going to stay. The servant who opened the door told me that tea was being served in the garden, and led me through a low dark-panelled hall, with a large open fireplace, on to a cheerful green lawn set round with flower beds. There were grouped about the tea-table a small party of people, but they were all strangers to me except one, who was a school-fellow called Jack Stone, clearly the son of the house, and he introduced me to his mother and father and a couple of sisters. I was, I remember, somewhat astonished to find myself here, for the boy in question was scarcely known to me, and I rather disliked what I knew of him; moreover, he had left school nearly a year before. The afternoon was very hot, and an intolerable oppression reigned. On the far side of the lawn ran a red-brick wall, with an iron gate in its center, outside which stood a walnut tree. We sat in the shadow of the house opposite a row of long windows, inside which I could see a table with cloth laid, glimmering with glass and silver. This garden front of the house was very long, and at one end of it stood a tower of three stories, which looked to me much older than the rest of the building.

Before long, Mrs. Stone, who, like the rest of the party, had sat in absolute silence, said to me, "Jack will show you your room: I have given you the room in the tower."

Quite inexplicably my heart sank at her words. I felt as if I had known that I should have the room in the tower, and that it contained something dreadful and significant. Jack instantly got up, and I understood that I had to follow him. In silence we passed through the hall, and mounted a great oak staircase with many corners, and arrived at a small landing with two doors set in it. He pushed one of these open for me to enter, and without coming in himself, closed it after me. Then I knew that my conjecture had been right: there was something awful in the room, and with the terror of nightmare growing swiftly and enveloping me, I awoke in a spasm of terror.

Now that dream or variations on it occurred to me intermittently for fifteen years. Most often it came in exactly this form, the arrival, the tea laid out on the lawn, the deadly silence succeeded by that one deadly sentence, the mounting with Jack Stone up to the room in the tower where horror dwelt, and it always came to a close in the nightmare of terror at that which was in the room, though I never saw what it was. At other times I experienced variations on this same theme. Occasionally, for instance, we would be sitting at dinner in the dining-room, into the windows of which I had looked on the first night when the dream of this house visited me, but wherever we were, there was the same silence, the same sense of dreadful oppression and foreboding. And the silence I knew would always be broken by Mrs. Stone saying to me, "Jack will show you your room: I have given you the room in the tower." Upon which (this was invariable) I had to follow him up the oak staircase with many corners, and enter the place that I dreaded more and more each time that I visited it in sleep. Or, again, I would find myself playing cards still in silence in a drawing-room lit with immense chandeliers, that gave a blinding illumination. What the game was I have no idea; what I remember, with a sense of miserable anticipation, was that soon Mrs. Stone would get up and say to me, "Jack will show you your room: I have given you the room in the tower." This drawing-room where we played cards was next to the dining-room, and, as I have said, was always brilliantly illuminated, whereas the rest of the house was full of dusk and shadows. And yet, how often, in spite of those bouquets of lights, have I not pored over the cards that were dealt me, scarcely able for some reason to see them. Their designs, too, were strange: there were no red suits, but all were black, and among them there were certain cards which were black all over. I hated and dreaded those.

As this dream continued to recur, I got to know the greater part of the house. There was a smoking-room beyond the drawing-room, at the end of a passage with a green baize door. It was always very dark there, and as often as I went there I passed somebody whom I could not see in the doorway coming out. Curious developments, too, took place in the characters that peopled the dream as might happen to living persons. Mrs. Stone, for instance, who, when I first saw her, had been black-haired, became gray, and instead of rising briskly, as she had done at first when she said, "Jack will show you your room: I have given you the room in the tower," got up very feebly, as if the strength was leaving her limbs. Jack also grew up, and became a rather ill-looking young man, with a brown moustache, while one of the sisters ceased to appear, and I understood she was married.

Then it so happened that I was not visited by this dream for six months or more, and I began to hope, in such inexplicable dread did I hold it, that it had passed away for good. But one night after this interval I again found myself being shown out onto the lawn for tea, and Mrs. Stone was not there, while the others were all dressed in black. At once I guessed the reason, and my heart leaped at the thought that perhaps this time I should not have to sleep in the room in the tower, and though we usually all sat in silence, on this occasion the sense of relief made me talk and laugh as I had never yet done. But even then matters were not altogether comfortable, for no one else spoke, but they all looked secretly at each other. And soon the foolish stream of my talk ran dry, and gradually an apprehension worse than anything I had previously known gained on me as the light slowly faded.

Suddenly a voice which I knew well broke the stillness, the voice of Mrs. Stone, saying, "Jack will show you your room: I have given you the room in the tower." It seemed to come from near the gate in the red-brick wall that bounded the lawn, and looking up, I saw that the grass outside was sown thick with gravestones. A curious greyish light shone from them, and I could read the lettering on the grave nearest me, and it was, "In evil memory of Julia Stone." And as usual Jack got up, and again I followed him through the hall and up the staircase with many corners. On this occasion it was darker than usual, and when I passed into the room in the tower I could only just see the furniture, the position of which was already familiar to me. Also there was a dreadful odor of decay in the room, and I woke screaming.

The dream, with such variations and developments as I have mentioned, went on at intervals for fifteen years. Sometimes I would dream it two or three nights in succession; once, as I have said, there was an intermission of six months, but taking a reasonable average, I should say that I dreamed it quite as often as once in a month. It had, as is plain, something of nightmare about it, since it always ended in the same appalling terror, which so far from getting less, seemed to me to gather fresh fear every time that I experienced it. There was, too, a strange and dreadful consistency about it. The characters in it, as I have mentioned, got regularly older, death and marriage visited this silent family, and I never in the dream, after Mrs. Stone had died, set eyes on her again. But it was always her voice that told me that the room in the tower was prepared for me, and whether we had tea out on the lawn, or the scene was laid in one of the rooms overlooking it, I could always see her gravestone standing just outside the iron gate. It was the same, too, with the married daughter; usually she was not present, but once or twice she returned again, in company with a man, whom I took to be her husband. He, too, like the rest of them, was always silent. But, owing to the constant repetition of the dream, I had ceased to attach, in my waking hours, any significance to it. I never met Jack Stone again during all those years, nor did I ever see a house that resembled this dark house of my dream. And then something happened.

I had been in London in this year, up till the end of July, and during the first week in August went down to stay with a friend in a house he had taken for the summer months, in the Ashdown Forest district of Sussex. I left London early, for John Clinton was to meet me at Forest Row Station, and we were going to spend the day golfing, and go to his house in the evening. He had his motor with him, and we set off, about five of the afternoon, after a thoroughly delightful day, for the drive, the distance being some ten miles. As it was still so early we did not have tea at the club house, but waited till we should get home. As we drove, the weather, which up till then had been, though hot, deliciously fresh, seemed to me to alter in quality, and become very stagnant and oppressive, and I felt that indefinable sense of ominous apprehension that I am accustomed to before thunder. John, however, did not share my views, attributing my loss of lightness to the fact that I had lost both my matches. Events proved, however, that I was right, though I do not think that the thunderstorm that broke that night was the sole cause of my depression.

Our way lay through deep high-banked lanes, and before we had gone very far I fell asleep, and was only awakened by the stopping of the motor. And with a sudden thrill, partly of fear but chiefly of curiosity, I found myself standing in the doorway of my house of dream. We went, I half wondering whether or not I was dreaming still, through a low oak-panelled hall, and out onto the lawn, where tea was laid in the shadow of the house. It was set in flower beds, a red-brick wall, with a gate in it, bounded one side, and out beyond that was a space of rough grass with a walnut tree. The façade of the house was very long, and at one end stood a three-storied tower, markedly older than the rest.

Here for the moment all resemblance to the repeated dream ceased. There was no silent and somehow terrible family, but a large assembly of exceedingly cheerful persons, all of whom were known to me. And in spite of the horror with which the dream itself had always filled me, I felt nothing of it now that the scene of it was thus reproduced before me. But I felt intensest curiosity as to what was going to happen.

Tea pursued its cheerful course, and before long Mrs. Clinton got up. And at that moment I think I knew what she was going to say. She spoke to me, and what she said was:

"Jack will show you your room: I have given you the room in the tower."

At that, for half a second, the horror of the dream took hold of me again. But it quickly passed, and again I felt nothing more than the most intense curiosity. It was not very long before it was amply satisfied.

John turned to me.

"Right up at the top of the house," he said, "but I think you'll be comfortable. We're absolutely full up. Would you like to go and see it now? By Jove, I believe that you are right, and that we are going to have a thunderstorm. How dark it has become."

I got up and followed him. We passed through the hall, and up the perfectly familiar staircase. Then he opened the door, and I went in. And at that moment sheer unreasoning terror again possessed me. I did not know for certain what I feared: I simply feared. Then like a sudden recollection, when one remembers a name which has long escaped the memory, I knew what I feared. I feared Mrs. Stone, whose grave with the sinister inscription, "In evil memory," I had so often seen in my dream, just beyond the lawn which lay below my window. And then once more the fear passed so completely that I wondered what there was to fear, and I found myself, sober and quiet and sane, in the room in the tower, the name of which I had so often heard in my dream, and the scene of which was so familiar.

I looked round it with a certain sense of proprietorship, and found that nothing had been changed from the dreaming nights in which I knew it so well. Just to the left of the door was the bed, lengthways along the wall, with the head of it in the angle. In a line with it was the fireplace and a small bookcase; opposite the door the outer wall was pierced by two lattice-paned windows, between which stood the dressing-table, while ranged along the fourth wall was the washing-stand and a big cupboard. My luggage had already been unpacked, for the furniture of dressing and undressing lay orderly on the wash-stand and toilet-table, while my dinner clothes were spread out on the coverlet of the bed. And then, with a sudden start of unexplained dismay, I saw that there were two rather conspicuous objects which I had not seen before in my dreams: one a life-sized oil painting of Mrs. Stone, the other a black-and-white sketch of Jack Stone, representing him as he had appeared to me only a week before in the last of the series of these repeated dreams, a rather secret and evil-looking man of about thirty. His picture hung between the windows, looking straight across the room to the other portrait, which hung at the side of the bed. At that I looked next, and as I looked I felt once more the horror of the nightmare seize me.

It represented Mrs. Stone as I had seen her last in my dreams: old and withered and white-haired. But in spite of the evident feebleness of body, a dreadful exuberance and vitality shone through the envelope of flesh, an exuberance wholly malign, a vitality that foamed and frothed with unimaginable evil. Evil beamed from the narrow, leering eyes; it laughed in the demon-like mouth. The whole face was instinct with some secret and appalling mirth; the hands, clasped together on the knee, seemed shaking with suppressed and nameless glee. Then I saw also that it was signed in the left-hand bottom corner, and wondering who the artist could be, I looked more closely, and read the inscription. "Julia Stone by Julia Stone."

There came a tap at the door, and John Clinton entered.

"Got everything you want?" he asked.

"Rather more than I want," said I, pointing to the picture.

He laughed.

"Hard-featured old lady," he said. "By herself, too, I remember. Anyhow she can't have flattered herself much."

"But don't you see?" said I. "It's scarcely a human face at all. It's the face of some witch, of some devil."

He looked at it more closely.

"Yes; it isn't very pleasant," he said. "Scarcely a bedside manner, eh? Yes; I can imagine getting the nightmare if I went to sleep with that close by my bed. I'll have it taken down if you like."

"I really wish you would," I said. He rang the bell, and with the help of a servant we detached the picture and carried it out onto the landing, and put it with its face to the wall.

"By Jove, the old lady is a weight," said John, mopping his forehead. "I wonder if she had something on her mind."

The extraordinary weight of the picture had struck me too. I was about to reply, when I caught sight of my own hand. There was blood on it, in considerable quantities, covering the whole palm.

"I've cut myself somehow," said I.

John gave a little startled exclamation.

"Why, I have too," he said.

Simultaneously the footman took out his handkerchief and wiped his hand with it. I saw that there was blood also on his handkerchief.

John and I went back into the tower room and washed the blood off; but neither on his hand nor on mine was there the slightest trace of a scratch or cut. It seemed to me that, having ascertained this, we both, by a sort of tacit consent, did not allude to it again. Something in my case had dimly occurred to me that I did not wish to think about. It was but a conjecture, but I fancied that I knew the same thing had occurred to him.

The heat and oppression of the air, for the storm we had expected was still undischarged, increased very much after dinner, and for some time most of the party, among whom were John Clinton and myself, sat outside on the path bounding the lawn, where we had had tea. The night was absolutely dark, and no twinkle of star or moon ray could penetrate the pall of cloud that overset the sky. By degrees our assembly thinned, the women went up to bed, men dispersed to the smoking or billiard room, and by eleven o'clock my host and I were the only two left. All the evening I thought that he had something on his mind, and as soon as we were alone he spoke.

"The man who helped us with the picture had blood on his hand, too, did you notice?" he said.

"I asked him just now if he had cut himself, and he said he supposed he had, but that he could find no mark of it. Now where did that blood come from?"

By dint of telling myself that I was not going to think about it, I had succeeded in not doing so, and I did not want, especially just at bedtime, to be reminded of it.

"I don't know," said I, "and I don't really care so long as the picture of Mrs. Stone is not by my bed."

He got up.

"But it's odd," he said. "Ha! Now you'll see another odd thing."

A dog of his, an Irish terrier by breed, had come out of the house as we talked. The door behind us into the hall was open, and a bright oblong of light shone across the lawn to the iron gate which led on to the rough grass outside, where the walnut tree stood. I saw that the dog had all his hackles up, bristling with rage and fright; his lips were curled back from his teeth, as if he was ready to spring at something, and he was growling to himself. He took not the slightest notice of his master or me, but stiffly and tensely walked across the grass to the iron gate. There he stood for a moment, looking through the bars and still growling. Then of a sudden his courage seemed to desert him: he gave one long howl, and scuttled back to the house with a curious crouching sort of movement.

"He does that half-a-dozen times a day," said John. "He sees something which he both hates and fears."

I walked to the gate and looked over it. Something was moving on the grass outside, and soon a sound which I could not instantly identify came to my ears. Then I remembered what it was: it was the purring of a cat. I lit a match, and saw the purrer, a big blue Persian, walking round and round in a little circle just outside the gate, stepping high and ecstatically, with tail carried aloft like a banner. Its eyes were bright and shining, and every now and then it put its head down and sniffed at the grass.

I laughed.

"The end of that mystery, I am afraid," I said. "Here's a large cat having Walpurgis night all alone."

"Yes, that's Darius," said John. "He spends half the day and all night there. But that's not the end of the dog mystery, for Toby and he are the best of friends, but the beginning of the cat mystery. What's the cat doing there? And why is Darius pleased, while Toby is terror-stricken?"

At that moment I remembered the rather horrible detail of my dreams when I saw through the gate, just where the cat was now, the white tombstone with the sinister inscription. But before I could answer the rain began, as suddenly and heavily as if a tap had been turned on, and simultaneously the big cat squeezed through the bars of the gate, and came leaping across the lawn to the house for shelter. Then it sat in the doorway, looking out eagerly into the dark. It spat and struck at John with its paw, as he pushed it in, in order to close the door.

Somehow, with the portrait of Julia Stone in the passage outside, the room in the tower had absolutely no alarm for me, and as I went to bed, feeling very sleepy and heavy, I had nothing more than interest for the curious incident about our bleeding hands, and the conduct of the cat and dog. The last thing I looked at before I put out my light was the square empty space by my bed where the portrait had been. Here the paper was of its original full tint of dark red: over the rest of the walls it had faded. Then I blew out my candle and instantly fell asleep.

My awaking was equally instantaneous, and I sat bolt upright in bed under the impression that some bright light had been flashed in my face, though it was now absolutely pitch dark. I knew exactly where I was, in the room which I had dreaded in dreams, but no horror that I ever felt when asleep approached the fear that now invaded and froze my brain. Immediately after a peal of thunder crackled just above the house, but the probability that it was only a flash of lightning which awoke me gave no reassurance to my galloping heart. Something I knew was in the room with me, and instinctively I put out my right hand, which was nearest the wall, to keep it away. And my hand touched the edge of a picture-frame hanging close to me.

I sprang out of bed, upsetting the small table that stood by it, and I heard my watch, candle, and matches clatter onto the floor. But for the moment there was no need of light, for a blinding flash leaped out of the clouds, and showed me that by my bed again hung the picture of Mrs. Stone. And instantly the room went into blackness again. But in that flash I saw another thing also, namely a figure that leaned over the end of my bed, watching me. It was dressed in some close-clinging white garment, spotted and stained with mold, and the face was that of the portrait.

Overhead the thunder cracked and roared, and when it ceased and the deathly stillness succeeded, I heard the rustle of movement coming nearer me, and, more horrible yet, perceived an odor of corruption and decay. And then a hand was laid on the side of my neck, and close beside my ear I heard quick-taken, eager breathing. Yet I knew that this thing, though it could be perceived by touch, by smell, by eye and by ear, was still not of this earth, but something that had passed out of the body and had power to make itself manifest. Then a voice, already familiar to me, spoke.

"I knew you would come to the room in the tower," it said. "I have been long waiting for you. At last you have come. Tonight I shall feast; before long we will feast together."

And the quick breathing came closer to me; I could feel it on my neck.

At that the terror, which I think had paralyzed me for the moment, gave way to the wild instinct of self-preservation. I hit wildly with both arms, kicking out at the same moment, and heard a little animal-squeal, and something soft dropped with a thud beside me. I took a couple of steps forward, nearly tripping up over whatever it was that lay there, and by the merest good-luck found the handle of the door. In another second I ran out on the landing, and had banged the door behind me. Almost at the same moment I heard a door open somewhere below, and John Clinton, candle in hand, came running upstairs.

"What is it?" he said. "I sleep just below you, and heard a noise as if— Good heavens, there's blood on your shoulder."

I stood there, so he told me afterwards, swaying from side to side, white as a sheet, with the mark on my shoulder as if a hand covered with blood had been laid there.

"It's in there," I said, pointing. "She, you know. The portrait is in there, too, hanging up on the place we took it from."

At that he laughed.

"My dear fellow, this is mere nightmare," he said.

He pushed by me, and opened the door, I standing there simply inert with terror, unable to stop him, unable to move.

"Phew! What an awful smell," he said.

Then there was silence; he had passed out of my sight behind the open door. Next moment he came out again, as white as myself, and instantly shut it.

"Yes, the portrait's there," he said, "and on the floor is a thing—a thing spotted with earth, like what they bury people in. Come away, quick, come away."

How I got downstairs I hardly know. An awful shuddering and nausea of the spirit rather than of the flesh had seized me, and more than once he had to place my feet upon the steps, while every now and then he cast glances of terror and apprehension up the stairs. But in time we came to his dressing-room on the floor below, and there I told him what I have here described.

The sequel can be made short; indeed, some of my readers have perhaps already guessed what it was, if they remember that inexplicable affair of the churchyard at West Fawley, some eight years ago, where an attempt was made three times to bury the body of a certain woman who had committed suicide. On each occasion the coffin was found in the course of a few days again protruding from the ground. After the third attempt, in order that the thing should not be talked about, the body was buried elsewhere in unconsecrated ground. Where it was buried was just outside the iron gate of the garden belonging to the house where this woman had lived. She had committed suicide in a room at the top of the tower in that house. Her name was Julia Stone.

Subsequently the body was again secretly dug up, and the coffin was found to be full of blood.

Ray Bradbury

(1920–)

Born in Waukegan, Illinois, Ray Douglas Bradbury lived briefly in Tucson, Arizona, and moved to Los Angeles when he was thirteen. After graduation from Los Angeles High School, he worked as a newsboy, selling papers on the city streets. "Hollerbrochen's Dilemma," his first published story, appeared in the fanzine *Imagination!* (1938), and within several years, he had become a full-time writer of science fiction, fantasy, and horror fiction. Many of his stories were dramatized on television with Bradbury adapting some sixty-five of his works for *The Ray Bradbury Theater*, a series he hosted from 1985 to 1992. Among the full-length films based on his work are *It Came from Outer Space* (1953), *The Beast from 20,000 Fathoms* (1953), *Fahrenheit 451* (1966), *The Illustrated Man* (1969), *Something Wicked This Way Comes* (1983), and *The Wonderful Ice Cream Suit* (1999). He has received the Bram Stoker Award, the World Fantasy and SFWA Lifetime Achievement awards, the National Medal of Arts, and the National Book Foundation's Medal for Distinguished Contribution to American Letters.

The Man Upstairs

(1947)

He remembered how carefully and expertly Grandmother would fondle the cold cut guts of the chicken and withdraw the marvels therein; the wet shining loops of meat-smelling intestine, the muscled lump of heart, the gizzard with the collection of seeds in it. How neatly and nicely Grandma would slit the chicken and push her fat little hand in to deprive it of its medals. These would be segregated, some in pans of water, others in paper to be thrown to the dog later, perhaps. And then the ritual of taxidermy, stuffing the bird with watered, seasoned bread, and performing surgery with a swift, bright needle, stitch after pulled-tight stitch.

This was one of the prime thrills of Douglas's eleven-year-old life span.

Altogether, he counted twenty knives in the various squeaking drawers of the magic kitchen table from which Grandma, a kindly, gentle-faced, white-haired old witch, drew paraphernalia for her miracles.

Douglas was to be quiet. He could stand across the table from Grandma, his freckled nose tucked over the edge, watching, but any loose boy-talk might interfere with the spell. It was a wonder when Grandma brandished silver shakers over the bird, supposedly sprinkling showers of mummy-dust and pulverized Indian bones, muttering mystical verses under her toothless breath.

"Grammy," said Douglas at last, breaking the silence. "Am I like that inside?" He pointed at the chicken.

"Yes," said Grandma. "A little more orderly and presentable, but just about the same. . . ."

"And more *of* it!" added Douglas, proud of his guts.

"Yes," said Grandma. "More of it."

"Grandpa has lots more'n me. His sticks out in front so he can rest his elbows on it."

Grandma laughed and shook her head.

Douglas said, "And Lucie Williams, down the street, she . . ."

"Hush, child!" cried Grandma.

"But she's got . . ."

"Never you mind what she's got! That's different."

"But why is *she* different?"

"A darning-needle dragon-fly is coming by some day and sew up your mouth," said Grandma firmly.

Douglas waited, then asked, "How do you know I've got insides like that, Grandma?"

"Oh, go 'way, now!"

The front doorbell rang.

Through the front-door glass as he ran down the hall, Douglas saw a straw hat. The bell jangled again and again. Douglas opened the door.

"Good morning, child, is the landlady at home?"

Cold gray eyes in a long, smooth, walnut-colored face gazed upon Douglas. The man was tall, thin, and carried a suitcase, a briefcase, an umbrella under one bent arm, gloves rich and thick and gray on his thin fingers, and wore a horribly new straw hat.

Douglas backed up. "She's busy."

"I wish to rent her upstairs room, as advertised."

"We've got ten boarders, and it's already rented; go away!"

"Douglas!" Grandma was behind him suddenly. "How do you do?" she said to the stranger. "Never mind this child."

Unsmiling, the man stepped stiffly in. Douglas watched them ascend out of sight up the stairs, heard Grandma detailing the conveniences of the upstairs room. Soon she hurried down to pile linens from the linen closet on Douglas and send him scooting up with them.

Douglas paused at the room's threshold. The room was changed oddly, simply because the stranger had been in it a moment. The straw hat lay brittle and terrible upon the bed, the umbrella leaned stiff against one wall like a dead bat with dark wings folded.

Douglas blinked at the umbrella.

The stranger stood in the center of the changed room, tall, tall.

"Here!" Douglas littered the bed with supplies. "We eat at noon sharp, and if you're late coming down the soup'll get cold. Grandma fixes it so it will, every time!"

The tall strange man counted out ten new copper pennies and tinkled them in Douglas's blouse pocket. "We shall be friends," he said, grimly.

It was funny, the man having nothing but pennies. Lots of them. No silver at all, no dimes, no quarters. Just new copper pennies.

Douglas thanked him glumly. "I'll drop these in my dime bank when I get them changed into a dime. I got six dollars and fifty cents in dimes all ready for my camp trip in August."

"I must wash now," said the tall strange man.

Once, at midnight, Douglas had wakened to hear a storm rumbling outside—the cold hard wind shaking the house, the rain driving against the window. And then a lightning bolt had landed outside the window with a silent, terrific concussion. He remembered that fear of looking about at his room, seeing it strange and awful in the instantaneous light.

So it was, now, in this room. He stood looking up at the stranger. This room was no longer the same, but changed indefinably because this man, quick as a lightning bolt, had shed his light about it. Douglas backed up slowly as the stranger advanced.

The door closed in his face.

The wooden fork went up with mashed potatoes, came down empty. Mr. Koberman, for that was his name, had brought the wooden fork and wooden knife and spoon with him when Grandma called lunch.

"Mrs. Spaulding," he said, quietly, "my own cutlery; please use it. I will have lunch today, but from tomorrow on, only breakfast and supper."

Grandma bustled in and out, bearing steaming tureens of soup and beans and mashed potatoes to impress her new boarder, while Douglas sat rattling his silverware on his plate, because he had discovered it irritated Mr. Koberman.

"I know a trick," said Douglas. "Watch." He picked a fork-tine with his fingernail. He pointed at various sectors of the table, like a magician. Wherever he pointed, the sound of the vibrating fork-tine emerged, like a metal elfin voice. Simply done, of course. He pressed the fork handle on the table-top, secretly. The vibration came from the wood like a sounding board. It looked quite magical. "There, there, and *there*!" exclaimed Douglas, happily plucking the fork again. He pointed at Mr. Koberman's soup and the noise came from it.

Mr. Koberman's walnut-colored face became hard and firm and awful. He pushed the soup bowl away violently, his lips twisting. He fell back in his chair.

Grandma appeared. "Why, what's wrong, Mr. Koberman?"

"I cannot eat this soup."

"Why?"

"Because I am full and can eat no more. Thank you."

Mr. Koberman left the room, glaring.

"What did you do, just then?" asked Grandma at Douglas, sharply.

"Nothing. Grandma, why does he eat with *wooden* spoons?"

"Yours not to question! When do you go back to school, anyway?"

"Seven weeks."

"Oh, my lord!" said Grandma.

Mr. Koberman worked nights. Each morning at eight he arrived mysteriously home, devoured a very small breakfast, and then slept soundlessly in his room all through the dreaming hot daytime, until the huge supper with all the other boarders at night.

Mr. Koberman's sleeping habits made it necessary for Douglas to be quiet. This was unbearable. So, whenever Grandma visited down the street, Douglas stomped up and down stairs beating a drum, bouncing golf balls, or just screaming for three minutes outside Mr. Koberman's door, or flushing the toilet seven times in succession.

Mr. Koberman never moved. His room was silent, dark. He did not complain. There was no sound. He slept on and on. It was very strange.

Douglas felt a pure white flame of hatred burn inside himself with a steady, unflickering beauty. Now that room was Koberman Land. Once it had been flowery bright when Miss Sadlowe lived there. Now it was stark, bare, cold, clean, everything in its place, alien and brittle.

Douglas climbed upstairs on the fourth morning.

Halfway to the second floor was a large sun-filled window, framed by six-inch panes of orange, purple, blue, red, and burgundy glass. In the enchanted early mornings when the sun fell through to strike the landing and slide down the stair banister, Douglas stood entranced at this window peering at the world through the multi-colored panes.

Now a blue world, a blue sky, blue people, blue streetcars, and blue trotting dogs.

He shifted panes. Now—an amber world! Two lemonish women glided by, resembling the daughters of Fu Manchu! Douglas giggled. This pane made even the sunlight more purely golden.

It was eight a.m. Mr. Koberman strolled by below, on the sidewalk, returning from his night's work, his umbrella looped over his elbow, straw hat glued to his head with patent oil.

Douglas shifted panes again. Mr. Koberman was a red man walking through a red world with red trees and red flowers and—something else.

Something about—Mr. Koberman.

Douglas squinted.

The red glass *did* things to Mr. Koberman. His face, his suit, his hands. The clothes seemed to melt away. Douglas almost believed, for one terrible instant, that he could see *inside* Mr. Koberman. And what he saw made him lean wildly against the small red pane, blinking.

Mr. Koberman glanced up just then, saw Douglas, and raised his umbrella angrily, as if to strike. He ran swiftly across the red lawn to the front door.

"Young man!" he cried, running up the stairs. "What were you doing?"

"Just looking," said Douglas, numbly.

"That's all, is it?" cried Mr. Koberman.

"Yes, sir. I look through all the glasses. All kinds of worlds. Blue ones, red ones, yellow ones. All different."

"All kinds of worlds, is it!" Mr. Koberman glanced at the little panes of glass, his face pale. He got hold of himself. He wiped his face with a handkerchief and pretended to laugh. "Yes. All kinds of worlds. All different." He walked to the door of his room. "Go right ahead; play," he said.

The door closed. The hall was empty. Mr. Koberman had gone in.

Douglas shrugged and found a new pane.

"Oh, everything's violet!"

Half an hour later, while playing in his sandbox behind the house, Douglas heard the crash and the shattering tinkle. He leaped up.

A moment later, Grandma appeared on the back porch, the old razor strop trembling in her hand.

"Douglas! I told you time and again never fling your basketball against the house! Oh, I could just cry!"

"I been sitting right here," he protested.

"Come see what you've done, you nasty boy!"

The great colored window panes lay shattered in a rainbow chaos on the upstairs landing. His basketball lay in the ruins.

Before he could even begin telling his innocence, Douglas was struck a dozen stinging blows upon his rump. Wherever he landed, screaming, the razor strop struck again.

Later, hiding his mind in the sandpile like an ostrich, Douglas nursed his dreadful pains. He knew who'd thrown that basketball. A man with a straw hat and a stiff umbrella and a cold, gray room. Yeah, yeah, yeah. He dribbled tears. Just wait. Just *wait.*

He heard Grandma sweeping up the broken glass. She brought it out and threw it in the trash bin. Blue, pink, yellow meteors of glass dropped brightly down.

When she was gone, Douglas dragged himself, whimpering, over to save out three pieces of the incredible glass. Mr. Koberman disliked the colored windows. These—he clinked them in his fingers—would be worth saving.

Grandfather arrived from his newspaper office each night, shortly ahead of the other boarders, at five o'clock. When a slow, heavy tread filled the hall, and a thick, mahogany cane thumped in the cane-rack, Douglas ran to embrace the large stomach and sit on Grandpa's knee while he read the evening paper.

"Hi, Grampa!"

"Hello, down there!"

"Grandma cut chickens again today. It's fun watching," said Douglas.

Grandpa kept reading. "That's twice this week, chickens. She's the chickenist woman. You like to watch her cut 'em, eh? Cold-blooded little pepper! Ha!"

"I'm just curious."

"You are," rumbled Grandpa, scowling. "Remember that day when that young lady was killed at the rail station? You just walked over and looked at her, blood and all." He laughed. "Queer duck. Stay that way. Fear nothing, ever in your life. I guess you get it from your father, him being a military man and all, and you so close to him before you came here to live last year." Grandpa returned to his paper.

A long pause. "Gramps?"

"Yes?"

"What if a man didn't have a heart or lungs or stomach but still walked around, alive?"

"That," rumbled Gramps, "would be a miracle."

"I don't mean a—a miracle. I mean, what if he was all *different* inside? Not like me."

"Well, he wouldn't be quite human then, would he, boy?"

"Guess not, Gramps. Gramps, you got a heart and lungs?"

Gramps chuckled. "Well, tell the truth, I don't *know*. Never seen them. Never had an X-ray, never been to a doctor. Might as well be potato-solid for all I know."

"Have *I* got a stomach?"

"You certainly have!" cried Grandma from the parlor entry. " 'Cause I feed it! And you've lungs, you scream loud enough to wake the crumblees. And you've dirty hands, go wash them! Dinner's ready. Grandpa, come on. Douglas, git!"

In the rush of boarders streaming downstairs, Grandpa, if he intended questioning Douglas further about the weird conversation, lost his opportunity. If dinner delayed an instant more, Grandma and the potatoes would develop simultaneous lumps.

The boarders, laughing and talking at the table—Mr. Koberman silent and sullen among them—were silenced when Grandfather cleared his throat. He talked politics a few minutes and then shifted over into the intriguing topic of the recent peculiar deaths in the town.

"It's enough to make an old newspaper editor prick up his ears," he said, eying them all. "That young Miss Larson, lived across the ravine, now. Found her dead three days ago for no reason, just funny kinds of tattoos all over her, and a facial expression that would make Dante cringe. And that other young lady, what was her name? Whitely? She disappeared and *never did* come back."

"Them things happen alla time," said Mr. Britz, the garage mechanic, chewing. "Ever peek inna Missing Peoples Bureau file? It's *that* long." He illustrated. "Can't tell *what* happens to most of 'em."

"Anyone want more dressing?" Grandma ladled liberal portions from the chicken's interior. Douglas watched, thinking about how that chicken had had two kinds of guts—God-made and Man-made.

Well, how about *three* kinds of guts?

Eh?

Why not?

Conversation continued about the mysterious death of so-and-so, and, oh, yes, remember a week ago, Marion Barsumian died of heart failure, but maybe that didn't connect up? or did it? you're crazy! forget it, why talk about it at the dinner table? So.

"Never can tell," said Mr. Britz. "Maybe we got a vampire in town."

Mr. Koberman stopped eating.

"In the year 1927?" said Grandma. "A vampire? Oh go on, now."

"Sure," said Mr. Britz. "Kill 'em with silver bullets. Anything silver for that matter. Vampires *hate* silver. I read it in a book somewhere, once. Sure, I did."

Douglas looked at Mr. Koberman who ate with wooden knives and forks and carried only new copper pennies in his pocket.

"It's poor judgment," said Grandpa, "to call anything by a name. We don't know what a hobgoblin or a vampire or a troll is. Could be lots of things. You can't heave them into categories with labels and say they'll act one way or another. That'd be silly. They're people. People who do things. Yes, that's the way to put it: people who *do* things."

"Excuse me," said Mr. Koberman, who got up and went out for his evening walk to work.

The stars, the moon, the wind, the clock ticking, and the chiming of the hours into dawn, the sun rising, and here it was another morning, another day, and Mr. Koberman coming along the sidewalk from his night's work. Douglas stood off like a small mechanism whirring and watching with carefully microscopic eyes.

At noon, Grandma went to the store to buy groceries.

As was his custom every day when Grandma was gone, Douglas yelled outside Mr. Koberman's door for a full three minutes. As usual, there was no response. The silence was horrible.

He ran downstairs, got the pass-key, a silver fork, and the

three pieces of colored glass he had saved from the shattered window. He fitted the key to the lock and swung the door slowly open.

The room was in half light, the shades drawn. Mr. Koberman lay atop his bedcovers, in slumber clothes, breathing gently, up and down. He didn't move. His face was motionless.

"Hello, Mr. Koberman!"

The colorless walls echoed the man's regular breathing.

"Mr. Koberman, hello!"

Bouncing a golf ball, Douglas advanced. He yelled. Still no answer. "Mr. Koberman!"

Bending over Mr. Koberman, Douglas poked the tines of the silver fork in the sleeping man's face.

Mr. Koberman winced. He twisted. He groaned bitterly.

Response. Good. Swell.

Douglas drew a piece of blue glass from his pocket. Looking through the blue glass fragment he found himself in a blue room, in a blue world different from the world he knew. As different as was the red world. Blue furniture, blue bed, blue ceiling and walls, blue wooden eating utensils atop the blue bureau, and the sullen dark blue of Mr. Koberman's face and arms and his blue chest rising, falling. Also . . .

Mr. Koberman's eyes were wide, staring at him with a hungry darkness.

Douglas fell back, pulled the blue glass from his eyes.

Mr. Koberman's eyes were shut.

Blue glass again—open. Blue glass away—shut. Blue glass again—open. Away—shut. Funny. Douglas experimented, trembling. Through the glass the eyes seemed to peer hungrily, avidly, through Mr. Koberman's closed lids. Without the blue glass they seemed tightly shut.

But it was the rest of Mr. Koberman's body . . .

Mr. Koberman's bedclothes dissolved off him. The blue glass had something to do with it. Or perhaps it was the clothes themselves, just being *on* Mr. Koberman. Douglas cried out.

He was looking through the wall of Mr. Koberman's stomach, right *inside* him!

Mr. Koberman was solid.

Or, nearly so, anyway.

There were strange shapes and sizes within him.

Douglas must have stood amazed for five minutes, thinking about the blue worlds, the red worlds, the yellow worlds side by side, living together like glass panes around the big white stair window. Side by side, the colored panes, the different worlds; Mr. Koberman had said so himself.

So this was why the colored window had been broken.

"Mr. Koberman, wake up!"

No answer.

"Mr. Koberman, where do you work at night? Mr. Koberman, where do you work?"

A little breeze stirred the blue window shade.

"In a red world or a green world or a yellow one, Mr. Koberman?"

Over everything was a blue glass silence.

"Wait there," said Douglas.

He walked down to the kitchen, pulled open the great squeaking drawer and picked out the sharpest, biggest knife.

Very calmly he walked into the hall, climbed back up the stairs again, opened the door to Mr. Koberman's room, went in, and closed it, holding the sharp knife in one hand.

Grandma was busy fingering a piecrust into a pan when Douglas entered the kitchen to place something on the table.

"Grandma, what's this?"

She glanced up briefly, over her glasses. "I don't know."

It was square, like a box, and elastic. It was bright orange in color. It had four square tubes, colored blue, attached to it. It smelled funny.

"Ever see anything like it, Grandma?"

"No."

"That's what *I* thought."

Douglas left it there, went from the kitchen. Five minutes later he returned with something else. "How about *this*?"

He laid down a bright pink linked chain with a purple triangle at one end.

"Don't bother me," said Grandma. "It's only a chain."

Next time he returned with two hands full. A ring, a square, a triangle, a pyramid, a rectangle, and—other shapes.

All of them were pliable, resilient, and looked as if they were made of gelatin. "This isn't all," said Douglas, putting them down. "There's more where this came from."

Grandma said, "Yes, yes," in a far-off tone, very busy.

"You were wrong, Grandma."

"About what?"

"About all people being the same inside."

"Stop talking nonsense."

"Where's my piggy-bank?"

"On the mantel, where you left it."

"Thanks."

He tromped into the parlor, reached up for his piggy-bank.

Grandpa came home from the office at five.

"Grandpa, come upstairs."

"Sure, son. Why?"

"Something to show you. It's not nice; but it's interesting."

Grandpa chuckled, following his grandson's feet up to Mr. Koberman's room.

"Grandma mustn't know about this; she wouldn't like it," said Douglas. He pushed the door wide open. "There."

Grandfather gasped.

Douglas remembered the next few hours all the rest of his life. Standing over Mr. Koberman's naked body, the coroner and his assistants. Grandma, downstairs, asking somebody, "What's going on up there?" and Grandpa saying, shakily, "I'll take Douglas away on a long vacation so he can forget this whole ghastly affair. Ghastly, ghastly affair!"

Douglas said, "Why should it be bad? I don't see anything bad. I don't feel bad."

The coroner shivered and said, "Koberman's dead, all right."

His assistant sweated. "Did you see those *things* in the pans of water and in the wrapping paper?"

"Oh, my God, my God, yes, I saw them."

"Christ."

The coroner bent over Mr. Koberman's body again. "This better be kept secret, boys. It wasn't murder. It was a mercy the boy acted. God knows what might have happened if he hadn't."

"What was Koberman? A vampire? A monster?"

"Maybe. I don't know. Something—not human." The coroner moved his hands deftly over the suture.

Douglas was proud of his work. He'd gone to much trouble. He had watched Grandmother carefully and remembered. Needle and thread and all. All in all, Mr. Koberman was as neat a job as any chicken ever popped into hell by Grandma.

"I heard the boy say that Koberman lived even after all those *things* were taken out of him." The coroner looked at the triangles and chains and pyramids floating in the pans of water. "Kept on *living*. God."

"Did the boy say that?"

"He did."

"Then, what *did* kill Koberman?"

The coroner drew a few strands of sewing thread from their bedding.

"This. . . ." he said.

Sunlight blinked coldly off a half-revealed treasure trove: six dollars and sixty cents' worth of silver dimes inside Mr. Koberman's chest.

"I think Douglas made a wise investment," said the coroner, sewing the flesh back up over the "dressing" quickly.

Ramsey Campbell

(1946–)

John Ramsey Campbell was born in Liverpool. Prior to becoming a full-time writer, he worked as a tax officer and an assistant librarian. He made use of his library experience in the story "Call First," in which he depicted a librarian whose dark adventure began when he became excessively curious about the telephone calls that an elderly library patron made from his desk before leaving for home. His first published story, "The Church in the High Street" (1962), was soon followed by a collection of tales, *The Inhabitant of the Lake and Less Welcome Tenants* (1964). Among his other story collections are *Demons by Daylight* (1973), *The Height of the Scream* (1976), *Scared Stiff: Tales of Sex and Death* (1987), *Waking Nightmares* (1991), *Ghosts and Grisly Things* (1998), and *Told by the Dead* (2003). Among his novels are *The Nameless* (1981), *Needing Ghosts* (1990), *The Last Voice They Hear* (1998), *The Grin of the Dark* (2007), *Thieving Fear* (2008), and *The Seven Days of Cain* (2010). Campbell has won several Bram Stoker and World Fantasy awards, the Horror Writers Association Lifetime Achievement Award, the H. P. Lovecraft Film Festival for Lifetime Achievement Award, and the International Horror Guild's Living Legend Award.

The Brood

(1980)

He'd had an almost unbearable day. As he walked home his self-control still oppressed him, like rusty armour. Climbing the stairs, he tore open his mail: a glossy pamphlet from a binoculars firm, a humbler folder from the Wild Life

Preservation Society. Irritably he threw them on the bed and sat by the window, to relax.

It was autumn. Night had begun to cramp the days. Beneath golden trees, a procession of cars advanced along Princes Avenue, as though to a funeral; crowds hurried home. The incessant anonymous parade, dwarfed by three stories, depressed him. Faces like these vague twilit miniatures—selfishly ingrown, convinced that nothing was their fault—brought their pets to his office.

But where were all the local characters? He enjoyed watching them, they fascinated him. Where was the man who ran about the avenue, chasing butterflies of litter and stuffing them into his satchel? Or the man who strode violently, head down in no gale, shouting at the air? Or the Rainbow Man, who appeared on the hottest days obese with sweaters, each of a different garish colour? Blackband hadn't seen any of these people for weeks.

The crowds thinned; cars straggled. Groups of streetlamps lit, tinting leaves sodium, unnaturally gold. Often that lighting had meant—Why, there she was, emerging from the side street almost on cue: the Lady of the Lamp.

Her gait was elderly. Her face was withered as an old blanched apple; the rest of her head was wrapped in a tattered grey scarf. Her voluminous ankle-length coat, patched with remnants of colour, swayed as she walked. She reached the central reservation of the avenue, and stood beneath a lamp.

Though there was a pedestrian crossing beside her, people deliberately crossed elsewhere. They would, Blackband thought sourly: just as they ignored the packs of stray dogs that were always someone else's responsibility—ignored them, or hoped someone would put them to sleep. Perhaps they felt the human strays should be put to sleep, perhaps that was where the Rainbow Man and the rest had gone!

The woman was pacing restlessly. She circled the lamp, as though the blurred disc of light at its foot were a stage. Her shadow resembled the elaborate hand of a clock.

Surely she was too old to be a prostitute. Might she have been one, who was now compelled to enact her memories? His binoculars drew her face closer: intent as a sleepwalker's, introverted as a foetus. Her head bobbed against gravel, foreshortened by the false perspective of the lenses. She moved offscreen.

Three months ago, when he'd moved to this flat, there had been two old women. One night he had seen them, circling adjacent lamps. The other woman had been slower, more sleepy. At last the Lady of the Lamp had led her home; they'd moved slowly as exhausted sleepers. For days he'd thought of the two women in their long faded coats, trudging around the lamps in the deserted avenue, as though afraid to go home in the growing dark.

The sight of the lone woman still unnerved him, a little. Darkness was crowding his flat. He drew the curtains, which the lamps stained orange. Watching had relaxed him somewhat. Time to make a salad.

The kitchen overlooked the old women's house. See The World from the Attics of Princes Avenue. All Human Life Is Here. Backyards penned in rubble and crumbling toilet sheds; on the far side of the back street, houses were lidless boxes of smoke. The house directly beneath his window was dark, as always. How could the two women—if both were still alive—survive in there? But at least they could look after themselves, or call for aid; they were human, after all. It was their pets that bothered him.

He had never seen the torpid woman again. Since she had vanished, her companion had begun to take animals home; he'd seen her coaxing them toward the house. No doubt they were company for her friend; but what life could animals enjoy in the lightless, probably condemnable house? And why so many? Did they escape to their homes, or stray again? He shook his head: the women's loneliness was no excuse. They cared as little for their pets as did those owners who came, whining like their dogs, to his office.

Perhaps the woman was waiting beneath the lamps for cats to drop from the trees, like fruit. He meant the thought as a joke. But when he'd finished preparing dinner, the idea troubled him sufficiently that he switched off the light in the main room and peered through the curtains.

The bright gravel was bare. Parting the curtains, he saw the woman hurrying unsteadily toward her street. She was carrying a kitten: her head bowed over the fur cradled in her arms; her whole body seemed to enfold it. As he emerged from the kitchen again, carrying plates, he heard her door creak open and shut. Another one, he thought uneasily.

By the end of the week she'd taken in a stray dog, and Blackband was wondering what should be done.

The women would have to move eventually. The houses adjoining theirs were empty, the windows shattered targets. But how could they take their menagerie with them? They'd set them loose to roam or, weeping, take them to be put to sleep.

Something ought to be done, but not by him. He came home to rest. He was used to removing chicken bones from throats; it was suffering the excuses that exhausted him—Fido always had his bit of chicken, it had never happened before, they couldn't understand. He would nod curtly, with a slight pained smile. "Oh yes?" he would repeat tonelessly. "Oh yes?"

Not that that would work with the Lady of the Lamp. But then, he didn't intend to confront her: what on earth could he have said? That he'd take all the animals off her hands? Hardly. Besides, the thought of confronting her made him uncomfortable.

She was growing more eccentric. Each day she appeared a little earlier. Often she would move away into the dark, then hurry back into the flat bright pool. It was as though light were her drug.

People stared at her, and fled. They disliked her because she was odd. All she had to do to please them, Blackband thought, was be normal: overfeed her pets until their stomachs scraped the ground, lock them in cars to suffocate in the heat, leave them alone in the house all day then beat them for chewing. Compared to most of the owners he met, she was Saint Francis.

He watched television. Insects were courting and mating. Their ritual dances engrossed and moved him: the play of colours, the elaborate racial patterns of the life-force which they instinctively decoded and enacted. Microphotography presented them to him. If only people were as beautiful and fascinating!

Even his fascination with the Lady of the Lamp was no longer unalloyed; he resented that. Was she falling ill? She walked painfully slowly, stooped over, and looked shrunken.

Nevertheless, each night she kept her vigil, wandering sluggishly in the pools of light like a sleepwalker.

How could she cope with her animals now? How might she be treating them? Surely there were social workers in some of the cars nosing home, someone must notice how much she needed help. Once he made for the door to the stairs, but already his throat was parched of words. The thought of speaking to her wound him tight inside. It wasn't his job, he had enough to confront. The spring in his guts coiled tighter, until he moved away from the door.

One night an early policeman appeared. Usually the police emerged near midnight, disarming people of knives and broken glass, forcing them into the vans. Blackband watched eagerly. Surely the man must escort her home, see what the house hid. Blackband glanced back to the splash of light beneath the lamp. It was deserted.

How could she have moved so fast? He stared, baffled. A dim shape lurked at the corner of his eyes. Glancing nervously, he saw the woman standing on the bright disc several lamps away, considerably farther from the policeman than he'd thought. Why should he have been so mistaken?

Before he could ponder, sound distracted him: a loud fluttering, as though a bird were trapped and frantic in the kitchen. But the room was empty. Any bird must have escaped through the open window. Was that a flicker of movement below, in the dark house? Perhaps the bird had flown in there.

The policeman had moved on. The woman was trudging her island of light; her coat's hem dragged over the gravel. For a while Blackband watched, musing uneasily, trying to think what the fluttering had resembled more than the sound of a bird's wings.

Perhaps that was why, in the early hours, he saw a man stumbling through the derelict back streets. Jagged hurdles of rubble blocked the way; the man clambered, panting dryly, gulping dust as well as breath. He seemed only exhausted and uneasy, but Blackband could see what was pursuing him: a great wide shadow-colored stain, creeping vaguely over the rooftops. The stain was alive, for its face mouthed—though at first, from its color and texture, he thought the head was the moon. Its eyes gleamed hungrily.

As the fluttering made the man turn and scream, the face sailed down on its stain toward him.

Next day was unusually trying: a dog with a broken leg and a suffering owner, you'll hurt his leg, can't you be more gentle, oh come here, baby, what did the nasty man do to you; a senile cat and its protector, isn't the usual vet here today, he never used to do that, are you sure you know what you're doing. But later, as he watched the woman's obsessive trudging, the dream of the stain returned to him. Suddenly he realized he had never seen her during daylight.

So that was it! he thought, sniggering. She'd been a vampire all the time! A difficult job to keep when you hadn't a tooth in your head. He reeled in her face with the focusing-screw. Yes, she was toothless. Perhaps she used false fangs, or sucked through her gums. But he couldn't sustain his joke for long. Her face peered out of the frame of her grey scarf, as though from a web. As she circled she was muttering incessantly. Her tongue worked as though her mouth were too small for it. Her eyes were fixed as the heads of grey nails impaling her skull.

He laid the binoculars aside, and was glad that she'd become more distant. But even the sight of her trudging in miniature troubled him. In her eyes he had seen that she didn't want to do what she was doing.

She was crossing the roadway, advancing toward his gate. For a moment, unreasonably and with a sour uprush of dread, he was sure she intended to come in. But she was staring at the hedge. Her hands fluttered, warding off a fear; her eyes and her mouth were stretched wide. She stood quivering, then she stumbled toward her street, almost running.

He made himself go down. Each leaf of the hedge held an orange-sodium glow, like wet paint. But there was nothing among the leaves, and nothing could have struggled out, for the twigs were intricately bound by spiderwebs, gleaming like gold wire.

The next day was Sunday. He rode a train beneath the Mersey and went tramping the Wirral Way nature trail. Red-faced men, and women who had paralyzed their hair with spray, stared as though he'd invaded their garden. A few butterflies perched on flowers; their wings settled together delicately, then they flickered away above the banks of the abandoned railway cutting. They were too quick for him to enjoy, even with his binoculars; he kept remembering how near death their species were. His moping had slowed him, he felt barred from his surroundings by his inability to confront the old woman. He couldn't speak to her, there were no words he could use, but meanwhile her animals might be suffering. He dreaded going home to another night of helpless watching.

Could he look into the house while she was wandering? She might leave the door unlocked. At some time he had become intuitively sure that her companion was dead. Twilight gained on him, urging him back to Liverpool.

He gazed nervously down at the lamps. Anything was preferable to his impotence. But his feelings had trapped him into committing himself before he was ready. Could he really go down when she emerged? Suppose the other woman was still alive, and screamed? Good God, he needn't go in if he didn't want to. On the gravel, light lay bare as a row of plates on a shelf. He found himself thinking, with a secret eagerness, that she might already have had her wander.

As he made dinner, he kept hurrying irritably to the front window. Television failed to engross him; he watched the avenue instead. Discs of light dwindled away, impaled by their lamps. Below the kitchen window stood a block of night and silence. Eventually he went to bed, but heard fluttering—flights of litter in the derelict streets, no doubt. His dreams gave the litter a human face.

Throughout Monday he was on edge, anxious to hurry home and be done; he was distracted. Oh poor Chubbles, is the man hurting you! He managed to leave early. Day was trailing down the sky as he reached the avenue. Swiftly he brewed coffee and sat sipping, watching.

The caravan of cars faltered, interrupted by gaps. The last homecomers hurried away, clearing the stage. But the woman failed to take her cue. His cooking of dinner was fragmented; he hurried repeatedly back to the window. Where was the bloody woman, was she on strike? Not until the following night, when she had still not appeared, did he begin to suspect he'd seen the last of her.

His intense relief was short-lived. If she had died of whatever had been shrinking her, what would happen to her animals? Should he find out what was wrong? But there was no reason to think she'd died. Probably she, and her friend before her, had gone to stay with relatives. No doubt the animals had escaped long before—he'd never seen or heard any of them since she had taken them in. Darkness stood hushed and bulky beneath his kitchen window.

For several days the back streets were quiet, except for the flapping of litter or birds. It became easier to glance at the dark house. Soon they'd demolish it; already children had shattered all the windows. Now, when he lay awaiting sleep, the thought of the vague house soothed him, weighed his mind down gently.

That night he awoke twice. He'd left the kitchen window ajar, hoping to lose some of the unseasonable heat. Drifting through the window came a man's low moaning. Was he trying to form words? His voice was muffled, blurred as a dying radio. He must be drunk; perhaps he had fallen, for there was a faint scrape of rubble. Blackband hid within his eyelids, courting sleep. At last the shapeless moaning faded. There was silence, except for the feeble, stony scraping. Blackband lay and grumbled, until sleep led him to a face that crept over heaps of rubble.

Some hours later he woke again. The lifelessness of four o'clock surrounded him, the dim air seemed sluggish and ponderous. Had he dreamed the new sound? It returned, and made him flinch: a chorus of thin, piteous wailing, reaching weakly upward toward the kitchen. For a moment, on the edge of dream, it sounded like babies. How could babies be crying in an abandoned house? The voices were too thin. They were kittens.

He lay in the heavy dark, hemmed in by shapes that the night deformed. He willed the sounds to cease, and eventually they did. When he awoke again, belatedly, he had time only to hurry to work.

In the evening the house was silent as a draped cage. Someone must have rescued the kittens. But in the early hours the crying woke him: fretful, bewildered, famished. He couldn't go down now, he had no light. The crying was muffled, as though beneath stone. Again it kept him awake, again he was late for work.

His loss of sleep nagged him. His smile sagged impatiently, his nods were contemptuous twitches. "Yes," he agreed with a woman who said she'd been careless to slam her dog's paw in a door, and when she raised her eyebrows haughtily: "Yes, I can see that." He could see her deciding to find another vet. Let her, let someone else suffer her. He had problems of his own.

He borrowed the office flashlight, to placate his anxiety. Surely he wouldn't need to enter the house, surely someone else— He walked home, toward the darker sky. Night thickened like soot on the buildings.

He prepared dinner quickly. No need to dawdle in the kitchen, no point in staring down. He was hurrying; he dropped a spoon, which reverberated shrilly in his mind, nerve-racking. Slow down, slow down. A breeze piped incessantly outside, in the rubble. No, not a breeze. When he made himself raise the sash he heard the crying, thin as wind in crevices.

It seemed weaker now, dismal and desperate: intolerable. Could nobody else hear it, did nobody care? He gripped the windowsill; a breeze tried feebly to tug at his fingers. Suddenly, compelled by vague anger, he grabbed the flashlight and trudged reluctantly downstairs.

A pigeon hobbled on the avenue, dangling the stump of one leg, twitching clogged wings; cars brisked by. The back street was scattered with debris, as though a herd had moved on, leaving its refuse to manure the paving stones. His flashlight groped over the heaped pavement, trying to determine which house had been troubling him.

Only by standing back to align his own window with the house could he decide, and even then he was unsure. How could the old woman have clambered over the jagged pile that blocked the doorway? The front door sprawled splintered in the hall, on a heap of the fallen ceiling, amid peelings of wallpaper. He must be mistaken. But as his flashlight dodged about the hall, picking up debris then letting it drop back into the dark, he heard the crying, faint and muffled. It was somewhere within.

He ventured forward, treading carefully. He had to drag the door into the street before he could proceed. Beyond the door the floorboards were cobbled with rubble. Plaster swayed about him, glistening. His light wobbled ahead of him, then led him toward a gaping doorway on the right. The light spread into the room, dimming.

A door lay on its back. Boards poked like exposed ribs through the plaster of the ceiling; torn paper dangled. There was no carton full of starving kittens; in fact, the room was bare. Moist stains engulfed the walls.

He groped along the hall, to the kitchen. The stove was fat with grime. The wallpaper had collapsed entirely, draping indistinguishable shapes that stirred as the flashlight glanced at them. Through the furred window, he made out the light in his own kitchen, orange-shaded, blurred. How could two women have survived here?

At once he regretted that thought. The old woman's face loomed behind him: eyes still as metal, skin the colour of pale bone. He turned nervously; the light capered. Of course there was only the quivering mouth of the hall. But the face was present now, peering from behind the draped shapes around him.

He was about to give up—he was already full of the gasp of relief he would give when he reached the avenue—when he heard the crying. It was almost breathless, as though close to death: a shrill feeble wheezing. He couldn't bear it. He hurried into the hall.

Might the creatures be upstairs? His light showed splintered holes in most of the stairs; through them he glimpsed a huge symmetrical stain on the wall. Surely the woman could never have climbed up there—but that left only the cellar.

The door was beside him. The flashlight, followed by his hand, groped for the knob. The face was near him in the shadows; its fixed eyes gleamed. He dreaded finding her fallen on the cellar steps. But the crying pleaded. He dragged the door open; it scraped over rubble. He thrust the flashlight into the dank opening. He stood gaping, bewildered.

Beneath him lay a low stone room. Its walls glistened darkly. The place was full of debris: bricks, planks, broken lengths of wood. Draping the debris, or tangled beneath it, were numerous old clothes. Threads of a white substance were tethered to everything, and drifted feebly now the door was opened.

In one corner loomed a large pale bulk. His light twitched toward it. It was a white bag of some material, not cloth. It had been torn open; except for a sifting of rubble, and a tangle of what might have been fragments of dully painted cardboard, it was empty.

The crying wailed, somewhere beneath the planks. Several sweeps of the light showed that the cellar was otherwise deserted. Though the face mouthed behind him, he ventured down. For God's sake, get it over with; he knew he would never dare return. A swath had been cleared through the dust on the steps, as though something had dragged itself out of the cellar, or had been dragged in.

His movements disturbed the tethered threads; they rose like feelers, fluttering delicately. The white bag stirred, its torn mouth worked. Without knowing why, he stayed as far from that corner as he could.

The crying had come from the far end of the cellar. As he picked his way hurriedly over the rubble he caught sight of a group of clothes. They were violently coloured sweaters, which the Rainbow Man had worn. They slumped over planks; they nestled inside one another, as though the man had withered or had been sucked out.

Staring uneasily about, Blackband saw that all the clothes were stained. There was blood on all of them, though not a great deal on any. The ceiling hung close to him, oppressive and vague. Darkness had blotted out the steps and the door. He caught at them with the light, and stumbled toward them.

The crying made him falter. Surely there were fewer voices, and they seemed to sob. He was nearer the voices than the steps. If he could find the creatures at once, snatch them up and flee— He clambered over the treacherous debris, toward a gap in the rubble. The bag mouthed emptily; threads plucked at him, almost impalpably. As he thrust the flashlight's beam into the gap, darkness rushed to surround him.

Beneath the debris a pit had been dug. Parts of its earth walls had collapsed, but protruding from the fallen soil he could see bones. They looked too large for an animal's. In the centre of the pit, sprinkled with earth, lay a cat. Little of it remained, except for its skin and bones; its skin was covered with deep pock-marks. But its eyes seemed to move feebly.

Appalled, he stooped. He had no idea what to do. He never knew, for the walls of the pit were shifting. Soil trickled scattering as a face the size of his fist emerged. There were several; their limbless mouths, their sharp tongues flickered out toward the cat. As he fled they began wailing dreadfully.

He chased the light toward the steps. He fell, cutting his knees. He thought the face with its gleaming eyes would meet him in the hall. He ran from the cellar, flailing his flashlight at the air. As he stumbled down the street he could still see the faces that had crawled from the soil: rudimentary beneath translucent skin, but beginning to be human.

He leaned against his gatepost in the lamplight, retching. Images and memories tumbled disordered through his mind. The face crawling over the roofs. Only seen at night. Vampire. The fluttering at the window. Her terror at the hedge full of spiders. *Calyptra*, what was it, *Calyptra eustrigata.* Vampire moth.

Vague though they were, the implications terrified him. He fled into his building, but halted fearfully on the stairs. The things must be destroyed: to delay would be insane. Suppose their hunger brought them crawling out of the cellar tonight, toward his flat— Absurd though it must be, he couldn't forget that they might have seen his face.

He stood giggling, dismayed. Whom did you call in these circumstances? The police, an exterminator? Nothing would relieve his horror until he saw the brood destroyed, and the only way to see that was to do the job himself. Burn. Petrol. He dawdled on the stairs, delaying, thinking he knew none of the other tenants from whom to borrow the fuel.

He ran to the nearby garage. "Have you got any petrol?"

The man glared at him, suspecting a joke. "You'd be surprised. How much do you want?"

How much indeed! He restrained his giggling. Perhaps he should ask the man's advice! Excuse me, how much petrol do you need for—"A gallon," he stammered.

As soon as he reached the back street he switched on his flashlight. Crowds of rubble lined the pavements. Far above the dark house he saw his orange light. He stepped over the debris into the hall. The swaying light brought the face forward to meet him. Of course the hall was empty.

He forced himself forward. Plucked by the flashlight, the

cellar door flapped soundlessly. Couldn't he just set fire to the house? But that might leave the brood untouched. Don't think, go down quickly. Above the stairs the stain loomed.

In the cellar nothing had changed. The bag gaped, the clothes lay emptied. Struggling to unscrew the cap of the petrol can, he almost dropped the flashlight. He kicked wood into the pit and began to pour the petrol. At once he heard the wailing beneath him. "Shut up!" he screamed, to drown out the sound. "Shut up! Shut up!"

The can took its time in gulping itself empty; the petrol seemed thick as oil. He hurled the can clattering away, and ran to the steps. He fumbled with matches, gripping the flashlight between his knees. As he threw them, the lit matches went out. Not until he ventured back to the pit, clutching a ball of paper from his pocket, did he succeed in making a flame that reached his goal. There was a whoof of fire, and a chorus of interminable feeble shrieking.

As he clambered sickened toward the hall, he heard a fluttering above him. Wallpaper, stirring in a wind: it sounded moist. But there was no wind, for the air clung clammily to him. He slithered over the rubble into the hall, darting his light about. Something white bulked at the top of the stairs.

It was another torn bag. He hadn't been able to see it before. It slumped emptily. Beside it the stain spread over the wall. That stain was too symmetrical; it resembled an inverted coat. Momentarily he thought the paper was drooping, tugged perhaps by his unsteady light, for the stain had begun to creep down toward him. Eyes glared at him from its dangling face. Though the face was upside down he knew it at once. From its gargoyle mouth a tongue reached for him.

He whirled to flee. But the darkness that filled the front door was more than night, for it was advancing audibly. He stumbled, panicking, and rubble slipped from beneath his feet. He fell from the cellar steps, onto piled stone. Though he felt almost no pain, he heard his spine break.

His mind writhed helplessly. His body refused to heed it in any way, and lay on the rubble, trapping him. He could hear cars on the avenue, radio sets and the sounds of cutlery in flats, distant and indifferent. The cries were petering out now. He tried to scream, but only his eyes could move. As they struggled, he glimpsed through a slit in the cellar wall the orange light in his kitchen.

His flashlight lay on the steps, dimmed by its fall. Before long a rustling darkness came slowly down the steps, blotting out the light. He heard sounds in the dark, and something that was not flesh nestled against him. His throat managed a choked shriek that was almost inaudible, even to him. Eventually the face crawled away toward the hall, and the light returned. From the corner of his eye he could see what surrounded him. They were round, still, practically featureless: as yet, hardly even alive.

Angela Carter

(1940–92)

Angela Olive Stalker Carter was born in Eastbourne, but as a result of the Nazi bombing during World War II, she was sent to live with her grandmother in Yorkshire. She was graduated from the University of Bristol in 1965, becoming a journalist and essayist and publishing the first of her nine novels, *Shadow Dance*, in 1965. Fluent in French and German, she traveled widely in Europe, in Asia, where she lived in Tokyo for two years, and in the United States. At Sheffield University, she was the Arts Council of Great Britain Fellow in Creative Writing (1976–78), and later held writer-in-residence positions at Brown University, the University of Adelaide, and the University of East Anglia. Among her novels are *The Magic Toyshop* (1967), *The Infernal Desire Machines of Doctor Hoffman* (1972), *Nights at the Circus* (1984), and *Wise Children* (1991). Her three story collections are *The Bloody Chamber* (1979), *Fireworks: Nine Profane Pieces* (1984), and *Saints and Strangers* (1985). She won the John Llewellyn Rhys Prize, the Somerset Maugham Award, the Cheltenham Festival of Literature Award, and the James Tait Black Memorial Prize.

The Company of Wolves

(1979)

One beast and only one howls in the woods by night.

The wolf is carnivore incarnate and he's as cunning as he is ferocious; once he's had a taste of flesh then nothing else will do.

At night, the eyes of wolves shine like candle flames, yellowish, reddish, but that is because the pupils of their eyes fatten on darkness and catch the light from your lantern to flash it back to you—red for danger; if a wolf's eyes reflect only moonlight, then they gleam a cold and unnatural green, a mineral, a piercing colour. If the benighted traveller spies those luminous, terrible sequins stitched suddenly on the black thickets, then he knows he must run, if fear has not struck him stock-still.

But those eyes are all you will be able to glimpse of the forest assassins as they cluster invisibly round your smell of meat as you go through the wood unwisely late. They will be like shadows, they will be like wraiths, grey members of a congregation of nightmare; hark! his long, wavering howl . . . an aria of fear made audible.

The wolfsong is the sound of the rending you will suffer, in itself a murdering.

It is winter and cold weather. In this region of mountain and forest, there is now nothing for the wolves to eat. Goats and sheep are locked up in the byre, the deer departed for the remaining pasturage on the southern slopes—wolves grow lean and famished. There is so little flesh on them that you could count the starveling ribs through their pelts, if they gave you time before they pounced. Those slavering jaws; the lolling tongue; the rime of saliva on the grizzled chops—of all the teeming perils of the night and the forest, ghosts, hobgoblins, ogres that grill babies upon gridirons, witches that fatten their captives in cages for cannibal tables, the wolf is worst for he cannot listen to reason.

You are always in danger in the forest, where no people are. Step between the portals of the great pines where the shaggy branches tangle about you, trapping the unwary traveller in nets as if the vegetation itself were in a plot with the wolves who live there, as though the wicked trees go fishing on behalf of their friends—step between the gateposts of the forest with the greatest trepidation and infinite precautions, for if you stray from the path for one instant, the wolves will eat you. They are grey as famine, they are as unkind as plague.

The grave-eyed children of the sparse villages always carry knives with them when they go out to tend the little flocks of goats that provide the homesteads with acrid milk and rank, maggoty cheeses. Their knives are half as big as they are, the blades are sharpened daily.

But the wolves have ways of arriving at your own hearthside. We try and try but sometimes we cannot keep them out. There is no winter's night the cottager does not fear to see a lean, grey, famished snout questing under the door, and there was a woman once bitten in her own kitchen as she was straining the macaroni.

Fear and flee the wolf; for, worst of all, the wolf may be more than he seems.

There was a hunter once, near here, that trapped a wolf in a pit. This wolf had massacred the sheep and goats; eaten up a mad old man who used to live by himself in a hut halfway up the mountain and sing to Jesus all day; pounced on a girl looking after the sheep, but she made such a commotion that men came with rifles and scared him away and tried to track him into the forest but he was cunning and easily gave them the slip. So this hunter dug a pit and put a duck in it, for bait, all alive-oh; and he covered the pit with straw smeared with wolf dung. Quack, quack! went the duck and a wolf came slinking out of the forest, a big one, a heavy one, he weighed as much as a grown man and the straw gave way beneath him—into the pit he tumbled. The hunter jumped down after him, slit his throat, cut off all his paws for a trophy.

And then no wolf at all lay in front of the hunter but the bloody trunk of a man, headless, footless, dying, dead.

A witch from up the valley once turned an entire wedding party into wolves because the groom had settled on another girl. She used to order them to visit her, at night, from spite, and they would sit and howl around her cottage for her, serenading her with their misery.

Not so very long ago, a young woman in our village married a man who vanished clean away on her wedding night. The bed was made with new sheets and the bride lay down in it; the groom said, he was going out to relieve himself, insisted on it, for the sake of decency, and she drew the coverlet up to her chin and she lay there. And she waited and she waited and then she waited again—surely he's been gone a long time? Until she jumps up in bed and shrieks to hear a howling, coming on the wind from the forest.

That long-drawn, wavering howl has, for all its fearful

resonance, some inherent sadness in it, as if the beasts would love to be less beastly if only they knew how and never cease to mourn their own condition. There is a vast melancholy in the canticles of the wolves, melancholy infinite as the forest, endless as these long nights of winter and yet that ghastly sadness, that mourning for their own, irremediable appetites, can never move the heart for not one phrase in it hints at the possibility of redemption; grace could not come to the wolf from its own despair, only through some external mediator, so that, sometimes, the beast will look as if he half welcomes the knife that despatches him.

The young woman's brothers searched the outhouses and the haystacks but never found any remains so the sensible girl dried her eyes and found herself another husband not too shy to piss into a pot who spent the nights indoors. She gave him a pair of bonny babies and all went right as a trivet until, one freezing night, the night of the solstice, the hinge of the year when things do not fit together as well as they should, the longest night, her first good man came home again.

A great thump on the door announced him as she was stirring the soup for the father of her children and she knew him the moment she lifted the latch to him although it was years since she'd worn black for him and now he was in rags and his hair hung down his back and never saw a comb, alive with lice.

"Here I am again, missus," he said. "Get me my bowl of cabbage and be quick about it."

Then her second husband came in with wood for the fire and when the first one saw she'd slept with another man and, worse, clapped his red eyes on her little children who'd crept into the kitchen to see what all the din was about, he shouted: "I wish I were a wolf again, to teach this whore a lesson!" So a wolf he instantly became and tore off the eldest boy's left foot before he was chopped up with the hatchet they used for chopping logs. But when the wolf lay bleeding and gasping its last, the pelt peeled off again and he was just as he had been, years ago, when he ran away from his marriage bed, so that she wept and her second husband beat her.

They say there's an ointment the Devil gives you that

turns you into a wolf the minute you rub it on. Or, that he was born feet first and had a wolf for his father and his torso is a man's but his legs and genitals are a wolf's. And he has a wolf's heart.

Seven years is a werewolf's natural span but if you burn his human clothing you condemn him to wolfishness for the rest of his life, so old wives hereabouts think it some protection to throw a hat or an apron at the werewolf, as if clothes made the man. Yet by the eyes, those phosphorescent eyes, you know him in all his shapes; the eyes alone unchanged by metamorphosis.

Before he can become a wolf, the lycanthrope strips stark naked. If you spy a naked man among the pines, you must run as if the Devil were after you.

It is midwinter and the robin, the friend of man, sits on the handle of the gardener's spade and sings. It is the worst time in all the year for wolves but this strong-minded child insists she will go off through the wood. She is quite sure the wild beasts cannot harm her although, well-warned, she lays a carving knife in the basket her mother has packed with cheeses. There is a bottle of harsh liquor distilled from brambles; a batch of flat oatcakes baked on the hearthstone; a pot or two of jam. The flaxen-haired girl will take these delicious gifts to a reclusive grandmother so old the burden of her years is crushing her to death. Granny lives two hours' trudge through the winter woods; the child wraps herself up in her thick shawl, draws it over her head. She steps into her stout wooden shoes; she is dressed and ready and it is Christmas Eve. The malign door of the solstice still swings upon its hinges but she has been too much loved ever to feel scared.

Children do not stay young for long in this savage country. There are no toys for them to play with so they work hard and grow wise but this one, so pretty and the youngest of her family, a little late-comer, had been indulged by her mother and the grandmother who'd knitted her the red shawl that, today, has the ominous if brilliant look of blood on snow. Her breasts have just begun to swell; her hair is like lint, so fair it hardly makes a shadow on her pale forehead; her cheeks are an emblematic scarlet and white and she has just started her woman's bleeding, the clock inside her that will strike, henceforward, once a month.

She stands and moves within the invisible pentacle of her own virginity. She is an unbroken egg; she is a sealed vessel; she has inside her a magic space the entrance to which is shut tight with a plug of membrane; she is a closed system; she does not know how to shiver. She has her knife and she is afraid of nothing.

Her father might forbid her, if he were home, but he is away in the forest, gathering wood, and her mother cannot deny her.

The forest closed upon her like a pair of jaws.

There is always something to look at in the forest, even in the middle of winter—the huddled mounds of birds, succumbed to the lethargy of the season, heaped on the creaking boughs and too forlorn to sing; the bright frills of the winter fungi on the blotched trunks of the trees; the cuneiform slots of rabbits and deer, the herringbone tracks of the birds, a hare as lean as a rasher of bacon streaking across the path where the thin sunlight dapples the russet brakes of last year's bracken.

When she heard the freezing howl of a distant wolf, her practised hand sprang to the handle of her knife, but she saw no sign of a wolf at all, nor of a naked man, neither, but then she heard a clattering among the brushwood and there sprang on to the path a fully clothed one, a very handsome young one, in the green coat and wideawake hat of a hunter, laden with carcasses of game birds. She had her hand on her knife at the first rustle of twigs but he laughed with a flash of white teeth when he saw her and made her a comic yet flattering little bow; she'd never seen such a fine fellow before, not among the rustic clowns of her native village. So on they went together, through the thickening light of the afternoon.

Soon they were laughing and joking like old friends. When he offered to carry her basket, she gave it to him although her knife was in it because he told her his rifle would protect them. As the day darkened, it began to snow again; she felt the first flakes settle on her eyelashes but now there was only half a mile to go and there would be a fire, and hot tea, and a welcome, a warm one, surely, for the dashing huntsman as well as for herself.

This young man had a remarkable object in his pocket. It was a compass. She looked at the little round glass face in the palm of his hand and watched the wavering needle with a vague wonder. He assured her this compass had taken him safely through the wood on his hunting trip because the needle always told him with perfect accuracy where the north was. She did not believe it; she knew she should never leave the path on the way through the wood or else she would be lost instantly. He laughed at her again; gleaming trails of spittle clung to his teeth. He said, if he plunged off the path into the forest that surrounded them, he could guarantee to arrive at her grandmother's house a good quarter of an hour before she did, plotting his way through the undergrowth with his compass, while she trudged the long way, along the winding path.

I don't believe you. Besides, aren't you afraid of the wolves?

He only tapped the gleaming butt of his rifle and grinned.

Is it a bet? he asked her. Shall we make a game of it? What will you give me if I get to your grandmother's house before you?

What would you like? she asked disingenuously.

A kiss.

Commonplaces of a rustic seduction; she lowered her eyes and blushed.

He went through the undergrowth and took her basket with him but she forgot to be afraid of the beasts, although now the moon was rising, for she wanted to dawdle on her way to make sure the handsome gentleman would win his wager.

Grandmother's house stood by itself a little way out of the village. The freshly falling snow blew in eddies about the kitchen garden and the young man stepped delicately up the snowy path to the door as if he were reluctant to get his feet wet, swinging his bundle of game and the girl's basket and humming a little tune to himself.

There is a faint trace of blood on his chin; he has been snacking on his catch.

He rapped upon the panels with his knuckles.

Aged and frail, granny is three-quarters succumbed to the mortality the ache in her bones promises her and almost ready to give in entirely. A boy came out from the village to build up her hearth for the night an hour ago and the kitchen crackles with busy firelight. She has her Bible for company, she is a pious old woman. She is propped up on several pillows in the bed set into the wall peasant-fashion, wrapped up in the patchwork quilt she made before she was married, more years ago than she cares to remember. Two china spaniels with liver-coloured blotches on their coats and black noses sit on either side of the fireplace. There is a bright rug of woven rags on the pantiles. The grandfather clock ticks away her eroding time.

We keep the wolves outside by living well.

He rapped upon the panels with his hairy knuckles.

It is your granddaughter, he mimicked in a high soprano.

Lift up the latch and walk in, my darling.

You can tell them by their eyes, eyes of a beast of prey, nocturnal, devastating eyes as red as a wound; you can hurl your Bible at him and your apron after, granny, you thought that was a sure prophylactic against these infernal vermin . . . now call on Christ and his mother and all the angels in heaven to protect you but it won't do you any good.

His feral muzzle is sharp as a knife; he drops his golden burden of gnawed pheasant on the table and puts down your dear girl's basket, too. Oh, my God, what have you done with her?

Off with his disguise, that coat of forest-coloured cloth, the hat with the feather tucked into the ribbon; his matted hair streams down his white shirt and she can see the lice moving in it. The sticks in the hearth shift and hiss; night and the forest has come into the kitchen with darkness tangled in its hair.

He strips off his shirt. His skin is the colour and texture of vellum. A crisp stripe of hair runs down his belly, his nipples are ripe and dark as poison fruit but he's so thin you could count the ribs under his skin if only he gave you the time. He strips off his trousers and she can see how hairy his legs are. His genitals, huge. Ah! huge.

The last thing the old lady saw in all this world was a young man, eyes like cinders, naked as a stone, approaching her bed.

The wolf is carnivore incarnate.

When he had finished with her, he licked his chops and

quickly dressed himself again, until he was just as he had been when he came through her door. He burned the inedible hair in the fireplace and wrapped the bones up in a napkin that he hid away under the bed in the wooden chest in which he found a clean pair of sheets. These he carefully put on the bed instead of the tell-tale stained ones he stowed away in the laundry basket. He plumped up the pillows and shook out the patchwork quilt, he picked up the Bible from the floor, closed it and laid it on the table. All was as it had been before except that grandmother was gone. The sticks twitched in the grate, the clock ticked and the young man sat patiently, deceitfully beside the bed in granny's nightcap.

Rat-a-tap-tap.

Who's there, he quavers in granny's antique falsetto.

Only your granddaughter.

So she came in, bringing with her a flurry of snow that melted in tears on the tiles, and perhaps she was a little disappointed to see only her grandmother sitting beside the fire. But then he flung off the blanket and sprang to the door, pressing his back against it so that she could not get out again.

The girl looked round the room and saw there was not even the indentation of a head on the smooth cheek of the pillow and how, for the first time she'd seen it so, the Bible lay closed on the table. The tick of the clock cracked like a whip. She wanted her knife from her basket but she did not dare reach for it because his eyes were fixed upon her—huge eyes that now seemed to shine with a unique, interior light, eyes the size of saucers, saucers full of Greek fire, diabolic phosphorescence.

What big eyes you have.

All the better to see you with.

No trace at all of the old woman except for a tuft of white hair that had caught in the bark of an unburned log. When the girl saw that, she knew she was in danger of death.

Where is my grandmother?

There's nobody here but we two, my darling.

Now a great howling rose up all around them, near, very near, as close as the kitchen garden, the howling of a multitude of wolves; she knew the worst wolves are hairy on the inside and she shivered, in spite of the scarlet shawl she pulled more closely round herself as if it could protect her although it was as red as the blood she must spill.

Who has come to sing us carols, she said.

Those are the voices of my brothers, darling; I love the company of wolves. Look out of the window and you'll see them.

Snow half-caked the lattice and she opened it to look into the garden. It was a white night of moon and snow; the blizzard whirled round the gaunt, grey beasts who squatted on their haunches among the rows of winter cabbage, pointing their sharp snouts to the moon and howling as if their hearts would break. Ten wolves; twenty wolves—so many wolves she could not count them, howling in concert as if demented or deranged. Their eyes reflected the light from the kitchen and shone like a hundred candles.

It is very cold, poor things, she said; no wonder they howl so.

She closed the window on the wolves' threnody and took off her scarlet shawl, the colour of poppies, the colour of sacrifices, the colour of her menses, and, since her fear did her no good, she ceased to be afraid.

What shall I do with my shawl?

Throw it on the fire, dear one. You won't need it again.

She bundled up her shawl and threw it on the blaze, which instantly consumed it. Then she drew her blouse over her head; her small breasts gleamed as if the snow had invaded the room.

What shall I do with my blouse?

Into the fire with it, too, my pet.

The thin muslin went flaring up the chimney like a magic bird and now off came her skirt, her woollen stockings, her shoes, and on to the fire they went, too, and were gone for good. The firelight shone through the edges of her skin; now she was clothed only in her untouched integument of flesh. This dazzling, naked she combed out her hair with her fingers; her hair looked white as the snow outside. Then went directly to the man with red eyes in whose unkempt mane the lice moved; she stood up on tiptoe and unbuttoned the collar of his shirt.

What big arms you have.

All the better to hug you with.

Every wolf in the world now howled a prothalamion outside the window as she freely gave the kiss she owed him.

What big teeth you have!

She saw how his jaw began to slaver and the room was full of the clamour of the forest's Liebestod but the wise child never flinched, even when he answered:

All the better to eat you with.

The girl burst out laughing; she knew she was nobody's meat. She laughed at him full in the face, she ripped off his shirt for him and flung it into the fire, in the fiery wake of her own discarded clothing. The flames danced like dead souls on Walpurgisnacht and the old bones under the bed set up a terrible clattering but she did not pay them any heed.

Carnivore incarnate, only immaculate flesh appeases him.

She will lay his fearful head on her lap and she will pick out the lice from his pelt and perhaps she will put the lice into her mouth and eat them, as he will bid her, as she would do in a savage marriage ceremony.

The blizzard will die down.

The blizzard died down, leaving the mountains as randomly covered with snow as if a blind woman had thrown a sheet over them, the upper branches of the forest pines limed, creaking, swollen with the fall.

Snowlight, moonlight, a confusion of paw-prints.

All silent, all still.

Midnight; and the clock strikes. It is Christmas Day, the werewolves' birthday, the door of the solstice stands wide open; let them all sink through.

See! sweet and sound she sleeps in granny's bed, between the paws of the tender wolf.

Charles Dickens

(1812–70)

Born the son of a dockyard clerk in Portsmouth, England, Dickens was under the care of a young nursemaid named Mary Weller from the time that he was five until he was eleven. Fond of grim tales of death, demons, and ghosts, she filled the head of her young charge with a range of vivid stories of the supernatural. Dickens's comfortable childhood came to an abrupt end when he was twelve years old. His father was imprisoned for debt, and Dickens was sent to work at a London shoe-blacking factory. After his father's release from prison, Dickens was sent to school and rose from a clerkship in a law office to a journalist who covered the House of Commons to a writer of sketches. His first sketch was published in 1833, and by 1836, his immensely popular first novel, *The Pickwick Papers*, had been serialized in monthly installments. Interestingly, it contained five interpolated ghost stories. Among the novels that followed, often in serialized segments, were *Oliver Twist* (1837–38), *Nicholas Nickleby* (1838–39), *The Old Curiosity Shop* (1840–41), *Martin Chuzzlewit* (1843–44), *David Copperfield* (1849–50), *Bleak House* (1852–53), *Hard Times* (1854), and *Great Expectations* (1860–61). *A Christmas Carol* (1843) is the best known of his many ghost tales.

The Lawyer and the Ghost

(1836)

I knew a man—let me see—forty years ago now—who took an old, damp, rotten set of chambers, in one of the most ancient Inns, that had been shut up and empty for years and years before. There were lots of old women's stories about the place, and it certainly was very far from being a cheerful one; but he was poor, and the rooms were cheap, and that would have been quite a sufficient reason for him, if they had been ten times worse than they really were.

The man was obliged to take some mouldering fixtures that were on the place, and, among the rest, was a great lumbering wooden press for papers, with large glass doors, and a green curtain inside; a pretty useless thing for him, for he had no papers to put in it; and as to his clothes, he carried them about with him, and that wasn't very hard work, either.

Well, he had moved in all his furniture—it wasn't quite a truck-full—and had sprinkled it about the room, so as to make the four chairs look as much like a dozen as possible, and was sitting down before the fire at night, drinking the first glass of two gallons of whiskey he had ordered on credit, wondering whether it would ever be paid for, and if so, in how many years' time, when his eyes encountered the glass doors of the wooden press.

"Ah," says he. "If I hadn't been obliged to take that ugly article at the old broker's valuation, I might have got something comfortable for the money. I'll tell you what it is, old fellow," he said, speaking aloud to the press, having nothing else to speak to; "If it wouldn't cost more to break up your old carcase, than it would ever be worth afterwards, I'd have a fire out of you in less than no time."

He had hardly spoken the words, when a sound resembling a faint groan, appeared to issue from the interior of the case. It startled him at first, but thinking, on a moment's reflection, that it must be some young fellow in the next chamber, who had been dining out, he put his feet on the fender, and raised the poker to stir the fire.

At that moment, the sound was repeated: and one of the glass doors slowly opening, disclosed a pale and emaciated figure in soiled and worn apparel, standing erect in the press. The figure was tall and thin, and the countenance expressive of care and anxiety; but there was something in the hue of the skin, and gaunt and unearthly appearance of the whole form, which no being of this world was ever seen to wear.

"Who are you?" said the new tenant, turning very pale; poising the poker in his hand, however, and taking a very decent aim at the countenance of the figure. "Who are you?"

"Don't throw that poker at me," replied the form: "If you hurled it with ever so sure an aim, it would pass through me, without resistance, and expend its force on the wood behind. I am a spirit!"

"And, pray, what do you want here?" faltered the tenant.

"In this room," replied the apparition, "my worldly ruin was worked, and I and my children beggared. In this press, the papers in a long, long suit, which accumulated for years, were deposited. In this room, when I had died of grief, and long-deferred hope, two wily harpies divided the wealth for which I had contested during a wretched existence, and of which, at last, not one farthing was left for my unhappy descendants. I terrified them from the spot, and since that day have prowled by night—the only period at which I can revisit the earth—about the scenes of my long-protracted misery. This apartment is mine: leave it to me!"

"If you insist upon making your appearance here," said the tenant, who had had time to collect his presence of mind during this prosy statement of the ghost's, "I shall give up possession with the greatest pleasure, but I should like to ask you one question, if you will allow me."

"Say on," said the apparition, sternly.

"Well," said the tenant, "I don't apply the observation personally to you, because it is equally applicable to most of the ghosts I ever heard of; but it does appear to me somewhat inconsistent, that when you have an opportunity of visiting the fairest spots of earth—for I suppose space is nothing to you—you should always return exactly to the very places where you have been most miserable."

"Egad, that's very true; I never thought of that before," said the ghost.

"You see, sir," pursued the tenant, "this is a very uncomfortable room. From the appearance of that press, I should be disposed to say that it is not wholly free from bugs; and I really think you might find more comfortable quarters: to say nothing of the climate of London, which is extremely disagreeable."

"You are very right, sir," said the ghost politely, "it never struck me till now; I'll try a change of air directly."

In fact, he began to vanish as he spoke: his legs, indeed, had quite disappeared!

"And if, sir," said the tenant, calling after him, "if you *would* have the goodness to suggest to the other ladies and gentlemen who are now engaged in haunting old empty houses, that they might be much more comfortable elsewhere, you will confer a very great benefit on society."

"I will," replied the ghost, "we must be dull fellows, very dull fellows, indeed; I can't imagine how we can have been so stupid."

With these words, the spirit disappeared, and what is rather remarkable, he never came back again.

Sir Arthur Conan Doyle

(1859–1930)

Best known as the creator of the brilliant detective Sherlock Holmes and his sidekick, Dr. Watson, Sir Arthur Ignatius Conan Doyle was born in Edinburgh. One of ten children, he attended a Catholic preparatory school and Stonyhurst College, and studied to become a doctor at the University of Edinburgh. At age nineteen, he published his first story in *Chambers's Edinburgh Journal*, and since, initially, his medical practice was not very successful, he was able to spend a considerable amount of time writing fiction. Among his Sherlock Holmes books are *The Sign of Four* (1890), *The Adventures of Sherlock Holmes* (1892), *The Memoirs of Sherlock Holmes* (1894), *The Return of Sherlock Holmes* (1905), *His Last Bow* (1917), and *The Case-Book of Sherlock Holmes* (1927). His story collections include *My Friend the Murderer and Other Mysteries and Adventures* (1893), *Round the Fire Stories* (1908), *Danger! and Other Stories* (1918), *The Great Keinplatz Experiment and Other Tales of Twilight and the Unseen* (1919), and *The Black Doctor and Other Tales of Terror and Mystery* (1925). He was an avid believer in spiritualism and supporter of spiritualist groups such as the Spiritualists' National Union and The Ghost Club.

Lot No. 249

(1892)

Of the dealings of Edward Bellingham with William Monkhouse Lee, and of the cause of the great terror of Abercrombie Smith, it may be that no absolute and final judgment will ever be delivered. It is true that we have the full and clear narrative of Smith himself, and such corroboration as he could look for from Thomas Styles the servant, from the Reverend Plumptree Peterson, Fellow of Old's, and from such other people as chanced to gain some passing glance at this or that incident in a singular chain of events. Yet, in the main, the story must rest upon Smith alone, and the most will think that it is more likely that one brain, however outwardly sane, has some subtle warp in its texture, some strange flaw in its workings, than that the path of Nature has been overstepped in open day in so famed a center of learning and light as the University of Oxford. Yet when we think how narrow and how devious this path of Nature is, how dimly we can trace it, for all our lamps of science, and how from the darkness that girds it round great and terrible possibilities loom ever shadowly upward, it is a bold and confident man who will put a limit to the strange bypaths into which the human spirit may wander.

In a certain wing of what we will call Old College in Oxford there is a corner turret of an exceeding great age. The heavy arch that spans the open door has bent downward in the center under the weight of its years, and the gray, lichen-blotched blocks of stone are bound and knitted together with withes and strands of ivy, as though the old mother had set herself to brace them up against wind and weather. From the door a stone stair curves upward spirally, passing two landings, and terminating in a third one, its steps all shapeless and hollowed by the tread of so many generations of the seekers after knowledge. Life has flowed like water down this winding stair, and, waterlike, has left these smooth-worn grooves behind it. From the long-gowned, pedantic scholars of Plantagenet days down to the young bloods of a later age, how full and strong had been that tide of young, English life. And what was left now of all those hopes, those strivings, those fiery energies, save here and there in some old world churchyard a few scratches upon a stone, and perchance a handful of dust in a moldering coffin? Yet here were the silent stair and the gray, old wall, with bend and saltire and many another heraldic device still to be read upon its surface, like grotesque shadows thrown back from the days that had passed.

In the month of May, in the year 1884, three young men occupied the sets of rooms which opened on to the separate landings of the old stair. Each set consisted simply of a sitting room and of a bedroom, while the two corresponding rooms upon the ground floor were used, the one as a coal cellar, and the other as the living room of the servant, or scout, Thomas Styles, whose duty it was to wait upon the three men above him. To right and to left was a line of lecture rooms and of offices, so that the dwellers in the old turret enjoyed a certain seclusion, which made the chambers popular among the more studious undergraduates. Such were the three who occupied them now—Abercrombie Smith above, Edward Bellingham beneath him, and William Monkhouse Lee upon the lowest story.

It was ten o'clock on a bright, spring night, and Abercrombie Smith lay back in his armchair, his feet upon the fender, and his brierroot pipe between his lips. In a similar chair, and equally at his ease, there lounged on the other side of the fireplace his old school friend Jephro Hastie. Both men were in flannels, for they had spent their evening upon the river, but apart from their dress no one could look at their hard-cut, alert faces without seeing that they were open-air men—men whose minds and tastes turned naturally to all that was manly and robust. Hastie, indeed, was stroke of his college boat, and Smith was an even better oar, but a coming examination had already cast its shadow over him and held him to his work, save for the few hours a week which health demanded. A litter of medical books upon the table, with scattered bones, models, and anatomical plates, pointed to the extent as well as the nature of his studies, while a couple of single sticks and a set of boxing gloves above the mantelpiece hinted at the means by which, with Hastie's help, he might take his exercise in its most compressed and least distant form. They knew each other very well—so well that they could sit now in that soothing silence which is the very highest development of companionship.

"Have some whisky," said Abercrombie Smith at last between two cloudbursts. "Scotch in the jug and Irish in the bottle."

"No, thanks. I'm in for the sculls. I don't liquor when I'm training. How about you?"

"I'm reading hard. I think it best to leave it alone."

Hastie nodded, and they relapsed into a contented silence.

"By the way, Smith," asked Hastie, presently, "have you made the acquaintance of either of the fellows on your stair yet?"

"Just a nod when we pass. Nothing more."

"Hum! I should be inclined to let it stand at that. I know something of them both. Not much, but as much as I want. I don't think I should take them to my bosom if I were you. Not that there's much amiss with Monkhouse Lee."

"Meaning the thin one?"

"Precisely. He is a gentlemanly little fellow. I don't think there is any vice in him. But then you can't know him without knowing Bellingham."

"Meaning the fat one?"

"Yes, the fat one. And he's a man whom I, for one, would rather not know."

Abercrombie Smith raised his eyebrows and glanced across at his companion.

"What's up, then?" he asked. "Drink? Cards? Cad? You used not to be censorious."

"Ah! you evidently don't know the man, or you wouldn't ask. There's something damnable about him—something reptilian. My gorge always rises at him. I should put him down as a man with secret vices—an evil liver. He's no fool, though. They say that he is one of the best men in his line that they have ever had in the college."

"Medicine or classics?"

"Eastern languages. He's a demon at them. Chillingworth met him somewhere above the second cataract last summer vacation, and he told me that he just prattled to the Arabs as if he had been born and nursed and weaned among them. He talked Coptic to the Copts, and Hebrew to the Jews, and Arabic to the Bedouins, and they were all ready to kiss the hem of his frock coat. There are some old hermit johnnies up in those parts who sit on rocks and scowl and spit at the casual stranger. Well, when they saw this chap Bellingham, before he had said five words they just lay down on their bellies and wriggled. Chillingworth said that he never saw anything like it. Bellingham seemed to take it as his right, too, and strutted about among them and talked down to them like a Dutch uncle. Pretty good for an undergrad of Old's, wasn't it?"

"Why do you say you can't know Lee without knowing Bellingham?"

"Because Bellingham is engaged to his sister Eveline. Such a bright little girl, Smith! I know the whole family well. It's disgusting to see that brute with her. A toad and a dove, that's what they always remind me of."

Abercrombie Smith grinned and knocked his ashes out against the side of the grate.

"You show every card in your hand, old chap," said he. "What a prejudiced, green-eyed, evil-thinking old man it is! You have really nothing against the fellow except that."

"Well, I've known her ever since she was as long as that cherrywood pipe, and I don't like to see her taking risks. And it is a risk. He looks beastly. And he has a beastly temper, a venomous temper. You remember his row with Long Norton?"

"No; you always forget that I am a freshman."

"Ah, it was last winter. Of course. Well, you know the towpath along by the river. There were several fellows going along it, Bellingham in front, when they came on an old market woman coming the other way. It had been raining—you know what those fields are like when it has rained—and the path ran between the river and a great puddle that was nearly as broad. Well, what does this swine do but keep the path, and push the old girl into the mud, where she and her marketings came to terrible grief. It was a blackguard thing to do, and Long Norton, who is as gentle a fellow as ever stepped, told him what he thought of it. One word led to another, and it ended in Norton laying his stick across the fellow's shoulders. There was the deuce of a fuss about it, and it's a treat to see the way in which Bellingham looks at Norton when they meet now. By Jove, Smith, it's nearly eleven o'clock!"

"No hurry. Light your pipe again."

"Not I. I'm supposed to be in training. Here I've been sitting gossiping when I ought to have been safely tucked up. I'll borrow your skull, if you can share it. Williams has had mine for a month. I'll take the little bones of your ear, too, if you are sure you won't need them. Thanks very much. Never mind a bag, I can carry them very well under my arm. Good night, my son, and take my tip as to your neighbor."

When Hastie, bearing his anatomical plunder, had clattered off down the winding stair, Abercrombie Smith hurled his pipe into the wastepaper basket, and drawing his chair nearer to the lamp, plunged into a formidable, green-covered volume, adorned with great, colored maps of that strange, internal kingdom of which we are the hapless and helpless monarchs. Though a freshman at Oxford, the student was not so in medicine, for he had worked for four years at Glasgow and at Berlin, and this coming examination would place him finally as a member of his profession. With his firm mouth, broad forehead, and clear-cut, somewhat hard-featured face, he was a man who, if he had no brilliant talent, was yet so dogged, so patient, and so strong that he might in the end overtop a more showy genius. A man who can hold his own among Scotchmen and North Germans is not a man to be easily set back. Smith had left a name at Glasgow and at Berlin, and he was bent upon doing as much at Oxford, if hard work and devotion could accomplish it.

He had sat reading for about an hour, and the hands of the noisy carriage clock upon the side table were rapidly closing together upon the twelve, when a sudden sound fell upon his student's ear—a sharp, rather shrill sound, like the hissing intake of a man's breath who gasps under some strong emotion. Smith laid down his book and slanted his ear to listen. There was no one on either side or above him, so that the interruption came certainly from the neighbor beneath—the same neighbor of whom Hastie had given so unsavory an account. Smith knew him only as a flabby, pale-faced man of silent and studious habits, a man whose lamp threw a golden bar from the old turret even after he had extinguished his own. This community in lateness had formed a certain silent bond between them. It was soothing to Smith when the hours stole on toward dawn to feel that there was another so close who set as small a value upon his sleep as he did. Even now, as his thoughts turned toward him, Smith's feelings were kindly. Hastie was a good fellow, but he was rough, strong-fibered, with no imagination or sympathy. He could not tolerate departures from what he looked upon as the model type of manliness. If a man could not be measured by a public school standard, then he was beyond the pale with Hastie. Like so many who are themselves robust, he was apt to confuse the constitution with the character, to ascribe to want of principle what was really a want of circulation. Smith, with his stronger mind, knew his friend's habit, and made allowance for it now as his thoughts turned toward the man beneath him.

There was no return of the singular sound, and Smith was about to turn to his work once more, when suddenly there broke out in the silence of the night a hoarse cry, a positive scream—the call of a man who is moved and shaken beyond all control. Smith sprang out of his chair and dropped his book. He was a man of fairly firm fiber, but there was something in this sudden, uncontrollable shriek of horror that chilled his blood and pringled in his skin. Coming in such a place and at such an hour, it brought a thousand fantastic possibilities into his head. Should he rush down, or was it better to wait? He had all the national hatred of making a scene, and he knew so little of his neighbor that he would not lightly intrude upon his affairs. For a moment he stood in doubt and even as he balanced the matter there was a quick rattle of footsteps upon the stairs, and young Monkhouse Lee, half dressed and as white as ashes, burst into his room.

"Come down!" he gasped. "Bellingham's ill."

Abercrombie Smith followed him closely downstairs into the sitting room which was beneath his own, and intent as he was upon the matter in hand, he could not but take an amazed glance around him as he crossed the threshold. It was such a chamber as he had never seen before—a museum rather than a study. Walls and ceiling were thickly covered with a thousand strange relics from Egypt and the East. Tall, angular figures bearing burdens or weapons stalked in an uncouth frieze round the apartment. Above were bull-headed, stork-headed, cat-headed, owl-headed statues, with viper-crowned, almond-eyed monarchs, and strange, beetlelike deities cut out of the blue Egyptian lapis lazuli. Horus and Isis and Osiris peeped down from every niche and shelf, while across the ceiling a true son of Old Nile, a great, hanging-jawed crocodile, was slung in a double noose.

In the center of this singular chamber was a large, square table, littered with papers, bottles, and the dried leaves of some graceful, palmlike plant. These varied objects had all been heaped together in order to make room for a mummy case, which had been conveyed from the wall, as was evident from the gap there, and laid across the front of the table. The mummy itself, a horrid, black, withered thing, like a charred head on a gnarled bush, was lying half out of the case, with its clawlike hand and bony forearm resting upon the table. Propped up against the sarcophagus was an old, yellow scroll of papyrus, and in front of it, in a wooden armchair, sat the owner of the room, his head thrown back, his widely opened eyes directed in a horrified stare to the crocodile above him, and his blue, thick lips puffing loudly with every expiration.

"My God! He's dying!" cried Monkhouse Lee, distractedly.

He was a slim, handsome young fellow, olive-skinned and dark-eyed, of a Spanish rather than of an English type, with a Celtic intensity of manner which contrasted with the Saxon phlegm of Abercrombie Smith.

"Only a faint, I think," said the medical student. "Just give me a hand with him. You take his feet. Now onto the sofa. Can you kick all those little wooden devils off? What a litter it is! Now he will be all right if we undo his collar and give him some water. What has he been up to at all?"

"I don't know. I heard him cry out. I ran up. I know him pretty well, you know. It is very good of you to come down."

"His heart is going like a pair of castanets," said Smith, laying his hand on the breast of the unconscious man. "He seems to me to be frightened all to pieces. Chuck the water over him! What a face he has got on him!"

It was indeed a strange and most repellent face, for color and outline were equally unnatural. It was white, not with the ordinary pallor of fear, but with an absolutely bloodless white, like the underside of a sole. He was very fat, but gave the impression of having at some time been considerably fatter, for his skin hung loosely in creases and folds, and was shot with a meshwork of wrinkles. Short, stubby brown hair bristled up from his scalp, with a pair of thick, wrinkled ears protruding at the sides. His light gray eyes were still open, the pupils dilated and the balls projecting in a fixed and horrid stare. It seemed to Smith as he looked down upon him that he had never seen Nature's danger signals flying so plainly upon a man's countenance, and his thoughts turned more seriously to the warning which Hastie had given him an hour before.

"What the deuce can have frightened him so?" he asked.

"It's the mummy."

"The mummy? How, then?"

"I don't know. It's beastly and morbid. I wish he would drop it. It's the second fright he has given me. It was the same last winter. I found him just like this, with that horrid thing in front of him."

"What does he want with the mummy, then?"

"Oh, he's a crank, you know. It's his hobby. He knows more about these things than any man in England. But I wish he wouldn't! Ah, he's beginning to come to."

A faint tinge of color had begun to steal back into Bellingham's ghastly cheeks, and his eyelids shivered like a sail after a calm. He clasped and unclasped his hands, drew a long, thin breath between his teeth, and suddenly jerking up his head, threw a glance of recognition around him. As his eyes fell upon the mummy, he sprang off the sofa, seized the roll of papyrus, thrust it into a drawer, turned the key, and then staggered back onto the sofa.

"What's up?" he asked. "What do you chaps want?"

"You've been shrieking out and making no end of a fuss," said Monkhouse Lee. "If our neighbor here from above hadn't come down, I'm sure I don't know what I should have done with you."

"Ah, it's Abercrombie Smith," said Bellingham, glancing up at him. "How very good of you to come in! What a fool I am! Oh, my God, what a fool I am!"

He sank his head on to his hands, and burst into peal after peal of hysterical laughter.

"Look here! Drop it!" cried Smith, shaking him roughly by the shoulder.

"Your nerves are all in a jangle. You must drop these little midnight games with mummies, or you'll be going off your chump. You're all on wires now."

"I wonder," said Bellingham, "whether you would be as cool as I am if you had seen—"

"What then?"

"Oh, nothing. I meant that I wonder if you could sit up at night with a mummy without trying your nerves. I have no doubt that you are quite right. I dare say that I have been taking it out of myself too much lately. But I am all right now. Please don't go, though. Just wait for a few minutes until I am quite myself."

"The room is very close," remarked Lee, throwing open the window and letting in the cool night air.

"It's balsamic resin," said Bellingham. He lifted up one of the dried palmate leaves from the table and frizzled it over the chimney of the lamp. It broke away into heavy smoke wreaths, and a pungent, biting odor filled the chamber. "It's the sacred plant—the plant of the priests," he remarked. "Do you know anything of Eastern languages, Smith?"

"Nothing at all. Not a word."

The answer seemed to lift a weight from the Egyptologist's mind.

"By the way," he continued, "how long was it from the time that you ran down, until I came to my senses?"

"Not long. Some four or five minutes."

"I thought it could not be very long," said he, drawing a long breath. "But what a strange thing unconsciousness is! There is no measurement to it. I could not tell from my own sensations if it were seconds or weeks. Now that gentleman on the table was packed up in the days of the Eleventh Dynasty, some forty centuries ago, and yet if he could find his tongue, he would tell us that this lapse of time has been but a closing of the eyes and a reopening of them. He is a singularly fine mummy, Smith."

Smith stepped over to the table and looked down with a professional eye at the black and twisted form in front of him. The features, though horribly discolored, were perfect, and two little nutlike eyes still lurked in the depths of the black, hollow sockets. The blotched skin was drawn tightly from bone to bone, and a tangled wrap of black, coarse hair fell over the ears. Two thin teeth, like those of a rat, overlay the shriveled lower lip. In its crouching position, with bent joints and craned head, there was a suggestion of energy about the horrid thing which made Smith's gorge rise. The gaunt ribs, with their parchmentlike covering, were exposed, and the sunken, leaden-hued abdomen, with the long slit where the embalmer had left his mark; but the lower limbs were wrapped round with coarse, yellow bandages. A number of little clovelike pieces of myrrh and of cassia were sprinkled over the body, and lay scattered on the inside of the case.

"I don't know his name," said Bellingham, passing his hand over the shriveled head. "You see the outer sarcophagus with the inscriptions is missing. Lot 249 is all the title he has now. You see it printed on his case. That was his number in the auction at which I picked him up."

"He has been a very pretty sort of fellow in his day," remarked Abercrombie Smith.

"He has been a giant. His mummy is six feet seven in length, and that would be a giant over there, for they were never a very robust race. Feel these great, knotted bones, too. He would be a nasty fellow to tackle."

"Perhaps these very hands helped to build the stones into the pyramids," suggested Monkhouse Lee, looking down with disgust in his eyes at the crooked, unclean talons.

"No fear. This fellow has been pickled in natron, and looked after in the most approved style. They did not serve hodsmen in that fashion. Salt or bitumen was enough for them. It has been calculated that this sort of thing cost about seven hundred and thirty pounds in our money. Our friend was a noble at the least. What do you make of that small inscription near his feet, Smith?"

"I told you that I know no Eastern tongue."

"Ah, so you did. It is the name of the embalmer, I take it. A very conscientious worker he must have been. I wonder how many modern works will survive four thousand years?"

He kept on speaking lightly and rapidly, but it was evident to Abercrombie Smith that he was still palpitating with fear. His hands shook, his lower lip trembled, and look where he would, his eye always came sliding round to his gruesome companion. Through all his fear, however, there was a suspicion of triumph in his tone and manner. His eyes shone, and his footstep, as he paced the room, was brisk and jaunty. He gave the impression of a man who has gone through an ordeal, the marks of which he still bears upon him, but which has helped him to his end.

"You're not going yet?" he cried, as Smith rose from the sofa.

At the prospect of solitude, his fears seemed to crowd back upon him, and he stretched out a hand to detain him.

"Yes, I must go. I have my work to do. You are all right

now. I think that with your nervous system you should take up some less morbid study."

"Oh, I am not nervous as a rule; and I have unwrapped mummies before."

"You fainted last time," observed Monkhouse Lee.

"Ah, yes, so I did. Well, I must have a nerve tonic or a course of electricity. You are not going, Lee?"

"I'll do whatever you wish, Ned."

"Then I'll come down with you and have a shakedown on your sofa. Good night, Smith. I am so sorry to have disturbed you with my foolishness."

They shook hands, and as the medical student stumbled up the spiral and irregular stair he heard a key turn in a door, and the steps of his two new acquaintances as they descended to the lower floor.

In this strange way began the acquaintance between Edward Bellingham and Abercrombie Smith, an acquaintance which the latter, at least, had no desire to push further. Bellingham, however, appeared to have taken a fancy to his rough-spoken neighbor, and made his advances in such a way that he could hardly be repulsed without absolute brutality. Twice he called to thank Smith for his assistance, and many times afterward he looked in with books, papers, and such other civilities as two bachelor neighbors can offer each other. He was, as Smith soon found, a man of wide reading, with catholic tastes and an extraordinary memory. His manner, too, was so pleasing and suave that one came, after a time, to overlook his repellent appearance. For a jaded and wearied man he was no unpleasant companion, and Smith found himself, after a time, looking forward to his visits, and even returning them.

Clever as he undoubtedly was, however, the medical student seemed to detect a dash of insanity in the man. He broke out at times into a high, inflated style of talk which was in contrast with the simplicity of his life.

"It is a wonderful thing," he cried, "to feel that one can command powers of good and of evil—a ministering angel or a demon of vengeance." And again, of Monkhouse Lee, he said—"Lee is a good fellow, an honest fellow, but he is without strength or ambition. He would not make a fit partner for a man with a great enterprise. He would not make a fit partner for me."

At such hints and innuendoes stolid Smith, puffing solemnly at his pipe, would simply raise his eyebrows and shake his head, with little interjections of medical wisdom as to earlier hours and fresher air.

One habit Bellingham had developed of late which Smith knew to be a frequent herald of a weakening mind. He appeared to be forever talking to himself. At late hours of the night, when there could be no visitor with him, Smith could still hear his voice beneath him in a low, muffled monologue, sunk almost to a whisper, and yet very audible in the silence. This solitary babbling annoyed and distracted the student, so that he spoke more than once to his neighbor about it. Bellingham, however, flushed up at the charge, and denied curtly that he had uttered a sound; indeed, he showed more annoyance over the matter than the occasion seemed to demand.

Had Abercrombie Smith had any doubt as to his own ears he had not to go far to find corroboration. Tom Styles, the little wrinkled manservant who had attended to the wants of the lodgers in the turret for a longer time than any man's memory could carry him, was sorely put to it over the same matter.

"If you please, sir," said he, as he tidied down the top chamber one morning, "do you think Mr. Bellingham is all right, sir?"

"All right, Styles?"

"Yes, sir. Right in his head, sir."

"Why should he not be, then?"

"Well, I don't know, sir. His habits has changed of late. He's not the same man he used to be, though I make free to say that he was never quite one of my gentlemen, like Mr. Hastie or yourself, sir. He's took to talkin' to himself something awful. I wonder it don't disturb you. I don't know what to make of him, sir."

"I don't know what business it is of yours, Styles."

"Well, I takes an interest, Mr. Smith. It may be forward of me, but I can't help it. I feel sometimes as if I was mother and father to my young gentlemen. It all falls on me when things go wrong and the relations come. But Mr. Bellingham, sir. I want to know what it is that walks about his room sometimes when he's out and when the door's locked on the outside."

"Eh? You're talking nonsense, Styles."

"Maybe so, sir; but I heard it more'n once with my own ears."

"Rubbish, Styles."

"Very good, sir. You'll ring the bell if you want me."

Abercrombie Smith gave little heed to the gossip of the old manservant, but a small incident occurred a few days later which left an unpleasant effect upon his mind, and brought the words of Styles forcibly to his memory.

Bellingham had come up to see him late one night, and was entertaining him with an interesting account of the rock tombs of Beni Hassan in Upper Egypt, when Smith, whose hearing was remarkably acute, distinctly heard the sound of a door opening on the landing below.

"There's some fellow gone in or out of your room," he remarked.

Bellingham sprang up and stood helpless for a moment, with the expression of a man who is half incredulous and half afraid.

"I surely locked it. I am almost positive that I locked it," he stammered. "No one could have opened it."

"Why, I hear someone coming up the steps now," said Smith.

Bellingham rushed out through the door, slammed it loudly behind him, and hurried down the stairs. About halfway down Smith heard him stop, and thought he caught the sound of whispering. A moment later the door beneath him shut, a key creaked in a lock, and Bellingham, with beads of moisture upon his pale face, ascended the stairs once more, and reentered the room.

"It's all right," he said, throwing himself down in a chair. "It was that fool of a dog. He had pushed the door open. I don't know how I came to forget to lock it."

"I didn't know you kept a dog," said Smith, looking very thoughtfully at the disturbed face of his companion.

"Yes, I haven't had him long. I must get rid of him. He's a great nuisance."

"He must be, if you find it so hard to shut him up. I should have thought that shutting the door would have been enough, without locking it."

"I want to prevent old Styles from letting him out. He's of some value, you know, and it would be awkward to lose him."

"I am a bit of a dog fancier myself," said Smith, still gazing hard at his companion from the corner of his eyes. "Perhaps you'll let me have a look at it."

"Certainly. But I am afraid it cannot be tonight; I have an appointment. Is that clock right? Then I am a quarter of an hour late already. You'll excuse me, I am sure."

He picked up his cap and hurried from the room. In spite of his appointment, Smith heard him reenter his own chamber and lock his door upon the inside.

This interview left a disagreeable impression upon the medical student's mind. Bellingham had lied to him, and lied so clumsily that it looked as if he had desperate reasons for concealing the truth. Smith knew that his neighbor had no dog. He knew, also, that the step which he had heard upon the stairs was not the step of an animal. But if it were not, then what could it be? There was old Styles's statement about the something that used to pace the room at times when the owner was absent. Could it be a woman? Smith rather inclined to the view. If so, it would mean disgrace and expulsion to Bellingham if it were discovered by the authorities, so that his anxiety and falsehoods might be accounted for. And yet it was inconceivable that an undergraduate could keep a woman in his rooms without being instantly detected. Be the explanation what it might, there was something ugly about it, and Smith determined, as he turned to his books, to discourage all further attempts at intimacy on the part of his soft-spoken and ill-favored neighbor.

But his work was destined to interruption that night. He had hardly caught up the broken threads when a firm, heavy footfall came three steps at a time from below, and Hastie, in blazer and flannels, burst into the room.

"Still at it!" said he, plumping down into his wonted armchair. "What a chap you are to stew! I believe an earthquake might come and knock Oxford into a cocked hat, and you would sit perfectly placid with your books among the ruins. However, I won't bore you long. Three whiffs of baccy, and I am off."

"What's the news, then?" asked Smith, cramming a plug of bird's-eye into his brier with his forefinger.

"Nothing very much. Wilson made seventy for the freshmen against the eleven. They say that they will play him instead of Buddicomb, for Buddicomb is clean off color. He used to be able to bowl a little, but it's nothing but half volleys and long hops now."

"Medium right," suggested Smith, with the intense gravity that comes upon a varsity man when he speaks of athletics.

"Inclining to fast, with a work from leg. Comes with the arm about three inches or so. He used to be nasty on a wet wicket. Oh, by the way, have you heard about Long Norton?"

"What's that?"

"He's been attacked."

"Attacked?"

"Yes, just as he was turning out of the High Street, and within a hundred yards of the gate of Old's."

"But who—"

"Ah, that's the rub! If you said 'what,' you would be more grammatical. Norton swears that it was not human, and, indeed, from the scratches on his throat, I should be inclined to agree with him."

"What, then? Have we come down to spooks?"

Abercrombie Smith puffed his scientific contempt.

"Well, no; I don't think that is quite the idea, either. I am inclined to think that if any showman has lost a great ape lately, and the brute is in these parts, a jury would find a true bill against it. Norton passes that way every night, you know, about the same hour. There's a tree that hangs low over the path—the big elm from Rainy's garden. Norton thinks the thing dropped on him out of the tree. Anyhow, he was nearly strangled by two arms, which, he says, were as strong and as thin as steel bands. He saw nothing; only those beastly arms that tightened and tightened on him. He yelled his head off, and a couple of chaps came running, and the thing went over the wall like a cat. He never got a fair sight of it the whole time. It gave Norton a shake up, I can tell you. I tell him it has been as good as a change at the seaside for him."

"A garroter, most likely," said Smith.

"Very possibly. Norton says not; but we don't mind what he says. The garroter has long nails, and was pretty smart at swinging himself over walls. By the way, your beautiful neighbor would be pleased if he heard about it. He had a grudge against Norton, and he's not a man, from what I know of him, to forget his little debts. But hallo, old chap, what have you got in your noddle?"

"Nothing," Smith answered curtly.

He had started in his chair, and the look had flashed over his face which comes upon a man who is struck suddenly by some unpleasant idea.

"You looked as if something I had said had taken you on the raw. By the way, you have made the acquaintance of Master B. since I looked in last, have you not? Young Monkhouse Lee told me something to that effect."

"Yes; I know him slightly. He has been up here once or twice."

"Well, you're big enough and ugly enough to take care of yourself. He's not what I should call exactly a healthy sort of johnny, though, no doubt, he's very clever, and all that. But you'll soon find out for yourself. Lee is all right; he's a very decent little fellow. Well, so long, old chap! I row Mullins for the vice chancellor's pot on Wednesday week, so mind you come down, in case I don't see you before."

Bovine Smith laid down his pipe and turned stolidly to his books once more. But with all the will in the world, he found it very hard to keep his mind upon his work. It would slip away to brood upon the man beneath him, and upon the little mystery which hung round his chambers. Then his thoughts turned to this singular attack of which Hastie had spoken, and to the grudge which Bellingham was said to owe the object of it. The two ideas would persist in rising together in his mind, as though there were some close and intimate connection between them. And yet the suspicion was so dim and vague that it could not be put down in words.

"Confound the chap!" cried Smith, as he shied his book on pathology across the room. "He has spoiled my night's reading, and that's reason enough, if there were no other, why I should steer clear of him in the future."

For ten days the medical student confined himself so closely to his studies that he neither saw nor heard anything of either of the men beneath him. At the hours when Bellingham had been accustomed to visit him, he took care to sport his oak, and though he more than once heard a knocking at his outer door, he resolutely refused to answer it. One afternoon, however, he was descending the stairs when, just as he was passing it, Bellingham's door flew open, and young Monkhouse Lee came out with his eyes sparkling and a dark flush of anger upon his olive cheeks. Close at his heels followed Bellingham, his fat, unhealthy face all quivering with malignant passion.

"You fool!" he hissed. "You'll be sorry."

"Very likely," cried the other. "Mind what I say. It's off! I won't hear of it!"

"You've promised, anyhow."

"Oh, I'll keep that! I won't speak. But I'd rather little Eva was in her grave. Once for all, it's off. She'll do what I say. We don't want to see you again."

So much Smith could not avoid hearing, but he hurried on, for he had no wish to be involved in their dispute. There had been a serious breach between them, that was clear enough, and Lee was going to cause the engagement with his sister to be broken off. Smith thought of Hastie's comparison of the toad and the dove, and was glad to think that the matter was at an end. Bellingham's face when he was in a passion was not pleasant to look upon. He was not a man to whom an innocent girl could be trusted for life. As he walked, Smith wondered languidly what could have caused the quarrel, and what the promise might be which Bellingham had been so anxious that Monkhouse Lee should keep.

It was the day of the sculling match between Hastie and Mullins, and a stream of men were making their way down to the banks of the Isis. A May sun was shining brightly, and the yellow path was barred with the black shadows of the tall elm trees. On either side the gray colleges lay back from the road, the hoary old mothers of minds looking out from their high, mullioned windows at the tide of young life which swept so merrily past them. Black-clad tutors, prim officials, pale, reading men, brown-faced, straw-hatted young athletes in white sweaters or many-colored blazers, all were hurrying toward the blue, winding river which curves through the Oxford meadows.

Abercrombie Smith, with the intuition of an old oarsman, chose his position at the point where he knew that the struggle, if there were a struggle, would come. Far off he heard the hum that announced the start, the gathering roar of the approach, the thunder of running feet, and the shouts of the men in the boats beneath him. A spray of half-clad, deep-breathing runners shot past him, and craning over their shoulders, he saw Hastie pulling a steady thirty-six, while his opponent, with a jerky forty, was a good boat's length behind him. Smith gave a cheer for his friend, and pulling out his watch, was starting off again for his chambers, when he felt a touch upon his shoulder, and found that young Monkhouse Lee was beside him.

"I saw you there," he said, in a timid, deprecating way. "I wanted to speak to you, if you could spare me a half hour. This cottage is mine. I share it with Harrington of King's. Come in and have a cup of tea."

"I must be back presently," said Smith. "I am hard on the grind at present. But I'll come in for a few minutes with pleasure. I wouldn't have come out only Hastie is a friend of mine."

"So he is of mine. Hasn't he a beautiful style? Mullins wasn't in it. But come into the cottage. It's a little den of a place, but it is pleasant to work in during the summer months."

It was a small, square, white building, with green doors and shutters, and a rustic trelliswork porch, standing back some fifty yards from the river's bank. Inside, the main room was roughly fitted up as a study—deal table, unpainted shelves with books, and a few cheap oleographs upon the wall. A kettle sang upon a spirit-stove, and there were tea things upon a tray on the table.

"Try that chair and have a cigarette," said Lee. "Let me pour you out a cup of tea. It's so good of you to come in, for I know that your time is a good deal taken up. I wanted to say to you that, if I were you, I should change my rooms at once."

"Eh?"

Smith sat staring with a lighted match in one hand and his unlit cigarette in the other.

"Yes; it must seem very extraordinary, and the worst of it is that I cannot give my reasons, for I am under a solemn promise—a very solemn promise. But I may go so far as to say that I don't think Bellingham is a very safe man to live near. I intend to camp out here as much as I can for a time."

"Not safe! What do you mean?"

"Ah, that's what I mustn't say. But do take my advice and

move your rooms. We had a grand row today. You must have heard us, for you came down the stairs."

"I saw that you had fallen out."

"He's a horrible chap, Smith. That is the only word for him. I have had doubts about him ever since that night when he fainted—you remember, when you came down. I taxed him today, and he told me things that made my hair rise, and wanted me to stand in with him. I'm not strait-laced, but I am a clergyman's son, you know, and I think there are some things which are quite beyond the pale. I only thank God that I found him out before it was too late, for he was to have married into my family."

"This is all very fine, Lee," said Abercrombie Smith curtly. "But either you are saying a great deal too much or a great deal too little."

"I give you a warning."

"If there is real reason for warning, no promise can bind you. If I see a rascal about to blow a place up with dynamite no pledge will stand in my way of preventing him."

"Ah, but I cannot prevent him, and I can do nothing but warn you."

"Without saying what you warn me against."

"Against Bellingham."

"But that is childish. Why should I fear him, or any man?"

"I can't tell you. I can only entreat you to change your rooms. You are in danger where you are. I don't even say that Bellingham would wish to injure you. But it might happen, for he is a dangerous neighbor just now."

"Perhaps I know more than you think," said Smith, looking keenly at the young man's boyish, earnest face. "Suppose I tell you that someone else shares Bellingham's rooms."

Monkhouse Lee sprang from his chair in uncontrollable excitement.

"You know, then?" he gasped.

"A woman."

Lee dropped back again with a groan.

"My lips are sealed," he said. "I must not speak."

"Well, anyhow," said Smith, rising, "it is not likely that I should allow myself to be frightened out of rooms which suit me very nicely. It would be a little too feeble for me to move out all my goods and chattels because you say that Bellingham might in some unexplained way do me an injury. I think that I'll just take my chance, and stay where I am, and as I see that it's nearly five o'clock, I must ask you to excuse me."

He bade the young student adieu in a few curt words, and made his way homeward through the sweet spring evening, feeling half ruffled, half amused, as any other strong, unimaginative man might who has been menaced by a vague and shadowy danger.

There was one little indulgence which Abercrombie Smith always allowed himself, however closely his work might press upon him. Twice a week, on the Tuesday and the Friday, it was his invariable custom to walk over to Farlingford, the residence of Dr. Plumptree Peterson, situated about a mile and a half out of Oxford. Peterson had been a close friend of Smith's elder brother, Francis, and as he was a bachelor, fairly well-to-do, with a good cellar and a better library, his house was a pleasant goal for a man who was in need of a brisk walk. Twice a week, then, the medical student would swing out there along the dark country roads and spend a pleasant hour in Peterson's comfortable study, discussing, over a glass of old port, the gossip of the varsity or the latest developments of medicine or of surgery.

On the day that followed his interview with Monkhouse Lee, Smith shut up his books at a quarter past eight, the hour when he usually started for his friend's house. As he was leaving his room, however, his eyes chanced to fall upon one of the books which Bellingham had lent him, and his conscience pricked him for not having returned it. However repellent the man might be, he should not be treated with discourtesy. Taking the book, he walked downstairs and knocked at his neighbor's door. There was no answer; but on turning the handle he found that it was unlocked. Pleased at the thought of avoiding an interview, he stepped inside, and placed the book with his card upon the table.

The lamp was turned half down, but Smith could see the details of the room plainly enough. It was all much as he had seen it before—the frieze, the animal-headed gods, the hanging crocodile, and the table littered over with papers and dried leaves. The mummy case stood upright against the wall, but the mummy itself was missing. There was no sign of any second occupant of the room, and he felt as he withdrew that he had probably done Bellingham an injustice. Had he a guilty secret to preserve, he would hardly leave his door open so that all the world might enter.

The spiral stair was as black as pitch, and Smith was slowly making his way down its irregular steps, when he was suddenly conscious that something had passed him in the darkness. There was a faint sound, a whiff of air, a light brushing past his elbow, but so slight that he could scarcely be certain of it. He stopped and listened, but the wind was rustling among the ivy outside, and he could hear nothing else.

"Is that you, Styles?" he shouted.

There was no answer, and all was still behind him. It must have been a sudden gust of air, for there were crannies and cracks in the old turret. And yet he could almost have sworn that he heard a footfall by his very side. He had emerged into the quadrangle, still turning the matter over in his head, when a man came running swiftly across the smooth-cropped lawn.

"Is that you, Smith?"

"Hullo, Hastie!"

"For God's sake come at once! Young Lee is drowned! Here's Harrington of King's with the news. The doctor is out. You'll do, but come along at once. There may be life in him."

"Have you brandy?"

"No."

"I'll bring some. There's a flask on my table."

Smith bounded up the stairs, taking three at a time, seized the flask, and was rushing down with it, when, as he passed Bellingham's room, his eyes fell upon something which left him gasping and staring upon the landing.

The door, which he had closed behind him, was now open, and right in front of him, with the lamplight shining upon it, was the mummy case. Three minutes ago it had been empty. He could swear to that. Now it framed the lank body of its horrible occupant, who stood, grim and stark, with his black, shriveled face toward the door. The form was lifeless and inert, but it seemed to Smith as he gazed that there still lingered a lurid spark of vitality, some faint sign of consciousness in the little eyes which lurked in the depths of the hollow sockets. So astounded and shaken was he that he had forgotten his errand, and was still staring at the lean, sunken figure when the voice of his friend below recalled him to himself.

"Come on, Smith!" he shouted. "It's life and death, you know. Hurry up! Now, then," he added, as the medical student reappeared, "let us do a sprint. It is well under a mile, and we should do it in five minutes. A human life is better worth running for than a pot."

Neck and neck they dashed through the darkness, and did not pull up until, panting and spent, they had reached the little cottage by the river. Young Lee, limp and dripping like a broken water plant, was stretched upon the sofa, the green scum of the river upon his black hair, and a fringe of white foam upon his leaden-hued lips. Beside him knelt his fellow student, Harrington, endeavoring to chafe some warmth back into his rigid limbs.

"I think there's life in him," said Smith, with his hand to the lad's side. "Put your watch glass to his lips. Yes, there's dimming on it. You take one arm, Hastie. Now work it as I do, and we'll soon pull him round."

For ten minutes they worked in silence, inflating and depressing the chest of the unconscious man. At the end of that time a shiver ran through his body, his lips trembled, and he opened his eyes. The three students burst out into an irrepressible cheer.

"Wake up, old chap. You've frightened us quite enough."

"Have some brandy. Take a sip from the flask."

"He's all right now," said his companion Harrington. "Heavens, what a fright I got! I was reading here, and he had gone out for a stroll as far as the river, when I heard a scream and a splash. Out I ran, and by the time I could find him and fish him out, all life seemed to have gone. Then Simpson couldn't get a doctor, for he has a game leg, and I had to run, and I don't know what I'd have done without you fellows. That's right, old chap. Sit up."

Monkhouse Lee had raised himself on his hands, and looked wildly about him.

"What's up?" he asked. "I've been in the water. Ah, yes; I remember."

A look of fear came into his eyes, and he sank his face into his hands.

"How did you fall in?"

"I didn't fall in."

"How then?"

"I was thrown in. I was standing by the bank, and something from behind picked me up like a feather and hurled me in. I heard nothing, and I saw nothing. But I know what it was, for all that."

"And so do I," whispered Smith.

Lee looked up with a quick glance of surprise.

"You've learned, then?" he said. "You remember the advice I gave you?"

"Yes, and I begin to think that I shall take it."

"I don't know what the deuce you fellows are talking about," said Hastie, "but I think, if I were you, Harrington, I should get Lee to bed at once. It will be time enough to discuss the why and the wherefore when he is a little stronger. I think, Smith, you and I can leave him alone now. I am walking back to college; if you are coming in that direction, we can have a chat."

But it was little chat that they had upon their homeward path. Smith's mind was too full of the incidents of the evening, the absence of the mummy from his neighbor's rooms, the step that passed him on the stair, the reappearance—the extraordinary, inexplicable reappearance—of the grisly thing, and then this attack upon Lee, corresponding so closely to the previous outrage upon another man against whom Bellingham bore a grudge. All this settled in his thoughts, together with the many little incidents which had previously turned him against his neighbor, and the singular circumstances under which he was first called in to him. What had been a dim suspicion, a vague, fantastic conjecture, had suddenly taken form, and stood out in his mind as a grim fact, a thing not to be denied. And yet, how monstrous it was! how unheard of! how entirely beyond all bounds of human experience. An impartial judge, or even the friend who walked by his side, would simply tell him that his eyes had deceived him, that the mummy had been there all the time, that young Lee had tumbled into the river as any other man tumbles into a river, and the blue pill was the best thing for a disordered liver. He felt that he would have said as much if the positions had been reversed. And yet he could swear that Bellingham was a murderer at heart, and that he wielded a weapon such as no man had ever used in all the grim history of crime.

Hastie had branched off to his rooms with a few crisp and emphatic comments upon his friend's unsociability, and Abercrombie Smith crossed the quadrangle to his corner turret with a strong feeling of repulsion for his chambers and their associations. He would take Lee's advice, and move his quarters as soon as possible, for how could a man study when his ear was ever straining for every murmur or footstep in the room below? He observed, as he crossed over the lawn, that the light was still shining in Bellingham's window, and as he passed up the staircase the door opened, and the man himself looked out at him. With his fat, evil face he was like some bloated spider fresh from the weaving of his poisonous web.

"Good evening," said he. "Won't you come in?"

"No," cried Smith fiercely.

"No? You are as busy as ever? I wanted to ask you about Lee. I was sorry to hear that there was a rumor that something was amiss with him."

His features were grave, but there was the gleam of a hidden laugh in his eyes as he spoke. Smith saw it, and he could have knocked him down for it.

"You'll be sorrier still to hear that Monkhouse Lee is doing very well, and is out of all danger," he answered. "Your hellish tricks have not come off this time. Oh, you needn't try to brazen it out. I know all about it."

Bellingham took a step back from the angry student, and half closed the door as if to protect himself.

"You are mad," he said. "What do you mean? Do you assert that I had anything to do with Lee's accident?"

"Yes," thundered Smith. "You and that bag of bones behind you; you worked it between you. I tell you what it is, Master B., they have given up burning folk like you, but we still keep a hangman, and, by George! if any man in this college meets his death while you are here, I'll have you up, and if you don't swing for it, it won't be my fault. You'll find that your filthy Egyptian tricks won't answer in England."

"You're a raving lunatic," said Bellingham.

"All right. You just remember what I say, for you'll find that I'll be better than my word."

The door slammed, and Smith went fuming up to his chamber, where he locked the door upon the inside, and spent half the night in smoking his old brier, and brooding over the strange events of the evening.

Next morning Abercrombie Smith heard nothing of his neighbor, but Harrington called upon him in the afternoon to say that Lee was almost himself again. All day Smith stuck fast to his work, but in the evening he determined to pay the visit to his friend Dr. Peterson upon which he had started the night before. A good walk and a friendly chat would be welcome to his jangled nerves.

Bellingham's door was shut as he passed, but glancing back when he was some distance from the turret, he saw his neighbor's head at the window outlined against the lamplight, his face pressed apparently against the glass as he gazed out into the darkness. It was a blessing to be away from all contact with him, if but for a few hours, and Smith stepped out briskly, and breathed the soft spring air into his lungs. The half moon lay in the west between two Gothic pinnacles, and threw upon the silvered street a dark tracery from the stonework above. There was a brisk breeze, and light, fleecy clouds drifted swiftly across the sky. Old's was on the very border of the town, and in five minutes Smith found himself beyond the houses and between the hedges of a May-scented, Oxfordshire lane.

It was a lonely and little-frequented road which led to his friend's house. Early as it was, Smith did not meet a single soul upon his way. He walked briskly along until he came to the avenue gate, which opened into the long, gravel drive leading up to Farlingford. In front of him he could see the cozy, red light of the windows glimmering through the foliage. He stood with his hand upon the iron latch of the swinging gate, and he glanced back at the road along which he had come. Something was coming swiftly down it.

It moved in the shadow of the hedge, silently and furtively, a dark, crouching figure, dimly visible against the black background. Even as he gazed back at it, it had lessened its distance by twenty paces, and was fast closing upon him. Out of the darkness he had a glimpse of a scraggy neck, and of two eyes that will ever haunt him in his dreams. He turned, and with a cry of terror he ran for his life up the avenue. There were the red lights, the signals of safety, almost within a stone's throw of him. He was a famous runner, but never had he run as he ran that night.

The heavy gate had swung into place behind him but he heard it dash open again before his pursuer. As he rushed madly and wildly through the night, he could hear a swift, dry patter behind him, and could see, as he threw back a glance, that this horror was bounding like a tiger at his heels, with blazing eyes and one stringy arm outthrown. Thank God, the door was ajar. He could see the thin bar of light which shot from the lamp in the hall. Nearer yet sounded the clatter from behind. He heard a hoarse gurgling at his very shoulder. With a shriek he flung himself against the door, slammed and bolted it behind him, and sank half fainting on the hall chair.

"My goodness, Smith, what's the matter?" asked Peterson, appearing at the door of his study.

"Give me some brandy."

Peterson disappeared, and came rushing out again with a glass and a decanter.

"You need it," he said, as his visitor drank off what he poured out for him. "Why, man, you are as white as a cheese."

Smith laid down his glass, rose up, and took a deep breath.

"I am my own man again now," said he. "I was never so unmanned before. But, with your leave, Peterson, I will sleep here tonight, for I don't think I could face that road again except by daylight. It's weak, I know, but I can't help it."

Peterson looked at his visitor with a very questioning eye.

"Of course you shall sleep here if you wish. I'll tell Mrs. Burney to make up the spare bed. Where are you off to now?"

"Come up with me to the window that overlooks the door. I want you to see what I have seen."

They went up to the window of the upper hall whence they could look down upon the approach to the house. The drive and the fields on either side lay quiet and still, bathed in the peaceful moonlight.

"Well, really, Smith," remarked Peterson, "it is well that I know you to be an abstemious man. What in the world can have frightened you?"

"I'll tell you presently. But where can it have gone? Ah, now, look, look! See the curve of the road just beyond your gate."

"Yes, I see; you needn't pinch my arm off. I saw someone pass. I should say a man, rather thin, apparently, and tall, very tall. But what of him? And what of yourself? You are still shaking like an aspen leaf."

"I have been within handgrip of the devil, that's all. But come down to your study, and I shall tell you the whole story."

He did so. Under the cherry lamplight with a glass of wine on the table beside him, and the portly form and florid face of his friend in front, he narrated, in their order, all the events, great and small, which had formed so singular a chain, from the night on which he had found Bellingham fainting in front of the mummy case until this horrid experience of an hour ago.

"There now," he said as he concluded, "that's the whole, black business. It is monstrous and incredible, but it is true."

Dr. Plumptree Peterson sat for some time in silence with a very puzzled expression upon his face.

"I never heard of such a thing in my life, never!" he said at last. "You have told me the facts. Now tell me your inferences."

"You can draw your own."

"But I should like to hear yours. You have thought over the matter, and I have not."

"Well, it must be a little vague in detail, but the main points seem to me to be clear enough. This fellow Bellingham, in his Eastern studies, has got hold of some infernal secret by which a mummy—or possibly only this particular mummy—can be temporarily brought to life. He was trying this disgusting business on the night when he fainted. No doubt the sight of the creature moving had shaken his nerve, even though he had expected it. You remember that almost the first words he said were to call out upon himself as a fool. Well, he got more hardened afterward, and carried the matter through without fainting. The vitality which he could put into it was evidently only a passing thing, for I have seen it continually in its case as dead as this table. He has some elaborate process, I fancy, by which he brings the thing to pass. Having done it, he naturally bethought him that he might use the creature as an agent. It has intelligence and it has strength. For some purpose he took Lee into his confidence; but Lee, like a decent Christian, would have nothing to do with such a business. Then they had a row, and Lee vowed that he would tell his sister of Bellingham's true character. Bellingham's game was to prevent him, and he nearly managed it, by setting this creature of his on his track. He had already tried its powers upon another man—Norton—toward whom he had a grudge. It is the merest chance that he has not two murders upon his soul. Then, when I taxed him with the matter, he had the strongest reasons for wishing to get me out of the way before I could convey my knowledge to anyone else. He got his chance when I went out, for he knew my habits and where I was bound for. I have had a narrow shave, Peterson, and it is mere luck you didn't find me on your doorstep in the morning. I'm not a nervous man as a rule, and I never thought to have the fear of death put upon me as it was tonight."

"My dear boy, you take the matter too seriously," said his companion. "Your nerves are out of order with your work, and you make too much of it. How could such a thing as this stride about the streets of Oxford, even at night, without being seen?"

"It has been seen. There is quite a scare in the town about an escaped ape, as they imagine the creature to be. It is the talk of the place."

"Well, it's a striking chain of events. And yet, my dear fellow, you must allow that each incident in itself is capable of a more natural explanation."

"What! even my adventure of tonight?"

"Certainly. You come out with your nerves all unstrung, and your head full of this theory of yours. Some gaunt, half famished tramp steals after you, and seeing you run, is emboldened to pursue you. Your fears and imagination do the rest."

"It won't do, Peterson; it won't do."

"And again, in the instance of your finding the mummy case empty, and then a few moments later with an occupant, you know that it was lamplight, that the lamp was half turned down, and that you had no special reason to look hard at the case. It is quite possible that you may have overlooked the creature in the first instance."

"No, no; it is out of the question."

"And then Lee may have fallen into the river, and Norton been garroted. It is certainly a formidable indictment that you have against Bellingham; but if you were to place it before a police magistrate, he would simply laugh in your face."

"I know he would. That is why I mean to take the matter into my own hands."

"Eh?"

"Yes; I feel that a public duty rests upon me, and, besides, I must do it for my own safety, unless I choose to allow myself to be hunted by this beast out of the college, and that would be a little too feeble. I have quite made up my mind what I shall do. And first of all, may I use your paper and pens for an hour?"

"Most certainly. You will find all that you want upon that side table."

Abercrombie Smith sat down before a sheet of foolscap, and for an hour, and then for a second hour, his pen traveled swiftly over it. Page after page was finished and tossed aside while his friend leaned back in his armchair, looking across at him with patient curiosity. At last, with an exclamation of satisfaction, Smith sprang to his feet, gathered his papers up into order, and laid the last one upon Peterson's desk.

"Kindly sign this as a witness," he said.

"A witness? Of what?"

"Of my signature, and of the date. The date is the most important. Why, Peterson, my life might hang upon it."

"My dear Smith, you are talking wildly. Let me beg you to go to bed."

"On the contrary, I never spoke so deliberately in my life. And I will promise to go to bed the moment you have signed it."

"But what is it?"

"It is a statement of all that I have been telling you to-night. I wish you to witness it."

"Certainly," said Peterson, signing his name under that of his companion. "There you are! But what is the idea?"

"You will kindly retain it, and produce it in case I am arrested."

"Arrested? For what?"

"For murder. It is quite on the cards. I wish to be ready for every event. There is only one course open to me, and I am determined to take it."

"For heaven's sake, don't do anything rash!"

"Believe me, it would be far more rash to adopt any other course. I hope that we won't need to bother you, but it will ease my mind to know that you have this statement of my motives. And now I am ready to take your advice and to go to roost, for I want to be at my best in the morning."

Abercrombie Smith was not an entirely pleasant man to have as an enemy. Slow and easy tempered, he was formidable when driven to action. He brought to every purpose in life the same deliberate resoluteness that had distinguished him as a scientific student. He had laid his studies aside for a day, but he intended that the day should not be wasted. Not a word did he say to his host as to his plans, but by nine o'clock he was well on his way to Oxford.

In the High Street he stopped at Clifford's, the gunmaker's, and bought a heavy revolver, with a box of center-fire cartridges. Six of them he slipped into the chambers, and half cocking the weapon, placed it in the pocket of his coat. He then made his way to Hastie's rooms, where the big oarsman was lounging over his breakfast, with the *Sporting Times* propped up against the coffeepot.

"Hullo! What's up?" he asked. "Have some coffee?"

"No, thank you. I want you to come with me, Hastie, and do what I ask you."

"Certainly, my boy."

"And bring a heavy stick with you."

"Hullo!" Hastie stared. "Here's a hunting crop that would fell an ox."

"One other thing. You have a box of amputating knives. Give me the longest of them."

"There you are. You seem to be fairly on the war trail. Anything else?"

"No; that will do." Smith placed the knife inside his coat, and led the way to the quadrangle. "We are neither of us chickens, Hastie," said he. "I think I can do this job alone, but I take you as a precaution. I am going to have a little talk with Bellingham. If I have only him to deal with, I won't, of course, need you. If I shout, however, up you come, and lam out with your whip as hard as you can lick. Do you understand?"

"All right. I'll come if I hear you bellow."

"Stay here, then. I may be a little time, but don't budge until I come down."

"I'm a fixture."

Smith ascended the stairs, opened Bellingham's door and stepped in. Bellingham was seated behind his table, writing. Beside him, among his litter of strange possessions, towered the mummy case, with its sale number 249 still stuck upon its front, and its hideous occupant stiff and stark within it. Smith looked very deliberately round him, closed the door, and then, stepping across to the fireplace, struck a match and set the fire alight. Bellingham sat staring, with amazement and rage upon his bloated face.

"Well, really now, you make yourself at home," he gasped.

Smith sat himself deliberately down, placing his watch upon the table, drew out his pistol, cocked it, and laid it in his lap. Then he took the long amputating knife from his bosom, and threw it down in front of Bellingham.

"Now, then," said he, "just get to work and cut up that mummy."

"Oh, is that it?" said Bellingham with a sneer.

"Yes, that is it. They tell me that the law can't touch you. But I have a law that will set matters straight. If in five minutes you have not set to work, I swear by the God who made me that I will put a bullet through your brain!"

"You would murder me?"

Bellingham had half risen, and his face was the color of putty.

"Yes."

"And for what?"

"To stop your mischief. One minute has gone."

"But what have I done?"

"I know and you know."

"This is mere bullying."

"Two minutes are gone."

"But you must give reasons. You are a madman—a dangerous madman. Why should I destroy my own property? It is a valuable mummy."

"You must cut it up, and you must burn it."

"I will do no such thing."

"Four minutes are gone."

Smith took up the pistol and he looked toward Bellingham with an inexorable face. As the second hand stole round, he raised his hand, and the finger twitched upon the trigger.

"There! there! I'll do it!" screamed Bellingham.

In frantic haste he caught up the knife and hacked at the figure of the mummy, ever glancing round to see the eye and the weapon of his terrible visitor bent upon him. The creature crackled and snapped under every stab of the keen blade. A thick, yellow dust rose up from it. Spices and dried essences rained down upon the floor. Suddenly, with a rending crack, its backbone snapped asunder, and it fell, a brown heap of sprawling limbs, upon the floor.

"Now into the fire!" said Smith.

The flames leaped and roared as the dried and tinderlike debris was piled upon it. The little room was like the stokehole of a steamer and the sweat ran down the faces of the two men; but still the one stooped and worked, while the other sat watching him with a set face. A thick, fat smoke oozed out from the fire, and a heavy smell of burned resin and singed hair filled the air. In a quarter of an hour a few charred and brittle sticks were all that was left of Lot No. 249.

"Perhaps that will satisfy you," snarled Bellingham, with hate and fear in his little gray eyes as he glanced back at his tormentor.

"No; I must make a clean sweep of all your materials. We must have no more devil's tricks. In with all these leaves! They may have something to do with it."

"And what now?" asked Bellingham, when the leaves also had been added to the blaze.

"Now the roll of papyrus which you had on the table that night. It is in that drawer, I think."

"No, no," shouted Bellingham. "Don't burn that! Why, man, you don't know what you do. It is unique; it contains wisdom which is nowhere else to be found."

"Out with it!"

"But look here, Smith, you can't really mean it. I'll share the knowledge with you. I'll teach you all that is in it. Or, stay, let me only copy it before you burn it!"

Smith stepped forward and turned the key in the drawer. Taking out the yellow, curled roll of paper, he threw it into the fire, and pressed it down with his heel. Bellingham screamed, and grabbed at it; but Smith pushed him back and stood over it until it was reduced to a formless, gray ash.

"Now, Master B.," said he, "I think I have pretty well drawn your teeth. You'll hear from me again, if you return to your old tricks. And now good morning, for I must go back to my studies."

And such is the narrative of Abercrombie Smith as to the singular events that occurred in Old College, Oxford, in the spring of '84. As Bellingham left the university immediately afterward, and was last heard of in the Sudan, there is no one who can contradict his statement. But the wisdom of men is small, and the ways of Nature are strange, and who shall put a bound to the dark things that may be found by those who seek for them?

Ellen Glasgow

(1873–1945)

One of ten children, Ellen Anderson Gholson Glasgow was born in Richmond, Virginia, into a well-respected Southern family. At the age of sixteen, her hearing began to fail, and doctors were unable to prevent her from becoming deaf. Although she lived in New York City for a time, she spent most of her life in Richmond. Her first novel, *The Descendant*, which she began at the age of seventeen, was published anonymously in 1897. Among the novels that followed are *Phases of an Inferior Planet* (1898), *The Battle-Ground* (1902), *The Ancient Law* (1908), *Barren Ground* (1925), *The Romantic Comedians* (1926), *They Stooped to Folly* (1929), and *Vein of Iron* (1935). *In This Our Life* (1941) was awarded the Pulitzer Prize. She also published literary criticism, poems, and a collection of short stories, *The Shadowy Third and Other Stories* (1923).

The Shadowy Third

(1916)

When the call came I remember that I turned from the telephone in a romantic flutter. Though I had spoken only once to the great surgeon, Roland Maradick, I felt on that December afternoon that to speak to him only once—to watch him in the operating-room for a single hour—was an adventure which drained the colour and the excitement from the rest of life. After all these years of work on typhoid and pneumonia cases, I can still feel the delicious tremor of my young pulses; I can still see the winter sunshine slanting through the hospital windows over the white uniforms of the nurses.

"He didn't mention me by name. Can there be a mistake?" I stood, incredulous yet ecstatic, before the superintendent of the hospital.

"No, there isn't a mistake. I was talking to him before you came down." Miss Hemphill's strong face softened while she looked at me. She was a big, resolute woman, a distant Canadian relative of my mother's, and the kind of nurse I had discovered in the month since I had come up from Richmond, that Northern hospital boards, if not Northern patients, appear instinctively to select. From the first, in spite of her hardness, she had taken a liking—I hesitate to use the word "fancy" for a preference so impersonal—to her Virginia cousin. After all, it isn't every Southern nurse, just out of training, who can boast a kinswoman in the superintendent of a New York hospital.

"And he made you understand positively that he meant me?" The thing was so wonderful that I simply couldn't believe it.

"He asked particularly for the nurse who was with Miss Hudson last week when he operated. I think he didn't even remember that you had a name. When I asked if he meant Miss Randolph, he repeated that he wanted the nurse who had been with Miss Hudson. She was small, he said, and cheerful-looking. This, of course, might apply to one or two of the others, but none of these was with Miss Hudson."

"Then I suppose it is really true?" My pulses were tingling. "And I am to be there at six o'clock?"

"Not a minute later. The day nurse goes off duty at that hour, and Mrs. Maradick is never left by herself for an instant."

"It is her mind, isn't it? And that makes it all the stranger that he should select me, for I have had so few mental cases."

"So few cases of any kind." Miss Hemphill was smiling, and when she smiled I wondered if the other nurses would know her. "By the time you have gone through the treadmill in New York, Margaret, you will have lost a good many things besides your inexperience. I wonder how long you will keep your sympathy and your imagination? After all, wouldn't you have made a better novelist than a nurse?"

"I can't help putting myself into my cases. I suppose one ought not to?"

"It isn't a question of what one ought to do, but of what one must. When you are drained of every bit of sympathy and enthusiasm, and have got nothing in return for it, not even thanks, you will understand why I try to keep you from wasting yourself."

"But surely in a case like this—for Doctor Maradick?"

"Oh, well, of course—for Doctor Maradick." She must have seen that I implored her confidence, for, after a minute, she let fall carelessly a gleam of light on the situation: "It is a very sad case when you think what a charming man and a great surgeon Doctor Maradick is."

Above the starched collar of my uniform I felt the blood leap in bounds to my cheeks. "I have spoken to him only once," I murmured, "but he is charming, and so kind and handsome, isn't he?"

"His patients adore him."

"Oh, yes, I've seen that. Everyone hangs on his visits." Like the patients and the other nurses, I also had come by delightful, if imperceptible, degrees to hang on the daily visits of Doctor Maradick. He was, I suppose, born to be a hero to women. From my first day in his hospital, from the moment when I watched, through closed shutters, while he stepped out of his car, I have never doubted that he was assigned to the great part in the play. If I had been ignorant of his spell—of the charm he exercised over his hospital—I should have felt it in the waiting hush, like a drawn breath, which followed his ring at the door and preceded his imperious footstep on the stairs. My first impression of him, even after the terrible events of the next year, records a memory that is both careless and splendid. At that moment, when, gazing through the chinks in the shutters, I watched him, in his coat of dark fur, cross the pavement over the pale streaks of sunshine, I knew beyond any doubt—I knew with a sort of infallible prescience—that my fate was irretrievably bound up with his in the future. I knew this, I repeat, though Miss Hemphill would still insist that my foreknowledge was merely a sentimental gleaning from indiscriminate novels. But it wasn't only first love, impressionable as my kinswoman believed me to be. It wasn't only the way he looked. Even more than his appearance—more than the shining dark of his eyes, the silvery brown of his hair, the dusky glow in his face—even more than his charm and his magnificence, I think, the beauty and sympathy in his voice won my heart. It was a voice, I heard someone say afterwards, that ought always to speak poetry.

So you will see why—if you do not understand at the beginning, I can never hope to make you believe impossible things!—so you will see why I accepted the call when it came as an imperative summons. I couldn't have stayed away after he sent for me. However much I may have tried not to go, I know that in the end I must have gone. In those days, while I was still hoping to write novels, I used to talk a great deal about "destiny" (I have learned since then how silly all such talk is), and I suppose it was my "destiny" to be caught in the web of Roland Maradick's personality. But I am not the first nurse to grow lovesick about a doctor who never gave her a thought.

"I am glad you got the call, Margaret. It may mean a great deal to you. Only try not to be too emotional." I remember that Miss Hemphill was holding a bit of rose-geranium in her hand while she spoke—one of the patients had given it to her from a pot she kept in her room, and the scent of the flower is still in my nostrils—or my memory. Since then—oh, long since then—I have wondered if she also had been caught in the web.

"I wish I knew more about the case." I was pressing for light. "Have you ever seen Mrs. Maradick?"

"Oh, dear, yes. They have been married only a little over a year, and in the beginning she used to come sometimes to the hospital and wait outside while the doctor made his visits. She was a very sweet-looking woman then—not exactly pretty, but fair and slight, with the loveliest smile, I think, I have ever seen. In those first months she was so much in love that we used to laugh about it among ourselves. To see her face light up when the doctor came out of the hospital and crossed the pavement to his car, was as good as a play. We never tired of watching her—I wasn't superintendent then, so I had more time to look out of the window while I was on day duty. Once or twice she brought her little girl in to see one of the patients. The child was so much like her that you would have known them anywhere for mother and daughter."

I had heard that Mrs. Maradick was a widow, with one child, when she first met the doctor, and I asked now, still seeking an illumination I had not found, "There was a great deal of money, wasn't there?"

"A great fortune. If she hadn't been so attractive, people would have said, I suppose, that Doctor Maradick married her for her money. Only," she appeared to make an effort of memory, "I believe I've heard somehow that it was all left in trust away from Mrs. Maradick if she married again. I can't, to save my life, remember just how it was; but it was a queer will, I know, and Mrs. Maradick wasn't to come into the money unless the child didn't live to grow up. The pity of it——"

A young nurse came into the office to ask for something—the keys, I think, of the operating-room, and Miss Hemphill broke off inconclusively as she hurried out of the door. I was sorry that she left off just when she did. Poor Mrs. Maradick! Perhaps I was too emotional, but even before I saw her I had begun to feel her pathos and her strangeness.

My preparations took only a few minutes. In those days I always kept a suitcase packed and ready for sudden calls; and it was not yet six o'clock when I turned from Tenth Street into Fifth Avenue, and stopped for a minute, before ascending the steps, to look at the house in which Doctor Maradick lived. A fine rain was falling, and I remember thinking, as I turned the corner, how depressing the weather must be for Mrs. Maradick. It was an old house, with damp-looking walls (though that may have been because of the rain) and a spindle-shaped iron railing which ran up the stone steps to the black door, where I noticed a dim flicker through the old-fashioned fanlight. Afterwards I discovered that Mrs. Maradick had been born in the house—her maiden name was Calloran—and that she had never wanted to live anywhere else. She was a woman—this I found out when I knew her better—of strong attachments to both persons and places; and though Doctor Maradick had tried to persuade her to move uptown after her marriage, she had clung, against his wishes, to the old house in lower Fifth Avenue. I dare say she was obstinate about it in spite of her gentleness and her passion for the doctor. Those sweet, soft women, especially when they have always been rich, are sometimes amazingly obstinate. I have nursed so many of them since—women with strong affections and weak intellects—that I have come to recognize the type as soon as I set eyes upon it.

My ring at the bell was answered after a little delay, and when I entered the house I saw that the hall was quite dark except for the waning glow from an open fire which burned in the library. When I gave my name, and added that I was the night nurse, the servant appeared to think my humble presence unworthy of illumination. He was an old negro butler, inherited perhaps from Mrs. Maradick's mother, who, I learned afterwards, was from South Carolina; and while he passed me on his way up the staircase, I heard him vaguely muttering that he "wa'n't gwinter tu'n on dem lights twel de chile had done playin'."

To the right of the hall, the soft glow drew me into the library, and crossing the threshold timidly, I stooped to dry my wet coat by the fire. As I bent there, meaning to start up at the first sound of a footstep, I thought how cosy the room was after the damp walls outside to which some bared creepers were clinging; and I was watching the strange shapes and patterns the firelight made on the old Persian rug, when the lamps of a slowly turning motor flashed on me through the white shades at the window. Still dazzled by the glare, I looked round in the dimness and saw a child's ball of red and blue rubber roll towards me out of the gloom of the adjoining room. A moment later, while I made a vain attempt to capture the toy as it spun past me, a little girl darted airily, with peculiar lightness and grace, through the doorway, and stopped quickly, as if in surprise at the sight of a stranger. She was a small child—so small and slight that her footsteps made no sound on the polished floor of the threshold; and I remember thinking while I looked at her that she had the gravest and sweetest face I had ever seen. She couldn't—I decided this afterwards—have been more than six or seven years old, yet she stood there with a curious prim dignity, like the dignity of an elderly person, and gazed up at me with enigmatical eyes. She was dressed in Scotch plaid, with a bit of red ribbon in her hair, which was cut in a fringe over her forehead and hung very straight to her shoulders. Charming as she was, from her uncurled brown hair to the white socks and black slippers on her little feet, I recall most vividly the singular look in her eyes, which appeared in the shifting light to be of an indeterminate colour. For the odd thing about this look was that it was not the look of childhood at all. It was the look of profound experience, of bitter knowledge.

"Have you come for your ball?" I asked; but while the friendly question was still on my lips, I heard the servant returning. In my confusion I made a second ineffectual grasp at the plaything, which had rolled away from me into the dusk of the drawing-room. Then, as I raised my head, I saw that the child also had slipped from the room; and without looking after her I followed the old negro into the pleasant study above, where the great surgeon awaited me.

Ten years ago, before hard nursing had taken so much out of me, I blushed very easily, and I was aware at the moment when I crossed Doctor Maradick's study that my cheeks were the colour of peonies. Of course, I was a fool—no one knows this better than I do—but I had never been alone, even for an instant, with him before, and the man was more than a hero to me, he was—there isn't any reason now why I should blush over the confession—almost a god. At that age I was mad about the wonders of surgery, and Roland Maradick in the operating-room was magician enough to have turned an older and more sensible head than mine. Added to his great reputation and his marvelous skill, he was, I am sure of this, the most splendid-looking man, even at forty-five, that one could imagine. Had he been ungracious—had he been positively rude to me, I should still have adored him; but when he held out his hand, and greeted me in the charming way he had with women, I felt that I would have died for him. It is no wonder that a saying went about the hospital that every woman he operated on fell in love with him. As for the nurses—well, there wasn't a single one of them who had escaped his spell—not even Miss Hemphill, who could have been scarcely a day under fifty.

"I am glad you could come, Miss Randolph. You were with Miss Hudson last week when I operated?"

I bowed. To save my life I couldn't have spoken without blushing the redder.

"I noticed your bright face at the time. Brightness, I think, is what Mrs. Maradick needs. She finds her day nurse depressing." His eyes rested so kindly upon me that I have suspected since that he was not entirely unaware of my worship. It was a small thing, heaven knows, to flatter his vanity—a nurse just out of a training-school—but to some men no tribute is too insignificant to give pleasure.

"You will do your best, I am sure." He hesitated an instant—just long enough for me to perceive the anxiety beneath the genial smile on his face—and then added gravely, "We wish to avoid, if possible, having to send her away."

I could only murmur in response, and after a few carefully chosen words about his wife's illness, he rang the bell and directed the maid to take me upstairs to my room. Not until I was ascending the stairs to the third storey did it occur to me that he had really told me nothing. I was as perplexed about the nature of Mrs. Maradick's malady as I had been when I entered the house.

I found my room pleasant enough. It had been arranged—at Doctor Maradick's request, I think—that I was to sleep in the house, and after my austere little bed of the hospital, I was agreeably surprised by the cheerful look of the apartment into which the maid led me. The walls were papered in roses, and there were curtains of flowered chintz at the window, which looked down on a small formal garden at the rear of the house. This the maid told me, for it was too dark for me to distinguish more than a marble fountain and a fir tree, which looked old, though I afterwards learned that it was replanted almost every season.

In ten minutes I had slipped into my uniform and was ready to go to my patient; but for some reason—to this day I have never found out what it was that turned her against me at the start—Mrs. Maradick refused to receive me. While I stood outside her door I heard the day nurse trying to persuade her to let me come in. It wasn't any use, however, and in the end I was obliged to go back to my room and wait until the poor lady got over her whim and consented to see me. That was long after dinner—it must have been nearer eleven than ten o'clock—and Miss Peterson was quite worn out by the time she came for me.

"I'm afraid you'll have a bad night," she said as we went downstairs together. That was her way, I soon saw, to expect the worst of everything and everybody.

"Does she often keep you up like this?"

"Oh, no, she is usually very considerate. I never knew a sweeter character. But she still has this hallucination——"

Here again, as in the scene with Doctor Maradick, I felt that the explanation had only deepened the mystery. Mrs. Maradick's hallucination, whatever form it assumed, was evidently a subject for evasion and subterfuge in the household. It was on the tip of my tongue to ask, "What is her hallucination?"—but before I could get the words past my lips we had reached Mrs. Maradick's door, and Miss Peterson motioned me to be silent. As the door opened a little way to admit me, I saw that Mrs. Maradick was already in bed, and that the lights were out except for a night-lamp burning on a candle-stand beside a book and a carafe of water.

"I won't go in with you," said Miss Peterson in a whisper; and I was on the point of stepping over the threshold when I saw the little girl, in the dress of Scotch plaid, slip by me from the dusk of the room into the electric light of the hall. She held a doll in her arms, and as she went by she dropped a doll's work-basket in the doorway. Miss Peterson must have picked up the toy, for when I turned in a minute to look for it I found that it was gone. I remember thinking that it was late for a child to be up—she looked delicate, too—but, after all, it was no business of mine, and four years in a hospital had taught me never to meddle in things that do not concern me. There is nothing a nurse learns quicker than not to try to put the world to rights in a day.

When I crossed the floor to the chair by Mrs. Maradick's bed, she turned over on her side and looked at me with the sweetest and saddest smile.

"You are the night nurse," she said in a gentle voice; and from the moment she spoke I knew that there was nothing hysterical or violent about her mania—or hallucination, as they called it. "They told me your name, but I have forgotten it."

"Randolph—Margaret Randolph." I liked her from the start, and I think she must have seen it.

"You look very young, Miss Randolph."

"I am twenty-two, but I suppose I don't look quite my age. People usually think I am younger."

For a minute she was silent, and while I settled myself in the chair by the bed, I thought how strikingly she resembled the little girl I had seen first in the afternoon, and then leaving her room a few moments before. They had the same small, heart-shaped faces, coloured ever so faintly; the same straight, soft hair, between brown and flaxen; and the same large, grave eyes, set very far apart under arched eyebrows. What surprised me most, however, was that they both looked at me with that enigmatical and vaguely wondering expression—only in Mrs. Maradick's face the vagueness seemed to change now and then to a definite fear—a flash, I had almost said, of startled horror.

I sat quite still in my chair, and until the time came for Mrs. Maradick to take her medicine not a word passed between us. Then, when I bent over her with the glass in my hand, she raised her head from the pillow and said in a whisper of suppressed intensity:

"You look kind. I wonder if you could have seen my little girl?"

As I slipped my arm under the pillow I tried to smile cheerfully down on her. "Yes, I've seen her twice. I'd know her anywhere by her likeness to you."

A glow shone in her eyes, and I thought how pretty she must have been before illness took the life and animation out of her features. "Then I know you're good." Her voice was so strained and low that I could barely hear it. "If you weren't good you couldn't have seen her."

I thought this queer enough, but all I answered was, "She looked delicate to be sitting up so late."

A quiver passed over her thin features, and for a minute I thought she was going to burst into tears. As she had taken the medicine, I put the glass back on the candle-stand, and bending over the bed, smoothed the straight brown hair, which was as fine and soft as spun silk, back from her forehead. There was something about her—I don't know what it was—that made you love her as soon as she looked at you.

"She always had that light and airy way, though she was never sick a day in her life," she answered calmly after a pause. Then, groping for my hand, she whispered passionately, "You must not tell him—you must not tell anyone that you have seen her!"

"I must not tell anyone?" Again I had the impression that had come to me first in Doctor Maradick's study, and afterwards with Miss Peterson on the staircase, that I was seeking a gleam of light in the midst of obscurity.

"Are you sure there isn't any one listening—that there isn't any one at the door?" she asked, pushing aside my arm and raising herself on the pillows.

"Quite, quite sure. They have put out the lights in the hall."

"And you will not tell him? Promise me that you will not tell him." The startled horror flashed from the vague wonder of her expression. "He doesn't like her to come back, because he killed her."

"Because he killed her!" Then it was that light burst on me in a blaze. So this was Mrs. Maradick's hallucination! She believed that her child was dead—the little girl I had seen with my own eyes leaving her room; and she believed that her husband—the great surgeon we worshipped in the hospital—had murdered her. No wonder they veiled the dreadful obsession in mystery! No wonder that even Miss Peterson had not dared to drag the horrid thing out into the light! It was the kind of hallucination one simply couldn't stand having to face.

"There is no use telling people things that nobody believes," she resumed slowly, still holding my hand in a grasp that would have hurt me if her fingers had not been so fragile. "Nobody believes that he killed her. Nobody believes that she comes back every day to the house. Nobody believes—and yet you saw her——"

"Yes, I saw her—but why should your husband have killed her?" I spoke soothingly, as one would speak to a person who was quite mad. Yet she was not mad, I could have sworn this while I looked at her.

For a moment she moaned inarticulately, as if the horror of her thoughts were too great to pass into speech. Then she flung out her thin, bare arm with a wild gesture.

"Because he never loved me!" she said. "He never loved me!"

"But he married you," I urged gently while I stroked her hair. "If he hadn't loved you, why should he have married you?"

"He wanted the money—my little girl's money. It all goes to him when I die."

"But he is rich himself. He must make a fortune from his profession."

"It isn't enough. He wanted millions." She had grown

stern and tragic. "No, he never loved me. He loved someone else from the beginning—before I knew him."

It was quite useless, I saw, to reason with her. If she wasn't mad, she was in a state of terror and despondency so black that it had almost crossed the borderline into madness. I thought once that I would go upstairs and bring the child down from her nursery; but, after a moment's hesitation, I realized that Miss Peterson and Doctor Maradick must have long ago tried all these measures. Clearly, there was nothing to do except soothe and quiet her as much as I could; and this I did until she dropped into a light sleep which lasted well into the morning.

By seven o'clock I was worn out—not from work but from the strain on my sympathy—and I was glad, indeed, when one of the maids came in to bring me an early cup of coffee. Mrs. Maradick was still sleeping—it was a mixture of bromide and chloral I had given her—and she did not wake until Miss Peterson came on duty an hour or two later. Then, when I went downstairs, I found the dining-room deserted except for the old housekeeper, who was looking over the silver. Doctor Maradick, she explained to me presently, had his breakfast served in the morning-room on the other side of the house.

"And the little girl? Does she take her meals in the nursery?" She threw me a startled glance. Was it, I questioned afterwards, one of distrust or apprehension?

"There isn't any little girl. Haven't you heard?"

"Heard? No. Why, I saw her only yesterday."

The look she gave me—I was sure of it now—was full of alarm.

"The little girl—she was the sweetest child I ever saw—died just two months ago of pneumonia."

"But she couldn't have died." I was a fool to let this out, but the shock had completely unnerved me. "I tell you I saw her yesterday."

The alarm in her face deepened. "That is Mrs. Maradick's trouble. She believes that she still sees her."

"But don't you see her?" I drove the question home bluntly.

"No." She set her lips tightly. "I never see anything."

So I had been wrong, after all, and the explanation, when it came, only accentuated the terror. The child was dead—

she had died of pneumonia two months ago—and yet I had seen her, with my own eyes, playing ball in the library; I had seen her slipping out of her mother's room, with her doll in her arms.

"Is there another child in the house? Could there be a child belonging to one of the servants?" A gleam had shot through the fog in which I was groping.

"No, there isn't any other. The doctors tried bringing one once, but it threw the poor lady into such a state she almost died of it. Besides, there wouldn't be any other child as quiet and sweet-looking as Dorothea. To see her skipping along in her dress of Scotch plaid used to make me think of a fairy, though they say that fairies wear nothing but white or green."

"Has anyone else seen her—the child, I mean—any of the servants?"

"Only old Gabriel, the coloured butler, who came with Mrs. Maradick's mother from South Carolina. I've heard that negroes often have a kind of second sight—though I don't know that that is just what you would call it. But they seem to believe in the supernatural by instinct, and Gabriel is so old and dotty—he does no work except answer the doorbell and clean the silver—that nobody pays much attention to anything that he sees——"

"Is the child's nursery kept as it used to be?"

"Oh, no. The doctor had all the toys sent to the children's hospital. That was a great grief to Mrs. Maradick; but Doctor Brandon thought, and all the nurses agreed with him, that it was best for her not to be allowed to keep the room as it was when Dorothea was living."

"Dorothea? Was that the child's name?"

"Yes, it means the gift of God, doesn't it? She was named after the mother of Mrs. Maradick's first husband, Mr. Ballard. He was the grave, quiet kind—not the least like the doctor."

I wondered if the other dreadful obsession of Mrs. Maradick's had drifted down through the nurses or the servants to the housekeeper; but she said nothing about it, and since she was, I suspected, a garrulous person, I thought it wiser to assume that the gossip had not reached her.

A little later, when breakfast was over and I had not yet gone upstairs to my room, I had my first interview with

Doctor Brandon, the famous alienist who was in charge of the case. I had never seen him before, but from the first moment that I looked at him I took his measure almost by intuition. He was, I suppose, honest enough—I have always granted him that, bitterly as I have felt towards him. It wasn't his fault that he lacked red blood in his brain, or that he had formed the habit, from long association with abnormal phenomena, of regarding all life as a disease. He was the sort of physician—every nurse will understand what I mean—who deals instinctively with groups instead of with individuals. He was long and solemn and very round in the face; and I hadn't talked to him ten minutes before I knew he had been educated in Germany, and that he had learned over there to treat every emotion as a pathological manifestation. I used to wonder what he got out of life—what any one got out of life who had analyzed away everything except the bare structure.

When I reached my room at last, I was so tired that I could barely remember either the questions Doctor Brandon had asked or the directions he had given me. I fell asleep, I know, almost as soon as my head touched the pillow; and the maid who came to enquire if I wanted luncheon decided to let me finish my nap. In the afternoon, when she returned with a cup of tea, she found me still heavy and drowsy. Though I was used to night nursing, I felt as if I had danced from sunset to daybreak. It was fortunate, I reflected, while I drank my tea, that every case didn't wear on one's sympathies as acutely as Mrs. Maradick's hallucination had worn on mine.

Through the day I did not see Doctor Maradick; but at seven o'clock when I came up from my early dinner on my way to take the place of Miss Peterson, who had kept on duty an hour later than usual, he met me in the hall and asked me to come into his study. I thought him handsomer than ever in his evening clothes, with a white flower in his buttonhole. He was going to some public dinner, the housekeeper told me, but, then, he was always going somewhere. I believe he didn't dine at home a single evening that winter.

"Did Mrs. Maradick have a good night?" He had closed the door after us, and turning now with the question, he smiled kindly, as if he wished to put me at ease in the beginning.

"She slept very well after she took the medicine. I gave her that at eleven o'clock."

For a minute he regarded me silently, and I was aware that his personality—his charm—was focused upon me. It was almost as if I stood in the centre of converging rays of light, so vivid was my impression of him.

"Did she allude in any way to her—to her hallucination?" he asked.

How the warning reached me—what invisible waves of sense-perception transmitted the message—I have never known; but while I stood there, facing the splendour of the doctor's presence, every intuition cautioned me that the time had come when I must take sides in the household. While I stayed there I must stand either with Mrs. Maradick or against her.

"She talked quite rationally," I replied after a moment.

"What did she say?"

"She told me how she was feeling, that she missed her child, and that she walked a little every day about her room."

His face changed—how I could not at first determine.

"Have you seen Doctor Brandon?"

"He came this morning to give me his directions."

"He thought her less well today. He has advised me to send her to Rosedale."

I have never, even in secret, tried to account for Doctor Maradick. He may have been sincere. I tell you only what I know—not what I believe or imagine—and the human is sometimes as inscrutable, as inexplicable, as the supernatural.

While he watched me I was conscious of an inner struggle, as if opposing angels warred somewhere in the depths of my being. When at last I made my decision, I was acting less from reason, I knew, than in obedience to the pressure of some secret current of thought. Heaven knows, even then, the man held me captive while I defied him.

"Doctor Maradick," I lifted my eyes for the first time frankly to his, "I believe that your wife is as sane as I am—or as you are."

He started. "Then she did not talk freely to you?"

"She may be mistaken, unstrung, piteously distressed in mind"—I brought this out with emphasis—"but she is not—I am willing to stake my future on it—a fit subject for an asylum. It would be foolish—it would be cruel to send her to Rosedale."

"Cruel, you say?" A troubled look crossed his face, and his voice grew very gentle. "You do not imagine that I could be cruel to her?"

"No, I do not think that." My voice also had softened.

"We will let things go on as they are. Perhaps Doctor Brandon may have some other suggestion to make." He drew out his watch and compared it with the clock—nervously, I observed, as if his action were a screen for his discomfiture or perplexity. "I must be going now. We will speak of this again in the morning."

But in the morning we did not speak of it, and during the month that I nursed Mrs. Maradick I was not called again into her husband's study. When I met him in the hall or on the staircase, which was seldom, he was as charming as ever; yet, in spite of his courtesy, I had a persistent feeling that he had taken my measure on that evening, and that he had no further use for me.

As the days went by Mrs. Maradick seemed to grow stronger. Never, after our first night together, had she mentioned the child to me; never had she alluded by so much as a word to her dreadful charge against her husband. She was like any woman recovering from a great sorrow, except that she was sweeter and gentler. It is no wonder that everyone who came near her loved her; for there was a mysterious loveliness about her like the mystery of light, not of darkness. She was, I have always thought, as much of an angel as it is possible for a woman to be on this earth. And yet, angelic as she was, there were times when it seemed to me that she both hated and feared her husband. Though he never entered her room while I was there, and I never heard his name on her lips until an hour before the end, still I could tell by the look of terror in her face whenever his step passed down the hall that her very soul shivered at his approach.

During the whole month I did not see the child again, though one night, when I came suddenly into Mrs. Maradick's room, I found a little garden, such as children make out of pebbles and bits of box, on the window-sill. I did not mention it to Mrs. Maradick, and a little later, as the maid lowered the shades, I noticed that the garden had vanished. Since then I have often wondered if the child were invisible only to the rest of us, and if her mother still saw her. But there was no way of finding out except by questioning, and Mrs. Maradick was so well and patient that I hadn't the heart to question. Things couldn't have been better with her than they were, and I was beginning to tell myself that she might soon go out for an airing, when the end came so suddenly.

It was a mild January day—the kind of day that brings the foretaste of spring in the middle of winter, and when I came downstairs in the afternoon, I stopped a minute by the window at the end of the hall to look down on the box maze in the garden. There was an old fountain, bearing two laughing boys in marble, in the centre of the gravelled walk, and the water, which had been turned on that morning for Mrs. Maradick's pleasure, sparkled now like silver as the sunlight splashed over it. I had never before felt the air quite so soft and springlike in January; and I thought, as I gazed down on the garden, that it would be a good idea for Mrs. Maradick to go out and bask for an hour or so in the sunshine. It seemed strange to me that she was never allowed to get any fresh air except the air that came through her windows.

When I went into her room, however, I found that she had no wish to go out. She was sitting, wrapped in shawls, by the open window, which looked down on the fountain; and as I entered she glanced up from a little book she was reading. A pot of daffodils stood on the window-sill—she was very fond of flowers and we tried always to keep some growing in her room.

"Do you know what I am reading, Miss Randolph?" she asked in her soft voice; and she read aloud a verse while I went over to the candle-stand to measure out a dose of medicine.

"'If thou hast two loaves of bread, sell one and buy daffodils, for bread nourisheth the body, but daffodils delight the soul.' That is very beautiful, don't you think so?"

I said, "Yes," that it was beautiful; and then I asked her if she wouldn't go downstairs and walk about in the garden.

"He wouldn't like it," she answered; and it was the first time she had mentioned her husband to me since the night I came to her. "He doesn't want me to go out."

I tried to laugh her out of the idea; but it was no use, and after a few minutes I gave up and began talking of other things. Even then it did not occur to me that her fear of Doctor Maradick was anything but a fancy. I could see, of course, that she wasn't out of her head; but sane persons, I knew, sometimes have unaccountable prejudices, and I accepted her dislike as a mere whim or aversion. I did not understand then and—I may as well confess this before the end comes—I do not understand any better today. I am writing down the things I actually saw, and I repeat that I have never had the slightest twist in the direction of the miraculous.

The afternoon slipped away while we talked—she talked brightly when any subject came up that interested her—and it was the last hour of day—that grave, still hour when the movement of life seems to droop and falter for a few precious minutes—that brought us the thing I had dreaded silently since my first night in the house. I remember that I had risen to close the window, and was leaning out for a breath of the mild air, when there was the sound of steps, consciously softened, in the hall outside, and Doctor Brandon's usual knock fell on my ears. Then, before I could cross the room, the door opened, and the doctor entered with Miss Peterson. The day nurse, I knew, was a stupid woman; but she had never appeared to me so stupid, so armoured and encased in her professional manner, as she did at that moment.

"I am glad to see that you are taking the air." As Doctor Brandon came over to the window, I wondered maliciously what devil of contradictions had made him a distinguished specialist in nervous diseases.

"Who was the other doctor you brought this morning?" asked Mrs. Maradick gravely; and that was all I ever heard about the visit of the second alienist.

"Someone who is anxious to cure you." He dropped into a chair beside her and patted her hand with his long, pale fingers. "We are so anxious to cure you that we want to send you away to the country for a fortnight or so. Miss Peterson has come to help you to get ready, and I've kept my car waiting for you. There couldn't be a nicer day for a trip, could there?"

The moment had come at last. I knew at once what he

meant, and so did Mrs. Maradick. A wave of colour flowed and ebbed in her thin checks, and I felt her body quiver when I moved from the window and put my arms on her shoulders. I was aware again, as I had been aware that evening in Doctor Maradick's study, of a current of thought that beat from the air around into my brain. Though it cost me my career as a nurse and my reputation for sanity, I knew that I must obey that invisible warning.

"You are going to take me to an asylum," said Mrs. Maradick.

He made some foolish denial or evasion; but before he had finished I turned from Mrs. Maradick and faced him impulsively. In a nurse this was flagrant rebellion, and I realized that the act wrecked my professional future. Yet I did not care—I did not hesitate. Something stronger than I was driving me on.

"Doctor Brandon," I said, "I beg you—I implore you to wait until tomorrow. There are things I must tell you."

A queer look came into his face, and I understood, even in my excitement, that he was mentally deciding in which group he should place me—to which class of morbid manifestations I must belong.

"Very well, very well, we will hear everything," he replied soothingly; but I saw him glance at Miss Peterson, and she went over to the wardrobe for Mrs. Maradick's fur coat and hat.

Suddenly, without warning, Mrs. Maradick threw the shawls away from her, and stood up. "If you send me away," she said, "I shall never come back. I shall never live to come back."

The grey of twilight was just beginning, and while she stood there, in the dusk of the room, her face shone out as pale and flower-like as the daffodils on the window-sill. "I cannot go away!" she cried in a sharper voice. "I cannot go away from my child!"

I saw her face clearly; I heard her voice; and then—the horror of the scene sweeps back over me!—I saw the door open slowly and the little girl run across the room to her mother. I saw the child lift her little arms, and I saw the mother stoop and gather her to her bosom. So closely locked were they in that passionate embrace that their forms seemed to mingle in the gloom that enveloped them.

"After this can you doubt?" I threw out the words almost savagely—and then, when I turned from the mother and child to Doctor Brandon and Miss Peterson, I knew breathlessly—oh, there was a shock in the discovery!—that they were blind to the child. Their blank faces revealed the consternation of ignorance, not of conviction. They had seen nothing except the vacant arms of the mother and the swift, erratic gesture with which she stooped to embrace some invisible presence. Only my vision—and I have asked myself since if the power of sympathy enabled me to penetrate the web of material fact and see the spiritual form of the child—only my vision was not blinded by the clay through which I looked.

"After this can you doubt?" Doctor Brandon had flung my words back to me. Was it his fault, poor man, if life had granted him only the eyes of flesh? Was it his fault if he could see only half of the thing there before him?

But they couldn't see, and since they couldn't see I realized that it was useless to tell them. Within an hour they took Mrs. Maradick to the asylum; and she went quietly, though when the time came for parting from me she showed some faint trace of feeling. I remember that at the last, while we stood on the pavement, she lifted her black veil, which she wore for the child, and said: "Stay with her, Miss Randolph, as long as you can. I shall never come back."

Then she got into the car and was driven off, while I stood looking after her with a sob in my throat. Dreadful as I felt it to be, I didn't, of course, realize the full horror of it, or I couldn't have stood there quietly on the pavement. I didn't realize it, indeed, until several months afterwards when word came that she had died in the asylum. I never knew what her illness was, though I vaguely recall that something was said about "heart failure"—a loose enough term. My own belief is that she died simply of the terror of life.

To my surprise Doctor Maradick asked me to stay on as his office nurse after his wife went to Rosedale; and when the news of her death came there was no suggestion of my leaving. I don't know to this day why he wanted me in the house. Perhaps he thought I should have less opportunity to gossip if I stayed under his roof; perhaps he still wished to test the power of his charm over me. His vanity was incredible in so great a man. I have seen him flush with pleasure when people turned to look at him in the street, and I know that he was not above playing on the sentimental weakness of his patients. But he was magnificent, heaven knows! Few men, I imagine, have been the objects of so many foolish infatuations.

The next summer Doctor Maradick went abroad for two months, and while he was away I took my vacation in Virginia. When we came back the work was heavier than ever—his reputation by this time was tremendous—and my days were so crowded with appointments, and hurried flittings to emergency cases, that I had scarcely a minute left in which to remember poor Mrs. Maradick. Since the afternoon when she went to the asylum the child had not been in the house; and at last I was beginning to persuade myself that the little figure had been an optical illusion—the effect of shifting lights in the gloom of the old rooms—not the apparition I had once believed it to be. It does not take long for a phantom to fade from the memory—especially when one leads the active and methodical life I was forced into that winter. Perhaps—who knows?—(I remember telling myself) the doctors may have been right, after all, and the poor lady may have actually been out of her mind. With this view of the past, my judgement of Doctor Maradick insensibly altered. It ended, I think, in my acquitting him altogether. And then, just as he stood clear and splendid in my verdict of him, the reversal came so precipitately that I grow breathless now whenever I try to live it over again. The violence of the next turn in affairs left me, I often fancy, with a perpetual dizziness of the imagination.

It was in May that we heard of Mrs. Maradick's death, and exactly a year later, on a mild and fragrant afternoon, when the daffodils were blooming in patches around the old fountain in the garden, the housekeeper came into the office, where I lingered over some accounts, to bring me news of the doctor's approaching marriage.

"It is no more than we might have expected," she concluded rationally. "The house must be lonely for him—he is such a sociable man. But I can't help feeling," she brought out slowly after a pause in which I felt a shiver pass over me, "I can't help feeling that it is hard for that other woman to have all the money poor Mrs. Maradick's first husband left her."

"There is a great deal of money, then?" I asked curiously.

"A great deal." She waved her hand, as if words were futile to express the sum. "Millions and millions!"

"They will give up this house, of course?"

"That's done already, my dear. There won't be a brick left of it by this time next year. It's to be pulled down and an apartment-house built on the ground."

Again the shiver passed over me. I couldn't bear to think of Mrs. Maradick's old home falling to pieces.

"You didn't tell me the name of the bride," I said. "Is she someone he met while he was in Europe?"

"Dear me, no! She is the very lady he was engaged to before he married Mrs. Maradick, only she threw him over, so people said, because he wasn't rich enough. Then she married some lord or prince from over the water; but there was a divorce, and now she has turned again to her old lover. He is rich enough now, I guess, even for her!"

It was all perfectly true, I suppose; it sounded as plausible as a story out of a newspaper; and yet while she told me I felt, or dreamed that I felt, a sinister, an impalpable hush in the air. I was nervous, no doubt; I was shaken by the suddenness with which the housekeeper had sprung her news on me; but as I sat there I had quite vividly an impression that the old house was listening—that there was a real, if invisible, presence somewhere in the room or the garden. Yet, when an instant afterwards I glanced through the long window which opened down to the brick terrace, I saw only the faint sunshine over the deserted garden, with its maze of box, its marble fountain, and its patches of daffodils.

The housekeeper had gone—one of the servants, I think, came for her—and I was sitting at my desk when the words of Mrs. Maradick on that last evening floated into my mind. The daffodils brought her back to me; for I thought, as I watched them growing, so still and golden in the sunshine, how she would have enjoyed them. Almost unconsciously I repeated the verse she had read to me:

"If thou hast two loaves of bread, sell one and buy daffodils"—and it was at this very instant, while the words were still on my lips, that I turned my eyes to the box maze, and saw the child skipping rope along the gravelled path to the fountain. Quite distinctly, as clear as day, I saw her come, with what children call the dancing step, between the low box borders to the place where the daffodils bloomed by the fountain. From her straight brown hair to her frock of Scotch plaid and her little feet, which twinkled in white socks and black slippers over the turning rope, she was as real to me as the ground on which she trod or the laughing marble boys under the splashing water. Starting up from my chair, I made a single step to the terrace. If I could only reach her—only speak to her—I felt that I might at last solve the mystery. But with the first flutter of my dress on the terrace, the airy little form melted into the quiet dusk of the maze. Not a breath stirred the daffodils, not a shadow passed over the sparkling flow of the water; yet, weak and shaken in every nerve, I sat down on the brick step of the terrace and burst into tears. I must have known that something terrible would happen before they pulled down Mrs. Maradick's home.

The doctor dined out that night. He was with the lady he was going to marry, the housekeeper told me; and it must have been almost midnight when I heard him come in and go upstairs to his room. I was downstairs because I had been unable to sleep, and the book I wanted to finish I had left that afternoon in the office. The book—I can't remember what it was—had seemed to me very exciting when I began it in the morning; but after the visit of the child I found the romantic novel as dull as a treatise on nursing. It was impossible for me to follow the lines, and I was on the point of giving up and going to bed, when Doctor Maradick opened the front door with his latchkey and went up the staircase. "There can't be a bit of truth in it," I thought over and over again as I listened to his even step ascending the stairs. "There can't be a bit of truth in it." And yet, though I assured myself that "there couldn't be a bit of truth in it," I shrank, with a creepy sensation, from going through the house to my room in the third storey. I was tired out after a hard day, and my nerves must have reacted morbidly to the silence and the darkness. For the first time in my life I knew what it was to be afraid of the unknown, of the unseen; and while I bent over my book, in the glare of the electric light,

I became conscious presently that I was straining my senses for some sound in the spacious emptiness of the rooms overhead. The noise of a passing motor-car in the street jerked me back from the intense hush of expectancy; and I can recall the wave of relief that swept over me as I turned to my book again and tried to fix my distracted mind on its pages.

I was still sitting there when the telephone on my desk rang, with what seemed to my overwrought nerves a startling abruptness, and the voice of the superintendent told me hurriedly that Doctor Maradick was needed at the hospital. I had become so accustomed to these emergency calls in the night that I felt reassured when I had rung up the doctor in his room and had heard the hearty sound of his response. He had not yet undressed, he said, and would come down immediately while I ordered back his car, which must just have reached the garage.

"I'll be with you in five minutes!" he called as cheerfully as if I had summoned him to his wedding.

I heard him cross the floor of his room; and before he could reach the head of the staircase, I opened the door and went out into the hall in order that I might turn on the light and have his hat and coat waiting. The electric button was at the end of the hall, and as I moved towards it, guided by the glimmer that fell from the landing above, I lifted my eyes to the staircase, which climbed dimly, with its slender mahogany balustrade, as far as the third storey. Then it was, at the very moment when the doctor, humming gaily, began his quick descent of the steps, that I distinctly saw—I will swear to this on my deathbed—a child's skipping rope lying loosely coiled, as if it had dropped from a careless little hand, in the bend of the staircase. With a spring I had reached the electric button, flooding the hall with light; but as I did so, while my arm was still outstretched behind me, I heard the humming voice change to a cry of surprise or terror, and the figure on the staircase tripped heavily and stumbled with groping hands into emptiness. The scream of warning died in my throat while I watched him pitch forward down the long flight of stairs to the floor at my feet. Even before I bent over him, before I wiped the blood from his brow and felt for his silent heart, I knew that he was dead.

Something—it may have been, as the world believes, a misstep in the dimness, or it may have been, as I am ready to bear witness, an invisible judgement—something had killed him at the very moment when he most wanted to live.

Derek Gunn

(1964–)

Born in Dublin, Derek Gunn as a boy avidly read science fiction, horror stories, thrillers, fantasy, and Westerns while collecting American Marvel and DC comics. A graduate of the College of Marketing and Design and the Marketing Institute of Ireland, he has been designing communication networks for international businesses for over twenty years as a consultant for a major global telecommunications company. He is the author of four novels of a postapocalyptic thriller series, *Vampire Apocalypse: A World Torn Asunder* (2006), *Descent into Chaos* (2008), *Fallout* (2009), and *The Estuary* (2009), as well as numerous short stories. A member of the Horror Writers Association and the International Thriller Writers Association, he is a contributing editor for the latter, publishing a monthly column in which he interviews and reviews the work of a range of authors.

The Third Option

(2007)

"I fucking hate dead people," Deputy William Boyle whined as he reached for his hat. Outside the wind howled and threw sand against the windows of the small jail, the sound crackling like bacon sizzling on a pan. "I mean why can't we just put them back in the ground where they belong?"

Sheriff Amos Carter waited impatiently for his deputy and tried to ignore the pounding in his head. Boyle was a good man but inexperienced. He also asked way too many questions, but he had just become a father yesterday and they had celebrated far too much the previous night. Carter decided he would allow him a little leeway, but only as much as his throbbing head would tolerate, and his limit was fast approaching. "Now, Will," Carter sighed, "you know as well as I do that the Governor has ordered that these dead folk be left alone until they can decide whether they have a legal right to walk around."

"And what if they decide that they don't?" Boyle pressed him.

"Then," Carter sighed and slapped his thigh impatiently, "you can put them back in the ground. Now hurry up. We have to let him know about our town rules before he goes and breaks any of 'em."

"I'm coming," Boyle pouted, "but I still can't figure out what the good Lord was thinking 'bout when he sent 'em back to clutter up the place."

"It had nothing to do with the Lord's work as you well know." Carter pushed the younger man out the door where his startled cry was ripped from his mouth by the wind.

The day was young. The sun was still climbing in the sky. Sand swirled around the two men and forced them to pull their bandanas up over their noses and mouths. Carter cursed as his eyes were assaulted by the sand and he hunched up further as the wind snapped at him. It was June. Normally the sun would already be hot enough to fry an egg, but the sand was so thick after a dry month that the wind had whipped it up easily and it was blocking most of the heat. He squinted upward but could only see a vague outline of the sun through the storm. The weak glow cast the town in an eerie, diffused light.

The two men hurried to the saloon. Carter was thankful the storm cut off any further questions Boyle might have had. The subject of the dead walking around was confusing enough to him without having to come up with answers for an overeager deputy as well.

Of course it would be easier to just kill them all, but one of the buggers had petitioned the Governor that the dead still had rights. He had argued that the fact that they no longer breathed did not necessarily change their legal status and the Governor's legal experts did not have any counter to that argument. Until the lawyers got their act together, they would have to put up with their share of visitors, although few of them came this far upstate.

It had all started two years ago as an act of final defiance by an Indian shaman before his tribe had been kicked off their land. Nobody knew for certain what had happened. The accepted version was that an Indian shaman had put a curse on the white man that "the dead would rise and ravage that which he held most dear." Carter assumed that the Shaman had meant for the dead to kill the living but something had gone wrong. The dead *did* crave that which the white man held most dear, there was no argument about that, it was just that the shaman had miscalculated on the white man's priorities. It wasn't life that the white man held most precious. Out here in the west, it was gold that men lusted after. Gold meant power. Of course some idiot had gone and killed the shaman in the meantime so the curse could not be reversed. So for now at least, they were stuck with the dead folk.

The two men reached the wooden boardwalk, which stretched from Tracy's Hardware to the hotel. The saloon was about halfway along, past a barbershop, a few houses and the doctor's office. The path boasted a wooden canopy so they were shielded from the brunt of the storm as they continued walking. Unfortunately this also meant that it afforded Boyle the opportunity to launch into another question and, as if on cue, he did just that. "It's kind'a weird, don't you think?"

"What's that?" Carter rolled his eyes and reminded himself that Boyle was the only able-bodied man in the town willing to work for the wages that the state paid.

"This gold thing."

The dead craved gold and needed it to survive. They needed it as surely as man needed food. "Is there anything in particular or is it everything in general that you find weird?"

"Well, why do they drink it?"

Carter could understand the young man's confusion. He had been incredulous himself when he had heard it. He had since found out that hundreds of years ago kings and queens in Europe frequently took gold in the same fashion, believing that anything so expensive must be good for them. The problem now was that the living also coveted gold, and so trouble had begun almost as soon as the dead's cravings became common knowledge.

Carter sighed and stopped. Boyle didn't notice for a moment and continued on and had to hurry back. He smiled sheepishly. "Look. These things are dead. If we left them alone they'd eventually rot away and solve all our problems. Unfortunately that shaman worked some weird shit and gold slows their rotting. And before you ask I don't know how." Carter put his hand up to enforce his statement. "Anyway their teeth ain't as strong as they used to be so they have to take it in a drink or as a handful of finely shaved dust." Carter had had enough questions. "Bill," he placed a shoulder on the young man's shoulders. "I'll handle this. You go on over to Muriel in the hotel and let her know the Governor will be here later today. No doubt he'll want his usual suite."

"That's the fourth time this month." Boyle grinned lasciviously. "Those bedsprings must be bust by now."

"The Governor's sexual antics are no concern of yours," Carter admonished him and then grinned. "Mind you keep your mouth shut though. If his wife finds out he'll probably fire us just for spite."

The younger man grinned and headed off toward the hotel, giving Carter a moment to collect his thoughts before he entered the saloon. He pushed open the battered swinging doors to the saloon and winced as the hinges creaked and sent pain stabbing through his already delicate head. He stood for a moment and breathed a sigh of relief as he brushed dust and grit from his clothes. Outside, the church began summoning the faithful to worship and the incessant tolling of the bells reverberated painfully in his head.

Carter looked around the saloon, taking in his surroundings in a practised glance. He hadn't survived twenty years as a lawman by being stupid. He had long ago perfected the ability to read the occupants in a room by their stance or the looks on their faces when he entered a room, even when he was suffering from a hangover. Long slabs of wood lay on top of numerous barrels and dominated the room in front of him. The wooden planks acted as a bar until the new one arrived from St. Louis. The owner had promised the town a beautiful mahogany bar, with brass fittings, though Carter would miss this beer-stained monstrosity when it went, it had a certain charm. Large ornate oil lamps hung from the low ceiling. They burned merrily and cast deep shadows into the corners of the room. Tables lay scattered around the room in a chaotic jumble that seemed to have no plan other than to fit as many customers as possible into a relatively small space.

His eyes were drawn immediately to three Mexicans in the corner. The three men leaned in on the table conspiratorially with their elbows on the edges. Their quick, furtive glances toward Peterson behind the bar intimated some illicit activity, though their harsh accented voices and guttural laughter were far too loud to suggest anything he needed to be involved in. They were probably looking for somewhere to ride out the storm and had their own bottle hidden under the table rather than pay the exorbitant prices Peterson charged. Their clothes were simple and of poor quality. They did not appear to have weapons of any kind. His eyes continued to scan the room.

It was early yet so only two girls prowled the floor. Their gaudy colours and heavy makeup were more suited to the dim lighting of the evening. The morning's brightness, though somewhat subdued from the storm, illuminated their tired faces and lustreless hair more than they probably would have liked. They looked up with hope in their eyes as the doors creaked and announced his entry but they quickly lost interest when they saw him. The "moral majority" in the town constantly put him under pressure to run the girls out, but the law still tolerated their profession. Until that changed he could do nothing, though he did make sure that he was seen as neutral and that meant keeping his distance from both groups.

John Peterson stood behind the bar in his usual boiled white shirt and brocaded vest. He sported an overly-large moustache as if to compensate for the lack of hair on his head. His ruddy complexion hinted at an addiction to the liquor he sold. He rubbed furiously at a glass and moved his head toward the far corner of the bar. Carter nodded and glanced over toward the indicated table near the window where a lone man sat.

He spent another moment casually brushing dust from his clothes and used the time to look the stranger over. The man's boots and jeans were almost the same color, with the natural fading of the materials and the dirt encrusted liberally over them both. He wore a dark blue shirt of good quality, though the material was worn in places and the collar was frayed. A black vest with three silver buttons, dulled from lack of attention, completed the man's wardrobe. He also wore a matching black hat that cast a shadow over his face but Carter could see that he was relatively clean shaven and that his hair was still quite short, the ends only curling slightly above the frayed collar.

Not dead that long then, he mused as he continued to study the figure. Hair had become the accepted method of judging the duration of a dead person's existence. Hair seemed to grow for quite a while after death, so many of them had long hair and uneven, scraggly beards. The dead seemed to have no interest in hygiene, so most of them smelled foul, somewhere between rotten meat and an open sewer. Their hair was usually matted and infested with all kinds of parasites.

Carter came to a stop at the table. The man moved his head slowly and regarded him with a cool appraisal of his own. The man had a strong jawline but his desiccated skin was pulled too taut over the bone. This made the man's face angular rather than strong. His nose seemed too long and narrow with the flesh having receded in death, giving him a hawkish appearance that threw shadows over his already sunken eye sockets. His eyes bore the hallmark of the dead. Skin stretched tightly at the sides, making them appear as if they were constantly squinting. The high cheekbones, where the bone protruded and stretched the skin around his mouth, gave the stranger an insane-looking grin. It was unnerving, looking at someone who grinned constantly, but it was the eyes that held him, as they always did. They were yellow with a small bead of black in the centre. There was no sense of life in those eyes as they regarded him, nothing but dark ovals of purest black.

The recent Civil and Indian wars had left thousands dead. The graveyards full to capacity. When the dead had begun to rise, there had been no shortage of corpses. Suddenly towns and cities filled with ambling corpses that, while they seemed to pose no immediate threat to the population, did make everyone uncomfortable. The first response had been to kill them. Thousands died, again, but the dead did not simply stand still and let it happen. Once they got over the shock of finding themselves walking around, the dead began to regain their wits and began to protect themselves. They were also bloody difficult to kill. They could survive almost any wound and only finally died when their brains were destroyed.

The figure nodded to him and Carter nodded back as he finished his appraisal. The man might be dirty and rotting but the two Colts strapped to his sides were in beautiful condition. Even the holster shone with a recent oiling and the weapons' worn bone handles testified to long years of use. He also noted that both guns were tied low on the man's thighs. *A gunfighter.* Carter cursed his luck. He was not slow on the draw himself but he just knew as he looked into the stranger's eyes that he would be no match for this man. Dead or not, this man exuded competence. The dead tended to move more slowly than they had in life—something to do with the blood stagnating in their veins he had been told—but this corpse did not look slow. He had moved with an easy grace when he turned to face Carter and not the exaggerated slowness of many of his kind. Carter also noted that the man had cut his fingernails short to accommodate a fast draw and he felt his heart beat faster.

People had begun to grow worried when the dead began to defend themselves. It was assumed that, strange as it was, the phenomenon was still an isolated incident and once they killed off the walking corpses, things would return to normal. It was only when they realized that even those who had recently died also rose again that things had gone to hell. The government had been forced to call for a cessation of hostilities on both sides until something could be done. The most popular solution seemed to be that a reservation, similar to that put in place for the Indians, would be provided and everyone seemed to calm down while plans were laid.

The subsequent discovery that the dead needed gold to survive threw everything into chaos. Hostilities broke out again. It had been at that point that one of the dead had written a legal paper citing that the dead still had rights and as such should have access to all the protection that the law could provide. The paper also called for the return of all the dead's assets. The banks disagreed. The banks had gotten used to keeping the money and assets that the dead left behind, when no beneficiaries were involved, and they did not want to have to give these assets back. Cases were brought against the banks by a growing number of dead people, but until the question of their rights was addressed there could be no decision on who owned the money. This of course meant that the dead had no means of purchasing the gold they required to survive.

That left the dead with few choices. If they wanted to continue to exist they only had two options; either they earned their money or they would have to steal it. Most of the living would not employ the dead, so many of them were forced into crime to survive. It was this fact that branded all of them as criminals. This had the result of the dead being shunned. Violence had a habit of breaking out regularly when they came to town. While Carter was not allowed to throw the dead out of his jurisdiction, just because they were dead, he did make sure to warn any who came through that he took a dim view of anyone causing trouble in his town.

He took a deep breath and addressed the man. "Morning," Carter managed finally, pleased that his voice didn't break. The corpse nodded back, his mouth still grinning insanely at him. As a law officer he was not allowed merely to kill the stranger on a whim. Until the lawyers ruled one way or the other, this corpse had as many rights as any of the town's citizens. His hands were tied.

Only the elite Texas Rangers could kill without recourse, and they hardly ever came this far north. The Governor had made the Rangers exempt in an attempt to mollify his richest supporters. He had dressed it up in fancy language extolling the Rangers' proud history and supporting their judgment when on missions. It just wasn't practical, he had stated in his address to the papers, to force these men to check in before they acted. It would be suicide for these trusted men to be second-guessed for every decision. The result was that the Rangers had become untouchable. Carter had heard stories of Rangers combing the state and quietly executing the dead. It seemed that the Governor was making sure that whatever might be decided by the government about the issue of the dead's rights, it would not have an impact on the Governor's own finances.

Stories were becoming more frequent of Ranger death-squads sweeping the state trying to accomplish their mission before the lawyers came to any decisions. Carter didn't really care one way or the other. The dead were dead. Who cared if they were put back in the ground? Carter knew more than most about the current situation because the Governor's mistress lived in his town. Each time he came to visit, Carter made sure that he got an update from the Governor's bodyguards.

Carter shifted on his feet nervously. Most of the dead he dealt with were easy prey. He could intimidate them easily, but this corpse seemed far too confident. He had never seen such confidence in the dead before, and it worried him. He cursed himself for letting Boyle go on to the hotel. He could have done with the younger man's support. Outside the bells finally stopped tolling and he sighed in relief as the pounding in his head began to subside. The sun flared briefly outside in momentary relief from the wind and its glare blazed through the glass and reflected off something on the man's chest.

Carter frowned as he blinked and then the glare suddenly stopped as the wind picked up and the sand once again drew its veil over the sun. He studied the man's chest and saw that there was a badge there of some sort. *Was he a lawman too?* That would certainly make things easier. A lawman, even a dead one, would understand his predicament. He looked harder at the badge; the edges were not pointed like his own and it was more rounded just like. . .

Oh shit! Realization flooded through him. He's a Texas Ranger. A *dead* Texas Ranger. No one had foreseen that. Did that mean he still had his immunity to the law? *Shit.* He had to warn the Governor.

Suddenly a terrible thought struck him. If this Ranger killed the Governor, would the Governor still retain his powers of office after death? That could turn the whole state upside down. The dead already outnumbered the living in the state. If they were in charge, they might be able to pass laws that would make living in the state almost impossible. Up till now the dead had been limited to two options to obtain the gold they coveted—employment, which was unlikely, and crime, which gave the living an excuse to kill them. It struck Carter they had discovered a third option to their problem. If they controlled the law, they could control the gold. Up till now people had considered the dead to be stupid, merely an inconvenience rather than any real threat. If they were capable of such planning, it showed an intelligence that sent a cold feeling of fear flooding through his veins.

These thoughts flooded his throbbing head in a flash. The Ranger merely smiled insanely at him.

He had to do something. He dropped his hand to his own weapon, adrenaline speeding his reflexes. The Ranger moved in a blur and suddenly Carter was staring at the barrel of the Ranger's colt before he even slapped leather. He looked into the Ranger's dead eyes and thought for a moment that he saw a widening of the corpse's grin. Maybe that damn shaman had got it right after all! By making the dead dependant on gold he had forced them to strike at the cornerstones of the country itself—its wealth and power. For a second he wondered what it would be like being dead.

Then he heard the shot. Darkness swept over him.

Joe Hill

(1972–)

Joseph Hillstrom King, one of three children of acclaimed horror writer Stephen King, spent his childhood in Bangor, Maine. A graduate of Vassar College, he began publishing short stories with "The Lady Rests" in 1997. In 2005, he published *20th Century Ghosts*, a collection of stories that was awarded the Bram Stoker Award for Best Fiction and was reprinted with an additional story in 2007. He has published the chapbooks *Voluntary Committal* (2005), *Pop Art* (2007), and *Thumbprint* (2007) and the novels *Heart-Shaped Box* (2007) and *Horns* (2010). His series of comic book/graphic novels titled *Locke & Key* began appearing in 2008. Among his many awards, Hill is a recipient of the Ray Bradbury Fellowship, a World Fantasy Award for Best Novella, the British Fantasy Award for Best Collection and Best Short Story, and the British Fantasy Society's Sydney J. Bounds Best Newcomer Award.

20th Century Ghost

(2002)

The best time to see her is when the place is almost full.

There is the well-known story of the man who wanders in for a late show and finds the vast six-hundred-seat theater almost deserted. Halfway through the movie, he glances around and discovers her sitting next to him, in a chair that only moments before had been empty. Her witness stares at her. She turns her head and stares back. She has a nosebleed. Her eyes are wide, stricken. My head hurts, *she whispers.* I have to step out for a moment. Will you tell me what I miss?

It is in this instant that the person looking at her realizes she is as insubstantial as the shifting blue ray of light cast by the projector. It is possible to see the next seat over through her body. As she rises from her chair, she fades away.

Then there is the story about the group of friends who go into the Rosebud together on a Thursday night. One of the bunch sits down next to a woman by herself, a woman in blue. When the movie doesn't start right away, the person who sat down beside her decides to make conversation. What's playing tomorrow? *he asks her.* The theater is dark tomorrow, *she whispers.* This is the last show. *Shortly after the movie begins she vanishes. On the drive home, the man who spoke to her is killed in a car accident.*

These, and many of the other best-known legends of the Rosebud, are false . . . the ghost stories of people who have seen too many horror movies and who think they know exactly how a ghost story should be.

Alec Sheldon, who was one of the first to see Imogene Gilchrist, owns the Rosebud, and at seventy-three still operates the projector most nights. He can always tell, after talking to someone for just a few moments, whether or not they really saw her, but what he knows he keeps to himself, and he never publicly discredits anyone's story . . . that would be bad for business.

He knows, though, that anyone who says they could see right through her didn't see her at all. Some of the put-on artists talk about blood pouring from her nose, her ears, her eyes; they say she gave them a pleading look, and asked for them to find somebody, to bring help. But she doesn't bleed that way, and when she wants to talk, it isn't to tell someone to bring a doctor. A lot of the pretenders begin their stories by saying, You'll never believe what I just saw. *They're right. He won't, although he will listen to all that they have to say, with a patient, even encouraging, smile.*

The ones who have seen her don't come looking for Alec to tell him about it. More often than not he finds them, *comes across them wandering the lobby on unsteady legs; they've had a bad shock, they don't feel well. They need to sit down a while. They don't ever say,* You won't believe what I just saw. *The experience is still too immediate. The idea that they might not be believed doesn't occur to them until later. Often they are in a state that might be described as subdued, even submissive. When he thinks about the effect she has on those who encounter her, he thinks of Steven Greenberg coming out of* The Birds *one cool Sunday afternoon in 1963. Steven was just twelve then, and it would be another twelve years before he went and got so famous; he was at that time not a golden boy, but just a boy.*

Alec was in the alley behind the Rosebud, having a smoke, when he heard the fire door into the theater clang open behind him. He turned to see a lanky kid leaning in the doorway—just leaning there, not going in or out. The boy squinted into the harsh white sunshine, with the confused, wondering look of a small child who has just been shaken out of a deep sleep. Alec could see past him into a darkness filled with the shrill sounds of thousands of squeaking sparrows. Beneath that, he could hear a few in the audience stirring restlessly, beginning to complain.

Hey, kid, in or out? *Alec said.* You're lettin' the light in.

The kid—Alec didn't know his name then—turned his head and stared back into the theater for a long, searching moment. Then he stepped out and the door settled shut behind him, closing gently on its pneumatic hinge. And still he didn't go anywhere, didn't say anything. The Rosebud had been showing The Birds *for two weeks, and although Alec had seen others walk out before it was over, none of the early exits had been twelve-year-old boys. It was the sort of film most boys of that age waited all year to see, but who knew? Maybe the kid had a weak stomach.*

I left my Coke in the theater, *the kid said, his voice distant, almost toneless.* I still had a lot of it left.

You want to go back in and look for it?

And the kid lifted his eyes and gave Alec a bright look of alarm, and then Alec knew. No.

Alec finished his cigarette, pitched it.

I sat with the dead lady, *the kid blurted.*

Alec nodded.

She talked to me.

What did she say?

He looked at the kid again, and found him staring back with eyes that were now wide and round with disbelief.

I need someone to talk to, she said. When I get excited about a movie I need to talk.

Alec knows when she talks to someone she always wants

to talk about the movies. She usually addresses herself to men, although sometimes she will sit and talk with a woman—Lois Weisel most notably. Alec has been working on a theory of what it is that causes her to show herself. He has been keeping notes in a yellow legal pad. He has a list of who she appeared to and in what movie and when (Leland King, Harold and Maude, *'72; Joel Harlowe,* Eraserhead, *'77; Hal Lash,* Blood Simple, *'85; and all the others). He has, over the years, developed clear ideas about what conditions are most likely to produce her, although the specifics of his theory are constantly being revised.*

As a young man, thoughts of her were always on his mind, or simmering just beneath the surface; she was his first and most strongly felt obsession. Then for a while he was better—when the theater was a success, and he was an important businessman in the community, chamber of commerce, town planning board. In those days he could go weeks without thinking about her; and then someone would see her, or pretend to have seen her, and stir the whole thing up again.

But following his divorce—she kept the house, he moved into the one-bedroom under the theater—and not long after the 8-screen cineplex opened just outside of town, he began to obsess again, less about her than about the theater itself (is there any difference, though? Not really, he supposes, thoughts of one always circling around to thoughts of the other). He never imagined he would be so old and owe so much money. He has a hard time sleeping, his head is so full of ideas—wild, desperate ideas—about how to keep the theater from failing. He keeps himself awake thinking about income, staff, salable assets. And when he can't think about money anymore, he tries to picture where he will go if the theater closes. He envisions an old folks' home, mattresses that reek of Ben-Gay, hunched geezers with their dentures out, sitting in a musty common room watching daytime sitcoms; he sees a place where he will passively fade away, like wallpaper that gets too much sunlight and slowly loses its color.

This is bad. What is more terrible is when he tries to imagine what will happen to her if the Rosebud closes. He sees the theater stripped of its seats, an echoing empty space, drifts of dust in the corners, petrified wads of gum stuck fast to the cement. Local teens have broken in to drink and screw; he sees scattered liquor bottles, ignorant graffiti on the walls, a single, grotesque, used condom on the floor in front of the stage. He sees the lonely and violated place where she will fade away.

Or won't fade . . . the worst thought of all.

Alec saw her—spoke to her—for the first time when he was fifteen, six days after he learned his older brother had been killed in the South Pacific. President Truman had sent a letter expressing his condolences. It was a form letter, but the signature on the bottom—that was really his. Alec hadn't cried yet. He knew, years later, that he spent that week in a state of shock, that he had lost the person he loved most in the world and it had badly traumatized him. But in 1945 no one used the word "trauma" to talk about emotions, and the only kind of shock anyone discussed was "shell—."

He told his mother he was going to school in the mornings. He wasn't going to school. He was shuffling around downtown looking for trouble. He shoplifted candy-bars from the American Luncheonette and ate them out at the empty shoe factory—the place closed down, all the men off in France, or the Pacific. With sugar zipping in his blood, he launched rocks through the windows, trying out his fastball.

He wandered through the alley behind the Rosebud and looked at the door into the theater and saw that it wasn't firmly shut. The side facing the alley was a smooth metal surface, no door handle, but he was able to pry it open with his fingernails. He came in on the 3:30 P.M. show, the place crowded, mostly kids under the age of ten and their mothers. The fire door was halfway up the theater, recessed into the wall, set in shadow. No one saw him come in. He slouched up the aisle and found a seat in the back.

"I heard Jimmy Stewart went to the Pacific," his brother had told him while he was home on leave, before he shipped out. They were throwing the ball around out back. "Mr. Smith is probably carpet-bombing the red fuck out of Tokyo right this instant. How's that for a crazy thought?" Alec's brother, Ray, was a self-described film freak. He and Alec went to every single movie that opened during his monthlong leave: *Bataan*, *The Fighting Seabees*, *Going My Way*.

Alec waited through an episode of a serial concerning the latest adventures of a singing cowboy with long eyelashes and a mouth so dark his lips were black. It failed to interest him. He picked his nose and wondered how to get a Coke with no money. The feature started.

At first Alec couldn't figure out what the hell kind of movie it was, although right off he had the sinking feeling it was going to be a musical. First the members of an orchestra filed onto a stage against a bland blue backdrop. Then a starched shirt came out and started telling the audience all about the brand-new kind of entertainment they were about to see. When he started blithering about Walt Disney and his artists, Alec began to slide downwards in his seat, his head sinking between his shoulders. The orchestra surged into big dramatic blasts of strings and horns. In another moment his worst fears were realized. It wasn't just a musical; it was also a *cartoon*. Of course it was a cartoon, he should have known—the place crammed with little kids and their mothers—a 3:30 show in the middle of the week that led off with an episode of The Lipstick Kid, singing sissy of the high plains.

After a while he lifted his head and peeked at the screen through his fingers, watched some abstract animation: silver raindrops falling against a background of roiling smoke, rays of molten light shimmering across an ashen sky. Eventually he straightened up to watch in a more comfortable position. He was not quite sure what he was feeling. He was bored, but interested too, almost a little mesmerized. It would have been hard not to watch. The visuals came at him in a steady hypnotic assault: ribs of red light, whirling stars, kingdoms of cloud glowing in the crimson light of a setting sun.

The little kids were shifting around in their seats. He heard a little girl whisper loudly, "Mom, when is there going to be *Mickey*?" For the kids it was like being in school. But by the time the movie hit the next segment, the orchestra shifting from Bach to Tchaikovsky, he was sitting all the way up, even leaning forward slightly, his forearms resting on his knees. He watched fairies flitting through a dark forest, touching flowers and spiderwebs with enchanted wands and spreading sheets of glittering, incandescent dew. He felt a kind of baffled wonder watching them fly around, a curious feeling of yearning. He had the sudden idea he could sit there and watch forever.

"I could sit in this theater forever," whispered someone beside him. It was a girl's voice. "Just sit here and watch and never leave."

He didn't know there was someone sitting beside him and jumped to hear a voice so close. He thought—no, he knew—that when he sat down, the seats on either side of him were empty. He turned his head.

She was only a few years older than him, couldn't have been more than twenty, and his first thought was that she was very close to being a fox; his heart beat a little faster to have such a girl speaking to him. He was already thinking, *Don't blow it.* She wasn't looking at him. She was staring up at the movie, and smiling in a way that seemed to express both admiration and a child's dazed wonder. He wanted desperately to say something smooth, but his voice was trapped in his throat.

She leaned towards him without glancing away from the screen, her left hand just touching the side of his arm on the armrest.

"I'm sorry to bother you," she whispered. "When I get excited about a movie I want to talk. I can't help it."

In the next moment he became aware of two things, more or less simultaneously. The first was that her hand against his arm was cold. He could feel the deadly chill of it through his sweater, a cold so palpable it startled him a little. The second thing he noticed was a single teardrop of blood on her upper lip, under her left nostril.

"You have a nosebleed," he said, in a voice that was too loud. He immediately wished he hadn't said it. You only had one opportunity to impress a fox like this. He should have found something for her to wipe her nose with, and handed it to her, murmured something real Sinatra: *You're bleeding, here.* He pushed his hands into his pockets, feeling for something she could wipe her nose with. He didn't have anything.

But she didn't seem to have heard him, didn't seem the slightest bit aware he had spoken. She absentmindedly brushed the back of one hand under her nose, and left a dark smear of blood over her upper lip . . . and Alec froze with his hands in his pockets, staring at her. It was the first he knew there was something wrong about the girl sitting next to him, something slightly *off* about the scene playing out between them. He instinctively drew himself up and slightly away from her without even knowing he was doing it.

She laughed at something in the movie, her voice soft, breathless. Then she leaned towards him and whispered, "This is all wrong for kids. Harry Parcells loves this theater, but he plays all the wrong movies—Harry Parcells who runs the place?"

There was a fresh runner of blood leaking from her left nostril and blood on her lips, but by then Alec's attention had turned to something else. They were sitting directly under the projector beam, and there were moths and other insects whirring through the blue column of light above. A white moth had landed on her face. It was crawling up her cheek. She didn't notice, and Alec didn't mention it to her. There wasn't enough air in his chest to speak.

She whispered, "He thinks just because it's a cartoon they'll like it. It's funny he could be so crazy for movies and know so little about them. He won't run the place much longer."

She glanced at him and smiled. She had blood staining her teeth. Alec couldn't get up. A second moth, ivory white, landed just inside the delicate cup of her ear.

"Your brother Ray would have loved this," she said.

"Get away," Alec whispered hoarsely.

"You belong here, Alec," she said. "You belong here with me."

He moved at last, shoved himself up out of his seat. The first moth was crawling into her hair. He thought he heard himself moan, just faintly. He started to move away from her. She was staring at him. He backed a few feet down the aisle and bumped into some kid's legs, and the kid yelped. He glanced away from her for an instant, down at a fattish boy in a striped T-shirt who was glaring back at him: *Watch where you're going, meathead.*

Alec looked at her again and now she was slumped very low in her seat. Her head rested on her left shoulder. Her legs hung lewdly open. There were thick strings of blood, dried and crusted, running from her nostrils, bracketing her thin-lipped mouth. Her eyes were rolled back in her head. In her lap was an overturned carton of popcorn.

Alec thought he was going to scream. He didn't scream. She was perfectly motionless. He looked from her to the kid he had almost tripped over. The fat kid glanced casually in the direction of the dead girl, showed no reaction. He turned his gaze back to Alec, his eyes questioning, one corner of his mouth turned up in a derisive sneer.

"Sir," said a woman, the fat kid's mother. "Can you move, *please?* We're trying to watch the movie."

Alec threw another look towards the dead girl, only now the chair where she had been was empty, the seat folded up. He started to retreat, bumping into knees, almost falling over once, grabbing someone for support. Then suddenly the room erupted into cheers, applause. His heart throbbed. He cried out, looked wildly around. It was Mickey, up there on the screen in droopy red robes—Mickey had arrived at last.

He backed up the aisle, swatted through the padded leather doors into the lobby. He flinched at the late-afternoon brightness, narrowed his eyes to squints. He felt dangerously sick. Then someone was holding his shoulder, turning him, walking him across the room, over to the staircase up to balcony-level. Alec sat down on the bottom step, sat down hard.

"Take a minute," someone said. "Don't get up. Catch your breath. Do you think you're going to throw up?"

Alec shook his head.

"Because if you think you're going to throw up, hold on till I can get you a bag. It isn't so easy to get stains out of this carpet. Also when people smell vomit they don't want popcorn."

Whoever it was lingered beside him for another moment, then without a word turned and shuffled away. He returned maybe a minute later.

"Here. On the house. Drink it slow. The fizz will help with your stomach."

Alec took a wax cup sweating beads of cold water, found the straw with his mouth, sipped icy cola bubbly with carbonation. He looked up. The man standing over him was tall and slope-shouldered, with a sagging roll around the middle. His hair was cropped to a dark bristle and his eyes, behind his absurdly thick glasses, were small and pale and uneasy.

Alec said, "There's a dead girl in there." He didn't recognize his own voice.

The color drained out of the big man's face and he cast an unhappy glance back at the doors into the theater. "She's never been in a matinee before. I thought only night shows, I thought—for God's sake, it's a kid's movie. What's she trying to do to me?"

Alec opened his mouth, didn't even know what he was going to say, something about the dead girl, but what came out instead was: "It's not really a kid's film."

The big man shot him a look of mild annoyance. "Sure it is. It's Walt Disney."

Alec stared at him for a long moment, then said, "You must be Harry Parcells."

"Yeah. How'd you know?"

"Lucky guesser," Alec said. "Thanks for the Coke."

Alec followed Harry Parcells behind the concessions counter, through a door and out onto a landing at the bottom of some stairs. Harry opened a door to the right and let them into a small, cluttered office. The floor was crowded with steel film cans. Fading film posters covered the walls, overlapping in places: *Boys Town*, *David Copperfield*, *Gone With the Wind*.

"Sorry she scared you," Harry said, collapsing into the office chair behind his desk. "You sure you're all right? You look kind of peaked."

"Who is she?"

"Something blew out in her brain," he said, and pointed a finger at his left temple, as if pretending to hold a gun to his head. "Six years ago. During *The Wizard of Oz*. The very first show. It was the most terrible thing. She used to come in all the time. She was my steadiest customer. We used to talk, kid around with each other—" His voice wandered off, confused and distraught. He squeezed his plump hands together on the desktop in front of him, said finally, "Now she's trying to bankrupt me."

"You've seen her." It wasn't a question.

Harry nodded. "A few months after she passed away. She told me I don't belong here. I don't know why she wants to scare me off when we used to get along so great. Did she tell you to go away?"

"Why is she here?" Alec said. His voice was still hoarse, and it was a strange kind of question to ask. For a while, Harry just peered at him through his thick glasses with what seemed to be total incomprehension.

Then he shook his head and said, "She's unhappy. She died before the end of *The Wizard* and she's still miserable about it. I understand. That was a good movie. I'd feel robbed too."

"Hello?" someone shouted from the lobby. "Anyone there?"

"Just a minute," Harry called out. He gave Alec a pained look. "My concession-stand girl told me she was quitting yesterday. No notice or anything."

"Was it the ghost?"

"Heck no. One of her paste-on nails fell into someone's food so I told her not to wear them anymore. No one wants to get a fingernail in a mouthful of popcorn. She told me a lot of boys she knows come in here and if she can't wear her nails she wasn't going to work for me no more so now I got to do everything myself." He said this as he was coming around the desk. He had something in one hand, a newspaper clipping. "This will tell you about her." And then he gave Alec a look—it wasn't a glare exactly, but there was at least a measure of dull warning in it—and he added: "Don't run off on me. We still have to talk."

He went out, Alec staring after him, wondering what that last funny look was about. He glanced down at the clipping. It was an obituary—her obituary. The paper was creased, the edges worn, the ink faded; it looked as if it had been handled often. Her name was Imogene Gilchrist, she had died at nineteen, she worked at Water Street Stationery. She was survived by her parents, Colm and Mary. Friends and family spoke of her pretty laugh, her infectious sense of humor. They talked about how she loved the movies. She saw all the movies, saw them on opening day, first show. She could recite the entire cast from almost any picture you cared to name, it was like a party trick—she even knew the names of actors who had had just one line. She was president of the drama club in high school, acted in all the plays, built sets, arranged lighting. "I always thought she'd be a movie star," said her drama professor. "She had those looks and that laugh. All she needed was someone to point a camera at her and she would have been famous."

When Alec finished reading he looked around. The office was still empty. He looked back down at the obituary, rubbing the corner of the clipping between thumb and forefinger. He felt sick at the unfairness of it, and for a moment there was a pressure at the back of his eyeballs, a tingling, and he had the ridiculous idea he might start crying. He felt ill to live in a world where a nineteen-year-old girl full of laughter and life could be struck down like that, for no reason. The intensity of what he was feeling didn't really make sense, considering he had never known her when she was alive; didn't make sense until he thought about Ray, thought about Harry Truman's letter to his mom, the words *died with bravery, defending freedom, America is proud of him.* He thought about how Ray had taken him to *The Fighting Seabees*, right here in this theater, and they sat together with their feet up on the seats in front of them, their shoulders touching. "Look at John Wayne," Ray said. "They oughta have one bomber to carry him, and another one to carry his balls." The stinging in his eyes was so intense he couldn't stand it, and it hurt to breathe. He rubbed at his wet nose, and focused intently on crying as soundlessly as possible.

He wiped his face with the tail of his shirt, put the obituary on Harry Parcells' desk, looked around. He glanced at the posters, and the stacks of steel cans. There was a curl of film in the corner of the room, just eight or so frames—he wondered where it had come from—and he picked it up for a closer look. He saw a girl closing her eyes and lifting her face, in a series of little increments, to kiss the man holding her in a tight embrace; giving herself to him. Alec wanted to be kissed that way sometime. It gave him a curious thrill to be holding an actual piece of a movie. On impulse he stuck it into his pocket.

He wandered out of the office and back onto the landing at the bottom of the stairwell. He peered into the lobby. He expected to see Harry behind the concession stand, serving a customer, but there was no one there. Alec hesitated, wondering where he might have gone. While he was thinking it over, he became aware of a gentle whirring sound coming from the top of the stairs. He looked up them, and it clicked—the projector. Harry was changing reels.

Alec climbed the steps and entered the projection room, a dark compartment with a low ceiling. A pair of square windows looked into the theater below. The projector itself was pointed through one of them, a big machine made of brushed stainless steel, with the word VITAPHONE stamped on the case. Harry stood on the far side of it, leaning forward, peering out the same window through which the projector was casting its beam. He heard Alec at the door, shot him a brief look. Alec expected to be ordered away, but Harry said nothing, only nodded and returned to his silent watch over the theater.

Alec made his way to the VITAPHONE, picking a path carefully through the dark. There was a window to the left of the projector that looked down into the theater. Alec stared at it for a long moment, not sure if he dared, and then put his face close to the glass and peered into the darkened room beneath.

The theater was lit a deep midnight blue by the image on the screen: the conductor again, the orchestra in silhouette. The announcer was introducing the next piece. Alec lowered his gaze and scanned the rows of seats. It wasn't much trouble to find where he had been sitting, an empty cluster of seats close to the back, on the right. He half-expected to see her there, slid down in her chair, face tilted up towards the ceiling and blood all down it—her eyes turned perhaps to stare up at *him*. The thought of seeing her filled him with both dread and a strange nervous exhilaration, and when he realized she wasn't there, he was a little surprised by his own disappointment.

Music began: at first the wavering skirl of violins, rising and falling in swoops, and then a series of menacing bursts from the brass section, sounds of an almost military nature. Alec's gaze rose once more to the screen—rose and held there. He felt a chill race through him. His forearms prickled with gooseflesh. On the screen the dead were rising from their graves, an army of white and watery specters pouring out of the ground and into the night above. A square-shouldered demon, squatting on a mountaintop, beckoned them. They came to him, their ripped white shrouds fluttering around their gaunt bodies, their faces anguished, sorrowing. Alec caught his breath and held it, watched with a feeling rising in him of mingled shock and wonder.

The demon split a crack in the mountain, opened Hell. Fires leaped, the Damned jumped and danced, and Alec knew what he was seeing was about the war. It was about his brother dead for no reason in the South Pacific, *America is proud of him,* it was about bodies damaged beyond repair, bodies sloshing this way and that while they rolled in the surf at the edge of a beach somewhere in the Far East, getting soggy, bloating. It was about Imogene Gilchrist, who loved the movies and died with her legs spread open and her brain swelled full of blood and she was nineteen, her parents were Colm and Mary. It was about young people, young healthy bodies, punched full of holes and the life pouring out in arterial gouts, not a single dream realized, not a single ambition achieved. It was about young people who loved and were loved in return, going away, and not coming back, and the pathetic little remembrances that marked their departure, *my prayers are with you today, Harry Truman,* and *I always thought she'd be a movie star.*

A church bell rang somewhere, a long way off. Alec looked up. It was part of the film. The dead were fading away. The churlish and square-shouldered demon covered himself with his vast black wings, hiding his face from the coming of dawn. A line of robed men moved across the land below, carrying softly glowing torches. The music moved in gentle pulses. The sky was a cold, shimmering blue, light rising in it, the glow of sunrise spreading through the branches of birch trees and northern pine. Alec watched with a feeling in him like religious awe until it was over.

"I liked *Dumbo* better," Harry said.

He flipped a switch on the wall, and a bare lightbulb came on, filling the projection room with harsh white light. The last of the film squiggled through the VITAPHONE, and came out at the other end, where it was being collected on one of the reels. The trailing end whirled around and around and went *slap, slap, slap.* Harry turned the projector off, looked at Alec over the top of the machine.

"You look better. You got your color back."

"What did you want to talk about?" Alec remembered the vague look of warning Harry gave him when he told him not to go anywhere, and the thought occurred to him now that maybe Harry knew he had slipped in without buying a ticket, that maybe they were about to have a problem.

But Harry said, "I'm prepared to offer you a refund or two free passes to the show of your choice. Best I can do."

Alec stared. It was a long time before he could reply.

"For what?"

"For what? To shut up about it. You know what it would do to this place if it got out about her? I got reasons to think people don't want to pay money to sit in the dark with a chatty dead girl."

Alec shook his head. It surprised him that Harry thought it would keep people away if it got out that the Rosebud was haunted. Alec had an idea it would have the opposite effect. People were happy to pay for the opportunity to experience a little terror in the dark—if they weren't, there wouldn't be any business in horror pictures. And then he remembered what Imogene Gilchrist had said to him about Harry Parcells: *He won't run the place much longer.*

"So what do you want?" Harry asked. "You want passes?"

Alec shook his head.

"Refund then."

"No."

Harry froze with his hand on his wallet, flashed Alec a surprised, hostile look. "What do you want then?"

"How about a job? You need someone to sell popcorn. I promise not to wear my paste-on nails to work."

Harry stared at him for a long moment without any reply, then slowly removed his hand from his back pocket.

"Can you work weekends?" he asked.

In October, Alec hears that Steven Greenberg is back in New Hampshire, shooting exteriors for his new movie on the grounds of Phillips Exeter Academy—something with Tom Hanks and Haley Joel Osment, a misunderstood teacher inspiring troubled kid-geniuses. Alec doesn't need to know any more than that to know it smells like Steven might be on his way to winning another Oscar. Alec, though, preferred the earlier work, Steven's fantasies and suspense thrillers.

*He considers driving down to have a look, wonders if he could talk his way onto the set—*Oh yes, I knew Steven when he was a boy—*wonders if he might even be allowed to speak* *with Steven himself. But he soon dismisses the idea. There must be hundreds of people in this part of New England who could claim to have known Steven back in the day, and it isn't as if they were ever close. They only really had that one conversation, the day Steven saw her. Nothing before; nothing much after.*

So it is a surprise when one Friday afternoon close to the end of the month Alec takes a call from Steven's personal assistant, a cheerful, efficient-sounding woman named Marcia. She wants Alec to know that Steven was hoping to see him, and if he can drop in—is Sunday morning all right?—there will be a set pass waiting for him at Main Building, on the grounds of the Academy. They'll expect to see him around 10:00 A.M.*, she says in her bright chirp of a voice, before ringing off. It is not until well after the conversation has ended that Alec realizes he has received not an invitation, but a summons.*

A goateed P.A. meets Alec at Main and walks him out to where they're filming. Alec stands with thirty or so others, and watches from a distance, while Hanks and Osment stroll together across a green quad littered with fallen leaves, Hanks nodding pensively while Osment talks and gestures. In front of them is a dolly, with two men and their camera equipment sitting on it, and two men pulling it. Steven and a small group of others stand off to the side, Steven observing the shot on a video monitor. Alec has never been on a movie set before, and he watches the work of professional make-believe with great pleasure.

After he has what he wants, and has talked with Hanks for a few minutes about the shot, Steven starts over towards the crowd where Alec is standing. There is a shy, searching look on his face. Then he sees Alec and opens his mouth in a gap-toothed grin, lifts one hand in a wave, looks for a moment very much the lanky boy again. He asks Alec if he wants to walk to craft services with him, for a chili dog and a soda.

On the walk Steven seems anxious, jingling the change in his pockets and shooting sideways looks at Alec. Alec knows he wants to talk about Imogene, but can't figure how to broach the subject. When at last he begins to talk, it's about his memories of the Rosebud. He talks about how he loved the place, talks about all the great pictures he saw for the first time there. Alec smiles and nods, but is secretly a little as-

tounded at the depths of Steven's self-deception. Steven never went back after The Birds. *He didn't see any of the movies he says he saw there.*

At last, Steven stammers, What's going to happen to the place after you retire? Not that you should retire! I just mean—do you think you'll run the place much longer?

Not much longer, *Alec replies—it's the truth—but says no more. He is concerned not to degrade himself asking for a handout—although the thought is in him that this is in fact why he came. That ever since receiving Steven's invitation to visit the set he had been fantasizing that they would talk about the Rosebud, and that Steven, who is so wealthy, and who loves movies so much, might be persuaded to throw Alec a life preserver.*

The old movie houses are national treasures, *Steven says.* I own a couple, believe it or not. I run them as revival joints. I'd love to do something like that with the Rosebud someday. That's a dream of mine, you know.

Here is his chance, the opportunity Alec was not willing to admit he was hoping for. But instead of telling him that the Rosebud is in desperate straits, sure to close, Alec changes the subject . . . ultimately lacks the stomach to do what must be done.

What's your next project? *Alec asks.*

After this? I was considering a remake, *Steven says, and gives him another of those shifty sideways looks from the corners of his eyes.* You'd never guess what. *Then, suddenly, he reaches out, touches Alec's arm.* Being back in New Hampshire has really stirred some things up for me. I had a dream about our old friend, would you believe it?

Our old—*Alec starts, then realizes who he means.*

I had a dream the place was closed. There was a chain on the front doors, and boards in the windows. I dreamed I heard a girl crying inside, *Steven says, and grins nervously.* Isn't that the funniest thing?

Alec drives home with a cool sweat on his face, ill at ease. He doesn't know why he didn't say anything, why he couldn't *say anything; Greenberg was practically begging to give him some money. Alec thinks bitterly that he has become a very foolish and useless old man.*

At the theater there are nine messages on Alec's machine. The first is from Lois Weisel, whom Alec has not heard from in years. Her voice is brittle. She says, Hi, Alec, Lois Weisel at B.U. *As if he could have forgotten her. Lois saw Imogene in* Midnight Cowboy. *Now she teaches documentary filmmaking to graduate students. Alec knows these two things are not unconnected, just as it is no accident Steven Greenberg became what he became.* Will you give me a call? I wanted to talk to you about—I just—will you call me? *Then she laughs, a strange, frightened kind of laugh, and says,* This is crazy. *She exhales heavily.* I just wanted to find out if something was happening to the Rosebud. Something bad. So—call me.

The next message is from Dana Llewellyn, who saw her in The Wild Bunch. *The message after that is from Shane Leonard, who saw Imogene in* American Graffiti. *Darren Campbell, who saw her in* Reservoir Dogs. *Some of them talk about the dream, a dream identical to the one Steven Greenberg described, boarded-over windows, chain on the doors, girl crying. Some only say they want to talk. By the time the answering machine tape has played its way to the end, Alec is sitting on the floor of his office, his hands balled into fists—an old man weeping helplessly.*

Perhaps twenty people have seen Imogene in the last twenty-five years, and nearly half of them have left messages for Alec to call. The other half will get in touch with him over the next few days, to ask about the Rosebud, to talk about their dream. Alec will speak with almost everyone living who has ever seen her, all of those Imogene felt compelled to speak to: a drama professor, the manager of a video rental store, a retired financier who in his youth wrote angry, comical film reviews for The Lansdowne Record, *and others. A whole congregation of people who flocked to the Rosebud instead of church on Sundays, those whose prayers were written by Paddy Chayefsky and whose hymnals were composed by John Williams and whose intensity of faith is a call Imogene is helpless to resist. Alec himself.*

After the sale, the Rosebud is closed for two months to refurbish. New seats, state-of-the-art sound. A dozen artisans put up scaffolding and work with little paintbrushes to restore the crumbling plaster molding on the ceiling. Steven adds personnel to run the day-to-day operations. Although it's his place now, Alec has agreed to stay on to manage things for a little while.

Lois Weisel drives up three times a week to film a documentary about the renovation, using her grad students in various capacities, as electricians, sound people, grunts. Steven wants a gala reopening to celebrate the Rosebud's past. When Alec hears what he wants to show first—a double feature of The Wizard of Oz *and* The Birds*—his forearms prickle with gooseflesh; but he makes no argument.*

On reopening night, the place is crowded like it hasn't been since Titanic. *The local news is there to film people walking inside in their best suits. Of course, Steven is there, which is why all the excitement . . . although Alec thinks he would have a sellout even without Steven, that people would have come just to see the results of the renovation. Alec and Steven pose for photographs, the two of them standing under the marquee in their tuxedoes, shaking hands. Steven's tuxedo is Armani, bought for the occasion. Alec got married in his.*

Steven leans into him, pressing a shoulder against his chest. What are you going to do with yourself?

Before Steven's money, Alec would have sat behind the counter handing out tickets, and then gone up himself to start the projector. But Steven hired someone to sell tickets and run the projector. Alec says, Guess I'm going to sit and watch the movie.

Save me a seat, *Steven says.* I might not get in until *The Birds,* though. I have some more press to do out here.

Lois Weisel has a camera set up at the front of the theater, turned to point at the audience, and loaded with high-speed film for shooting in the dark. She films the crowd at different times, recording their reactions to The Wizard of Oz. *This was to be the conclusion of her documentary—a packed house enjoying a twentieth-century classic in this lovingly restored old movie palace—but her movie wasn't going to end like she thought it would.*

In the first shots on Lois's reel it is possible to see Alec sitting in the back left of the theater, his face turned up towards the screen, his glasses flashing blue in the darkness. The seat to the left of him, on the aisle, is empty, the only empty seat in the house. Sometimes he can be seen eating popcorn. Other times he is just sitting there watching, his mouth open slightly, an almost worshipful look on his face.

Then in one shot he has turned sideways to face the seat

to his left. He has been joined by a woman in blue. He is leaning over her. They are unmistakably kissing. No one around them pays them any mind. The Wizard of Oz *is ending. We know this because we can hear Judy Garland, reciting the same five words over and over in a soft, yearning voice, saying—well, you know what she is saying. They are only the loveliest five words ever said in all of film.*

In the shot immediately following this one, the house lights are up, and there is a crowd of people gathered around Alec's body, slumped heavily in his seat. Steven Greenberg is in the aisle, yelping hysterically for someone to bring a doctor. A child is crying. The rest of the crowd generates a low rustling buzz of excited conversation. But never mind this shot. The footage that came just before it is much more interesting.

It is only a few seconds long, this shot of Alec and his unidentified companion—a few hundred frames of film—but it is the shot that will make Lois Weisel's reputation, not to mention a large sum of money. It will appear on television shows about unexplained phenomena, it will be watched and rewatched at gatherings of those fascinated with the supernatural. It will be studied, written about, debunked, confirmed, and celebrated. Let's see it again.

He leans over her. She turns her face up to his, and closes her eyes and she is very young and she is giving herself to him completely. Alec has removed his glasses. He is touching her lightly at the waist. This is the way people dream of being kissed, a movie star kiss. Watching them one almost wishes the moment would never end. And over all this, Dorothy's small, brave voice fills the darkened theater. She is saying something about home. She is saying something everyone knows.

Henry James

(1843–1916)

Born in New York City, Henry James was the son of Henry James Sr., a theologian, lecturer, and author, and the younger brother of William James, a renowned professor, philosopher, and psychologist. Educated at private schools and by tutors, he was extraordinarily well traveled in Europe at an early age. In 1876, he chose to make his home in England, first in London and then in the village of Rye. A major influence on the style and structure of modern fiction, his first story, "A Tragedy of Error," was published in 1864. Among his many famous novels are *The American* (1877), *Washington Square* (1881), *The Portrait of a Lady* (1881), *The Wings of the Dove* (1902), and *The Golden Bowl* (1904). Of James's considerable number of ghost stories, probably the best known is the novella *The Turn of the Screw* (1898). His stories of the supernatural are collected in *The Ghostly Tales of Henry James* (1948) and *The Ghost Stories of Henry James* (2001).

The Ghostly Rental

(1876)

I was in my twenty-second year, and I had just left college. I was at liberty to choose my career, and I chose it with much promptness. I afterward renounced it, in truth, with equal ardor, but I have never regretted those two youthful years of perplexed and excited, but also of agreeable and fruitful experiment. I had a taste for theology, and during my college term I had been an admiring reader of Dr. Channing. This was theology of a grateful and succulent savor; it seemed to offer one the rose of faith delightfully stripped of its thorns. And then (for I rather think this had something to do with it), I had taken a fancy to the old Divinity School. I have always had an eye to the back scene in the human drama, and it seemed to me that I might play my part with a fair chance of applause (from myself at least), in that detached and tranquil home of mild casuistry, with its respectable avenue on one side, and its prospect of green fields and contact with acres of woodland on the other. Cambridge, for the lovers of woods and fields, has changed for the worse since those days, and the precinct in question has forfeited much of its mingled pastoral and scholastic quietude. It was then a College-hall in the woods—a charming mixture. What it is now has nothing to do with my story; and I have no doubt that there are still doctrine-haunted young seniors who, as they stroll near it in the summer dusk, promise themselves, later, to taste of its fine leisurely quality. For myself, I was not disappointed. I established myself in a great square, low-browed room, with deep window-benches; I hung prints from Overbeck and Ary Scheffer on the walls; I arranged my books, with great refinement of classification, in the alcoves beside the high chimney-shelf, and I began to read Plotinus and St. Augustine. Among my companions were two or three men of ability and of good fellowship, with whom I occasionally brewed a fireside bowl; and with adventurous reading, deep discourse, potations conscientiously shallow, and long country walks, my initiation into the clerical mystery progressed agreeably enough.

With one of my comrades I formed an especial friendship, and we passed a great deal of time together. Unfortunately he had a chronic weakness of one of his knees, which compelled him to lead a very sedentary life, and as I was a methodical pedestrian, this made some difference in our habits. I used often to stretch away for my daily ramble, with no companion but the stick in my hand or the book in my pocket. But in the use of my legs and the sense of unstinted open air, I have always found company enough. I should, perhaps, add that in the enjoyment of a very sharp pair of eyes, I found something of a social pleasure. My eyes and I were on excellent terms; they were indefatigable observers of all wayside incidents, and so long as they were amused I was contented. It is, indeed, owing to their inquisitive habits that I came into possession of this remarkable story. Much of the country about the old college town is pretty now, but it was prettier thirty years ago. That multitudinous eruption of domiciliary pasteboard which now graces the landscape, in the direction of the low, blue Waltham Hills, had not yet taken place; there were no genteel cottages to put the shabby meadows and scrubby orchards to shame—a juxtaposition by which, in later years, neither element of the contrast has gained. Certain crooked cross-roads, then, as I remember them, were more deeply and naturally rural, and the solitary dwellings on the long grassy slopes beside them, under the tall, customary elm that curved its foliage in mid-air like the outward dropping ears of a girdled wheat-sheaf, sat with their shingled hoods well pulled down on their ears, and no prescience whatever of the fashion of French roofs—weather-wrinkled old peasant women, as you might call them, quietly wearing the native coif, and never dreaming of mounting bonnets, and indecently exposing their venerable brows. That winter was what is called an "open" one; there was much cold, but little snow; the roads were firm and free, and I was rarely compelled by the weather to forego my exercise. One gray December afternoon I had sought it in the direction of the adjacent town of Medford, and I was retracing my steps at an even pace, and watching the pale, cold tints—the transparent amber and faded rose-color—which curtained, in wintry fashion, the western sky, and reminded me of a sceptical smile on the lips of a beautiful woman. I came, as dusk was falling, to a narrow road which I had never traversed and which I imagined offered me a short cut homeward. I was about three miles away; I was late, and would have been thankful to make them two. I diverged, walked some ten minutes, and then perceived that the road had a very unfrequented air. The wheel-ruts looked old; the stillness seemed peculiarly sensible. And yet down the road stood a house, so that it must in some degree have been a thoroughfare. On one side was a high, natural embankment, on the top of which was perched an apple-orchard, whose tangled boughs made a stretch of coarse black lace-work, hung across the coldly rosy west. In a short time I came to the house, and I immediately found myself interested in it. I stopped in front of it gazing hard, I hardly knew why, but with a vague mixture of curiosity and timidity. It was a house like most of the houses thereabouts, except that it was decidedly a handsome specimen of its class. It stood on a grassy slope, it had its tall, impartially drooping elm beside it, and its old black well-cover at its shoulder. But it was of very large proportions, and it had a striking look of solidity and stoutness of timber. It had lived to a good old age, too, for the wood-work on its doorway and under its eaves, carefully and abundantly carved, referred it to the middle, at the latest, of the last century. All this had once been painted white, but the broad back of time, leaning against the door-posts for a hundred years, had laid bare the grain of the wood. Behind the house stretched an orchard of apple-trees, more gnarled and fantastic than usual, and wearing, in the deepening dusk, a blighted and exhausted aspect. All the windows of the house had rusty shutters, without slats, and these were closely drawn. There was no sign of life about it; it looked blank, bare and vacant, and yet, as I lingered near it, it seemed to have a familiar meaning—an audible eloquence. I have always thought of the impression made upon me at first sight, by that gray colonial dwelling, as a proof that induction may sometimes be near akin to divination; for after all, there was nothing on the face of the matter to warrant the very serious induction that I made. I fell back and crossed the road. The last red light of the sunset disengaged itself, as it was about to vanish, and rested faintly for a moment on the time-silvered front of the old house. It touched, with perfect regularity, the series of small panes in the fan-shaped window above the door, and twinkled there fantastically. Then it died away, and left the place more intensely somber. At this moment, I said to myself with the accent of profound conviction—"The house is simply haunted!"

Somehow, immediately, I believed it, and so long as I was not shut up inside, the idea gave me pleasure. It was implied in the aspect of the house, and it explained it. Half an hour before, if I had been asked, I would have said, as befitted a young man who was explicitly cultivating cheerful views of the supernatural, that there were no such things as haunted houses. But the dwelling before me gave a vivid meaning to the empty words; it had been spiritually blighted.

The longer I looked at it, the intenser seemed the secret that it held. I walked all round it, I tried to peep here and there, through a crevice in the shutters, and I took a puerile satisfaction in laying my hand on the door-knob and gently turning it. If the door had yielded, would I have gone in?—would I have penetrated the dusky stillness? My audacity, fortunately, was not put to the test. The portal was admirably solid, and I was unable even to shake it. At last I turned away, casting many looks behind me. I pursued my way, and, after a longer walk than I had bargained for, reached the high-road. At a certain distance below the point at which the long lane I have mentioned entered it, stood a comfortable, tidy dwelling, which might have offered itself as the model of the house which is in no sense haunted—which has no sinister secrets, and knows nothing but blooming prosperity. Its clean white paint stared placidly through the dusk, and its vine-covered porch had been dressed in straw for the winter. An old, one-horse chaise, freighted with two departing visitors, was leaving the door, and through the undraped windows, I saw the lamp-lit sitting-room, and the table spread with the early "tea," which had been improvised for the comfort of the guests. The mistress of the house had come to the gate with her friends; she lingered there after the chaise had wheeled creakingly away, half to watch them down the road, and half to give me, as I passed in the twilight, a questioning look. She was a comely, quick young woman, with a sharp, dark eye, and I ventured to stop and speak to her.

"That house down that side-road," I said, "about a mile from here—the only one—can you tell me whom it belongs to?"

She stared at me a moment, and, I thought, colored a little. "Our folks never go down that road," she said, briefly.

"But it's a short way to Medford," I answered.

She gave a little toss of her head. "Perhaps it would turn out a long way. At any rate, we don't use it."

This was interesting. A thrifty Yankee household must have good reasons for this scorn of time-saving processes. "But you know the house, at least?" I said.

"Well, I have seen it."

"And to whom does it belong?"

She gave a little laugh and looked away, as if she were

aware that, to a stranger, her words might seem to savor of agricultural superstition. "I guess it belongs to them that are in it."

"But is there any one in it? It is completely closed."

"That makes no difference. They never come out, and no one ever goes in." And she turned away.

But I laid my hand on her arm, respectfully. "You mean," I said, "that the house is haunted?"

She drew herself away, colored, raised her finger to her lips, and hurried into the house, where, in a moment, the curtains were dropped over the windows.

For several days, I thought repeatedly of this little adventure, but I took some satisfaction in keeping it to myself. If the house was not haunted, it was useless to expose my imaginative whims, and if it was, it was agreeable to drain the cup of horror without assistance. I determined, of course, to pass that way again; and a week later—it was the last day of the year—I retraced my steps. I approached the house from the opposite direction, and found myself before it at about the same hour as before. The light was failing, the sky low and gray; the wind wailed along the hard, bare ground, and made slow eddies of the frost-blackened leaves. The melancholy mansion stood there, seeming to gather the winter twilight around it, and mask itself in it, inscrutably. I hardly knew on what errand I had come, but I had a vague feeling that if this time the door-knob were to turn and the door to open, I should take my heart in my hands, and let them close behind me. Who were the mysterious tenants to whom the good woman at the corner had alluded? What had been seen or heard—what was related? The door was as stubborn as before, and my impertinent fumblings with the latch caused no upper window to be thrown open, nor any strange, pale face to be thrust out. I ventured even to raise the rusty knocker and give it half-a-dozen raps, but they made a flat, dead sound, and aroused no echo. Familiarity breeds contempt; I don't know what I should have done next, if, in the distance, up the road (the same one I had followed), I had not seen a solitary figure advancing. I was unwilling to be observed hanging about this ill-famed dwelling, and I sought refuge among the dense shadows of a grove of pines near by, where I might peep forth, and yet remain invisible. Presently, the new-comer drew near, and I perceived that he was making straight for the house. He was a little, old man, the most striking feature of whose appearance was a voluminous cloak, of a sort of military cut. He carried a walking-stick, and advanced in a slow, painful, somewhat hobbling fashion, but with an air of extreme resolution. He turned off from the road, and followed the vague wheel-track, and within a few yards of the house he paused. He looked up at it, fixedly and searchingly, as if he were counting the windows, or noting certain familiar marks. Then he took off his hat, and bent over slowly and solemnly, as if he were performing an obeisance. As he stood uncovered, I had a good look at him. He was, as I have said, a diminutive old man, but it would have been hard to decide whether he belonged to this world or to the other. His head reminded me, vaguely, of the portraits of Andrew Jackson. He had a crop of grizzled hair, as stiff as a brush, a lean, pale, smooth-shaven face, and an eye of intense brilliancy, surmounted with thick brows, which had remained perfectly black. His face, as well as his cloak, seemed to belong to an old soldier; he looked like a retired military man of a modest rank; but he struck me as exceeding the classic privilege of even such a personage to be eccentric and grotesque. When he had finished his salute, he advanced to the door, fumbled in the folds of his cloak, which hung down much further in front than behind, and produced a key. This he slowly and carefully inserted into the lock, and then, apparently, he turned it. But the door did not immediately open; first he bent his head, turned his ear, and stood listening, and then he looked up and down the road. Satisfied or re-assured, he applied his aged shoulder to one of the deep-set panels, and pressed a moment. The door yielded—opening into perfect darkness. He stopped again on the threshold, and again removed his hat and made his bow. Then he went in, and carefully closed the door behind him.

Who in the world was he, and what was his errand? He might have been a figure out of one of Hoffmann's tales. Was he vision or a reality—an inmate of the house, or a familiar, friendly visitor? What had been the meaning, in either case, of his mystic genuflexions, and how did he propose to proceed, in that inner darkness? I emerged from my retirement, and observed narrowly, several of the windows.

In each of them, at an interval, a ray of light became visible in the chink between the two leaves of the shutters. Evidently, he was lighting up; was he going to give a party—a ghostly revel? My curiosity grew intense, but I was quite at a loss how to satisfy it. For a moment I thought of rapping peremptorily at the door; but I dismissed this idea as unmannerly, and calculated to break the spell, if spell there was. I walked round the house and tried, without violence, to open one of the lower windows. It resisted, but I had better fortune, in a moment, with another. There was a risk, certainly, in the trick I was playing—a risk of being seen from within, or (worse) seeing, myself, something that I should repent of seeing. But curiosity, as I say, had become an inspiration, and the risk was highly agreeable. Through the parting of the shutters I looked into a lighted room—a room lighted by two candles in old brass flambeaux, placed upon the mantel-shelf. It was apparently a sort of back parlor, and it had retained all its furniture. This was of a homely, old-fashioned pattern, and consisted of hair-cloth chairs and sofas, spare mahogany tables, and framed samplers hung upon the walls. But although the room was furnished, it had a strangely uninhabited look; the tables and chairs were in rigid positions, and no small, familiar objects were visible. I could not see everything, and I could only guess at the existence, on my right, of a large folding-door. It was apparently open, and the light of the neighboring room passed through it. I waited for some time, but the room remained empty. At last I became conscious that a large shadow was projected upon the wall opposite the folding-door—the shadow, evidently, of a figure in the adjoining room. It was tall and grotesque, and seemed to represent a person sitting perfectly motionless, in profile. I thought I recognized the perpendicular bristles and far-arching nose of my little old man. There was a strange fixedness in his posture; he appeared to be seated, and looking intently at something. I watched the shadow a long time, but it never stirred. At last, however, just as my patience began to ebb, it moved slowly, rose to the ceiling, and became indistinct. I don't know what I should have seen next, but by an irresistible impulse, I closed the shutter. Was it delicacy?—was it pusillanimity? I can hardly say. I lingered, nevertheless, near the house, hoping that my friend would re-appear. I was not disappointed; for he at last emerged, looking just as when he had gone in, and taking his leave in the same ceremonious fashion. (The lights, I had already observed, had disappeared from the crevice of each of the windows.) He faced about before the door, took off his hat, and made an obsequious bow. As he turned away I had a hundred minds to speak to him, but I let him depart in peace. This, I may say, was pure delicacy;—you will answer, perhaps, that it came too late. It seemed to me that he had a right to resent my observation; though my own right to exercise it (if ghosts were in the question) struck me as equally positive. I continued to watch him as he hobbled softly down the bank, and along the lonely road. Then I musingly retreated in the opposite direction. I was tempted to follow him, at a distance, to see what became of him; but this, too, seemed indelicate; and I confess, moreover, that I felt the inclination to coquet a little, as it were, with my discovery—to pull apart the petals of the flower one by one.

I continued to smell the flower, from time to time, for its oddity of perfume had fascinated me. I passed by the house on the cross-road again, but never encountered the old man in the cloak, or any other wayfarer. It seemed to keep observers at a distance, and I was careful not to gossip about it: one inquirer, I said to myself, may edge his way into the secret, but there is no room for two. At the same time, of course, I would have been thankful for any chance side-light that might fall across the matter—though I could not well see whence it was to come. I hoped to meet the old man in the cloak elsewhere, but as the days passed by without his re-appearing, I ceased to expect it. And yet I reflected that he probably lived in that neighborhood, inasmuch as he had made his pilgrimage to the vacant house on foot. If he had come from a distance, he would have been sure to arrive in some old deep-hooded gig with yellow wheels—a vehicle as venerably grotesque as himself. One day I took a stroll in Mount Auburn cemetery—an institution at that period in its infancy, and full of a sylvan charm which it has now completely forfeited. It contained more maple and birch than willow and cypress, and the sleepers had ample elbow room. It was not a city of the dead, but at the most a village, and a meditative pedestrian might stroll there without too importunate reminder of the grotesque side of our claims to posthumous consideration. I had come out to enjoy the first foretaste of Spring—one of those mild days of late winter, when the torpid earth seems to draw the first long breath that marks the rupture of the spell of sleep. The sun was veiled in haze, and yet warm, and the frost was oozing from its deepest lurking-places. I had been treading for half an hour the winding ways of the cemetery, when suddenly I perceived a familiar figure seated on a bench against a southward-facing ever-green hedge. I call the figure familiar, because I had seen it often in memory and in fancy; in fact, I had beheld it but once. Its back was turned to me, but it wore a voluminous cloak, which there was no mistaking. Here, at last, was my fellow-visitor at the haunted house, and here was my chance, if I wished to approach him! I made a circuit, and came toward him from in front. He saw me, at the end of the alley, and sat motionless, with his hands on the head of his stick, watching me from under his black eyebrows as I drew near. At a distance these black eyebrows looked formidable; they were the only thing I saw in his face. But on a closer view I was re-assured, simply because I immediately felt that no man could really be as fantastically fierce as this poor old gentleman looked. His face was a kind of caricature of martial truculence. I stopped in front of him, and respectfully asked leave to sit and rest upon his bench. He granted it with a silent gesture, of much dignity, and I placed myself beside him. In this position I was able, covertly, to observe him. He was quite as much an oddity in the morning sunshine, as he had been in the dubious twilight. The lines in his face were as rigid as if they had been hacked out of a block by a clumsy woodcarver. His eyes were flamboyant, his nose terrific, his mouth implacable. And yet, after a while, when he slowly turned and looked at me, fixedly, I perceived that in spite of this portentous mask, he was a very mild old man. I was sure he even would have been glad to smile, but, evidently, his facial muscles were too stiff—they had taken a different fold, once for all. I wondered whether he was demented, but I dismissed the idea; the fixed glitter in his eye was not that of insanity. What his face really expressed was deep and simple sadness; his heart perhaps was broken, but his brain was intact.

His dress was shabby but neat, and his old blue cloak had known half a century's brushing.

I hastened to make some observation upon the exceptional softness of the day, and he answered me in a gentle, mellow voice, which it was almost startling to hear proceed from such bellicose lips.

"This is a very comfortable place," he presently added.

"I am fond of walking in graveyards," I rejoined deliberately; flattering myself that I had struck a vein that might lead to something.

I was encouraged; he turned and fixed me with his duskily glowing eyes. Then very gravely—"Walking, yes. Take all your exercise now. Some day you will have to settle down in a graveyard in a fixed position."

"Very true," said I. "But you know there are some people who are said to take exercise even after that day."

He had been looking at me still; at this he looked away.

"You don't understand?" I said, gently.

He continued to gaze straight before him.

"Some people, you know, walk about after death," I went on.

At last he turned, and looked at me more portentously than ever. "You don't believe that," he said simply.

"How do you know I don't?"

"Because you are young and foolish." This was said without acerbity—even kindly; but in the tone of an old man whose consciousness of his own heavy experience made everything else seem light.

"I am certainly young," I answered; "but I don't think that, on the whole, I am foolish. But say I don't believe in ghosts—most people would be on my side."

"Most people are fools!" said the old man.

I let the question rest, and talked of other things. My companion seemed on his guard, he eyed me defiantly, and made brief answers to my remarks; but I nevertheless gathered an impression that our meeting was an agreeable thing to him, and even a social incident of some importance. He was evidently a lonely creature, and his opportunities for gossip were rare. He had had troubles, and they had detached him from the world, and driven him back upon himself; but the social chord in his antiquated soul was not entirely broken, and I was sure he was gratified to find that it could still feebly resound. At last, he began to ask questions himself; he inquired whether I was a student.

"I am a student of divinity," I answered.

"Of divinity?"

"Of theology. I am studying for the ministry."

At this he eyed me with peculiar intensity—after which his gaze wandered away again. "There are certain things you ought to know, then," he said at last.

"I have a great desire for knowledge," I answered. "What things do you mean?"

He looked at me again awhile, but without heeding my question.

"I like your appearance," he said. "You seem to me a sober lad."

"Oh, I am perfectly sober!" I exclaimed—yet departing for a moment from my soberness.

"I think you are fair-minded," he went on.

"I don't any longer strike you as foolish, then?" I asked.

"I stick to what I said about people who deny the power of departed spirits to return. They *are* fools!" And he rapped fiercely with his staff on the earth.

I hesitated a moment, and then, abruptly, "You have seen a ghost!" I said.

He appeared not at all startled.

"You are right, sir!" he answered with great dignity. "With me it's not a matter of cold theory—I have not had to pry into old books to learn what to believe. *I know!* With these eyes I have beheld the departed spirit standing before me as near as you are!" And his eyes, as he spoke, certainly looked as if they had rested upon strange things.

I was irresistibly impressed—I was touched with credulity.

"And was it very terrible?" I asked.

"I am an old soldier—I am not afraid!"

"When was it?—where was it?" I asked.

He looked at me mistrustfully, and I saw that I was going too fast.

"Excuse me from going into particulars," he said. "I am not at liberty to speak more fully. I have told you so much, because I cannot bear to hear this subject spoken of lightly. Remember in future, that you have seen a very honest old man who told you—on his honor—that he had seen a ghost!" And he got up, as if he thought he had said enough. Reserve, shyness, pride, the fear of being laughed at, the memory, possibly, of former strokes of sarcasm—all this, on one side, had its weight with him; but I suspected that on the other, his tongue was loosened by the garrulity of old age, the sense of solitude, and the need of sympathy—and perhaps, also, by the friendliness which he had been so good as to express toward myself. Evidently it would be unwise to press him, but I hoped to see him again.

"To give greater weight to my words," he added, "let me mention my name—Captain Diamond, sir. I have seen service."

"I hope I may have the pleasure of meeting you again," I said.

"The same to you, sir!" And brandishing his stick portentously—though with the friendliest intentions—he marched stiffly away.

I asked two or three persons—selected with discretion—whether they knew anything about Captain Diamond, but they were quite unable to enlighten me. At last, suddenly, I smote my forehead, and, dubbing myself a dolt, remembered that I was neglecting a source of information to which I had never applied in vain. The excellent person at whose table I habitually dined, and who dispensed hospitality to students at so much a week, had a sister as good as herself, and of conversational powers more varied. This sister, who was known as Miss Deborah, was an old maid in all the force of the term. She was deformed, and she never went out of the house; she sat all day at the window, between a bird-cage and a flower-pot, stitching small linen articles—mysterious bands and frills. She wielded, I was assured, an exquisite needle, and her work was highly prized. In spite of her deformity and her confinement, she had a little, fresh, round face, and an imperturbable serenity of spirit. She had also a very quick little wit of her own, she was extremely observant, and she had a high relish for a friendly chat. Nothing pleased her so much as to have you—especially, I think, if you were a young divinity student—move your chair near her sunny window, and settle yourself for twenty minutes' "talk." "Well, sir," she used always to say, "what is the latest monstrosity in Biblical criticism?"—for she used to pretend to be horrified at the rationalistic tendency of the age. But she was an inexorable little philosopher, and I am convinced that she was a keener rationalist than any of us, and that, if she had chosen, she could have propounded questions that would have made the boldest of us wince. Her window commanded the whole town—or rather, the whole country. Knowledge came to her as she sat singing, with her little, cracked voice, in her low rocking-chair. She was the first to learn everything, and the last to forget it. She had the town gossip at her fingers' ends, and she knew everything about people she had never seen. When I asked her how she had acquired her learning, she said simply—"Oh, I observe!" "Observe closely enough," she once said, "and it doesn't matter where you are. You may be in a pitch-dark closet. All you want is something to start with; one thing leads to another, and all things are mixed up. Shut me up in a dark closet and I will observe after a while, that some places in it are darker than others. After that (give me time), and I will tell you what the President of the United States is going to have for dinner." Once I paid her a compliment. "Your observation," I said, "is as fine as your needle, and your statements are as true as your stitches."

Of course Miss Deborah had heard of Captain Diamond. He had been much talked about many years before, but he had survived the scandal that attached to his name.

"What was the scandal?" I asked.

"He killed his daughter."

"Killed her?" I cried; "How so?"

"Oh, not with a pistol, or a dagger, or a dose of arsenic! With his tongue. Talk of women's tongues! He cursed her—with some horrible oath—and she died!"

"What had she done?"

"She had received a visit from a young man who loved her, and whom he had forbidden the house."

"The house," I said—"ah yes! The house is out in the country, two or three miles from here, on a lonely cross-road."

Miss Deborah looked sharply at me, as she bit her thread.

"Ah, you know about the house?" she said.

"A little," I answered; "I have seen it. But I want you to tell me more."

But here Miss Deborah betrayed an incommunicativeness which was most unusual.

"You wouldn't call me superstitious, would you?" she asked.

"You?—you are the quintessence of pure reason."

"Well, every thread has its rotten place, and every needle its grain of rust. I would rather not talk about that house."

"You have no idea how you excite my curiosity!" I said.

"I can feel for you. But it would make me very nervous."

"What harm can come to you?" I asked.

"Some harm came to a friend of mine." And Miss Deborah gave a very positive nod.

"What had your friend done?"

"She had told me Captain Diamond's secret, which he had told her with a mighty mystery. She had been an old flame of his, and he took her into his confidence. He bade her tell no one, and assured her that if she did, something dreadful would happen to her."

"And what happened to her?"

"She died."

"Oh, we are all mortal!" I said. "Had she given him a promise?"

"She had not taken it seriously, she had not believed him. She repeated the story to me, and three days afterward, she was taken with inflammation of the lungs. A month afterward, here where I sit now, I was stitching her grave-clothes. Since then, I have never mentioned what she told me."

"Was it very strange?"

"It was strange, but it was ridiculous too. It is a thing to make you shudder and to make you laugh, both. But you can't worry it out of me. I am sure that if I were to tell you, I should immediately break a needle in my finger, and die the next week of lock-jaw."

I retired, and urged Miss Deborah no further; but every two or three days, after dinner, I came and sat down by her rocking-chair. I made no further allusion to Captain Diamond; I sat silent, clipping tape with her scissors. At last, one day, she told me I was looking poorly. I was pale.

"I am dying of curiosity," I said. "I have lost my appetite. I have eaten no dinner."

"Remember Blue Beard's wife!" said Miss Deborah.

"One may as well perish by the sword as by famine!" I answered.

Still she said nothing, and at last I rose with a melodramatic sigh and departed. As I reached the door she called me and pointed to the chair I had vacated. "I never was hard-hearted," she said. "Sit down, and if we are to perish, may we at least perish together." And then, in very few words, she communicated what she knew of Captain Diamond's secret. "He was a very high-tempered old man, and though he was very fond of his daughter, his will was law. He had picked out a husband for her, and given her due notice. Her mother was dead, and they lived alone together. The house had been Mrs. Diamond's own marriage portion; the Captain, I believe, hadn't a penny. After his marriage they had come to live there, and he had begun to work the farm. The poor girl's lover was a young man with whiskers from Boston. The Captain came in one evening and found them together; he collared the young man, and hurled a terrible curse at the poor girl. The young man cried that she was his wife, and he asked her if it was true. She said, No! Thereupon Captain Diamond, his fury growing fiercer, repeated his imprecation, ordered her out of the house, and disowned her forever. She swooned away, but her father went raging off and left her. Several hours later, he came back and found the house empty. On the table was a note from the young man telling him that he had killed his daughter, repeating the assurance that she was his own wife, and declaring that he himself claimed the sole right to commit her remains to earth. He had carried the body away in a gig! Captain Diamond wrote him a dreadful note in answer, saying that he didn't believe his daughter was dead, but that, whether or no, she was dead to him. A week later, in the middle of the night, he saw her ghost. Then, I suppose, he was convinced. The ghost reappeared several times, and finally began regularly to haunt the house. It made the old man very uncomfortable, for little by little his passion had passed away, and he was given up to grief. He determined at last to leave the place, and tried to sell it or rent it; but meanwhile the story had gone abroad, the ghost had been seen by other persons, the house had a bad name, and it was impossible to dispose of it. With the farm, it was the old man's only property, and his only means of subsistence; if he could neither live in it nor rent it he was beggared. But the ghost had no mercy, as he had had none. He struggled for six months, and at last he broke down. He put on his old blue cloak and took up his staff, and prepared to wander away and beg his bread. Then the ghost relented, and proposed a compromise. 'Leave the house to me!' it said; 'I have marked it for my own. Go off and live elsewhere. But to enable you to live, I will be your tenant, since you can find no other. I will hire the house of you and pay you a certain rent.' And the ghost named a sum. The old man consented, and he goes every quarter to collect his rent!"

I laughed at this recital, but I confess I shuddered too, for my own observation had exactly confirmed it. Had I not been witness of one of the Captain's quarterly visits, had I not all but seen him sit watching his spectral tenant count out the rent-money, and when he trudged away in the dark, had he not a little bag of strangely gotten coin hidden in the folds of his old blue cloak? I imparted none of these reflections to Miss Deborah, for I was determined that my observations should have a sequel, and I promised myself the pleasure of treating her to my story in its full maturity. "Captain Diamond," I asked, "has no other known means of subsistence?"

"None whatever. He toils not, neither does he spin—his ghost supports him. A haunted house is valuable property!"

"And in what coin does the ghost pay?"

"In good American gold and silver. It has only this peculiarity—that the pieces are all dated before the young girl's death. It's a strange mixture of matter and spirit!"

"And does the ghost do things handsomely; is the rent large?"

"The old man, I believe, lives decently, and has his pipe and his glass. He took a little house down by the river; the door is sidewise to the street, and there is a little garden before it. There he spends his days, and has an old colored woman to do for him. Some years ago, he used to wander about a good deal, he was a familiar figure in the town, and most people knew his legend. But of late he has drawn back into his shell; he sits over his fire, and curiosity has forgotten him. I suppose he is falling into his dotage. But I am sure, I trust," said Miss Deborah in conclusion, "that he won't outlive his faculties or his powers of locomotion, for, if I remember rightly, it was part of the bargain that he should come in person to collect his rent."

We neither of us seemed likely to suffer any especial penalty for Miss Deborah's indiscretion; I found her, day after day, singing over her work, neither more nor less active than usual. For myself, I boldly pursued my observations. I went again, more than once, to the great graveyard, but I was disappointed in my hope of finding Captain Diamond there. I had a prospect, however, which afforded me compensation. I shrewdly inferred that the old man's quarterly pilgrimages were made upon the last day of the old quarter. My first sight of him had been on the 31st of December, and it was probable that he would return to his haunted home on the last day of March. This was near at hand; at last it arrived. I betook myself late in the afternoon to the old house on the cross-road, supposing that the hour of twilight was the appointed season. I was not wrong. I had been hovering about for a short time, feeling very much like a restless ghost myself, when he appeared in the same manner as before, and wearing the same costume. I again concealed myself, and saw him enter the house with the ceremonial which he had used on the former occasion. A light appeared successively in the crevice of each pair of shutters, and I opened the window which had yielded to my importunity before. Again I saw the great shadow on the wall, motionless and solemn. But I saw nothing else. The old man re-appeared at last, made his fantastic salaam before the house, and crept away into the dusk.

One day, more than a month after this, I met him again at Mount Auburn. The air was full of the voice of spring; the birds had come back and were twittering over their winter's travels, and a mild west wind was making a thin murmur in the raw verdure. He was seated on a bench in the sun, still muffled in his enormous mantle, and he recognized me as soon as I approached him. He nodded at me as if he were an old Bashaw giving the signal for my decapitation, but it was apparent that he was pleased to see me.

"I have looked for you here more than once," I said. "You don't come often."

"What did you want of me?" he asked.

"I wanted to enjoy your conversation. I did so greatly when I met you here before."

"You found me amusing?"

"Interesting!" I said.

"You didn't think me cracked?"

"Cracked?—My dear sir—!" I protested.

"I'm the sanest man in the country. I know that is what insane people always say; but generally they can't prove it. I can!"

"I believe it," I said. "But I am curious to know how such a thing can be proved."

He was silent awhile.

"I will tell you. I once committed, unintentionally, a great crime. Now I pay the penalty. I give up my life to it. I don't shirk it; I face it squarely, knowing perfectly what it is. I haven't tried to bluff it off; I haven't begged off from it; I haven't run away from it. The penalty is terrible, but I have accepted it. I have been a philosopher!

"If I were a Catholic, I might have turned monk, and spent the rest of my life in fasting and praying. That is no penalty; that is an evasion. I might have blown my brains out—I might have gone mad. I wouldn't do either. I would simply face the music, take the consequences. As I say, they are awful! I take them on certain days, four times a year. So it has been these twenty years; so it will be as long as I last. It's my business; it's my avocation. That's the way I feel about it. I call that reasonable!"

"Admirably so!" I said. "But you fill me with curiosity and with compassion."

"Especially with curiosity," he said, cunningly.

"Why," I answered, "if I know exactly what you suffer I can pity you more."

"I'm much obliged. I don't want your pity; it won't help me. I'll tell you something, but it's not for myself; it's for your own sake." He paused a long time and looked all round him, as if for chance eavesdroppers. I anxiously awaited his revelation, but he disappointed me. "Are you still studying theology?" he asked.

"Oh, yes," I answered, perhaps with a shade of irritation. "It's a thing one can't learn in six months."

"I should think not, so long as you have nothing but your

books. Do you know the proverb, 'A grain of experience is worth a pound of precept'? I'm a great theologian."

"Ah, you have had experience," I murmured sympathetically.

"You have read about the immortality of the soul; you have seen Jonathan Edwards and Dr. Hopkins chopping logic over it, and deciding, by chapter and verse, that it is true. But I have seen it with these eyes; I have touched it with these hands!" And the old man held up his rugged old fists and shook them portentously. "That's better!" he went on; "but I have bought it dearly. You had better take it from the books—evidently you always will. You are a very good young man; you will never have a crime on your conscience."

I answered with some juvenile fatuity, that I certainly hoped I had my share of human passions, good young man and prospective Doctor of Divinity as I was.

"Ah, but you have a nice, quiet little temper," he said. "So have I—now! But once I was very brutal—very brutal. You ought to know that such things are. I killed my own child."

"Your own child?"

"I struck her down to the earth and left her to die. They could not hang me, for it was not with my hand I struck her. It was with foul and damnable words. That makes a difference; it's a grand law we live under! Well, sir, I can answer for it that *her* soul is immortal. We have an appointment to meet four times a year, and then I catch it!"

"She has never forgiven you?"

"She has forgiven me as the angels forgive! That's what I can't stand—the soft, quiet way she looks at me. I'd rather she twisted a knife about in my heart—O Lord, Lord, Lord!" and Captain Diamond bowed his head over his stick, and leaned his forehead on his crossed hands.

I was impressed and moved, and his attitude seemed for the moment a check to further questions. Before I ventured to ask him anything more, he slowly rose and pulled his old cloak around him. He was unused to talking about his troubles, and his memories overwhelmed him. "I must go my way," he said; "I must be creeping along."

"I shall perhaps meet you here again," I said.

"Oh, I'm a stiff-jointed old fellow," he answered, "and this is rather far for me to come. I have to reserve myself. I have sat sometimes a month at a time smoking my pipe in my chair. But I should like to see you again." And he stopped and looked at me, terribly and kindly. "Some day, perhaps, I shall be glad to be able to lay my hand on a young, unperverted soul. If a man can make a friend, it is always something gained. What is your name?"

I had in my pocket a small volume of Pascal's "Thoughts," on the fly-leaf of which were written my name and address. I took it out and offered it to my old friend. "Pray keep this little book," I said. "It is one I am very fond of, and it will tell you something about me."

He took it and turned it over slowly, then looking up at me with a scowl of gratitude, "I'm not much of a reader," he said; "but I won't refuse the first present I shall have received since—my troubles; and the last. Thank you, sir!" And with the little book in his hand he took his departure.

I was left to imagine him for some weeks after that sitting solitary in his arm-chair with his pipe. I had not another glimpse of him. But I was awaiting my chance, and on the last day of June, another quarter having elapsed, I deemed that it had come. The evening dusk in June falls late, and I was impatient for its coming. At last, toward the end of a lovely summer's day, I revisited Captain Diamond's property. Everything now was green around it save the blighted orchard in its rear, but its own immitigable grayness and sadness were as striking as when I had first beheld it beneath a December sky. As I drew near it, I saw that I was late for my purpose, for my purpose had simply been to step forward on Captain Diamond's arrival, and bravely ask him to let me go in with him. He had preceded me, and there were lights already in the windows. I was unwilling, of course, to disturb him during his ghostly interview, and I waited till he came forth. The lights disappeared in the course of time; then the door opened and Captain Diamond stole out. That evening he made no bow to the haunted house, for the first object he beheld was his fair-minded young friend planted, modestly but firmly, near the doorstep. He stopped short, looking at me, and this time his terrible scowl was in keeping with the situation.

"I knew you were here," I said. "I came on purpose."

He seemed dismayed, and looked round at the house uneasily.

"I beg your pardon if I have ventured too far," I added, "but you know you have encouraged me."

"How did you know I was here?"

"I reasoned it out. You told me half your story, and I guessed the other half. I am a great observer, and I had noticed this house in passing. It seemed to me to have a mystery. When you kindly confided to me that you saw spirits, I was sure that it could only be here that you saw them."

"You are mighty clever," cried the old man. "And what brought you here this evening?"

I was obliged to evade this question.

"Oh, I often come; I like to look at the house—it fascinates me."

He turned and looked up at it himself. "It's nothing to look at outside." He was evidently quite unaware of its peculiar outward appearance, and this odd fact, communicated to me thus in the twilight, and under the very brow of the sinister dwelling, seemed to make his vision of the strange things within more real.

"I have been hoping," I said, "for a chance to see the inside. I thought I might find you here, and that you would let me go in with you. I should like to see what you see."

He seemed confounded by my boldness, but not altogether displeased. He laid his hand on my arm. "Do you know what I see?" he asked.

"How can I know, except as you said the other day, by experience? I want to have the experience. Pray, open the door and take me in."

Captain Diamond's brilliant eyes expanded beneath their dusky brows, and after holding his breath a moment, he indulged in the first and last apology for a laugh by which I was to see his solemn visage contorted. It was profoundly grotesque, but it was perfectly noiseless. "Take you in?" he softly growled. "I wouldn't go in again before my time's up for a thousand times that sum." And he thrust out his hand from the folds of his cloak and exhibited a small agglomeration of coin, knotted into the corner of an old silk pocket-handkerchief. "I stick to my bargain no less, but no more!"

"But you told me the first time I had the pleasure of talking with you that it was not so terrible."

"I don't say it's terrible—now. But it's damned disagreeable!"

This adjective was uttered with a force that made me hesitate and reflect. While I did so, I thought I heard a slight movement of one of the window-shutters above us. I looked up, but everything seemed motionless. Captain Diamond, too, had been thinking; suddenly he turned toward the house. "If you will go in alone," he said, "you are welcome."

"Will you wait for me here?"

"Yes, you will not stop long."

"But the house is pitch-dark. When you go you have lights."

He thrust his hand into the depths of his cloak and produced some matches. "Take these," he said. "You will find two candlesticks with candles on the table in the hall. Light them, take one in each hand and go ahead."

"Where shall I go?"

"Anywhere—everywhere. You can trust the ghost to find you."

I will not pretend to deny that by this time my heart was beating. And yet I imagine I motioned the old man with a sufficiently dignified gesture to open the door. I had made up my mind that there was in fact a ghost. I had conceded the premise. Only I had assured myself that once the mind was prepared, and the thing was not a surprise, it was possible to keep cool. Captain Diamond turned the lock, flung open the door, and bowed low to me as I passed in. I stood in the darkness, and heard the door close behind me. For some moments, I stirred neither finger nor toe; I stared bravely into the impenetrable dusk. But I saw nothing and heard nothing, and at last I struck a match. On the table were two old brass candlesticks rusty from disuse. I lighted the candles and began my tour of exploration.

A wide staircase rose in front of me, guarded by an antique balustrade of that rigidly delicate carving which is found so often in old New England houses. I postponed ascending it, and turned into the room on my right. This was an old-fashioned parlor, meagerly furnished, and musty with the absence of human life. I raised my two lights aloft and saw nothing but its empty chairs and its blank walls. Behind it was the room into which I had peeped from without, and which, in fact, communicated with it, as I had supposed, by folding doors. Here, too, I found myself confronted by no menacing specter. I crossed the hall again, and visited the rooms on the other side; a dining-room in front, where I might have written my name with my finger in the deep dust of the great square table; a kitchen behind with its pots and pans eternally cold. All this was hard and grim, but it was not formidable. I came back into the hall, and walked to the foot of the staircase, holding up my candles; to ascend required a fresh effort, and I was scanning the gloom above. Suddenly, with an inexpressible sensation, I became aware that this gloom was animated; it seemed to move and gather itself together. Slowly—I say slowly, for to my tense expectancy the instants appeared ages—it took the shape of a large, definite figure, and this figure advanced and stood at the top of the stairs. I frankly confess that by this time I was conscious of a feeling to which I am in duty bound to apply the vulgar name of fear. I may poetize it and call it Dread, with a capital letter; it was at any rate the feeling that makes a man yield ground. I measured it as it grew, and it seemed perfectly irresistible; for it did not appear to come from within but from without, and to be embodied in the dark image at the head of the staircase. After a fashion I reasoned—I remember reasoning. I said to myself, "I had always thought ghosts were white and transparent; this is a thing of thick shadows, densely opaque." I reminded myself that the occasion was momentous, and that if fear were to overcome me I should gather all possible impressions while my wits remained. I stepped back, foot behind foot, with my eyes still on the figure and placed my candles on the table. I was perfectly conscious that the proper thing was to ascend the stairs resolutely, face to face with the image, but the soles of my shoes seemed suddenly to have been transformed into leaden weights. I had got what I wanted; I was seeing the ghost. I tried to look at the figure distinctly so that I could remember it, and fairly claim, afterward, not to have lost my self-possession. I even asked myself how long it was expected I should stand looking, and how soon I could honorably retire. All this, of course, passed through my mind with extreme rapidity, and it was checked by a further movement on the part of the figure. Two white hands appeared in the dark perpendicular mass, and were slowly raised to what seemed to be the level of the head. Here they were pressed together, over the region of the face, and then they were removed, and the face was disclosed. It was dim, white, strange, in every way ghostly. It looked down at me for an instant, after which one of the hands was raised again, slowly, and waved to and fro before it. There was something very singular in this gesture; it seemed to denote resentment and dismissal, and yet it had a sort of trivial, familiar motion. Familiarity on the part of the haunting Presence had not entered into my calculations, and did not strike me pleasantly. I agreed with Captain Diamond that it was "damned disagreeable." I was pervaded by an intense desire to make an orderly, and, if possible, a graceful retreat. I wished to do it gallantly, and it seemed to me that it would be gallant to blow out my candles. I turned and did so, punctiliously, and then I made my way to the door, groped a moment and opened it. The outer light, almost extinct as it was, entered for a moment, played over the dusty depths of the house and showed me the solid shadow.

Standing on the grass, bent over his stick, under the early glimmering stars, I found Captain Diamond. He looked up at me fixedly for a moment, but asked no questions, and then he went and locked the door. This duty performed, he discharged the other—made his obeisance like the priest before the altar—and then without heeding me further, took his departure.

A few days later, I suspended my studies and went off for the summer's vacation. I was absent for several weeks, during which I had plenty of leisure to analyze my impressions of the supernatural. I took some satisfaction in the reflection that I had not been ignobly terrified; I had not bolted nor swooned—I had proceeded with dignity. Nevertheless, I was certainly more comfortable when I had put thirty miles between me and the scene of my exploit, and I continued for many days to prefer the daylight to the dark. My nerves had been powerfully excited; of this I was particularly conscious when, under the influence of the drowsy air of the seaside, my excitement began slowly to ebb. As it disappeared, I attempted to take a sternly rational view of my experience. Certainly I had seen *something*—that was not fancy; but what had I seen? I regretted extremely now that I had not been bolder, that I had not gone nearer and inspected the apparition more minutely. But it was very well to talk; I had done as much as any man in the circumstances would have dared; it was indeed a physical impossibility that I should have advanced. Was not this paralyzation of my powers in itself a supernatural influence? Not necessarily, perhaps, for a sham ghost that one accepted might do as much execution as a real ghost. But why had I so easily accepted the sable phantom that waved its hand? Why had it so impressed itself? Unquestionably, true or false, it was a very clever phantom. I greatly preferred that it should have been true—in the first place because I did not care to have shivered and shaken for nothing, and in the second place because to have seen a well-authenticated goblin is, as things go, a feather in a quiet man's cap. I tried, therefore, to let my vision rest and to stop turning it over. But an impulse stronger than my will recurred at intervals and set a mocking question on my lips. Granted that the apparition was Captain Diamond's daughter; if it was she it certainly was her spirit. But was it not her spirit and something more?

The middle of September saw me again established among the theologic shades, but I made no haste to revisit the haunted house.

The last of the month approached—the term of another quarter with poor Captain Diamond—and found me indisposed to disturb his pilgrimage on this occasion; though I confess that I thought with a good deal of compassion of the feeble old man trudging away, lonely, in the autumn dusk, on his extraordinary errand. On the thirtieth of September, at noonday, I was drowsing over a heavy octavo, when I heard a feeble rap at my door. I replied with an invitation to enter, but as this produced no effect I repaired to the door and opened it. Before me stood an elderly negress with her head bound in a scarlet turban, and a white handkerchief folded across her bosom. She looked at me intently and in silence; she had that air of supreme gravity and decency which aged persons of her race so often wear. I stood interrogative, and at last, drawing her hand from her ample pocket, she held up a little book. It was the copy of Pascal's "Thoughts" that I had given to Captain Diamond.

"Please, sir," she said, very mildly, "do you know this book?"

"Perfectly," said I, "my name is on the fly-leaf."

"It is your name—no other?"

"I will write my name if you like, and you can compare them," I answered.

She was silent a moment and then, with dignity—"It would be useless, sir," she said, "I can't read. If you will give me your word that is enough. I come," she went on, "from the gentleman to whom you gave the book. He told me to carry it as a token—a token—that is what he called it. He is right down sick, and he wants to see you."

"Captain Diamond—sick?" I cried. "Is his illness serious?"

"He is very bad—he is all gone."

I expressed my regret and sympathy, and offered to go to him immediately, if his sable messenger would show me the way. She assented deferentially, and in a few moments I was following her along the sunny streets, feeling very much like a personage in the Arabian Nights, led to a postern gate by an Ethiopian slave. My own conductress directed her steps toward the river and stopped at a decent little yellow house in one of the streets that descend to it. She quickly opened the door and led me in, and I very soon found myself in the presence of my old friend. He was in bed, in a darkened room, and evidently in a very feeble state. He lay back on his pillow staring before him, with his bristling hair more erect than ever, and his intensely dark and bright old eyes touched with the glitter of fever. His apartment was humble and scrupulously neat, and I could see that my dusky guide was a faithful servant. Captain Diamond, lying there rigid and pale on his white sheets, resembled some ruggedly carven figure on the lid of a Gothic tomb. He looked at me silently, and my companion withdrew and left us alone.

"Yes, it's you," he said, at last, "it's you, that good young man. There is no mistake, is there?"

"I hope not; I believe I'm a good young man. But I am very sorry you are ill. What can I do for you?"

"I am very bad, very bad; my poor old bones ache so!" and, groaning portentously, he tried to turn toward me.

I questioned him about the nature of his malady and the

length of time he had been in bed, but he barely heeded me; he seemed impatient to speak of something else. He grasped my sleeve, pulled me toward him, and whispered quickly:

"You know my time's up!"

"Oh, I trust not," I said, mistaking his meaning. "I shall certainly see you on your legs again."

"God knows!" he cried. "But I don't mean I'm dying; not yet a bit. What I mean is, I'm due at the house. This is rent-day."

"Oh, exactly! But you can't go."

"I can't go. It's awful. I shall lose my money. If I am dying, I want it all the same. I want to pay the doctor. I want to be buried like a respectable man."

"It is this evening?" I asked.

"This evening at sunset, sharp."

He lay staring at me, and, as I looked at him in return, I suddenly understood his motive in sending for me. Morally, as it came into my thought, I winced. But, I suppose I looked unperturbed, for he continued in the same tone. "I can't lose my money. Someone else must go. I asked Belinda; but she won't hear of it."

"You believe the money will be paid to another person?"

"We can try, at least. I have never failed before and I don't know. But, if you say I'm as sick as a dog, that my old bones ache, that I'm dying, perhaps she'll trust you. She don't want me to starve!"

"You would like me to go in your place, then?"

"You have been there once; you know what it is. Are you afraid?"

I hesitated.

"Give me three minutes to reflect," I said, "and I will tell you." My glance wandered over the room and rested on the various objects that spoke of the threadbare, decent poverty of its occupant. There seemed to be a mute appeal to my pity and my resolution in their cracked and faded sparseness. Meanwhile Captain Diamond continued, feebly:

"I think she'd trust you, as I have trusted you; she'll like your face; she'll see there is no harm in you. It's a hundred and thirty-three dollars, exactly. Be sure you put them into a safe place."

"Yes," I said at last, "I will go, and, so far as it depends upon me, you shall have the money by nine o'clock tonight."

He seemed greatly relieved; he took my hand and faintly pressed it, and soon afterward I withdrew. I tried for the rest of the day not to think of my evening's work, but, of course, I thought of nothing else. I will not deny that I was nervous; I was, in fact, greatly excited, and I spent my time in alternately hoping that the mystery should prove less deep than it appeared, and yet fearing that it might prove too shallow. The hours passed very slowly, but, as the afternoon began to wane, I started on my mission. On the way, I stopped at Captain Diamond's modest dwelling, to ask how he was doing, and to receive such last instructions as he might desire to lay upon me. The old negress, gravely and inscrutably placid, admitted me, and, in answer to my inquiries, said that the Captain was very low; he had sunk since the morning.

"You must be right smart," she said, "if you want to get back before he drops off."

A glance assured me that she knew of my projected expedition, though, in her own opaque black pupil, there was not a gleam of self-betrayal.

"But why should Captain Diamond drop off?" I asked. "He certainly seems very weak; but I cannot make out that he has any definite disease."

"His disease is old age," she said, sententiously.

"But he is not so old as that; sixty-seven or sixty-eight, at most."

She was silent a moment.

"He's worn out; he's used up; he can't stand it any longer."

"Can I see him a moment?" I asked; upon which she led me again to his room.

He was lying in the same way as when I had left him, except that his eyes were closed. But he seemed very "low," as she had said, and he had very little pulse. Nevertheless, I further learned the doctor had been there in the afternoon and professed himself satisfied. "He don't know what's been going on," said Belinda, curtly.

The old man stirred a little, opened his eyes, and after some time recognized me.

"I'm going, you know," I said. "I'm going for your money. Have you anything more to say?" He raised himself slowly, and with a painful effort, against his pillows; but he seemed hardly to understand me. "The house, you know," I said. "Your daughter."

He rubbed his forehead, slowly, awhile, and at last, his comprehension awoke. "Ah, yes," he murmured, "I trust you. A hundred and thirty-three dollars. In old pieces—all in old pieces." Then he added more vigorously, and with a brightening eye: "Be very respectful—be very polite. If not—if not—" and his voice failed again.

"Oh, I certainly shall be," I said, with a rather forced smile. "But, if not?"

"If not, I shall know it!" he said, very gravely. And with this, his eyes closed and he sunk down again.

I took my departure and pursued my journey with a sufficiently resolute step. When I reached the house, I made a propitiatory bow in front of it, in emulation of Captain Diamond. I had timed my walk so as to be able to enter without delay; night had already fallen. I turned the key, opened the door and shut it behind me. Then I struck a light, and found the two candlesticks I had used before, standing on the tables in the entry. I applied a match to both of them, took them up and went into the parlor. It was empty, and though I waited awhile, it remained empty. I passed then into the other rooms on the same floor, and no dark image rose before me to check my steps. At last, I came out into the hall again, and stood weighing the question of going upstairs. The staircase had been the scene of my discomfiture before, and I approached it with profound mistrust. At the foot, I paused, looking up, with my hand on the balustrade. I was acutely expectant, and my expectation was justified. Slowly, in the darkness above, the black figure that I had seen before took shape. It was not an illusion; it was a figure, and the same. I gave it time to define itself, and watched it stand and look down at me with its hidden face. Then, deliberately, I lifted up my voice and spoke.

"I have come in place of Captain Diamond, at his request," I said. "He is very ill; he is unable to leave his bed. He earnestly begs that you will pay the money to me; I will immediately carry it to him." The figure stood motionless, giving no sign. "Captain Diamond would have come if he were able to move," I added, in a moment, appealingly; "but, he is utterly unable."

At this the figure slowly unveiled its face and showed me a dim, white mask; then it began slowly to descend the stairs. Instinctively I fell back before it, retreating to the door of the front sitting-room. With my eyes still fixed on it, I moved backward across the threshold; then I stopped in the middle of the room and set down my lights. The figure advanced; it seemed to be that of a tall woman, dressed in vaporous black crape. As it drew near, I saw that it had a perfectly human face, though it looked extremely pale and sad. We stood gazing at each other; my agitation had completely vanished; I was only deeply interested.

"Is my father dangerously ill?" said the apparition.

At the sound of its voice—gentle, tremulous, and perfectly human—I started forward; I felt a rebound of excitement. I drew a long breath, I gave a sort of cry, for what I saw before me was not a disembodied spirit, but a beautiful woman, an audacious actress. Instinctively, irresistibly, by the force of reaction against my credulity, I stretched out my hand and seized the long veil that muffled her head. I gave it a violent jerk, dragged it nearly off, and stood staring at a large fair person, of about five-and-thirty. I comprehended her at a glance; her long black dress, her pale, sorrow-worn face, painted to look paler, her very fine eyes—the color of her father's—and her sense of outrage at my movement.

"My father, I suppose," she cried, "did not send you here to insult me!" and she turned away rapidly, took up one of the candles and moved toward the door. Here she paused, looked at me again, hesitated, and then drew a purse from her pocket and flung it down on the floor. "There is your money!" she said, majestically.

I stood there, wavering between amazement and shame, and saw her pass out into the hall. Then I picked up the purse. The next moment, I heard a loud shriek and a crash of something dropping, and she came staggering back into the room without her light.

"My father—my father!" she cried; and with parted lips and dilated eyes, she rushed toward me.

"Your father—where?" I demanded.

"In the hall, at the foot of the stairs."

I stepped forward to go out, but she seized my arm.

"He is in white," she cried, "in his shirt. It's not he!"

"Why, your father is in his house, in his bed, extremely ill," I answered.

She looked at me fixedly, with searching eyes.

"Dying?"

"I hope not," I stuttered.

She gave a long moan and covered her face with her hands.

"Oh, heavens, I have seen his ghost!" she cried.

She still held my arm; she seemed too terrified to release it. "His ghost!" I echoed, wondering.

"It's the punishment of my long folly!" she went on.

"Ah," said I, "it's the punishment of my indiscretion—of my violence!"

"Take me away, take me away!" she cried, still clinging to my arm. "Not there"—as I was turning toward the hall and the front door—"not there, for pity's sake! By this door—the back entrance." And snatching the other candles from the table, she led me through the neighboring room into the back part of the house. Here was a door opening from a sort of scullery into the orchard. I turned the rusty lock and we passed out and stood in the cool air, beneath the stars. Here my companion gathered her black drapery about her, and stood for a moment, hesitating. I had been infinitely flurried, but my curiosity touching her was uppermost. Agitated, pale, picturesque, she looked, in the early evening light, very beautiful.

"You have been playing all these years a most extraordinary game," I said.

She looked at me somberly, and seemed disinclined to reply. "I came in perfect good faith," I went on. "The last time—three months ago—you remember?—you greatly frightened me."

"Of course it was an extraordinary game," she answered at last. "But it was the only way."

"Had he not forgiven you?"

"So long as he thought me dead, yes. There have been things in my life he could not forgive."

I hesitated and then—"And where is your husband?" I asked.

"I have no husband—I have never had a husband."

She made a gesture which checked further questions, and moved rapidly away. I walked with her round the house to the road, and she kept murmuring—"It was he—it was he!" When we reached the road she stopped, and asked me which way I was going. I pointed to the road by which I had come, and she said—"I take the other. You are going to my father's?" she added.

"Directly," I said.

"Will you let me know to-morrow what you have found?"

"With pleasure. But how shall I communicate with you?"

She seemed at a loss, and looked about her. "Write a few words," she said, "and put them under that stone." And she pointed to one of the lava slabs that bordered the old well. I gave her my promise to comply, and she turned away. "I know my road," she said. "Everything is arranged. It's an old story."

She left me with a rapid step, and as she receded into the darkness, resumed, with the dark flowing lines of her drapery, the phantasmal appearance with which she had at first appeared to me. I watched her till she became invisible, and then I took my own leave of the place. I returned to town at a swinging pace, and marched straight to the little yellow house near the river. I took the liberty of entering without a knock, and, encountering no interruption, made my way to Captain Diamond's room. Outside the door, on a low bench, with folded arms, sat the sable Belinda.

"How is he?" I asked.

"He's gone to glory."

"Dead?" I cried.

She rose with a sort of tragic chuckle.

"He's as big a ghost as any of them now!"

I passed into the room and found the old man lying there irredeemably rigid and still. I wrote that evening a few lines which I proposed on the morrow to place beneath the stone, near the well; but my promise was not destined to be executed. I slept that night very ill—it was natural—and in my restlessness left my bed to walk about the room. As I did so I caught sight, in passing my window, of a red glow in the north-western sky. A house was on fire in the country, and evidently burning fast. It lay in the same direction as the scene of my evening's adventures, and as I stood watching the crimson horizon I was startled by a sharp memory. I had blown out the candle which lighted me, with my companion, to the door through which we escaped, but I had not accounted for the other light, which she had carried into the hall and dropped—heaven knew where—in her consternation. The next day I walked out with my folded letter and turned into the familiar cross-road. The haunted house was a mass of charred beams and smoldering ashes; the well-cover had been pulled off, in quest of water, by the few neighbors who had had the audacity to contest what they must have regarded as a demon-kindled blaze, the loose stones were completely displaced, and the earth had been trampled into puddles.

Stephen King

(1947–)

Stephen Edwin King was born in Portland, Maine, and earned a BS in English from the University of Maine. King began publishing stories with "I Was a Teenage Grave Robber" in *Comics Review* (1965) and "The Glass Floor" in *Startling Mystery Stories* (1967). His first published novel, *Carrie: A Novel of a Girl with a Frightening Power* (1974), was made into a highly successful film, as were the novels *The Shining* (1977), *Firestarter* (1980), *Pet Sematary* (1983), *Misery* (1987), and *The Green Mile* (1996). Among his other novels are *Needful Things* (1991), *Bag of Bones* (1998), *Cell* (2006), and *Under the Dome* (2009). His story and novella collections include *Skeleton Crew* (1985), *Nightmares and Dreamscapes* (1993), *Hearts in Atlantis* (1999), *Everything's Eventual* (2002), *Just After Sunset* (2008), and *Full Dark, No Stars* (2010). He has won numerous Bram Stoker and British Fantasy awards, the Mystery Writers of America Grand Master Award, the Shirley Jackson Award, and the National Book Foundation's Medal for Distinguished Contribution to American Letters.

Home Delivery

(1989)

Considering that it was probably the end of the world, Maddie Pace thought she was doing a good job. *Hell* of a good job. She thought that she just might be coping with the End of Everything better than anyone else on earth. And she was *positive* she was coping better than any other *pregnant* woman on earth.

Coping.

Maddie Pace, of all people.

Maddie Pace, who sometimes couldn't sleep if, after a visit from Reverend Peebles, she spied a dust-bunny under the dining room table—just the thought that Reverend Peebles *might* have seen that dust-bunny could be enough to keep her awake until two in the morning.

Maddie Pace, who, as Maddie Sullivan, used to drive her fiancé Jack crazy when she froze over a menu, debating entrées sometimes for as long as half an hour.

"Maddie, why don't you just flip a coin?" he'd asked her once after she had managed to narrow it down to a choice between the braised veal and the lamb chops . . . and then could get no further. "I've had five bottles of this goddam German beer already, and if you don't make up y'mind pretty damn quick, there's gonna be a drunk lobsterman under the table before we ever get any food *on* it!"

So she had smiled nervously, ordered the braised veal . . . and then lay awake until well past midnight, wondering if the chops might not have been better.

She'd had no trouble coping with Jack's proposal, however; she accepted it and him quickly, and with tremendous relief. Following the death of her father, Maddie and her mother had lived an aimless, cloudy sort of life on Deer Isle, off the coast of Maine. "If I wasn't around to tell them women where to squat and lean against the wheel," George Sullivan had been fond of saying while in his cups and among his friends at Buster's Tavern or in the back room of Daggett's Barber Shop, "I don't know what the hell they'd do."

When he died of a massive coronary, Maddie was nineteen and minding the town library weekday evenings at a salary of $41.50 a week. Her mother was minding the house—or had been, that was, when George reminded her (sometimes with a good, hard shot to the ear) that she had a house that needed minding.

He was right.

They didn't speak of it because it embarrassed them, but he was right and both of them knew it. Without George around to tell them where to squat and lean to the wheel, they didn't know what the hell to do. Money wasn't the problem; George had believed passionately in insurance, and when he dropped down dead during the tiebreaker frame of the League Bowl-Offs at Big Duke's Big Ten in

Yarmouth, his wife had come into better than a hundred thousand dollars. And island life was cheap, if you owned your own home and kept your garden weeded and knew how to put up your own vegetables come fall. The *problem* was having nothing to focus on. The *problem* was how the center seemed to have dropped out of their lives when George went facedown in his Island Amoco bowling shirt just over the foul line of lane nineteen in Big Duke's (and goddam if he hadn't picked up the spare they needed to win, too). With George gone their lives had become an eerie sort of blur.

It's like being lost in a heavy fog, Maddie thought sometimes. Only instead of looking for the road, or a house, or the village, or just some landmark like that lightning-struck pine in the Altons' woodlot, I am looking for the wheel. If I can ever find the wheel, maybe I can tell *myself* to squat and lean my shoulder to it.

At last she found her wheel; it turned out to be Jack Pace. Women marry their fathers and men their mothers, some say, and while such a broad statement can hardly be true all of the time, it was true in Maddie's case. Her father had been looked upon by his peers with fear and admiration—"Don't fool with George Sullivan, chummy," they'd say. "He's one hefty son of a bitch and he'd just as soon knock the nose off your face as fart downwind."

It was true at home, too. He'd been domineering and sometimes physically abusive . . . but he'd also known things to want, and work for, like the Ford pickup, the chain saw, or those two acres that bounded their place on the left. Pop Cook's land. George Sullivan had been known to refer to Pop Cook (out of his cups as well as in them) as one stinky old bastid, but there was some good hardwood left on those two acres. Pop didn't know it because he had gone to living on the mainland when his arthritis really got going and crippled him up bad, and George let it be known on the island that what that bastid Pop Cook didn't know wouldn't hurt him none, and furthermore, he would kill the man or woman that let light into the darkness of Pop's ignorance. No one did, and eventually the Sullivans got the land. And the wood, of course. The hardwood was logged off for the two wood stoves that heated the house in three years, but the land would remain. That was what George said and they believed him, believed *in* him, and they worked, all three of them. He said you got to put your shoulder to this wheel and *push* the bitch, you got to push ha'ad because she don't move easy. So that was what they did.

In those days Maddie's mother had kept a roadside stand, and there were always plenty of tourists who bought the vegetables she grew—the ones George *told* her to grow, of course, and even though they were never exactly what her mother called "the Gotrocks family," they made out. Even in years when lobstering was bad, they made out.

Jack Pace could be domineering when Maddie's indecision finally forced him to be, and she suspected that, loving as he was in their courtship, he might get around to the physical part—the twisted arm when supper was cold, the occasional slap or downright paddling—in time; when the bloom was off the rose, so as to speak. She saw the similarities . . . but she loved him. And needed him.

"I'm not going to be a lobsterman all my life, Maddie," he told her the week before they married, and she believed him. A year before, when he had asked her out for the first time (she'd had no trouble coping then, either—had said yes almost before all the words could get out of his mouth, and she had blushed to the roots of her hair at the sound of her own naked eagerness), he would have said, "I *ain't* going to be a lobsterman all my life." A small change . . . but all the difference in the world. He had been going to night school three evenings a week, taking the ferry over and back. He would be dog tired after a day of pulling pots, but he'd go just the same, pausing only long enough to shower off the powerful smells of lobster and brine and to gulp two No Doz with hot coffee. After a while, when she saw he really meant to stick to it, Maddie began putting up hot soup for him to drink on the ferry ride over. Otherwise, he would have had no supper at all.

She remembered agonizing over the canned soups in the store—there were so *many*! Would he want tomato? Some people didn't like tomato soup. In fact, some people *hated* tomato soup, even if you made it with milk instead of water. Vegetable soup? Turkey? Cream of chicken? Her helpless eyes roved the shelf display for nearly ten minutes before Charlene Nedeau asked if she could help her with something—only Charlene said it in a sarcastic way, and

Maddie guessed she would tell all her friends at high school tomorrow and they would giggle about it—about *her*—in the Girls' Room, because Charlene knew what was wrong; the same thing that was always wrong. It was just Maddie Sullivan, unable to make up her mind over so simple a thing as a can of *soup*. How she had ever been able to decide to accept Jack Pace's proposal was a wonder and a marvel to all of them . . . but of course they didn't know how, once you found the wheel, you had to have someone to tell you when to stoop and where exactly to lean against it.

Maddie had left the store with no soup and a throbbing headache.

When she worked up nerve enough to ask Jack what his favorite soup was, he had said: "Chicken noodle. Kind that comes in the can."

Were there any others he specially liked?

The answer was no, just chicken noodle—the kind that came in the can. That was all the soup Jack Pace needed in his life, and all the answer (on that one particular subject, at least) that Maddie needed in hers. Light of step and cheerful of heart, Maddie climbed the warped wooden steps of the store the next day and bought the four cans of chicken noodle soup that were on the shelf. When she asked Bob Nedeau if he had any more, he said he had a whole damn *case* of the stuff out back.

She bought the entire case and left him so flabbergasted that he actually carried the carton out to the truck for her and forgot all about asking why she had wanted all that chicken soup—a lapse for which his wife Margaret and his daughter Charlene took him sharply to task that evening.

"You just better believe it," Jack had said that time not long before the wedding—she never forgot. "More than a lobsterman. My dad says I'm full of shit. He says if it was good enough for his old man, and his old man's old man, and all the way back to the friggin' Garden of Eden to hear *him* tell it, if it was good enough for all of *them*, it ought to be good enough for me. But it ain't—*isn't*, I mean—and I'm going to do better." His eye fell on her, and it was a loving eye, but it was a stern eye, too. "More than a lobsterman is what I mean to be, and more than a lobsterman's wife is what I intend for you to be. You're going to have a house on the mainland."

"Yes, Jack."

"And I'm not going to have any friggin' Chevrolet." He took a deep breath: "I'm going to have an *Oldsmobile*." He looked at her, as if daring her to refute him. She did no such thing, of course; she said yes, Jack, for the third or fourth time that evening. She had said it to him thousands of times over the year they had spent courting, and she confidently expected to say it *millions* of times before death ended their marriage by taking one of them—or, hopefully, both of them together.

"More than a friggin' lobsterman, no matter what my old man says, I'm going to do it, and do you know who's going to help me?"

"Yes," Maddie had said. "Me."

"You," he responded with a grin, sweeping her into his arms, "are damned tooting."

So they were wed.

Jack knew what he wanted, and he would tell her how to help him get it and that was just the way she wanted things to be.

Then Jack died.

Then, not more than four months after, while she was still wearing weeds, dead folks started to come out of their graves and walk around. If you got too close, they bit you and you died for a little while and then *you* got up and started walking around, too.

Then, Russia and America came very, very close to blowing the whole world to smithereens, both of them accusing the other of causing the phenomenon of the walking dead. "How close?" Maddie heard one news correspondent from CNN ask about a month after dead people started to get up and walk around, first in Florida, then in Murmansk, then in Leningrad and Minsk, then in Elmira, Illinois; Rio de Janeiro; Biterad, Germany; New Delhi, India; and a small Australian hamlet on the edge of the outback.

(This hamlet went by the colorful name of Wet Noggin, and before the news got out of there, most of Wet Noggin's populace consisted of shambling dead folks and starving dogs. Maddie had watched most of these developments on the Pulsifers' TV. Jack had hated their satellite dish—maybe because they could not yet afford one themselves—but now, with Jack dead, none of that mattered.)

In answer to his own rhetorical question about how close the two countries had come to blowing the earth to smithereens, the commentator had said, "We'll never know, but that may be just as well. My guess is within a hair's breadth."

Then, at the last possible second, a British astronomer had discovered the satellite—the apparently *living* satellite—which became known as Star Wormwood.

Not one of ours, not one of theirs. Someone else's. Someone or something from the great big darkness Out There.

Well, they had swapped one nightmare for another, Maddie supposed, because *then*—the last *then* before the TV (even all the channels the Pulsifers' satellite dish could pull in) stopped showing anything but snow—the walking dead folks stopped only biting people if they came too close.

The dead folks started *trying* to get close.

The dead folks, it seemed, had discovered they *liked* what they were biting.

Before all the weird things started happening, Maddie discovered she was what her mother had always called "preg," a curt word that was like the sound you made when you had a throatful of snot and had to rasp some of it up (or at least that was how Maddie had always thought it sounded). She and Jack had moved to Genneseault Island, a nearby island simply called Jenny Island by those who lived there.

She had had one of her agonizing interior debates when she had missed her time of the month twice, and after four sleepless nights she had made a decision . . . and an appointment with Dr. McElwain on the mainland. Looking back, she was glad. If she had waited to see if she was going to miss a third period, Jack would not even have had one month of joy . . . and she would have missed the concerns and little kindnesses he had showered upon her.

Looking back—now that she was *coping*—her indecision seemed ludicrous, but her deeper heart knew that going to have the test had taken tremendous courage. She had wanted to be sick in the mornings so she could be surer; she had longed for nausea. She made the appointment when Jack was out dragging pots, and she went while he was out, but there was no such thing as *sneaking* over to the mainland on the ferry. Too many people saw you. Someone would mention casually to Jack that he or she had seen his wife on *The Gull* t'other day, and then Jack would want to know who and why and where, and if she'd made a mistake, Jack would look at her like she was a goose.

But it had been true, she was with child (and never mind that word that sounded like someone with a bad cold trying to rake snot off the sides of his throat), and Jack Pace had had exactly twenty-seven days of joy and looking forward before a bad swell had caught him and knocked him over the side of *My Lady-Love,* the lobster boat he had inherited from his Uncle Mike. Jack could swim, and he had popped to the surface like a cork, Dave Eamons had told her miserably, but just as he did, another heavy swell came, slewing the boat directly into Jack, and although Dave would say no more, Maddie had been born and brought up an island girl, and she knew: could, in fact, *hear* the hollow thud as the boat with its treacherous name smashed her husband's head, leaving blood and hair and bone and brain for the next swell to wash away from the boat's worn side.

Dressed in a heavy hooded parka and down-filled pants and boots, Jack Pace had sunk like a stone. They had buried an empty casket in the little cemetery at the north end of Jenny Island, and the Reverend Peebles (on Jenny you had your choice when it came to religion: you could be a Methodist, or if that didn't suit you, you could be a Methodist) had presided over this empty coffin, as he had so many others, and at the age of twenty-two Maddie had found herself a widow with an almost half-cooked bun in her oven and no one to tell her where the wheel was, let alone when to put her shoulder to it.

She thought she would go back to Deer Isle, back to her mother, to wait for her time, but she knew her mother was as lost—maybe even *more* lost—than she was herself, and held off.

"Maddie," Jack told her again and again, "the only thing you can ever decide on is not to decide."

Nor was her mother any better. They talked on the phone and Maddie waited and hoped for her mother to tell her to come home, but Mrs. Sullivan could tell no one over the age of ten anything. "Maybe you ought to come on back over here," she had said once in a tentative way, and Maddie couldn't tell if that meant *please come home* or *please don't take me up on an offer which was really just made for form's sake,* and she spent sleepless nights trying to decide and succeeding in doing only that thing of which Jack had accused her: deciding not to decide.

Then the weirdness started, and that was a mercy, because there was only the one small graveyard on Jenny (and so many of the graves filled with those empty coffins—a thing which had once seemed pitiful to her now seemed another blessing, a grace) and there were two on Deer Isle, bigger ones, and it seemed so much safer to stay on Jenny and wait.

She would wait and see if the world lived or died.

If it lived, she would wait for the baby.

That seemed like enough.

And now she was, after a life of passive obedience and vague resolves that passed like dreams an hour or two after getting out of bed, finally *coping.* She knew that part of this was nothing more than the effect of being slammed with one massive shock after another, beginning with the death of her husband and ending with one of the last broadcasts the Pulsifers' TV had picked up—a horrified young boy who had been pressed into service as an INS reporter, saying that it seemed certain that the president of the United States, the first lady, the secretary of state, the honorable senator from Oregon (which honorable senator the gibbering boy reporter didn't say), and the emir of Kuwait had been eaten alive in the White House ballroom by zombies.

"I want to repeat," the young reporter said, the fire-spots of his acne standing out on his forehead and chin like stigmata. His mouth and cheeks had begun to twitch; the microphone in his hand shook spastically. "I want to repeat that a bunch of dead people have just lunched up on the president and his wife and a whole lot of other political hotshots who were at the White House to eat poached salmon and cherries jubilee. Go, Yale! Boola-boola! Boola-fuckin-boola!" And then the young reporter with the fiery pimples had lost control of his face entirely, and he was screaming, only his screams were disguised as laughter, and he went on yelling *Go, Yale! Boola-boola* while Maddie and the Pulsifers sat in dismayed silence until the young man was suddenly swallowed by an ad for Boxcar Willy records, which were not available in any store, you could only get them if you dialed the 800 number on your screen, operators were standing by. One of little Cheyne Pulsifer's crayons was on the end table beside the place where Maddie was sitting, and she took down the number before Mr. Pulsifer got up and turned off the TV without a single word.

Maddie told them good night and thanked them for sharing their TV and their Jiffy Pop.

"Are you sure you're all right, Maddie dear?" Candi Pulsifer asked her for the fifth time that night, and Maddie said she was fine for the fifth time that night (and she was, she was *coping* for the first time in her life, and that really *was* fine, just as fine as paint), and Candi told her again that she could have that upstairs room that used to be Brian's anytime she wanted, and Maddie had declined her with the most graceful thanks she could find, and was at last allowed to escape. She had walked the windy half mile back to her own house and was in her own kitchen before she realized that she still had the scrap of paper on which she had jotted the 800 number in one hand. She dialed it, and there was nothing. No recorded voice telling her all circuits were currently busy or that number was out of service; no wailing siren sound that indicated a line interruption (had Jack told her that was what that sound meant? she tried to remember and couldn't, and really, it didn't matter a bit, did it?), no clicks and boops, no static. Just smooth silence.

That was when Maddie knew—knew for sure.

She hung up the telephone slowly and thoughtfully.

The end of the world had come. It was no longer in doubt. When you could no longer call the 800 number and order the Boxcar Willy records that were not available in any store, when there were for the first time in her living memory no Operators Standing By, the end of the world was a foregone conclusion.

She felt her rounding stomach as she stood there by the phone on the wall in the kitchen and said it out loud for the first time, unaware that she had spoken: "It will have to be a home delivery. But that's all right, as long as you remember, Maddie. There isn't any other way, not now. It will have to be a home delivery."

She waited for fear and none came.

"I can cope with this just fine," she said, and this time she heard herself and was comforted by the sureness of her own words.

A baby.

When the baby came, the end of the world would itself end.

"Eden," she said, and smiled. Her smile was sweet, the smile of a madonna. It didn't matter how many rotting dead people (maybe Boxcar Willy among them) were shambling around on the face of the world.

She would have a baby, she would have a home delivery, and the possibility of Eden would remain.

The first news had come out of a small Florida town on the Tamiami Trail. The name of this town was not as colorful as Wet Noggin, but it was still pretty good: Thumper. Thumper, Florida. It was reported in one of those lurid tabloids that fill the racks by the checkout aisles in supermarkets and discount drugstores. DEAD COME TO LIFE IN SMALL FLORIDA TOWN! the headline of *Inside View* read. And the subhead: *Horror Movie Comes to Life!* The subhead referred to a movie called *Night of the Living Dead*, which Maddie had never seen. It also mentioned another movie she had never seen. The title of this piece of cinema was *Macumba Love.* The article was accompanied by three photos. One was a still from *Night of the Living Dead*, showing what appeared to be a bunch of escapees from a lunatic asylum standing outside an isolated farmhouse at night. One was a still from *Macumba Love*, showing a woman with a great lot of blond hair and a small bit of bikini-top holding in breasts the size of prize-winning gourds. The woman was holding up her hands and screaming at what appeared to be a black man in a mask. The third purported to be a picture taken in Thumper, Florida. It was a blurred, grainy shot of a human whose sex was impossible to define. It was walking up the middle of a business street in a small town. The figure was described as being "wrapped in the cerements of the grave," but it could have been someone in a dirty sheet.

No big deal. Bigfoot Rapes Girl Scouts last week, the dead people coming back to life this week, the dwarf mass murderer next week.

No big deal until they started to come out everywhere.

No big deal until the first news film ("You may want to ask your children to leave the room," Dan Rather introduced gravely) showed up on network TV, creatures with naked bone showing through their dried skin, traffic accident victims, the morticians' concealing makeup sloughed away either in the dark passivity of the earth or in the clawing climb to escape it so that the ripped faces and bashed-in skulls showed, women with their hair teased into dirt-clogged beehives in which worms and beetles still squirmed and crawled, their faces alternately vacuous and informed with a kind of calculating, idiotic intelligence; no big deal until the first horrible stills in an issue of *People* magazine that had been sealed in shrink-wrap like girly magazines, an issue with an orange sticker that read *Not For Sale To Minors!*

Then it was a big deal.

When you saw a decaying man still dressed in the mud-streaked remnants of the Brooks Brothers suit in which he had been buried tearing at the breast of a screaming woman in a T-shirt that read *Property of the Houston Oilers,* you suddenly realized it might be a very big deal indeed.

Then the accusations and the saber rattling had started, and for three weeks the entire world had been diverted from the creatures escaping their graves like grotesque moths escaping diseased cocoons by the spectacle of the two great nuclear powers on what appeared to be an undivertable collision course.

There were no zombies in the United States, Tass declared: This was a self-serving lie to camouflage an unforgivable act of chemical warfare against the Union of Soviet Socialist Republics. Reprisals would follow if the dead comrades coming out of their graves did not fall down decently dead within ten days. All U.S. diplomatic people were expelled from the mother country and most of her satellites.

The president (who would not long after become a Zombie Blue Plate Special himself) responded by becoming a pot (which he had come to resemble, having put on at least fifty pounds since his second-term election) calling a kettle black. The U.S. government, he told the American people, had incontrovertible evidence that the only walking dead people in the USSR had been set loose deliberately, and while the premier might stand there with his bare face hanging out and claim there were over eight thousand lively corpses striding around Russia in search of the ultimate collectivism, *we* had definite proof that there were less than forty. It was the *Russians* who had committed an act—a *heinous* act—of chemical warfare, bringing loyal Americans back to life with no urge to consume anything but other loyal Americans, and if these Americans—some of whom had been good Democrats—did not lie down decently dead within the next *five* days, the USSR was going to be one large slag pit.

The president expelled all Soviet diplomatic people . . . with one exception. This was a young fellow who was teaching him how to play chess (and who was not at all averse to the occasional grope under the table).

Norad was at Defcon-2 when the satellite was spotted. Or the spaceship. Or the creature. Or whatever in hell's name it was. An amateur astronomer from Hinchly-on-Strope in the west of England spotted it first, and this fellow, who had a deviated septum, fallen arches, and balls the size of acorns (he was also going bald, and his expanding pate showcased his really horrible case of psoriasis admirably), probably saved the world from nuclear holocaust.

The missile silos were open all over the world as telescopes in California and Siberia trained on Star Wormwood; they closed only following the horror of Salyut/Eagle-I, which was launched with a crew of six Russians, three Americans, and one Briton only three days following the discovery of Star Wormwood by Humphrey Dagbolt, the amateur astronomer with the deviated septum, et al. He was, of course, the Briton.

And he paid.

They *all* paid.

The final sixty-one seconds of received transmission from the *Gorbachev/Truman* were considered too horrible for release by all three governments involved, and so no formal release was ever made. It didn't matter, of course; nearly twenty thousand ham operators had been monitoring the craft, and it seemed that at least nineteen thousand of them had been running tape decks when the craft had been—well, was there really any other word for it?—invaded.

Russian voice: Worms! It appears to be a massive ball of—

American voice: Christ! Look out! It's coming for us!
Dagbolt: Some sort of extrusion is occurring. The port-side window is—
Russian voice: Breach! Breach! Suits!
(Indecipherable gabble.)
American voice: —and appears to be eating its way in—
Female Russian voice (Olga Katinya): Oh stop it stop the eyes—
(Sound of an explosion.)
Dagbolt: Explosive decompression has occurred. I see three—no, four—dead—and there are worms . . . everywhere there are worms—
American voice: Faceplate! Faceplate! *Faceplate!*
(Screaming.)
Russian voice: Where is my mamma? Where—
(Screams. Sounds like a toothless old man sucking up mashed potatoes.)
Dagbolt: The cabin is full of worms—what appears to be worms, at any rate—which is to say that they really *are* worms, one realizes—they have extruded themselves from the main satellite—what we took to be—which is to say one means—the cabin is full of floating body parts. These space-worms apparently excrete some sort of aci—
(Booster rockets fired at this point; duration of the burn is seven point two seconds. This may or may not have been attempt to escape or possibly to ram the central object. In either case, the maneuver did not work. It seems likely that the chambers themselves were clogged with worms and Captain Vassily Task—or whichever officer was then in charge—believed an explosion of the fuel tanks themselves to be imminent as a result of the clog. Hence the shutdown.)
American voice: Oh my Christ they're in my head, they're eating my fuckin br—
(Static.)
Dagbolt: I am retreating to the aft storage compartment. At the present moment, this seems the most prudent of my severely limited choices. I believe the others are all dead. Pity. Brave bunch. Even that fat Russian who kept rooting around in his nose. But in another sense I don't think—
(Static.)
Dagbolt: —dead at all because the Russian woman—or

rather, the Russian woman's severed head, one means to say—just floated past me, and her eyes were open. She was looking at me from inside her—

(Static.)

Dagbolt: —keep you—

(Explosion. Static.)

Dagbolt: Is it possible for a severed penis to have an orgasm? I th—

(Static.)

Dagbolt: —around me, I repeat, all around me. Squirming things. They—I say, does anyone know if—

(Dagbolt, screaming and cursing, then just screaming. Sound of toothless old man again.)

Transmission ends.

The *Gorbachev/Truman* exploded three seconds later. The extrusion from the rough ball nicknamed Star Wormwood had been observed from better than three hundred telescopes earthside during the short and rather pitiful conflict. As the final sixty-one seconds of transmission began, the craft began to be obscured by something that certainly *looked* like worms. By the end of the final transmission, the craft itself could not be seen at all—only the squirming mass of things that had attached themselves to it. Moments after the final explosion, a weather satellite snapped a single picture of floating debris, some of which was almost certainly chunks of the worm-things. A severed human leg clad in a Russian space suit floating among them was a good deal easier to identify.

And in a way, none of it even mattered. The scientists and political leaders of both countries knew exactly where Star Wormwood was located: above the expanding hole in earth's ozone layer. It was sending something down from there, and it was not Flowers by Wire.

Missiles came next.

Star Wormwood jigged easily out of their way and then returned to its place over the hole.

More dead people got up and walked.

Now they were all biting.

The final effort to destroy the thing was made by the United States. At a cost of just under six hundred million dollars, four SDI "defensive weapons" satellites had been hoisted into orbit by the previous administration. The president of the current—and last—administration informed the Soviet premier of his intentions to use the SDI missiles, and got an enthusiastic approval (the Russian premier failed to note the fact that seven years before he had called these missiles "infernal engines of war and hate forged in the factories of hell").

It might even have worked . . . except not a single missile from a single SDI orbiter fired. Each satellite was equipped with six two-megaton warheads. Every goddamn one malfunctioned.

So much for modern technology.

Maddie supposed the horrible deaths of those brave men (and one woman) in space really hadn't been the last shock; there was the business of the one little graveyard right here on Jenny. But that didn't seem to count so much because, after all, she had not been there. With the end of the world now clearly at hand and the island cut off—*thankfully* cut off, in the opinion of the island's residents—from the rest of the world, old ways had reasserted themselves with a kind of unspoken but inarguable force. By then they all knew what was going to happen; it was only a question of when. That, and being ready when it did.

Women were excluded.

It was Bob Daggett, of course, who drew up the watch roster. That was only right, since Bob had been head selectman on Jenny since Hector was a pup. The day after the death of the president (the thought of him and the first lady wandering witlessly through the streets of Washington, D.C., gnawing on human arms and legs like people eating chicken legs at a picnic was not mentioned; it was a little too much to bear, even if the bastid and his big old blond wife *were* Democrats). Bob Daggett called the first men-only Town Meeting on Jenny since someplace before the Civil War. So Maddie wasn't there, but she heard. Dave Eamons told her all she needed to know.

"You men all know the situation," Bob said. He had always been a pretty hard fellow, but right then he looked as yellow as a man with jaundice, and people remembered his daughter, the one on the island, was only one of four. The other three were other places . . . which was to say, on the mainland.

But hell, if it came down to that, they *all* had folks on the mainland.

"We got one boneyard here on the island," Bob continued, "and nothin' ain't happened yet, but that don't mean nothin' *will.* Nothin' ain't happened yet lots of places . . . but it seems like once it starts, nothin' turns to somethin' pretty goddam quick."

There was a rumble of assent from the men gathered in the basement of the Methodist church. There were about seventy of them, ranging in age from Johnny Crane, who had just turned eighteen, to Bob's great-uncle Frank, who was eighty, had a glass eye, and chewed tobacco. There was no spittoon in the church basement and Frank Daggett knew it well enough, so he'd brought an empty mayonnaise jar to spit his juice into. He did so now.

"Git down to where the cheese binds, Bobby," he said. "You ain't got no office to run for, and time's a-wastin'."

There was another rumble of agreement, and Bob Daggett blushed. Somehow his great-uncle always managed to make him look like an ineffectual fool, and if there was anything in the world he hated worse than looking like an ineffectual fool, it was being called Bobby. He owned property, for Chrissake! He *supported* the old fart, for Chrissake.

But these were not things he could say. Frank's eyes were like pieces of flint.

"Okay," he said curtly. "Here it is. We want twelve men to a watch. I'm gonna set a roster in just a couple minutes. Four-hour shifts."

"I can stand watch a helluva lot longer'n four hours!" Matt Arsenault spoke up, and Davey told Maddie that Bob said after the meeting that no frog setting on a welfare lily pad like Matt Arsenault would have had the nerve enough to speak up like that if his great-uncle hadn't called him Bobby, like he was a kid instead of a man three months shy of his fiftieth birthday, in front of all the island men.

"Maybe so," Bob said, "but we got enough men to go around, and nobody's gonna fall asleep on sentry duty."

"I ain't gonna—"

"I didn't say *you,*" Bob said, but the way his eyes rested

on Matt Arsenault suggested that he *might* have meant him. "This is no kid's game. Sit down and shut up."

Matt Arsenault opened his mouth to say something more, then looked around at the other men—including old Frank Daggett—and wisely sat down again.

"If you got a rifle, bring it when it's your trick," Bob continued. He felt a little better with Frere Jacques out of the way. "Unless it's a twenty-two. If you got no rifle bigger'n that, or none at all, come and get one here."

"I didn't know Reverend Peebles kept a supply of 'em handy," Cal Partridge said, and there was a ripple of laughter.

"He don't now, but he's gonna," Bob said, "because every man jack of you with more than one rifle bigger than a twenty-two is gonna bring it here." He looked at Peebles. "Okay if we keep 'em in the rectory, Tom?"

Peebles nodded, dry-washing his hands in a distraught way.

"Shit on that," Orrin Campbell said. "I got a wife and two kids at home. Am I s'posed to leave 'em with nothin' if a bunch of cawpses come for an early Thanksgiving dinner while I'm on watch?"

"If we do our job at the boneyard, none will," Bob replied stonily. "Some of you got handguns. We don't want none of those. Figure out which women can shoot and which can't, and give 'em the pistols. We'll put 'em together in bunches."

"They can play Beano," old Frank cackled, and Bob smiled, too. That was more like it, by the Christ.

"Nights, we're gonna want trucks posted around so we got plenty of light." He looked over at Sonny Dotson, who ran Island Amoco, the only gas station on Jenny—Sonny's main business wasn't gassing cars and trucks—shit, there was no place much on the island to drive, and you could get your go ten cents cheaper on the mainland—but filling up lobster boats and the motorboats he ran out of his jackleg marina in the summer. "You gonna supply the gas, Sonny?"

"Am I gonna get cash slips?"

"You're gonna get your ass saved," Bob said. "When things get back to normal—if they ever do—I guess you'll get what you got coming."

Sonny looked around, saw only hard eyes, and shrugged.

He looked a bit sullen, but in truth he looked more confused than anything, Davey told Maddie the next day.

"Ain't got n'more'n four hunnert gallons of gas," he said. "Mostly diesel."

"There's five generators on the island," Burt Dorfman said (when Burt spoke everyone listened; as the only Jew on the island, he was regarded as a creature both quixotic and fearsome, like an oracle that works about half the time). "They all run on diesel. I can rig lights if I have to."

Low murmurs. If Burt said he could, he could. He was an electrician, and a damned good one . . . for a Jew, anyway.

"We're gonna light that place up like a friggin' stage," Bob said.

Andy Kinsolving stood up. "I heard on the news that sometimes you can shoot one of them . . . things . . . in the head and it'll stay down, and sometimes it won't."

"We got chain saws," Bob said stonily, "and what won't stay dead . . . why, we can make sure it won't move too far alive."

And, except for making out the duty roster, that was pretty much that.

Six days and nights passed and the sentries posted around the island graveyard were starting to feel a wee bit silly ("I dunno if I'm standin' guard or pullin' my pud," Orrin Campbell said one afternoon as a dozen men stood around a small cemetery where the most exciting thing happening was a caterpillar spinning a cocoon while a spider watched it and waited for the moment to pounce) when it happened . . . and when it happened, it happened fast.

Dave told Maddie that he heard a sound like the wind wailing in the chimney on a gusty night . . . and then the gravestone marking the final resting place of Mr. and Mrs. Fournier's boy Michael, who had died of leukemia at seventeen—bad go, that had been, him being their only get and them being such nice people and all—fell over. Then a shredded hand with a moss-caked Yarmouth Academy class ring on one finger rose out of the ground, shoving through the tough grass. The third finger had been torn off in the process.

The ground heaved like (like the belly of a pregnant woman getting ready to drop her load, Dave almost said, and hastily reconsidered) well, like the way a big wave heaves up on its way into a close cove, and then the boy himself sat up, only he wasn't nothing you could really recognize, not after almost two years in the ground. There was little pieces of wood sticking to him, Davey said, and pieces of blue cloth.

Later inspection proved these to be shreds of satin from the coffin in which the boy had been buried away.

("Thank Christ Richie Fournier dint have that trick," Bill Pulsifer said later, and they had all nodded shakily—many of them were still wiping their mouths, because almost all of them had puked at some point or other during that hellacious half hour . . . these were not things Dave Eamons could tell Maddie, but Maddie guessed more than Dave ever guessed she guessed.)

Gunfire tore Michael Fournier to shreds before he could do more than sit up; other shots, fired in wild panic, blew chips off his marble gravestone, and it was a goddam wonder someone on one side hadn't shot someone on one of the others, but they got off lucky. Bud Meechum found a hole torn in the sleeve of his shirt the next day, but liked to think that might have been nothing more than a thorn—there had been raspberry bushes on his side of the boneyard. Maybe that was really all it was, although the black smudges on the hole made him think that maybe it had been a thorn with a pretty large caliber.

The Fournier kid fell back, most of him lying still, other parts of him still twitching.

But by then the whole graveyard seemed to be rippling, as if an earthquake was going on there—but *only* there, no place else.

Just about an hour before dusk, this had happened.

Burt Dorfman had rigged up a siren to a tractor battery, and Bob Daggett flipped the switch. Within twenty minutes, most of the men in town were at the island cemetery.

Goddam good thing, too, because a few of the deaders almost got away. Old Frank Daggett, still two hours away from the heart attack that would carry him off after it was all over and the moon had risen, organized the men into a pair of angled flanks so they wouldn't shoot each other, and for the final ten minutes the Jenny boneyard sounded like Bull Run. By the end of the festivities, the powder smoke was so thick that some men choked on it. No one puked on it, because no one had anything left to puke up. The sour smell of vomit was almost heavier than the smell of gunsmoke ... it was sharper, too, and lingered longer.

And still some of them wriggled and squirmed like snakes with broken backs ... the fresher ones, for the most part.

"Burt," Frank Daggett said. "You got them chain saws?"

"I got 'em," Burt said, and then a long, buzzing sound came out of his mouth, a sound like a cicada burrowing its way into tree bark, as he dry-heaved. He could not take his eyes from the squirming corpses, the overturned gravestones, the yawning pits from which the dead had come. "In the truck."

"Gassed up?" Blue veins stood out on Frank's ancient, hairless skull.

"Yeah." Burt's hand was over his mouth. "I'm sorry."

"Work y'fuckin gut all you want," Frank said briskly. "But get them saws while you do. And you ... you ... you ... you ..."

The last "you" was his grandnephew Bob.

"I can't, Uncle Frank," Bob said sickly. He looked around and saw at least twenty men lying in the tall grass. They had swooned. Most of them had seen their own relatives rise out of the ground. Buck Harkness over there lying by an aspen tree had been part of the cross fire that had cut his late wife to ribbons before he fainted when her decayed brains exploded from the back of her head in a grisly gray fan. "I can't. I c—"

Frank's hand, twisted with arthritis but as hard as stone, cracked across his face.

"You can and you will, chummy," he said grimly.

Bob went with the rest of the men.

Frank Daggett watched them grimly and rubbed his chest.

"I was nearby when Frank spoke to Bob," Dave told Maddie. He wasn't sure if he should be telling her this—or any of it, for that matter, with her almost halfway to foaling time—but he was still too impressed with the old man's grim and quiet courage to forbear. "This was after ... you know ... we cleaned the mess up."

Maddie only nodded.

"I'll stop," Dave said, "if you can't bear it, Maddie."

"I can bear it," she said quietly, and Dave looked at her quickly, curiously, but she had averted her eyes before he could see the secret in them.

Davey didn't know the secret because no one on Jenny knew. That was the way Maddie wanted it, and the way she intended to keep it. There had been a time when she had, in the blue darkness of her shock, pretended to be *coping*. And then something happened that *made* her cope. Four days before the island cemetery vomited up its corpses, Maddie Pace was faced with a simple choice: cope or die.

She had been sitting in the living room, drinking a glass of the blueberry wine she and Jack had put up during August of the previous year—a time that now seemed impossibly distant—and doing something so trite it was laughable: She was Knitting Little Things (the second bootee of a pair this evening). But what else *was* there to do? It seemed that no one would be going across to the mall on the mainland for a long time.

Something had thumped the window.

A bat, she thought, looking up. Her needles paused in her hands, though. It seemed that something was moving out there in the windy dark. The oil lamp was turned up high and kicking too much reflection off the panes to be sure. She reached to turn it down and the thump came again. The panes shivered. She heard a little pattering of dried putty falling on the sash. Jack was going to reglaze all the windows this fall, she thought stupidly, and then: Maybe that's what he came back for. Because it was Jack. She knew that. Before Jack, no one from Jenny had drowned for nearly three years. Whatever was making them return apparently couldn't reanimate whatever was left of their bodies. But Jack . . .

Jack was still fresh.

She sat, poised, head cocked to one side, knitting in her hands. A little pink bootee. She had already made a blue set. All of a sudden it seemed she could hear so *much*. The wind. The faint thunder of surf on Cricket's Ledge. The house making little groaning sounds, like an elderly woman making herself comfortable in bed. The tick of the clock in the hallway.

It was Jack. She knew it.

"Jack?" she said, and the window burst inward and what came in was not really Jack but a skeleton with a few mouldering strings of flesh hanging from it.

His compass was still around his neck. It had grown a beard of moss.

The wind blew the curtains out in a cloud as he sprawled, then got up on his hands and knees and looked at her from black sockets in which barnacles had grown.

He made grunting sounds. His fleshless mouth opened and the teeth chomped down. He was hungry . . . but this time chicken noodle soup would not serve. Not even the kind that came in the can.

Gray stuff hung and swung beyond those dark barnacle-crusted holes, and she realized she was looking at whatever remained of Jack's brain. She sat where she was, frozen, as he got up and came toward her, leaving black kelpy tracks on the carpet, fingers reaching. He stank of salt and fathoms. His hands stretched. His teeth champed mechanically up and down. Maddie saw he was wearing the remains of the black-and-red-checked shirt she had bought him at L.L. Bean's last Christmas. It had cost the earth, but he had said again and again how warm it was, and look how well it had lasted, even under water all this time, even—

The cold cobwebs of bone which were all that remained of his fingers touched her throat before the baby kicked in her stomach—for the first time—and her shocked horror, which she had believed to be calmness, fled, and she drove one of the knitting needles into the thing's eye.

Making horrid, thick, draggling noises that sounded like the suck of a swill pump, he staggered backward, clawing at the needle, while the half-made pink bootee swung in front of the cavity where his nose had been. She watched as a sea slug squirmed from that nasal cavity and onto the bootee, leaving a trail of slime behind it.

Jack fell over the end table she'd gotten at a yard sale just after they had been married—she hadn't been able to make her mind up about it, had been in agonies about it, until Jack finally said either she was going to buy it for their living room or he was going to give the biddy running the sale twice what she was asking for the goddam thing and then bust it up into firewood with—

—with the—

He struck the floor and there was a brittle, cracking sound as his febrile, fragile form broke in two. The right hand tore the knitting needle, slimed with decaying brain tissue, from his eye socket and tossed it aside. His top half crawled toward her. His teeth gnashed steadily together.

She thought he was trying to grin, and then the baby kicked again and she thought: *You buy it, Maddie, for Christ's sake! I'm tired! Want to go home and get m'dinner! You want it, buy it! If you don't, I'll give that old bat twice what she wants to bust it up for firewood with my—*

Cold, dank hand clutching her ankle; polluted teeth poised to bite. To kill her and kill the baby.

She tore loose, leaving him with only her slipper, which he tried to chew and then spat out.

When she came back from the entry, he was crawling mindlessly into the kitchen—at least the top half of him was—with the compass dragging on the tiles. He looked up at the sound of her, and there seemed to be some idiot question in those black eye sockets before she brought the ax whistling down, cleaving his skull as he had threatened to cleave the end table.

His head fell in two pieces, brains dribbling across the tile like spoiled oatmeal, brains that squirmed with slugs and gelatinous sea worms, brains that smelled like a woodchuck exploded with gassy decay in a high-summer meadow.

Still his hands clashed and clittered on the kitchen tiles, making a sound like beetles.

She chopped . . . she chopped . . . she chopped.

At last there was no more movement.

A sharp pain rippled across her midsection and for a moment she was gripped by terrible panic: *Is it a miscarriage? Am I going to have a miscarriage?* But the pain left . . . and the baby kicked again, more strongly than before.

She went back into the living room, carrying an ax that now smelled like tripe.

His legs had somehow managed to stand.

"Jack, I loved you so much," she said, and brought the ax down in a whistling arc that split him at the pelvis, sliced the carpet, and drove deep into the solid oak floor beneath.

The legs separated, trembled wildly . . . and then lay still.

She carried him down to the cellar piece by piece, wearing her oven gloves and wrapping each piece with the insulating blankets Jack had kept in the shed and which she had never thrown away—he and the crew threw them over the pots on cold days so the lobsters wouldn't freeze.

Once a severed hand tried to close over her wrist . . . then loosened.

That was all.

There was an unused cistern, polluted, which Jack had been meaning to fill in. Maddie Pace slid the heavy concrete cover aside so that its shadow lay on the earthen floor like a partial eclipse and then threw the pieces of him down, listening to the splashes, then worked the heavy cover back into place.

"Rest in peace," she whispered, and an interior voice whispered back that her husband was resting in *pieces,* and then she began to cry, and her cries turned to hysterical shrieks, and she pulled at her hair and tore at her breasts until they were bloody, and she thought, I am insane, this is what it's like to be in—

But before the thought could be completed, she had fallen down in a faint that became a deep sleep, and the next morning she felt all right.

She would never tell, though.

Never.

She understood, of course, that David knew of this, and Dave would say nothing at all if she pressed. She kept her ears open, and she knew what he meant, and what they had apparently done. The dead folks and the . . . the *parts* of dead folks that wouldn't . . . wouldn't be still . . . had been chain-sawed like her father had chain-sawed the hardwood on Pop Cook's two acres after he had gotten the deed registered, and then those parts—some *still* squirming, hands with no arms attached to them clutching mindlessly, feet divorced from their legs digging at the bullet-chewed earth of the graveyard as if trying to run away—had been doused with diesel fuel and set afire. She had seen the pyre from the house.

Later, Jenny's one fire truck had turned its hose on the

dying blaze, although there wasn't much chance of the fire spreading, with a brisk easterly blowing the sparks off Jenny's seaward edge.

When there was nothing left but a stinking, tallowy lump (and still there were occasional bulges in this mass, like twitches in a tired muscle), Matt Arsenault fired up his old D-9 Caterpillar—above the nicked steel blade and under his faded pillowtick engineer's cap, Matt's face had been as white as cottage cheese—and plowed the whole hellacious mess under.

The moon was coming up when Frank took Bob Daggett, Dave Eamons, and Cal Partridge aside.

"I'm havin a goddam heart attack." he said.

"Now, Uncle Frank—"

"Never mind Uncle Frank this 'n' that," the old man said. "I ain't got time, and I ain't wrong. Seen half my friends go the same way. Beats hell out of getting whacked with the cancer-stick. Quicker. But when I go down, I intend to *stay* down. Cal, stick that rifle of yours in my left ear. Muzzle's gonna get some wax on it, but it won't be there after you pull the trigger. Dave, when I raise my left arm, you sock your thirty-thirty into my armpit, and see that you do it a right smart. And Bobby, you put yours right over my heart. I'm gonna say the Lawd's Prayer, and when I hit amen, you three fellows are gonna pull your triggers."

"Uncle Frank—" Bob managed. He was reeling on his heels.

"I told you not to start in on that," Frank said. "And don't you *dare* faint on me, you friggin pantywaist. If I'm goin' down, I mean to *stay* down. Now get over here."

Bob did.

Frank looked around at the three men, their faces as white as Matt Arsenault's had been when he drove the dozer over men and women he had known since he was a kid in short pants and Buster Browns.

"I ain't got long," Frank said, "and I only got enough jizzum left to get m' arm up once, so don't fuck up on me. And remember, I'd 'a' done the same for any of you. If that don't help, ask y'selves if *you'd* want to end up like those we just took care of."

"Go on," Bob said hoarsely. "I love you, Uncle Frank."

"You ain't the man your father was, Bobby Daggett, but I love you, too," Frank said calmly, and then, with a cry of pain, he threw his left hand up over his head like a guy in New York who has to have a cab in a rip of a hurry, and started in: "Our Father who art in heaven—*Christ,* that hurts!—hallow'd be Thy name—oh, son of a *gun, I*—Thy kingdom come, Thy will be done, on earth as it . . . as it . . ."

Frank's upraised left arm was wavering wildly now. Dave Eamons, with his rifle socked into the old geezer's armpit, watched it as carefully as a logger would watch a big tree that looked like it meant to fall the wrong way. Every man on the island was watching now. Big beads of sweat had formed on the old man's pallid face. His lips had pulled back from the even, yellowish white of his Roebuckers, and Dave had been able to smell the Polident on his breath.

". . . as it is in heaven!" the old man jerked out. "Lead us not into temptation butdeliverusfromevilohshitonitforever-andeverAMEN!"

All three of them fired, and both Cal Partridge and Bob Daggett fainted, but Frank never did try to get up and walk.

Frank Daggett intended to *stay* dead, and that was just what he did.

Once Dave started that story he had to go on with it, and so he cursed himself for ever starting. He'd been right the first time; it was no story for a pregnant woman.

But Maddie had kissed him and told him she thought he had done wonderfully, and Dave went out, feeling a little dazed, as if he had just been kissed on the cheek by a woman he had never met before.

As, in a way, he had.

She watched him go down the path to the dirt track that was one of Jenny's two roads and turn left. He was weaving a little in the moonlight, weaving with tiredness, she thought, but reeling with shock, as well. Her heart went out to him . . . to all of them. She had wanted to tell Dave she loved him and kiss him squarely on the mouth instead of just skimming his cheek with her lips, but he might have taken the wrong meaning from something like that, even though he was bone-weary and she was almost five months pregnant.

But she *did* love him, loved *all* of them, because they had gone through a hell she could only imagine dimly, and by going through that hell they had made the island safe for her.

Safe for her baby.

"It will be a home delivery," she said softly as Dave went out of sight behind the dark hulk of the Pulsifers' satellite dish. Her eyes rose to the moon. "It will be a home delivery . . . and it will be fine."

Rudyard Kipling

(1865–1936)

Joseph Rudyard Kipling was born in Bombay (now Mumbai) during the period of British rule of India. When he was five, he and his three-year-old sister were sent to England to be educated. Although he attended the United Services College at Westward Ho! (a Devon school that served to prepare boys for military careers), his poor sight prevented his having a career in the Indian Army. In 1882, he returned to India, where he began work as a journalist at a Lahore newspaper, the *Civil and Military Gazette*. Upon his marriage in 1892 to Caroline Balestier, an American, Kipling moved to the Brattleboro, Vermont, area, where the couple lived for the next four years before settling in England. Among his story collections are *Plain Tales from the Hills* (1888), *Life's Handicap* (1891), *The Jungle Book* (1894), *Just So Stories* (1902), *Actions and Reactions* (1909), and *Debits and Credits* (1926). His novels include *The Light That Failed* (1891), *Captains Courageous* (1896), and *Kim* (1901). He was awarded the Nobel Prize in Literature in 1907.

The Mark of the Beast

(1890)

Your Gods and my Gods
—do you or I know which are the stronger?
—*Native Proverb.*

East of Suez, some hold, the direct control of Providence ceases; Man being there handed over to the power of the Gods and Devils of Asia, and the Church of England Providence only exercising an occasional and modified supervision in the case of Englishmen.

This theory accounts for some of the more unnecessary horrors of life in India: it may be stretched to explain my story.

My friend Strickland of the Police, who knows as much of natives of India as is good for any man, can bear witness to the facts of the case. Dumoise, our doctor, also saw what Strickland and I saw. The inference which he drew from the evidence was entirely incorrect. He is dead now; he died in a rather curious manner, which has been elsewhere described.

When Fleete came to India he owned a little money and some land in the Himalayas, near a place called Dharmsala. Both properties had been left him by an uncle, and he came out to finance them. He was a big, heavy, genial, and inoffensive man. His knowledge of natives was, of course, limited, and he complained of the difficulties of the language.

He rode in from his place in the hills to spend New Year in the station, and he stayed with Strickland. On New Year's Eve there was a big dinner at the club, and the night was excusably wet. When men foregather from the uttermost ends of the Empire, they have a right to be riotous. The Frontier had sent down a contingent o' Catch-'em-Alive-O's who had not seen twenty white faces for a year, and were used to ride fifteen miles to dinner at the next Fort at the risk of a Khyberee bullet where their drinks should lie. They profited by their new security, for they tried to play pool with a curled-up hedgehog found in the garden, and one of them carried the marker round the room in his teeth. Half a dozen planters had come in from the south and were talking "horse" to the Biggest Liar in Asia, who was trying to cap all their stories at once. Everybody was there, and there was a general closing up of ranks and taking stock of our losses in dead or disabled that had fallen during the past year. It was a very wet night, and I remember that we sang "Auld Lang Syne" with our feet in the Polo Championship Cup, and our heads among the stars, and swore that we were all dear friends. Then some of us went away and annexed Burma, and some tried to open up the Soudan and were opened up by Fuzzies in that cruel scrub outside Suakim, and some found stars and medals, and some were married, which was bad, and some did other things which were worse, and the others of us stayed in our chains and strove to make money on insufficient experiences.

Fleete began the night with sherry and bitters, drank champagne steadily up to dessert, then raw, rasping Capri with all the strength of whiskey, took Benedictine with his coffee, four or five whiskies and sodas to improve his pool strokes, beer and bones at half-past two, winding up with old brandy. Consequently, when he came out, at half-past three in the morning, into fourteen degrees of frost, he was very angry with his horse for coughing, and tried to leapfrog into the saddle. The horse broke away and went to the stables; so Strickland and I formed a Guard of Dishonour to take Fleete home.

Our road lay through the bazar, close to a little temple of Hanuman, the Monkey-god, who is a leading divinity worthy of respect. All gods have good points, just as have all priests. Personally, I attach much importance to Hanuman, and am kind to his people—the great gray apes of the hills. One never knows when one may want a friend.

There was a light in the temple, and as we passed we could hear voices of men chanting hymns. In a native temple the priests rise at all hours of the night to do honour to their god. Before we could stop him, Fleete dashed up the steps, patted two priests on the back, and was gravely grinding the ashes of his cigar-butt into the forehead of the red stone image of Hanuman. Strickland tried to drag him out, but he sat down and said solemnly:

"Shee that? 'Mark of the B-beasht! *I* made it. Ishn't it fine?"

In half a minute the temple was alive and noisy, and Strickland, who knew what came of polluting gods, said that things might occur. He, by virtue of his official position, long residence in the country, and weakness for going among the natives, was known to the priests, and he felt unhappy. Fleete sat on the ground and refused to move. He said that "good old Hanuman" made a very soft pillow.

Then, without any warning, a Silver Man came out of a recess behind the image of the god. He was perfectly naked in that bitter, bitter cold, and his body shone like frosted silver, for he was what the Bible calls "a leper as white as snow." Also he had no face, because he was a leper of some years' standing, and his disease was heavy upon him. We two stooped to haul Fleete up, and the temple was filling and filling with folk who seemed to spring from the earth, when the Silver Man ran in under our arms, making a noise exactly like the mewing of an otter, caught Fleete round the body and dropped his head on Fleete's breast before we could wrench him away. Then he retired to a corner and sat mewing while the crowd blocked all the doors.

The priests were very angry until the Silver Man touched Fleete. That nuzzling seemed to sober them.

At the end of a few minutes' silence one of the priests came to Strickland and said, in perfect English, "Take your friend away. He has done with Hanuman, but Hanuman has not done with him." The crowd gave room and we carried Fleete into the road.

Strickland was very angry. He said that we might all three have been knifed, and that Fleete should thank his stars that he had escaped without injury.

Fleete thanked no one. He said that he wanted to go to bed. He was gorgeously drunk.

We moved on, Strickland silent and wrathful, until Fleete was taken with violent shivering fits and sweating. He said that the smells of the bazar were overpowering, and he wondered why slaughterhouses were permitted so near English residences. "Can't you smell the blood?" said Fleete.

We put him to bed at last, just as the dawn was breaking, and Strickland invited me to have another whiskey and soda. While we were drinking he talked of the trouble in the temple, and admitted that it baffled him completely. Strickland hates being mystified by natives, because his business in life is to overmatch them with their own weapons. He has not yet succeeded in doing this, but in fifteen or twenty years he will have made some small progress.

"They should have mauled us," he said, "instead of mewing at us. I wonder what they meant. I don't like it one little bit."

I said that the Managing Committee of the temple would in all probability bring a criminal action against us for insulting their religion. There was a section of the Indian Penal Code which exactly met Fleete's offence. Strickland said he only hoped and prayed that they would do this. Before I left I looked into Fleete's room, and saw him lying on his right side, scratching his left breast. Then I went to bed, cold, depressed, and unhappy at seven o'clock in the morning.

At one o'clock I rode over to Strickland's house to inquire after Fleete's head. I imagined that it would be a sore one. Fleete was breakfasting and seemed unwell. His temper was gone, for he was abusing the cook for not supplying him with an underdone chop. A man who can eat raw meat after a wet night is a curiosity. I told Fleete this, and he laughed.

"You breed queer mosquitos in these parts," he said. "I've been bitten to pieces, but only in one place."

"Let's have a look at the bite," said Strickland. "It may have gone down since this morning."

While the chops were being cooked, Fleete opened his shirt and showed us, just over his left breast, a mark, the perfect double of the black rosettes—the five or six irregular blotches arranged in a circle—on a leopard's hide. Strickland looked and said, "It was only pink this morning. It's grown black now."

Fleete ran to a glass.

"By Jove!" he said, "this is nasty. What is it?"

We could not answer. Here the chops came in, all red and juicy, and Fleete bolted three in a most offensive manner. He ate on his right grinders only, and threw his head over his right shoulder as he snapped the meat. When he had finished, it struck him that he had been behaving strangely, for he said apologetically, "I don't think I ever felt so hungry in my life. I've bolted like an ostrich."

After breakfast Strickland said to me, "Don't go. Stay here, and stay for the night."

Seeing that my house was not three miles from Strickland's, this request was absurd. But Strickland insisted, and was going to say something when Fleete interrupted by declaring in a shame-faced way that he felt hungry again. Strickland sent a man to my house to fetch over my bedding and a horse, and we three went down to Strickland's stables to pass the hours until it was time to go out for a ride. The man who has a weakness for horses never wearies of inspecting them; and when two men are killing time in this way they gather knowledge and lies the one from the other.

There were five horses in the stables, and I shall never

forget the scene as we tried to look them over. They seemed to have gone mad. They reared and screamed and nearly tore up their pickets; they sweated and shivered and lathered and were distraught with fear. Strickland's horses used to know him as well as his dogs; which made the matter more curious. We left the stable for fear of the brutes throwing themselves in their panic. Then Strickland turned back and called me. The horses were still frightened, but they let us "gentle" and make much of them, and put their heads in our bosoms.

"They aren't afraid of *us*," said Strickland. "D'you know, I'd give three months' pay if Outrage here could talk."

But Outrage was dumb, and could only cuddle up to his master and blow out his nostrils, as is the custom of horses when they wish to explain things but can't. Fleete came up when we were in the stalls, and as soon as the horses saw him their fright broke out afresh. It was all that we could do to escape from the place unkicked. Strickland said, "They don't seem to love you, Fleete."

"Nonsense," said Fleete; "my mare will follow me like a dog." He went to her; she was in a loose-box; but as he slipped the bars she plunged, knocked him down, and broke away into the garden. I laughed, but Strickland was not amused. He took his moustache in both fists and pulled at it till it nearly came out. Fleete, instead of going off to chase his property, yawned, saying that he felt sleepy. He went to the house to lie down, which was a foolish way of spending New Year's Day.

Strickland sat with me in the stables and asked if I had noticed anything peculiar in Fleete's manner. I said that he ate his food like a beast; but that this might have been the result of living alone in the hills out of the reach of society as refined and elevating as ours, for instance. Strickland was not amused. I do not think that he listened to me, for his next sentence referred to the mark on Fleete's breast, and I said that it might have been caused by blister-flies, or that it was possibly a birth-mark newly born and now visible for the first time. We both agreed that it was unpleasant to look at, and Strickland found occasion to say that I was a fool.

"I can't tell you what I think now," said he, "because you would call me a madman; but you must stay with me for the next few days, if you can. I want you to watch Fleete, but don't tell me what you think till I have made up my mind."

"But I am dining out to-night," I said.

"So am I," said Strickland, "and so is Fleete. At least if he doesn't change his mind."

We walked about the garden smoking, but saying nothing—because we were friends, and talking spoils good tobacco—till our pipes were out. Then we went to wake up Fleete. He was wide awake and fidgeting about his room.

"I say, I want some more chops," he said. "Can I get them?"

We laughed and said, "Go and change. The ponies will be round in a minute."

"All right," said Fleete. "I'll go when I get the chops—underdone ones, mind."

He seemed to be quite in earnest. It was four o'clock, and we had had breakfast at one; still, for a long time, he demanded those underdone chops. Then he changed into riding clothes and went out into the verandah. His pony—the mare had not been caught—would not let him come near. All three horses were unmanageable—mad with fear—and finally Fleete said that he would stay at home and get something to eat. Strickland and I rode out wondering. As we passed the temple of Hanuman, the Silver Man came out and mewed at us.

"He is not one of the regular priests of the temple," said Strickland. "I think I should peculiarly like to lay my hands on him."

There was no spring in our gallop on the racecourse that evening. The horses were stale, and moved as though they had been ridden out.

"The fright after breakfast has been too much for them," said Strickland.

That was the only remark he made through the remainder of the ride. Once or twice I think he swore to himself; but that did not count.

We came back in the dark at seven o'clock, and saw that there were no lights in the bungalow. "Careless ruffians my servants are!" said Strickland.

My horse reared at something on the carriage-drive, and Fleete stood up under its nose.

"What are you doing, grovelling about the garden?" said Strickland.

But both horses bolted and nearly threw us. We dismounted by the stables and returned to Fleete, who was on his hands and knees under the orange-bushes.

"What the devil's wrong with you?" said Strickland.

"Nothing, nothing in the world," said Fleete, speaking very quickly and thickly. "I've been gardening—botanising, you know. The smell of the earth is delightful. I think I'm going for a walk—a long walk—all night."

Then I saw that there was something excessively out of order somewhere, and I said to Strickland, "I am not dining out."

"Bless you!" said Strickland. "Here, Fleete, get up. You'll catch fever there. Come in to dinner and let's have the lamps lit. We'll all dine at home."

Fleete stood up unwillingly, and said, "No lamps—no lamps. It's much nicer here. Let's dine outside and have some more chops—lots of 'em and underdone—bloody ones with gristle."

Now a December evening in Northern India is bitterly cold, and Fleete's suggestion was that of a maniac.

"Come in," said Strickland sternly. "Come in at once."

Fleete came, and when the lamps were brought, we saw that he was literally plastered with dirt from head to foot. He must have been rolling in the garden. He shrank from the light and went to his room. His eyes were horrible to look at. There was a green light behind them, not in them, if you understand, and the man's lower lip hung down.

Strickland said, "There is going to be trouble—big trouble—to-night. Don't you change your riding-things."

We waited and waited for Fleete's reappearance, and ordered dinner in the meantime. We could hear him moving about his own room, but there was no light there. Presently from the room came the long-drawn howl of a wolf.

People write and talk lightly of blood running cold and hair standing up and things of that kind. Both sensations are too horrible to be trifled with. My heart stopped as though a knife had been driven through it, and Strickland turned as white as the tablecloth.

The howl was repeated, and was answered by another howl far across the fields.

That set the gilded roof on the horror. Strickland dashed into Fleete's room. I followed, and we saw Fleete getting out of the window. He made beast-noises in the back of his throat. He could not answer us when we shouted at him. He spat.

I don't quite remember what followed, but I think that Strickland must have stunned him with the long boot-jack or else I should never have been able to sit on his chest. Fleete could not speak, he could only snarl, and his snarls were those of a wolf, not of a man. The human spirit must have been giving way all day and have died out with the twilight. We were dealing with a beast that had once been Fleete.

The affair was beyond any human and rational experience. I tried to say "Hydrophobia," but the word wouldn't come, because I knew that I was lying.

We bound this beast with leather thongs of the punkah-rope, and tied its thumbs and big toes together, and gagged it with a shoe-horn, which makes a very efficient gag if you know how to arrange it. Then we carried it into the dining-room, and sent a man to Dumoise, the doctor, telling him to come over at once. After we had despatched the messenger and were drawing breath, Strickland said, "It's no good. This isn't any doctor's work." I, also, knew that he spoke the truth.

The beast's head was free, and it threw it about from side to side. Any one entering the room would have believed that we were curing a wolf's pelt. That was the most loathsome accessory of all.

Strickland sat with his chin in the heel of his fist, watching the beast as it wriggled on the ground, but saying nothing. The shirt had been torn open in the scuffle and showed the black rosette mark on the left breast. It stood out like a blister.

In the silence of the watching we heard something without mewing like a she-otter. We both rose to our feet, and, I answer for myself, not Strickland, felt sick—actually and physically sick. We told each other, as did the men in "Pinafore," that it was the cat.

Dumoise arrived, and I never saw a little man so unprofessionally shocked. He said that it was a heart-rending case of hydrophobia, and that nothing could be done. At least any palliative measures would only prolong the agony. The beast was foaming at the mouth. Fleete, as we told Dumoise, had been bitten by dogs once or twice. Any man who keeps half a dozen terriers must expect a nip now and again. Dumoise could offer no help. He could only certify that Fleete was dying of hydrophobia. The beast was then howling, for it had managed to spit out the shoe-horn. Dumoise said that he would be ready to certify to the cause of death, and that the end was certain. He was a good little man, and he offered to remain with us; but Strickland refused the kindness. He did not wish to poison Dumoise's New Year. He would only ask him not to give the real cause of Fleete's death to the public.

So Dumoise left, deeply agitated; and as soon as the noise of the cart-wheels had died away, Strickland told me, in a whisper, his suspicions. They were so wildly improbable that he dared not say them out aloud; and I, who entertained all Strickland's beliefs, was so ashamed of owning to them that I pretended to disbelieve.

"Even if the Silver Man had bewitched Fleete for polluting the image of Hanuman, the punishment could not have fallen so quickly."

As I was whispering this the cry outside the house rose again, and the beast fell into a fresh paroxysm of struggling till we were afraid that the thongs that held it would give way.

"Watch!" said Strickland. "If this happens six times I shall take the law into my own hands. I order you to help me."

He went into his room and came out in a few minutes with the barrels of an old shot-gun, a piece of fishing-line, some thick cord, and his heavy wooden bedstead. I reported that the convulsions had followed the cry by two seconds in each case, and the beast seemed perceptibly weaker.

Strickland muttered, "But he can't take away the life! He can't take away the life!"

I said, though I knew that I was arguing against myself, "It may be a cat. It must be a cat. If the Silver Man is responsible, why does he dare to come here?"

Strickland arranged the wood on the hearth, put the gun-barrels into the glow of the fire, spread the twine on the table, and broke a walking-stick in two. There was one yard of fishing-line, gut, lapped with wire, such as is used for *mahseer*-fishing, and he tied the two ends together in a loop.

Then he said, "How can we catch him? He must be taken alive and unhurt."

I said that we must trust in Providence, and go out softly with polo-sticks into the shrubbery at the front of the house. The man or animal that made the cry was evidently moving round the house as regularly as a nightwatchman. We could wait in the bushes till he came by, and knock him over.

Strickland accepted this suggestion, and we slipped out from a bath-room window into the front verandah and then across the carriage-drive into the bushes.

In the moonlight we could see the leper coming round the corner of the house. He was perfectly naked, and from time to time he mewed and stopped to dance with his shadow. It was an unattractive sight, and thinking of poor Fleete, brought to such degradation by so foul a creature, I put away all my doubts and resolved to help Strickland from the heated gun-barrels to the loop of twine—from the loins to the head and back again—with all tortures that might be needful.

The leper halted in the front porch for a moment and we jumped out on him with the sticks. He was wonderfully strong, and we were afraid that he might escape or be fatally injured before we caught him. We had an idea that lepers were frail creatures, but this proved to be incorrect. Strickland knocked his legs from under him, and I put my foot on his neck. He mewed hideously, and even through my riding-boots I could feel that his flesh was not the flesh of a clean man.

He struck at us with his hand and feet-stumps. We looped the lash of a dog-whip round him, under the arm-pits, and dragged him backwards into the hall and so into the dining-room where the beast lay. There we tied him with trunk-straps. He made no attempt to escape, but mewed.

When we confronted him with the beast the scene was beyond description. The beast doubled backwards into a bow, as though he had been poisoned with strychnine, and moaned in the most pitiable fashion. Several other things happened also, but they cannot be put down here.

"I think I was right," said Strickland. "Now we will ask him to cure this case."

But the leper only mewed. Strickland wrapped a towel round his hand and took the gun-barrels out of the fire. I put the half of the broken walking-stick through a loop of fishing-line and buckled the leper comfortably to Strickland's bedstead. I understood then how men and women and little children can endure to see a witch burnt alive; for the beast was moaning on the floor, and though the Silver Man had no face, you could see horrible feelings passing through the slab that took its place, exactly as waves of heat play across red-hot iron—gun-barrels for instance.

Strickland shaded his eyes with his hands for a moment, and we got to work. This part is not to be printed.

The dawn was beginning to break when the leper spoke. His mewings had not been satisfactory up to that point. The beast had fainted from exhaustion, and the house was very still. We unstrapped the leper and told him to take away the evil spirit. He crawled to the beast and laid his hand upon the left breast. That was all. Then he fell face down and whined, drawing in his breath as he did so.

We watched the face of the beast, and saw the soul of Fleete coming back into the eyes. Then a sweat broke out on the forehead, and the eyes—they were human eyes—closed. We waited for an hour, but Fleete still slept. We carried him to his room and bade the leper go, giving him the bedstead, and the sheet on the bedstead to cover his nakedness, the gloves and the towels with which we had touched him, and the whip that had been hooked round his body. He put the sheet about him and went out into the early morning without speaking or mewing.

Strickland wiped his face and sat down. A night-gong, far away in the city, made seven o'clock.

"Exactly four-and-twenty hours!" said Strickland. "And I've done enough to ensure my dismissal from the service, besides permanent quarters in a lunatic asylum. Do you believe that we are awake?"

The red-hot gun-barrel had fallen on the floor and was singeing the carpet. The smell was entirely real.

That morning at eleven we two together went to wake up Fleete. We looked and saw that the black leopard-rosette on his chest had disappeared. He was very drowsy and tired, but as soon as he saw us, he said, "Oh! Confound you fellows. Happy New Year to you. Never mix your liquors. I'm nearly dead."

"Thanks for your kindness, but you're over time," said Strickland. "To-day is the morning of the second. You've slept the clock round with a vengeance."

The door opened, and little Dumoise put his head in. He had come on foot, and fancied that we were laying out Fleete.

"I've brought a nurse," said Dumoise. "I suppose that she can come in for . . . what is necessary."

"By all means," said Fleete cheerily, sitting up in bed. "Bring on your nurses."

Dumoise was dumb. Strickland led him out and explained that there must have been a mistake in the diagnosis. Dumoise remained dumb and left the house hastily. He considered that his professional reputation had been injured, and was inclined to make a personal matter of the recovery. Strickland went out too. When he came back, he said that he had been to call on the temple of Hanuman to offer redress for the pollution of the god, and had been solemnly assured that no white man had ever touched the idol, and that he was an incarnation of all the virtues laboring under a delusion. "What do you think?" said Strickland.

I said, "There are more things . . ."

Fritz Leiber

(1910–92)

Son of two well-known Shakespearean actors, Fritz Reuter Leiber was born in Chicago. A graduate of the University of Chicago, he worked as an editor, drama teacher, and stage and film actor, appearing in *Camille* (1937), *The Great Garrick* (1937), and *The Hunchback of Notre Dame* (1939). An early work, "Two Sought Adventure" (1939), introduced two popular characters, Fahfrd and the Gray Mouser, to whom he would return for more than fifty years. His novel *Conjure Wife* (1943) was filmed as *Weird Woman* in 1944, as *Burn, Witch, Burn!* in 1962, and as *Witches' Brew* in 1980. "The Girl with the Hungry Eyes" was the basis of a 1995 film. Best known as a writer of horror fiction, he published fantasy, science fiction, and sword-and-sorcery works. Celebrated as a prolific and influential author, Leiber received the Bram Stoker Life Achievement Award, the World Fantasy Convention's Grandmaster Award, and numerous Nebula and Hugo awards. Among his novels are *Gather Darkness* (1943 and 1950), *The Big Time* (1958), *The Wanderer* (1964), and *Our Lady of Darkness* (1977). His stories are collected in *Night's Black Agents* (1947), *The Girl with the Hungry Eyes and Other Stories* (1949), *The World of Fritz Leiber* (1976), *The Ghost Light* (1984), and *The Leiber Chronicles* (1990).

The Girl with the Hungry Eyes

(1949)

All right, I'll tell you why the Girl gives me the creeps. Why I can't stand to go downtown and see the mob slavering up at her on the tower, with that pop bottle or pack of cigarettes or whatever it is beside her. Why I hate to look at magazines anymore because I know she'll turn up somewhere in a brassière or a bubble bath. Why I don't like to think of millions of Americans drinking in that poisonous half-smile. It's quite a story—more story than you're expecting.

No, I haven't suddenly developed any long-haired indignation at the evils of advertising and the national glamor-girl complex. That'd be a laugh for a man in my racket, wouldn't it? Though I think you'll agree there's something a little perverted about trying to capitalize on sex that way. But it's okay with me. And I know we've had the Face and the Body and the Look and what not else, so why shouldn't someone come along who sums it all up so completely, that we have to call her the Girl and blazon her on all the billboards from Times Square to Telegraph Hill?

But the Girl isn't like any of the others. She's unnatural. She's morbid. She's unholy.

Oh, these are modern times, you say, and the sort of thing I'm hinting at went out with witchcraft. But you see I'm not altogether sure myself what I'm hinting at, beyond a certain point. There are vampires and vampires, and not all of them suck blood.

And there were the murders, if they were murders. Besides, let me ask you this. Why, when America is obsessed with the Girl, don't we find out more about her? Why doesn't she rate a *Time* cover with a droll biography inside? Why hasn't there been a feature in *Life* or the *Post?* A profile in *The New Yorker?* Why hasn't *Charm* or *Mademoiselle* done her career saga? Not ready for it? Nuts!

Why haven't the movies snapped her up? Why hasn't she been on "Information, Please"? Why don't we see her kissing candidates at political rallies? Why isn't she chosen queen of some sort of junk or other at a convention?

Why don't we read about her tastes and hobbies, her views of the Russian situation? Why haven't the columnists interviewed her in a kimono on the top floor of the tallest hotel in Manhattan and told us who her boyfriends are?

Finally—and this is the real killer—why hasn't she ever been drawn or painted?

Oh no she hasn't. If you knew anything about commercial art, you'd know that. Every blessed one of those pictures was worked up from a photograph. Expertly? Of course. They've got the top artists on it. But that's how it's done.

And now I'll tell you the why of all that. It's because from the top to the bottom of the whole world of advertising, news, and business, there isn't a solitary soul who knows where the Girl came from, where she lives, what she does, who she is, even what her name is.

You heard me. What's more, not a single solitary soul ever sees her—except one poor damned photographer, who's making more money off her than he ever hoped to in his life and who's scared and miserable as hell every minute of the day.

No, I haven't the faintest idea who he is or where he has his studio. But I know there has to be such a man and I'm morally certain he feels just like I said.

Yes, I might be able to find her, if I tried. I'm not sure though—by now she probably has other safeguards. Besides, I don't want to.

Oh, I'm off my rocker, am I? That sort of thing can't happen in the Era of the Atom? People can't keep out of sight that way, not even Garbo?

Well, I happen to know they can, because last year I was that poor damned photographer I was telling you about. Yes, last year, when the Girl made her first poisonous splash right here in this big little city of ours.

Yes, I know you weren't here last year and you don't know about it. Even the Girl had to start small. But if you hunted through the files of the local newspapers, you'd find some ads, and I might be able to locate you some of the old displays—I think Lovelybelt is still using one of them. I used to have a mountain of photos myself, until I burned them.

Yes, I made my cut off her. Nothing like what that other photographer must be making, but enough so it still bought this whiskey. She was funny about money. I'll tell you about that.

But first picture me then. I had a fourth-floor studio in that rathole the Hauser Building, not far from Ardleigh Park.

I'd been working at the Marsh-Mason studios until I'd gotten my bellyful of it and decided to start in for myself.

The Hauser Building was awful—I'll never forget how the stairs creaked—but it was cheap and there was a skylight.

Business was lousy. I kept making the rounds of all the advertisers and agencies, and some of them didn't object to me too much personally, but my stuff never clicked. I was pretty near broke. I was behind on my rent. Hell, I didn't even have enough money to have a girl.

It was one of those dark gray afternoons. The building was very quiet—I'd just finished developing some pix I was doing on speculation for Lovelybelt Girdles and Budford's Pool and Playground. My model had left. A Miss Leon. She was a civics teacher at one of the high schools and modeled for me on the side, just lately on speculation, too. After one look at the prints, I decided that Miss Leon probably wasn't just what Lovelybelt was looking for—or my photography either. I was about to call it a day.

And then the street door slammed four storys down and there were steps on the stairs and she came in.

She was wearing a cheap, shiny black dress. Black pumps. No stockings. And except that she had a gray cloth coat over one of them, those skinny arms of hers were bare. Her arms are pretty skinny, you know, or can't you see things like that any more?

And then the thin neck, the slightly gaunt, almost prim face, the tumbling mass of dark hair, and looking out from under it the hungriest eyes in the world.

That's the real reason she's plastered all over the country today, you know—those eyes. Nothing vulgar, but just the same they're looking at you with a hunger that's all sex and something more than sex. That's what everybody's been looking for since the Year One—something a little more than sex.

Well, boys, there I was, alone with the Girl, in an office that was getting shadowy, in a nearly empty building. A situation that a million male Americans have undoubtedly pictured to themselves with various lush details. How was I feeling? Scared.

I know sex can be frightening. That cold heart-thumping when you're alone with a girl and feel you're going to touch her. But if it was sex this time, it was overlaid with something else.

At least I wasn't thinking about sex.

I remember that I took a backward step and that my hand jerked so that the photos I was looking at sailed to the floor.

There was the faintest dizzy feeling like something was being drawn out of me. Just a little bit.

That was all. Then she opened her mouth and everything was back to normal for a while.

"I see you're a photographer, mister," she said. "Could you use a model?"

Her voice wasn't very cultivated.

"I doubt it," I told her, picking up the pix. You see, I wasn't impressed. The commercial possibilities of her eyes hadn't registered on me yet, by a long shot. "What have you done?"

Well, she gave me a vague sort of story and I began to check her knowledge of model agencies and studios and rates and what not and pretty soon I said to her, "Look here, you never modeled for a photographer in your life. You just walked in here cold."

Well, she admitted that was more or less so.

All along through our talk I got the idea she was feeling her way, like someone in a strange place. Not that she was uncertain of herself, or of me, but just of the general situation.

"And you think anyone can model?" I asked her pityingly.

"Sure," she said.

"Look," I said, "a photographer can waste a dozen negatives trying to get one halfway human photo of an average woman. How many do you think he'd have to waste before he got a real catchy, glamorous photo of her?"

"I think I could do it," she said.

Well, I should have kicked her out right then. Maybe I admired the cool way she stuck to her dumb little guns. Maybe I was touched by her underfed look. More likely I was feeling mean on account of the way my pictures had been snubbed by everybody and I wanted to take it out on her by showing her up.

"Okay, I'm going to put you on the spot," I told her. "I'm going to try a couple of shots of you. Understand it's strictly on spec. If somebody should ever want to use a photo of you, which is about one chance in two million, I'll pay you regular rates for your time. Not otherwise."

She gave me a smile. The first. "That's swell by me," she said.

Well, I took three or four shots, close-ups of her face since I didn't fancy her cheap dress, and at least she stood up to my sarcasm. Then I remembered I still had the Lovely-belt stuff and I guess the meanness was still working in me because I handed her a girdle and told her to go behind the screen and get into it and she did, without getting flustered as I'd expected, and since we'd gone that far, I figured we might as well shoot the beach scene to round it out, and that was that.

All this time I wasn't feeling anything particular one way or the other, except every once in a while I'd get one of those faint dizzy flashes and wonder if there was something wrong with my stomach or if I could have been a bit careless with my chemicals.

Still, you know, I think the uneasiness was in me all the while.

I tossed her a card and pencil. "Write your name and address and phone," I told her and made for the darkroom.

A little later she walked out. I didn't call any good-byes. I was irked because she hadn't fussed around or seemed anxious about her poses, or even thanked me, except for that one smile.

I finished developing the negatives, made some prints, glanced at them, decided they weren't a great deal worse than Miss Leon. On an impulse I slipped them in with the pictures I was going to take on the rounds next morning.

By now I'd worked long enough, so I was a bit fagged and nervous, but I didn't dare waste enough money on liquor to help that. I wasn't very hungry. I think I went to a cheap movie.

I didn't think of the Girl at all, except maybe to wonder faintly why in my present womanless state I hadn't made a pass at her. She had seemed to belong to a—well, distinctly more approachable social strata than Miss Leon. But then, of course, there were all sorts of arguable reasons for my not doing that.

Next morning I made the rounds. My first stop was Munsch's Brewery. They were looking for a "Munsch Girl." Papa Munsch had a sort of affection for me, though he razzed my photography. He had a good natural judgment about that, too. Fifty years ago he might have been one of the shoestring boys who made Hollywood.

Right now he was out in the plant, pursuing his favorite occupation. He put down the beaded schooner, smacked his lips, gabbled something technical to someone about hops, wiped his fat hands on the big apron he was wearing, and grabbed my thin stack of pictures.

He was about halfway through, making noises with his tongue and teeth, when he came to her. I kicked myself for even having stuck her in.

"That's her," he said. "The photography's not so hot, but that's the girl."

It was all decided. I wonder now why Papa Munsch sensed what the Girl had right away, while I didn't. I think it was because I saw her first in the flesh, if that's the right word.

At the time I just felt faint.

"Who is she?" he asked.

"One of my new models." I tried to make it casual.

"Bring her out tomorrow morning," he told me. "And your stuff. We'll photograph her here.

"Here, don't look so sick," he added. "Have some beer."

Well, I went away telling myself it was just a fluke, so that she'd probably blow it tomorrow with her inexperience, and so on.

Just the same, when I reverently laid my next stack of pictures on Mr. Fitch, of Lovelybelt's, rose-colored blotter, I had hers on top.

Mr. Fitch went through the motions of being an art critic. He leaned over backward, squinted his eyes, waved his long fingers, and said, "Hmm. What do you think, Miss Willow? Here, in this light, of course, the photograph doesn't show the bias cut. And perhaps we should use the Lovelybelt Imp instead of the Angel. Still, the girl. . . . Come over here, Binns." More finger-waving. "I want a married man's reaction."

He couldn't hide the fact that he was hooked.

Exactly the same thing happened at Budford's Pool and Playground, except that Da Costa didn't need a married man's say-so.

"Hot stuff," he said, sucking his lips. "Oh boy, you photographers!"

I hotfooted it back to the office and grabbed up the card I'd given her to put down her name and address.

It was blank.

I don't mind telling you that the next five days were about the worst I ever went through, in an ordinary way. When next morning rolled around and I still hadn't got hold of her, I had to start stalling.

"She's sick," I told Papa Munsch over the phone.

"She at a hospital?" he asked me.

"Nothing that serious," I told him.

"Get her out here then. What's a little headache?"

"Sorry, I can't."

Papa Munsch got suspicious. "You really got this girl?"

"Of course I have."

"Well, I don't know, I'd think it was some New York model, except I recognized your lousy photography."

I laughed.

"Well, look, you get her here tomorrow morning, you hear?"

"I'll try."

"Try nothing. You get her out here."

He didn't know half of what I tried. I went around to all the model and employment agencies. I did some slick detective work at the photographic and art studios. I used up some of my last dimes putting advertisements in all three papers. I looked at high school yearbooks and at employee photos in local house organs. I went to restaurants and drugstores, looking at waitresses, and to dime stores and department stores, looking at clerks. I watched the crowds coming out of movie theaters. I roamed the streets.

Evenings, I spent quite a bit of time along Pickup Row. Somehow that seemed the right place.

The fifth afternoon I knew I was licked. Papa Munsch's deadline—he'd given me several, but this was it—was due to run out at six o'clock. Mr. Fitch had already canceled.

I was at the studio window, looking out at Ardleigh Park.

She walked in.

I'd gone over this moment so often in my mind that I had no trouble putting on my act. Even the faint dizzy feeling didn't throw me off.

"Hello," I said, hardly looking at her.

"Hello," she said.

"Not discouraged yet?"

"No." It didn't sound uneasy or defiant. It was just a statement.

I snapped a look at my watch, got up and said curtly, "Look here, I'm going to give you a chance. There's a client of mine looking for a girl your general type. If you do a real good job you might break into the modeling business.

"We can see him this afternoon if we hurry," I said. I picked up my stuff. "Come on. And next time if you expect favors, don't forget to leave your phone number."

"Uh-uh," she said, not moving.

"What do you mean?" I said.

"I'm not going out to see any client of yours."

"The hell you aren't," I said. "You little nut, I'm giving you a break."

She shook her head slowly. "You're not fooling me, baby. You're not fooling me at all. They want me." And she gave me the second smile.

At the time I thought she must have seen my newspaper ad. Now I'm not so sure.

"And now I'll tell you how we're going to work," she went on. "You aren't going to have my name or address or phone number. Nobody is. And we're going to do all the pictures right here. Just you and me."

You can imagine the roar I raised at that. I was everything—angry, sarcastic, patiently explanatory, off my nut, threatening, pleading.

I would have slapped her face off, except it was photographic capital.

In the end all I could do was phone Papa Munsch and tell him her conditions. I knew I didn't have a chance, but I had to take it.

He gave me a really angry bawling out, said "no" several times and hung up.

It didn't worry her. "We'll start shooting at ten o'clock tomorrow," she said.

It was just like her, using that corny line from the movie magazines.

About midnight Papa Munsch called me up.

"I don't know what insane asylum you're renting this girl

from," he said, "but I'll take her. Come around tomorrow morning and I'll try to get it through your head just how I want the pictures. And I'm glad I got you out of bed!"

After that it was a breeze. Even Mr. Fitch reconsidered and, after taking two days to tell me it was quite impossible, he accepted the conditions too.

Of course you're all under the spell of the Girl, so you can't understand how much self-sacrifice it represented on Mr. Fitch's part when he agreed to forego supervising the photography of my model in the Lovelybelt Imp or Vixen or whatever it was we finally used.

Next morning she turned up on time according to her schedule, and we went to work. I'll say one thing for her, she never got tired and she never kicked at the way I fussed over shots. I got along okay, except I still had that feeling of something being shoved away gently. Maybe you've felt it just a little, looking at her picture.

When we finished I found out there were still more rules. It was about the middle of the afternoon. I started with her to get a sandwich and coffee.

"Uh-uh," she said, "I'm going down alone. And look, baby, if you ever try to follow me, if you ever so much as stick your head out of that window when I go, you can hire yourself another model."

You can imagine how all this crazy stuff strained my temper—and my imagination. I remember opening the window after she was gone—I waited a few minutes first—and standing there getting some fresh air and trying to figure out what could be behind it, whether she was hiding from the police, or was somebody's ruined daughter, or maybe had got the idea it was smart to be temperamental, or more likely Papa Munsch was right and she was partly nuts.

But I had my pictures to finish up.

Looking back, it's amazing to think how fast her magic began to take hold of the city after that. Remembering what came after, I'm frightened of what's happening to the whole country—and maybe the world. Yesterday I read something in *Time* about the Girl's picture turning up on billboards in Egypt.

The rest of my story will help show you why I'm frightened in that big, general way. But I have a theory, too, that helps explain, though it's one of those things that's beyond that "certain point." It's about the Girl. I'll give it to you in a few words.

You know how modern advertising gets everybody's mind set in the same direction, wanting the same things, imagining the same things. And you know the psychologists aren't so skeptical of telepathy as they used to be.

Add up the two ideas. Suppose the identical desires of millions of people focussed on one telepathic person. Say a girl. Shaped her in their image.

Imagine her knowing the hiddenmost hungers of millions of men. Imagine her seeing deeper into those hungers than the people that had them, seeing the hatred and the wish for death behind the lust. Imagine her shaping herself in that complete image, keeping herself as aloof as marble. Yet imagine the hunger she might feel in answer to their hunger.

But that's getting a long way from the facts of my story. And some of those facts are darn solid. Like money. We made money.

That was the funny thing I was going to tell you. I was afraid the Girl was going to hold me up. She really had me over a barrel, you know.

But she didn't ask for anything but the regular rates. Later on I insisted on pushing more money at her, a whole lot. But she always took it with that same contemptuous look, as if she were going to toss it down the first drain when she got outside.

Maybe she did.

At any rate, I had money. For the first time in months I had money enough to get drunk, buy new clothes, take taxicabs. I could make a play for any girl I wanted to. I only had to pick.

And so of course I had to go and pick . . .

But first let me tell you about Papa Munsch.

Papa Munsch wasn't the first of the boys to try to meet my model but I think he was the first to really go soft on her. I could watch the change in his eyes as he looked at her pictures. They began to get sentimental, reverent. Mama Munsch had been dead for two years.

He was smart about the way he planned it. He got me to drop some information which told him when she came to work, and then one morning he came pounding up the stairs a few minutes before.

"I've got to see her, Dave," he told me.

I argued with him, I kidded him, I explained he didn't know just how serious she was about her crazy ideas. I even pointed out he was cutting both our throats. I even amazed myself by bawling him out.

He didn't take any of it in his usual way. He just kept repeating, "But, Dave, I've got to see her."

The street door slammed.

"That's her," I said, lowering my voice. "You've got to get out."

He wouldn't, so I shoved him in the darkroom. "And keep quiet," I whispered. "I'll tell her I can't work today."

I knew he'd try to look at her and probably come busting in, but there wasn't anything else I could do.

The footsteps came to the fourth floor. But she never showed at the door. I got uneasy.

"Get that bum out of there!" she yelled suddenly from beyond the door. Not very loud, but in her commonest voice.

"I'm going up to the next landing," she said. "And if that fat-bellied bum doesn't march straight down to the street, he'll never get another picture of me except spitting in his lousy beer."

Papa Munsch came out of the darkroom. He was white. He didn't look at me as he went out. He never looked at her pictures in front of me again.

That was Papa Munsch. Now it's me I'm telling about. I talked around the subject with her, I hinted, eventually I made my pass.

She lifted my hand off her as if it were a damp rag.

"No, baby," she said. "This is working time."

"But afterward . . ." I pressed.

"The rules still hold." And I got what I think was the fifth smile.

It's hard to believe, but she never budged an inch from that crazy line. I mustn't make a pass at her in the office, because our work was very important and she loved it and there mustn't be any distractions. And I couldn't see her anywhere else, because if I tried to, I'd never snap another picture of her—and all this with more money coming in all the time and me never so stupid as to think my photography had anything to do with it.

Of course I wouldn't have been human if I hadn't made more passes. But they always got the wet-rag treatment and there weren't any more smiles.

I changed. I went sort of crazy and light-headed—only sometimes I felt my head was going to burst. And I started to talk to her all the time. About myself.

It was like being in a constant delirium that never interfered with business. I didn't pay any attention to the dizzy feeling. It seemed natural.

I'd walk around and for a moment the reflector would look like a sheet of white-hot steel, or the shadows would seem like armies of moths, or the camera would be a big black coal car. But the next instant they'd come all right again.

I think sometimes I was scared to death of her. She'd seem the strangest, most horrible person in the world. But other times. . . .

And I talked. It didn't matter what I was doing—lighting her, posing her, fussing with props, snapping my pictures—or where she was—on the platform, behind the screen, relaxing with a magazine—I kept up a steady gab.

I told her everything I knew about myself. I told her about my first girl. I told her about my brother Bob's bicycle. I told her about running away on a freight, and the licking Pa gave me when I came home. I told her about shipping to South America and the blue sky at night. I told her about Betty. I told her about my mother dying of cancer. I told her about being beaten up in a fight in an alley behind a bar. I told her about Mildred. I told her about the first picture I ever sold. I told her how Chicago looked from a sailboat. I told her about the longest drunk I was ever on. I told her about Marsh-Mason. I told her about Gwen. I told her about how I met Papa Munsch. I told her about hunting her. I told her about how I felt now.

She never paid the slightest attention to what I said. I couldn't even tell if she heard me.

It was when we were getting our first nibble from national advertisers that I decided to follow her when she went home.

Wait, I can place it better than that. Something you'll remember from the out-of-town papers—those maybe murders I mentioned. I think there were six.

I say "maybe" because the police could never be sure they weren't heart attacks. But there's bound to be suspicion when attacks happen to people whose hearts have been okay, and always at night when they're alone and away from home and there's a question of what they were doing.

The six deaths created one of those "mystery poisoner" scares. And afterward there was a feeling that they hadn't really stopped, but were being continued in a less suspicious way.

That's one of the things that scares me now.

But at that time my only feeling was relief that I'd decided to follow her.

I made her work until dark one afternoon. I didn't need any excuses, we were snowed under with orders. I waited until the street door slammed; then I ran down. I was wearing rubber-soled shoes. I'd slipped on a dark coat she'd never seen me in, and a dark hat.

I stood in the doorway until I spotted her. She was walking by Ardleigh Park toward the heart of town. It was one of those warm fall nights. I followed her on the other side of the street. My idea for tonight was just to find out where she lived. That would give me a hold on her.

She stopped in front of a display window of Everley's department store, standing back from the flow. She stood there looking in.

I remembered we'd done a big photograph of her for Everley's, to make a flat model for a lingerie display. That was what she was looking at.

At the time it seemed all right to me that she should adore herself, if that was what she was doing.

When people passed she'd turn away a little or drift back farther into the shadows.

Then a man came by alone. I couldn't see his face very well, but he looked middle-aged. He stopped and stood looking in the window.

She came out of the shadows and stepped up beside him.

How would you boys feel if you were looking at a poster of the Girl and suddenly she was there beside you, her arm linked with yours?

This fellow's reaction showed plain as day. A crazy dream had come to life for him.

They talked for a moment. Then he waved a taxi to the curb. They got in and drove off.

I got drunk that night. It was almost as if she'd known I was following her and had picked that way to hurt me. Maybe she had. Maybe this was the finish.

But the next morning she turned up at the usual time and I was back in the delirium, only now with some new angles added.

That night when I followed her she picked a spot under a streetlight, opposite one of the Munsch Girl billboards.

Now it frightens me to think of her lurking that way.

After about twenty minutes a convertible slowed down going past her, backed up, swung into the curb.

I was closer this time. I got a good look at the fellow's face. He was a little younger, about my age.

Next morning the same face looked up at me from the front page of the paper. The convertible had been found parked on a side street. He had been in it. As in the other maybe-murders, the cause of death was uncertain.

All kinds of thoughts were spinning in my head that day, but there were only two things I knew for sure. That I'd got the first real offer from a national advertiser, and that I was going to take the Girl's arm and walk down the stairs with her when we quit work.

She didn't seem surprised. "You know what you're doing?" she said.

"I know."

She smiled. "I was wondering when you'd get around to it."

I began to feel good. I was kissing everything good-bye, but I had my arm around hers.

It was another of those warm fall evenings. We cut across into Ardleigh Park. It was dark there, but all around the sky was a sallow pink from the advertising signs.

We walked for a long time in the park. She didn't say anything and she didn't look at me, but I could see her lips twitching and after a while her hand tightened on my arm.

We stopped. We'd been walking across the grass. She dropped down and pulled me after her. She put her hands on my shoulders. I was looking down at her face. It was the faintest sallow pink from the glow in the sky. The hungry eyes were dark smudges.

I was fumbling with her blouse. She took my hand away, not like she had in the studio. "I don't want that," she said.

First I'll tell you what I did afterward. Then I'll tell you why I did it. Then I'll tell you what she said.

What I did was run away. I don't remember all of that because I was dizzy, and the pink sky was swinging against the dark trees. But after a while I staggered into the lights of the street. The next day I closed up the studio. The telephone was ringing when I locked the door and there were unopened letters on the floor. I never saw the Girl again in the flesh, if that's the right word.

I did it because I didn't want to die. I didn't want the life drawn out of me. There are vampires and vampires, and the ones that suck blood aren't the worst. If it hadn't been for the warning of those dizzy flashes, and Papa Munsch and the face in the morning paper, I'd have gone the way the others did. But I realized what I was up against while there was still time to tear myself away. I realized that wherever she came from, whatever shaped her, she's the quintessence of the horror behind the bright billboard. She's the smile that tricks you into throwing away your money and your life. She's the eyes that lead you on and on, and then show you death. She's the creature you give everything for and never really get. She's the being that takes everything you've got and gives nothing in return. When you yearn toward her face on the billboards, remember that. She's the lure. She's the bait. She's the Girl.

And this is what she said, "I want you. I want your high spots. I want everything that's made you happy and everything that's hurt you bad. I want your first girl. I want that shiny bicycle. I want that licking. I want that pinhole camera. I want Betty's legs. I want the blue sky filled with stars. I want your mother's death. I want your blood on the cobblestones. I want Mildred's mouth. I want the first picture you sold. I want the lights of Chicago. I want the gin. I want Gwen's hands. I want your wanting me. I want your life. Feed me, baby, feed me."

H. P. Lovecraft

(1890–1937)

Howard Phillips Lovecraft was born in Providence, Rhode Island. His father's hospitalization when Lovecraft was three years old and death when he was eight resulted in his being raised in the home of his maternal grandfather, where he lived with his mother and two aunts. He attended Hope High School in Providence, but never achieved his goal of becoming a qualified astronomer. Except for the several years of his marriage when he and his wife lived in New York, Lovecraft resided in Providence. In 1919, "Dagon," his first published story, appeared in *The Vagrant*. In 1923, he resold the same story to *Weird Tales*, a popular pulp magazine, bringing him to the attention of a somewhat wider audience. Primarily publishing his fiction in pulp magazines and a few anthologies, Lovecraft became an extraordinary influence on a number of writers after his death. His work was collected in two early volumes, *The Outsider and Others* (1939) and *Beyond the Wall of Sleep* (1939). More recent editions include *The Call of Cthulhu and Other Weird Stories* (1999), *The Thing on the Doorstep and Other Weird Stories* (2001), and *The Dreams in the Witch House and Other Weird Stories* (2005).

Cool Air

(1928)

You ask me to explain why I am afraid of a draught of cool air; why I shiver more than others upon entering a cold room, and seem nauseated and repelled when the chill of evening creeps through the heat of a mild autumn day. There are those who say I respond to cold as others do to a bad odour, and I am the last to deny the impression. What I will do is to relate the most horrible circumstance I ever encountered, and leave it to you to judge whether or not this forms a suitable explanation of my peculiarity.

It is a mistake to fancy that horror is associated inextricably with darkness, silence, and solitude. I found it in the glare of mid-afternoon, in the clangour of a metropolis, and in the teeming midst of a shabby and commonplace rooming-house with a prosaic landlady and two stalwart men by my side. In the spring of 1923 I had secured some dreary and unprofitable magazine work in the city of New York; and being unable to pay any substantial rent, began drifting from one cheap boarding establishment to another in search of a room which might combine the qualities of decent cleanliness, endurable furnishings, and very reasonable price. It soon developed that I had only a choice between different evils, but after a time I came upon a house in West Fourteenth Street which disgusted me much less than the others I had sampled.

The place was a four-story mansion of brownstone, dating apparently from the late forties, and fitted with woodwork and marble whose stained and sullied splendour argued a descent from high levels of tasteful opulence. In the rooms, large and lofty, and decorated with impossible paper and ridiculously ornate stucco cornices, there lingered a depressing mustiness and hint of obscure cookery; but the floors were clean, the linen tolerably regular, and the hot water not too often cold or turned off, so that I came to regard it as at least a bearable place to hibernate 'til one might really live again. The landlady, a slatternly, almost bearded Spanish woman named Herrero, did not annoy me with gossip or with criticisms of the late-burning electric light in my third floor front hall room; and my fellow-lodgers were as quiet and uncommunicative as one might desire, being mostly Spaniards a little above the coarsest and crudest grade. Only the din of street cars in the thoroughfare below proved a serious annoyance.

I had been there about three weeks when the first odd incident occurred. One evening at about eight I heard a spattering on the floor and became suddenly aware that I had been smelling the pungent odour of ammonia for some time. Looking about, I saw that the ceiling was wet and dripping; the soaking apparently proceeding from a corner on the side toward the street. Anxious to stop the matter at its source, I hastened to the basement to tell the landlady; and was assured by her that the trouble would quickly be set right.

"Doctair Muñoz," she cried as she rushed upstairs ahead of me, "he have speel hees chemicals. He ees too seeck for doctair heemself—seecker and seecker all the time—but he weel not have no othair for help. He ees vairy queer in hees seeckness—all day he take funnee-smelling baths, and he cannot get excite or warm. All hees own housework he do—hees leetle room are full of bottles and machines, and he do not work as doctair. But he was great once—my fathair in Barcelona have hear of heem—and only joost now he feex a arm of the plumber that get hurt of sudden. He nevair go out, only on roof, and my boy Esteban he breeng heem hees food and laundry and mediceens and chemicals. My God, the sal-ammoniac that man use for to keep heem cool!"

Mrs. Herrero disappeared up the staircase to the fourth floor, and I returned to my room. The ammonia ceased to drip, and as I cleaned up what had spilled and opened the window for air, I heard the landlady's heavy footsteps above me. Dr. Muñoz I had never heard, save for certain sounds as of some gasoline-driven mechanism; since his step was soft and gentle. I wondered for a moment what the strange affliction of this man might be, and whether his obstinate refusal of outside aid were not the result of a rather baseless eccentricity. There is, I reflected tritely, an infinite deal of pathos in the state of an eminent person who has come down in the world.

I might never have known Dr. Muñoz had it not been for the heart attack that suddenly seized me one forenoon as I sat writing in my room. Physicians had told me of the danger of those spells, and I knew there was no time to be lost; so remembering what the landlady had said about the invalid's help of the injured workman, I dragged myself upstairs and knocked feebly at the door above mine. My knock was answered in good English by a curious voice some distance to the right, asking my name and business; and these things being stated, there came an opening of the door next to the one I had sought.

A rush of cool air greeted me; and though the day was one of the hottest of late June, I shivered as I crossed the threshold into a large apartment whose rich and tasteful decoration surprised me in this nest of squalor and seediness. A folding couch now filled its diurnal role of sofa, and the mahogany furniture, sumptuous hangings, old paintings, and mellow bookshelves all bespoke a gentleman's study rather than a boarding-house bedroom. I now saw that the hall room above mine—the "leetle room" of bottles and machines which Mrs. Herrero had mentioned—was merely the laboratory of the doctor; and that his main living quarters lay in the spacious adjoining room whose convenient alcoves and large contiguous bathroom permitted him to hide all dressers and obtrusively utilitarian devices. Dr. Muñoz, most certainly, was a man of birth, cultivation, and discrimination.

The figure before me was short but exquisitely proportioned, and clad in somewhat formal dress of perfect cut and fit. A high-bred face of masterful though not arrogant expression was adorned by a short iron-grey full beard, and an old-fashioned pince-nez shielded the full, dark eyes and surmounted an aquiline nose which gave a Moorish touch to a physiognomy otherwise dominantly Celtiberian. Thick, well-trimmed hair that argued the punctual calls of a barber was parted gracefully above a high forehead; and the whole picture was one of striking intelligence and superior blood and breeding.

Nevertheless, as I saw Dr. Muñoz in that blast of cool air, I felt a repugnance which nothing in his aspect could justify. Only his lividly inclined complexion and coldness of touch could have afforded a physical basis for this feeling, and even these things should have been excusable considering the man's known invalidism. It might, too, have been the singular cold that alienated me; for such chilliness was abnormal on so hot a day, and the abnormal always excites aversion, distrust, and fear.

But repugnance was soon forgotten in admiration, for the strange physician's extreme skill at once became manifest despite the ice-coldness and shakiness of his bloodless-looking hands. He clearly understood my needs at a glance, and ministered to them with a master's deftness; the while reassuring me in a finely modulated though oddly hollow and timbreless voice that he was the bitterest of sworn enemies to death, and had sunk his fortune and lost all his friends in a lifetime of bizarre experiment devoted to its bafflement and extirpation. Something of the benevolent fanatic seemed to reside in him, and he rambled on almost garrulously as he sounded my chest and mixed a suitable draught of drugs fetched from the smaller laboratory room. Evidently he found the society of a well-born man a rare novelty in this dingy environment, and was moved to unaccustomed speech as memories of better days surged over him.

His voice, if queer, was at least soothing; and I could not even perceive that he breathed as the fluent sentences rolled urbanely out. He sought to distract my mind from my own seizure by speaking of his theories and experiments; and I remember his tactfully consoling me about my weak heart by insisting that will and consciousness are stronger than organic life itself, so that if a bodily frame be but originally healthy and carefully preserved, it may through a scientific enhancement of these qualities retain a kind of nervous animation despite the most serious impairments, defects, or even absences in the battery of specific organs. He might, he half jestingly said, some day teach me to live—or at least to possess some kind of conscious existence—without any heart at all! For his part, he was afflicted with a complication of maladies requiring a very exact regimen which included constant cold. Any marked rise in temperature might, if prolonged, affect him fatally; and the frigidity of his habitation—some fifty-five or fifty-six degrees Fahrenheit—was maintained by an absorption system of ammonia cooling, the gasoline engine of whose pumps I had often heard in my own room below.

Relieved of my seizure in a marvellously short while, I left the shivery place a disciple and devotee of the gifted recluse. After that I paid him frequent over-coated calls; listening while he told of secret researches and almost ghastly results, and trembling a bit when I examined the unconventional and astonishingly ancient volumes on his shelves. I was eventually, I may add, almost cured of my disease for all time by his skilful ministrations. It seems that he did not scorn the incantations of the mediaevalists, since he believed these cryptic formulae to contain rare psychological stimuli which might conceivably have singular effects on the substance of a nervous system from which organic pulsations had fled. I was touched by his account of the aged Dr. Torres of Valencia, who had shared his earlier experiments and nursed him through the great illness of eighteen years before, whence his present disorders proceeded. No sooner had the venerable practitioner saved his colleague than he himself succumbed to the grim enemy he had fought. Perhaps the strain had been too great; for Dr. Muñoz made it whisperingly clear—though not in detail—that the methods of healing had been most extraordinary, involving scenes and processes not welcomed by elderly and conservative Galens.

As the weeks passed, I observed with regret that my new friend was indeed slowly but unmistakably losing ground physically, as Mrs. Herrero had suggested. The livid aspect of his countenance was intensified, his voice became more hollow and indistinct, his muscular motions were less perfectly coordinated, and his mind and will displayed less resilience and initiative. Of this sad change he seemed by no means unaware, and little by little his expression and conversation both took on a gruesome irony which restored in me something of the subtle repulsion I had originally felt.

He developed strange caprices, acquiring a fondness for exotic spices and Egyptian incense 'til his room smelled like a vault of a sepulchred Pharaoh in the Valley of Kings. At the same time, his demands for cold air increased, and with my aid he amplified the ammonia piping of his room and modified the pumps and feed of his refrigerating machine 'til he could keep the temperature as low as thirty-four or forty degrees, and finally even twenty-eight degrees; the bathroom and laboratory, of course, being less chilled, in order that water might not freeze, and that chemical processes might not be impeded. The tenant adjoining him complained of the icy air from around the connecting door, so I helped him fit heavy hangings to obviate the difficulty. A kind of growing horror, of outré and morbid cast, seemed to possess him. He talked of death incessantly, but laughed hollowly when such things as burial or funeral arrangements were gently suggested.

All in all he became a disconcerting and even gruesome companion; yet in my gratitude for his healing I could not well abandon him to the strangers around him, and was careful to dust his room and attend to his needs each day, muffled in a heavy ulster which I bought especially for the purpose. I likewise did much of his shopping, and gasped in bafflement at some of the chemicals he ordered from druggists and laboratory supply houses.

An increasing and unexplained atmosphere of panic seemed to rise around his apartment. The whole house, as I have said, had a musty odour; but the smell in his room was worse, and in spite of all the spices and incense, and the pungent chemicals of the now incessant baths which he insisted on taking unaided, I perceived that it must be connected with his ailment, and shuddered when I reflected on what that ailment might be. Mrs. Herrero crossed herself when she looked at him, and gave him up unreservedly to me; not even letting her son Estcban continue to run errands for him. When I suggested other physicians, the sufferer would fly into as much of a rage as he seemed to dare to entertain. He evidently feared the physical effect of violent emotion, yet his will and driving force waxed rather than waned, and he refused to be confined to his bed. The lassitude of his earlier ill days gave place to a return of his fiery purpose, so that he seemed about to hurl defiance at the death-daemon even as that ancient enemy seized him. The pretence of eating, always curiously like a formality with him, he virtually abandoned; and mental power alone appeared to keep him from total collapse.

He acquired a habit of writing long documents of some sort, which he carefully sealed and filled with injunctions that I transmit them after his death to certain persons whom he named—for the most part lettered East Indians, but including a once celebrated French physician now generally thought dead, and about whom the most inconceivable things had been whispered. As it happened, I burned all these papers undelivered and unopened. His aspect and voice became utterly frightful, and his presence almost unbearable. One September day an unexpected glimpse of him induced an epileptic fit in a man who had come to repair his electric desk lamp; a fit for which he prescribed effectively whilst keeping himself well out of sight. That man, oddly enough, had been through the terrors of the Great War without having incurred any fright so thorough.

Then, in the middle of October, the horror of horrors

came with stupefying suddenness. One night about eleven the pump of the refrigerating machine broke down, so that within three hours the process of ammonia cooling became impossible. Dr. Muñoz summoned me by thumping on the floor, and I worked desperately to repair the injury while my host cursed in a tone whose lifeless, rattling hollowness surpassed description. My amateur efforts, however, proved of no use; and when I had brought in a mechanic from a neighbouring all-night garage, we learned that nothing could be done until morning, when a new piston would have to be obtained. The moribund hermit's rage and fear, swelling to grotesque proportions, seemed likely to shatter what remained of his failing physique; and once a spasm caused him to clap his hands to his eyes and rush into the bathroom. He groped his way out with face tightly bandaged, and I never saw his eyes again.

The frigidity of the apartment was now sensibly diminishing, and at about five in the morning, the doctor retired to the bathroom, commanding me to keep him supplied with all the ice I could obtain at all-night drug stores and cafeterias. As I would return from my sometimes discouraging trips and lay my spoils before the closed bathroom door, I could hear a restless splashing within, and a thick voice croaking out the order for "More—more!" At length a warm day broke, and the shops opened one by one. I asked Esteban either to help with the ice-fetching while I obtained the pump piston, or to order the piston while I continued with the ice; but instructed by his mother, he absolutely refused.

Finally I hired a seedy-looking loafer whom I encountered on the corner of Eighth Avenue to keep the patient supplied with ice from a little shop where I introduced him, and applied myself diligently to the task of finding a pump piston and engaging workmen competent to install it. The task seemed interminable, and I raged almost as violently as the hermit when I saw the hours slipping by in a breathless, foodless round of vain telephoning, and a hectic quest from place to place, hither and thither by subway and surface car. About noon I encountered a suitable supply house far downtown, and at approximately one-thirty that afternoon arrived at my boarding-place with the necessary paraphernalia and two sturdy and intelligent mechanics. I had done all I could, and hoped I was in time.

Black terror, however, had preceded me. The house was in utter turmoil, and above the chatter of awed voices I heard a man praying in a deep basso. Fiendish things were in the air, and lodgers told over the beads of their rosaries as they caught the odour from beneath the doctor's closed door. The lounger I had hired, it seems, had fled screaming and mad-eyed not long after his second delivery of ice: perhaps as a result of excessive curiosity. He could not, of course, have locked the door behind him; yet it was now fastened, presumably from the inside. There was no sound within save a nameless sort of slow, thick dripping.

Briefly consulting with Mrs. Herrero and the workmen despite a fear that gnawed my inmost soul, I advised the breaking down of the door; but the landlady found a way to turn the key from the outside with some wire device. We had previously opened the doors of all the other rooms on that hall, and flung all the windows to the very top. Now, noses protected by handkerchiefs, we tremblingly invaded the accursed south room which blazed with the warm sun of early afternoon.

A kind of dark, slimy trail led from the open bathroom door to the hall door, and thence to the desk, where a terrible little pool had accumulated. Something was scrawled there in pencil in an awful, blind hand on a piece of paper hideously smeared as though by the very claws that traced the hurried last words. Then the trail led to the couch and ended unutterably.

What was, or had been, on the couch I cannot and dare not say here. But this is what I shiveringly puzzled out on the stickily smeared paper before I drew a match and burned it to a crisp; what I puzzled out in terror as the landlady and two mechanics rushed frantically from that hellish place to babble their incoherent stories at the nearest police station. The nauseous words seemed well-nigh incredible in that yellow sunlight, with the clatter of cars and motor trucks ascending clamorously from crowded Fourteenth Street, yet I confess that I believed them then. Whether I believe them now I honestly do not know. There are things about which it is better not to speculate, and all that I can say is that I hate the smell of ammonia, and grow faint at a draught of unusually cool air.

"The end," ran that noisome scrawl, "is here. No more ice—the man looked and ran away. Warmer every minute, and the tissues can't last. I fancy you know—what I said about the will and the nerves and the preserved body after the organs ceased to work. It was good theory, but couldn't keep up indefinitely. There was a gradual deterioration I had not foreseen. Dr. Torres knew, but the shock killed him. He couldn't stand what he had to do; he had to get me in a strange, dark place when he minded my letter and nursed me back. And the organs never would work again. It had to be done my way—artificial preservation—*for you see I died that time eighteen years ago.*"

Yvonne Navarro

(1957–)

Born in Chicago, Yvonne Navarro worked at a wide range of jobs including secretary, bookkeeper, cashier, nurse's aide, and accounting clerk before selling her first short story to *The Horror Show Magazine* in 1984. In 1999, she decided to leave her job at a law firm to become a full-time writer, and in 2002, she moved to Arizona, where she now lives. Her first and second novels, *AfterAge* (1993) and *deadrush* (1995), were finalists for the Bram Stoker Award. Among her *Buffy the Vampire Slayer* novels are *Paleo* (2000), *Wicked Willow I: The Darkening* (2004), *Wicked Willow II: Shattered Twilight* (2004), and *Wicked Willow III: Broken Sunrise* (2004). Her other novels include *Final Impact* (1997) and a follow-up novel, *Redshadow* (1998), *That's Not My Name* (2000), *Mirror Me* (2004), and *Highborn* (2010).

For the Good of All

(2009)

Fida can hear their moans through the floor.

The boarders are restless and hungry—they're always hungry—but there isn't much she can do about that.

Broxton House doesn't do bed and breakfast anymore, doesn't even rent to new boarders. Hell, nobody needs to rent now that a good seventy percent of the city population is gone. If a person wants to move, they move; all you need to do is make sure the new place is empty of both the living and the dead.

The law now says that if you live in it, you own it, period.

Squatting is okay, taking it by force isn't. People work jobs just like before, but they make less money, and there's a clear division in classes.

Fida's in the lower class, and that's fine with her. She grows most of her own food and has learned to live without the electricity she can't afford anyway. There's a weekly flea market in the parking lot of the abandoned high school two suburbs over, nice and safe within a secure eight-foot iron fence. Someone with a sense of humor dubbed it the "Lock 'n' Swap" and the name stuck.

Fida goes over and does small sewing jobs. She picked up the talent from her grandmother (who died decades before this zombie mess), and it earns her money for firewood in the winter, candles, enough gasoline to go to a different church each Sunday, and the few other things she can't make on her own.

Fida is ready when the priest knocks on her door at a quarter-to-twelve, even though he's fifteen minutes early. She's glad he didn't forget or decide not to come, because when that happens—and it does occasionally—it always shakes up her faith. Faith is all she has, and she mustn't let it waver. Too much depends upon it.

"Good afternoon, Miss . . ." He falters for a moment because she never told him her last name.

"Just call me Fida," she tells him. "Long *e*, rhymes with Rita." She steps to the side and motions to him. "Please, come inside."

He nods, and Fida can see the relief in his eyes as he steps over the threshold. His car, a heavy sedan that, like almost everyone's, has mesh soldered over the windows, is parked at the curb. It had probably seemed like a very long way from the sidewalk to her door. No one without an armed escort wants to be outside too long nowadays.

Fida judiciously bolts the door, then leads him into the drawing room. "Make yourself comfortable." He obliges by settling on one of the two floral-printed couches and passing a white handkerchief across his forehead. It's impossible to tell if it's the June heat or fear that makes him sweat. Some people just do.

She's made a simple lunch, homemade flat bread baked pizza-style over a grating in the fireplace of the old-fashioned kitchen, then topped with a sliced tomato and green pepper from her little greenhouse (she's privately called it the "Lock 'n' Grow" since hearing the nickname of the swap meet). She hasn't had mozzarella cheese in years, but a sprinkling of dry Parmesan before it goes over the heat works well. She serves it to him along with a glass of room-temperature water freshened by a small sprig of mint. A good man should have a good meal before he gets on about his business. A man such as Father Stane.

They eat without saying much of anything. After about ten minutes, Fida can see the priest finally relaxing. Even though she's herded the boarders to the far end of the house, they have a tendency to fight amongst themselves and now and then one of them gets loud.

Occasionally a snarl sails along the upstairs air currents and drifts through the unused heating vents. The first time this happens, Father Stane visibly twitches; when all Fida does is meet his gaze and shrug, he appears to accept that she has made her home safe. The next couple of noises make him raise an eyebrow, but his deep brown eyes are wise and he knows that the time for discussion isn't long in coming.

She can tell by his black hair and heavy bone structure that he is perhaps Slavic or Serbian. A man from the old country, where the faith is ancient and strong. Excellent.

Fida sets the dishes aside and folds her hands on her lap. "I appreciate you coming all this way," she says. "I know it's troublesome to travel alone."

Father Stane tilts his head. "Indeed. You said there was something important you wanted to discuss?"

Fida nods, then picks at the rough edges of her fingernails as she considers the phrasing of her question. "Father, do you believe in forgiveness?"

"Of course," he answers without hesitation. "Forgiveness is the core of our faith. Christ died for us, so that we would all be redeemed." He studies her. "You attended my mass last Sunday, but I won't presume you're Christian."

"I'm Catholic."

"But do you believe? These are difficult times, Fida. Even the strongest man or woman of faith can stumble."

"I do believe, very strongly."

He nods. "Then what is it you wanted to discuss?"

Fida takes a deep breath. "Do you believe in redemption? That souls can be saved?"

"Of course," he says again. He leans forward. "Do you need to make a confession? Is that why you asked me to come here—for privacy?" She shakes her head, but he continues anyway. "These are terrible times, Fida. A lot of people have done . . . questionable things, just to stay alive." He reaches over and gives her a paternal pat on the hand. "Many don't want to be public about it. They feel hypocritical. I understand."

Hypocritical . . . like Jesus and the Pharisees and scribes? No, she does not equate herself with them. "I only try to save people," she replies, and both of them look toward the ceiling at the sound of a faraway thump.

Father Stane sits back. "Ah," he says. "You have . . ." He hesitates, unsure of his terminology.

"Boarders," Fida answers for him. "They all lived here . . ." Another pause. "Before."

The priest's forehead furrows. "They came back?"

She nods. "They came *home.* I don't believe that the living dead are just monsters, creatures without thought or purpose. They have memory. They seek comfort." Her hands are squeezing tightly together now, almost in supplication. "They didn't ask for this. They want to be rescued, to be *saved.*"

Father Stane rubs his chin. "Have you considered that their return might just be instinct? There have been studies—"

Fida waves away his words. "You mean the experiment labs, where they're dissected like lab rats, treated with chemicals and used as targets for the security forces to try out their latest and greatest weapons?" Heat climbs up her face. "And let's not forget that the science centers are the perfect place for people to drop off their relatives—parents, spouses, *children,* for God's sake—then walk away with a clean conscience, saying that what they're doing is for the good of all.

"You mentioned hypocrites? *Those* are the hypocrites, Father Stane. Those are the monsters. The ones who won't take responsibility for people they once loved." She crosses her arms so tightly that the muscles in her shoulders spasm.

"So much for *until death do us part.* The living dead, Father Stane. The *living* dead."

He takes a drink of water and puts it back on the coffee table, carefully centering it on a coaster. "All right. Let's say they are still alive, after a fashion. Then what?"

"They need to be *saved,*" she tells him firmly. "Forgiven, like Jesus forgave us all at the Last Supper. It was his body and blood—"

"Metaphorically," the priest reminds her.

"Obviously, Father. I was about to say 'via the bread and wine.'" Fida squashes her irritation, then picks up again. "That's how mankind was forgiven, through his love and sacrifice. That's how we continue to be forgiven." She rises and crosses the drawing room, lifts a photo album from a mahogany side-table next to the fireplace. She brings it back and opens it in front of Father Stane, pointing to the pictures.

"This is Patrick. A good Irish boy, first room at the top of the stairs. He's been out of work so he's a bit behind on his rent." She flips the page. "This is Manuella. She lives . . . *lived* here with her boy, Reynaldo, in the biggest room at the back. Reynaldo's gone, though. He was only six."

Father Stane nods his head sympathetically. She taps a fingernail against a picture of a sallow-skinned Asian man; his eyes are thin and mean and a gang tattoo curves around the back of his bald skull. "This is Cade. I have to admit that he tries my patience sometimes." She lifts her chin. "Still, I have hope."

"I see."

"Do you?" Her eyes burn as she flips a couple more pages, locking her voice, determined not to show too much emotion. "Jesse and Tina. They're only sixteen. She's four months pregnant and they're hiding from her father, who told her he was going to kill Jesse." Another turn of the page. "Max is a heroin addict, always trying to kick the habit and always blowing it. He's come back here four times because he knows I'll help him keep on trying. And the last one is Sylvie. She's thirteen and a runaway."

Father Stane frowns at her. "You let a thirteen-year-old runaway stay here?"

Fida's gaze doesn't waver. "Her mother turned her out as a prostitute when she was eleven."

The priest's jaw works but he says nothing as Fida puts the album back in its place. "These are my tenants, Father."

"You talk about them as if things never changed."

"I don't think they have, at least not to them. In their minds, they're just lost." She sits back down and clasps her hands again. "Don't you see? These are *my* family. My responsibility. If I don't care for them, don't keep them safe and try to save them, then *I* will be a hypocrite. No better than so many others."

Father Stane nods and, to his credit, she can see him struggling to comprehend her way of thinking. "So why did you call me here, Fida? What can I do to help you with this situation?"

He stumbles a bit on the word *situation* and Fida's stomach twists inside. Does he believe, truly? His faith must be complete. It must be pure. If it isn't, he might as well go on home now.

"Will you do something for me, Father?" On the other end of the couch is a large wicker basket covered with a simple, clean white cloth. She pulls the basket to her side and lifts the cotton; beneath is more freshly baked flat bread, five good loaves of it, and a round crystal decanter of dark red wine. "Bless this bread and wine," she says. "Consecrate it with all your faith and everything you believe in. Like you do the Eucharist at mass."

"And then what?" he asks sternly. His gaze rolls upward. "You feed it to them? There is no forgiveness without confession. You know that."

She shakes her head. "But we have to *try*. The body of Christ, the blood of Christ. Miracles *have* happened. That the dead can walk is in itself a miracle, don't you think? Who's to say that a—a *reverse* miracle can't occur?"

"And if it doesn't? Will you be the one to stop them?" He glances pointedly at the machete hanging at her belt.

Fida looks at her hands. Sometimes she feels so much sadness she can hardly speak the words. "To kill out of judgment is not my place." He doesn't reply and she turns her hands palm up. "It's a small thing that I'm asking, Father. A sacrifice of symbology. A spreading of the Word, the faith, the Sacrament."

"All right," he says after a few moments, but he sounds

tired. Is he doing it because he wants to, or because he feels it's what will be necessary for him to leave and feel as if he's done his best?

He reaches for the basket but she stands and lifts it with her. "Upstairs," she says. "In Patrick's room. They're all down at the end, where Manuella stays." She doesn't add that the Mexican woman, whose skin and eyes have gone as grey as old cement and whose mouth is rimmed with the dried blood of her son, spends most of every day moaning and standing over the daybed where the boy used to sleep.

Fida can tell by the expression on Father Stane's sturdy face that he wants to protest, but he doesn't. This gives her reason to hope; a faithless man would have refused, would have asked how dangerous it was and was she sure that the creatures were safely locked away. But Father Stane is a good man. A faithful man.

He follows her up the stairs and she hands him the basket, then opens the door to Patrick's room. The priest pulls back but the room is empty, the door that joins it to Jesse's closed. The bed is rumpled, as if the boy has slept in it, but she knows it isn't so. She makes it up every morning, even changes the sheets once a week, but the boarders only bump against it, or sometimes fall onto the antique quilt. They never sleep, though, just get up and wander away. There are no mirrors in this room because the living dead version of Patrick doesn't like his reflection and he always breaks them.

Fida takes the basket back and walks inside, then sets it on the dresser across from the door. She lifts the cloth reverently and stares at the contents for several seconds without saying anything, then backs away and looks at the priest. "Will you bless it now?" she asks.

Father Stane clears his throat. "Yes." He takes his place in front of the dresser, bows his head and begins to pray, and Fida relaxes a little as the familiar words coat the air with promises of holiness.

"On the night he was betrayed, he took bread and gave you thanks and praise. He broke the bread, gave it to his disciples, and said, take this, all of you, and eat it: this is my body which will be given up for you." Father Stane holds up

one of the loaves and breaks it into two. She smiles and nods when he glances at her, then says in a soft voice, "I'll be right back. I have to get my crucifix. Don't stop."

She feels his gaze as she slips out of the room, but when she leaves the door open, his voice resumes and she hears more confidence in it. Excellent.

"When supper was ended, he took the cup. Again he gave you thanks and praise, gave the cup to his disciples, and said, take this, all of you, and drink from it: this is the cup of my blood, the blood of the new and everlasting covenant. It will be shed for you and for all men so that sins may be forgiven. Do this in memory of me."

He has spoken only a few words by the time Fida gets to the end of the hallway and Manuella's door. She bends and sweeps aside the soiled clothing that has kept the living dead clustered there all day, then walks quickly back to Patrick's room. She knows just where to step so the floor doesn't creak—along the edges of the baseboards where the nails are strong and the old oak boards haven't sagged in the middle. As she silently reaches out, pulls the door shut and bolts it, she hears another part of the mass in her head—the words that are always said in preparation of the altar and the gifts. They are out of order, but there is nothing more appropriate.

May the Lord accept the sacrifice at your hands, for the praise and glory of his name, for our good, and the good of all . . .

It takes only about thirty seconds for her boarders, her *family,* to lurch down to Patrick's room, where the final door that separates them from Father Stane is not locked. A few seconds later, the priest begins to scream.

Fida sits on the hallway floor and stares at the crucifix she took off the wall down by Manuella's room, discouragement leaving yet another bitter taste in her mouth. She was wrong about Father Stane—his faith had *not* been strong enough, he hadn't been truly sacred and believing in the body and soul of Christ. If he had, he would have been spared, and her loved ones would have eaten the blessed bread and wine, and they would have been cured.

She'll just have to try again. There is another Catholic church, Saint Benedictine, about five miles away, and she can drive Father Stane's car there next Sunday.

After mass she will ask one of the priests to come to her home and speak to her in confidence. These days, the priests are always out in the community, ministering and spreading the word of God for the good of all.

No one thinks twice when they don't come back.

Joyce Carol Oates

(1938–)

Born in Lockport, New York, Joyce Carol Oates received a BA from Syracuse University and an MA from the University of Wisconsin. As an undergraduate, she won the renowned *Mademoiselle* magazine fiction contest. For many decades, she has successfully combined her profession as a famous writer of fiction and poetry with her position as the Roger S. Berlind Distinguished Professor of the Humanities at Princeton University. She is a recipient of the M. L. Rosenthal Award from the National Institute of Arts and Letters, a National Book Award, a Bram Stoker Award, the PEN/Malamud Award for Excellence in the Art of the Short Story, and the *Kenyon Review* Award for Literary Achievement. Among over three dozen collections of her stories are *By the North Gate* (1963), *The Seduction and Other Stories* (1975), *Last Days: Stories* (1984), *Haunted: Tales of the Grotesque* (1994), *Demon and Other Tales* (1996), *The Female of the Species: Tales of Mystery and Suspense* (2006), and *Dear Husband: Stories* (2009). Her novels include *A Garden of Earthly Delights* (1967), *Do with Me What You Will* (1973), *Bellefleur* (1980), *Nemesis* (1990), *Zombie* (1995), *We Were the Mulvaneys* (1996), *The Gravedigger's Daughter* (2007), and *A Fair Maiden* (2010).

Accursed Inhabitants of the House of Bly

(1994)

In life she'd been a modest girl, a sensible and sane young woman whose father was a poor country parson across the moors in Glyngden. How painful then to conceive of herself in this astonishing new guise, an object of horror, still less an object of disgust. Physical disgust if you saw her. Spiritual disgust at the thought of her. Condemned to the eternal motions of washing the mud-muck of the Sea of Azof off her body, in particular the private parts of her marmoreal body, with fanatic fastidiousness picking iridescent-shelled beetles out of her still-lustrous black hair with the stubborn curl her lover had called her "Scots curl" to flatter her—for the truth, too, can be flattery, uttered with design. And not only he, her lover, Master's valet, but Master himself had flattered her, so craftily: "*I* would trust *you,* ah! with any responsibility!"

She, twenty-year-old Miss Jessel, interviewed by Master in Harley Street, wearing her single really good dark cotton-serge dress, how hot her face, how brimming with moisture her eyes, how stricken with shyness at the rush of love, its impact scarcely less palpable than a slap in the buttocks would have been. And, later, in the House of Bly, so stricken-shy of love, or love's antics, Master's valet Peter Quint burst into laughter (not rude exactly, indeed affectionate, but indeed laughter) at the cringing nakedness of her, the shivers that rippled across her skin, the lovely smoky-dark eyes downcast, blind in maidenly shame. Oh, ridiculous! Now Jessel, as she bluntly calls herself, has to bite her lips to keep from howling with laughter like a beast at such memories; has to stop herself short imagining the sharp tug of a chain fixed to a collar tight around her neck, for otherwise she might drop to all fours to scramble after prey (terrified mice, judging from the sound of their tiny squeals and scurrying feet) here in the catacombs.

The catacombs!—as, bemusedly, bitterly, they call this damp, chill, lightless place with its smell of ancient stone and sweetly-sour decay to which *crossing over* has brought them: in fact, unromantically, their place of refuge is a corner, an abandoned storage area, in the cellar of the great ugly House of Bly.

By night, of course, they are free to roam. If compulsion overcomes them (she, passionate Jessel, being more susceptible than he, the coolly appalled Quint), they venture forth in stealthy forays even during the day. But nights, ah! nights! lawless, extravagant! by wind-ravaged moonlight Quint pursues Jessel naked across the very front lawn of Bly, lewd laughter issuing from his throat, he, too, near-naked, crouched like an ape. Jessel is likely to be in a blood-trance when at last he catches her on the shore of the marshy pond, he has to pry her delicate-boned but devilishly strong jaws open to extricate a limp, bloody, still-quivering furry creature (a baby rabbit?—Jessel dreads to know) caught between her teeth.

Are the children watching, from the house? Are their small, pale, eager faces pressed to the glass? What do little Flora and little Miles see, that the accursed lovers themselves cannot see?

In interludes of sanity Jessel considers: how is it possible that, as a girl, in the dour old stone parsonage on the Scots border, she'd been incapable of eating bread dipped in suet, gravy was repugnant to her as a thinly disguised form of blood, she'd eaten only vegetables, fruits, and grains with what might be called a healthy appetite; yet, now, scarcely a year later, in the catacombs of the House of Bly, she experiences an ecstatic shudder at the crunch of delicate bones, nothing tastes so sweet to her as the warm, rich, still-pulsing blood, her soul cries *Yes! yes! like this! only let it never end!* in a swoon of realization that her infinite hunger might be, if not satisfied, held at bay.

In life, a good pious scared-giggly Christian girl, virgin to the tips of her toes.

In death, for why mince words?—a ghoul.

Because, in a fury of self-disgust and abnegation, she'd dared to take her own life, is that the reason for the curse?—or is it that in taking her own life, in that marshy-mucky pond the children call the Sea of Azof, she'd taken also the life of the ghostly being in her womb?

Quint's seed, planted hot and deep. Searing flame at the conception and sorrow, pain, rage, defiance, soul-nausea to follow.

Yet there had seemed to Jessel no other way. An unwed mother, a despoiled virgin, a figure of ignominy, pity, shame—no other way.

Indeed, in that decent Christian world of which the great ugly House of Bly was the emblem, there *was* no other way.

Little Flora, seven years old at the time of her governess's death, was wild with grief, and mourns her still. *Her* Miss Jessel!

And I love you too, dear Flora, Jessel wills her words to fly, in silence, into the child's sleep—*please forgive me that there was no other way.*

Do children forgive?—of course, always.

Being children, and innocent.

Orphaned children, like little Flora, and little Miles, above all.

More strangely altered than Jessel, in a sense, by the rude shock of *crossing over,* is Master's flamey-haired and -whiskered valet Peter Quint—"That hound!" as Mrs. Grose calls him still, with a shiver of her righteous jowls.

In the old, rough, careless days, the bachelor days of a dissolute and protracted youth, Quint had cared not a tuppence for conscience; tall, supple-muscled, handsome in a redhead's luminous pale-skinned way, irresistible to weakly female eyes in certain purloined vests, tweeds, riding breeches and gleaming leather boots of Master's, he'd had his way, indeed his myriad-wallowing ways, with half the household staff at Bly. (Even Mrs. Grose, some believed. Yes, even Mrs. Grose, who now hates him with a fury hardly mitigated by the man's death.) It was rumored, or crudely boasted, that babes born to one or another of the married women belowstairs at Bly were in fact Quint's bastards, whether accursed by tell-tale red hair, or not; yes, and in the Village as well, and scattered through the county.

Hadn't Master, himself livened by drink, been in the habit of regaling Quint, one fellow to another, "Quint, my man, *you* must do my living for me, eh?"—all but nudging his valet in the ribs.

At which times the shrewd Quint, knowing how aristocrats may play at forgetting their station in life, as if to tempt another to forget, fatally, his own, maintained a servile propriety, commensurate with his erect posture and high-held head, saying, quietly, "Yes, sir. If you will explain how. I am at your command, sir."

But Master had only laughed, a sound as of wet gravel being roughly shoveled.

And now, how unexpected, in a way how perverse: Quint

finds himself considerably sobered by his change of fortune. His death, unlike poor Jessel's, was not deliberate; yet, a drunken misstep, a fall down a rocky slope midway between The Black Ox (a pub in the Village of Bly) and the House of Bly in the eerie pre-dawn of a morning shortly after Jessel's funeral, it was perhaps not accidental, either.

In the catacombs, where time, seemingly, has stopped, the fact of Quint's death is frequently discussed. Jessel muses, "You need not have done it, you know. No one would have expected it of you," and Quint says, with a shrug of irritation, "I don't do what is expected of me, only what I expect of myself."

"Then you do love me?"—the question, though reiterated often, is quaveringly posed.

"We are both accursed by love, it seems," Quint says, in a flat, hollow tone, stroking his bearded chin (and how unevenly trimmed his beard, once the pride of his manly bearing), "—for each other, and, you know, damn them—little Flora, and little Miles."

"Oh! don't speak so harshly. They are all we have."

"But we don't, you know, precisely 'have' them. They are still—"

Quint hesitates, with a fastidious frown, "—they have not yet *crossed over.*"

Jessel's luminous, mad eyes glare up at him, out of the sepulchral gloom. "Yes, as you say—not *yet.*"

Little Flora, and little Miles!—the living children, not of the lovers' union, but of their desire.

Quint would not wish to name it thus, but his attachment to them, as to Jessel, is that of a man blessed (some might say, accursed) by his love of his family.

Jessel, passionate and reckless now, as, in life, she'd been stricken by shyness as by a scarlet rash of the skin (a "nerve" rash, which had indeed afflicted her occasionally), spoke openly—"Flora is my soul, and I will not give her up. No, nor dear little Miles, either!"

Since *crossing over,* since the deaths, and alarms, and funerals, and hushed conversations from which the children were banned, Flora and Miles have grieved inwardly; forbidden to so much as speak of the "depraved, degenerate sinners"—as all in the vicinity of Bly call the dead couple—

they have had to contemplate Miss Jessel and Peter Quint, if at all, only at distances, and in their dreams.

The unhappy children, now eight and ten years old, were, years ago, tragically orphaned when their parents died of mysterious tropical diseases in India. Their uncle-guardian, Master of the House of Bly, resident of sumptuous bachelor's digs in Harley Street, London, always professes to be very, very fond of his niece and nephew, indeed devoted to them—their well-being, their educations, their "moral, Christian selves"; even as, when he speaks of them, his red-veined eyes glaze over.

Tremulous twenty-year-old Miss Jessel with the staring eyes, interviewed by the Master of Bly in his Harley Street townhouse, clasped her fingers so tightly in her cotton-serge lap, the bony knuckles glared white. She, a poor parson's daughter, educated at a governess's school in Norfolk, had never in her life been in such a presence!—gentlemanly, yet manly; of the landed aristocracy in bearing, if not in actual lineage, yet capable, a bit teasingly, of plain talk. It is a measure of the young governess's trust in her social superiors that she did not think it strange that the Master glided swiftly, indeed cursorily, over her duties as a governess, and over the bereaved children themselves, but reiterated several times, with an inscrutable smile that left her breathless, that the "prime responsibility" of her employment would be that she must never, under any circumstances, trouble him with problems.

In a sort of giddy daze Miss Jessel heard herself giggle, and inquire, almost inaudibly, "—*any* circumstances, sir?" and Master loftily and smilingly replied, "*I* would trust *you,* ah! with any responsibility!"

And so the interview, which required scarcely half an hour, came to an end.

Little Flora was Miss Jessel's delight. Miss Jessel's angel. Quite simply—so the ecstatic young woman wrote home, to Glyngden—the most beautiful, the most charming child she'd ever seen, with pale blond curls like silk, and thick-lashed blue eyes clear as washed glass, and a sweet melodic voice. Shy, initially—ah, tragically shy!—as if seemingly abandoned by her parents, and only barely tolerated by her uncle, Flora had no sense of her human worth. When first Miss Jessel set eyes upon her, introduced to her by the housekeeper Mrs. Grose, the child visibly shrank from the young woman's warm scrutiny. "Why, hello, Flora! I'm Miss Jessel: I am to be your friend," Miss Jessel said. She, too, was afflicted by shyness, but in this case gazed upon the perfect child with such a look of rapture that Flora must have seen, yes, here was her lost young mother restored to her, at last!

Within the space of a few blissful days, Miss Jessel and little Flora became inseparable companions.

Together they picnicked on the grassy bank of the pond—the "Sea of Azof," as Flora so charmingly called it. Together they walked white-gloved hand in hand to church a mile away. Together they ate every meal. Flora's organdy-ruffled little bed was established in a corner of Miss Jessel's room.

On bare Presbyterian knees, beside her own bed, in the dark, Miss Jessel fiercely prayed: *Dear God, I vow to devote my life to this child!—I will do far, far more than* he *has so much as hinted of my doing.*

No need, between Miss Jessel and an omniscient God, to identify this Olympian *he.*

Days and weeks passed in an oblivion of happiness. For what *is* happiness, save oblivion? The young governess from Glyngden with the pale, rather narrow, plain-pretty face and intense dark eyes, who had long forbade herself fantasy as a heathen sort of indulgence, now gave herself up in day-dreams of little Flora, and Master, and, yes, she herself. (For, at this time, little Miles was away at school.) *A new family, the most natural of families, why not?* Like every other young governess in England, Miss Jessel had avidly read her *Jane Eyre.*

These were the oblivious days before Peter Quint.

Little Miles, as comely and angelic a boy as his sister was perfection as a girl, was under the guidance, when at Bly, of Peter Quint, his uncle's trusted valet. The more censorious among the servants, in particular Mrs. Grose, thought this an unfortunate situation: cunning Quint played the gentleman at Bly and environs, a dashing figure (if you liked the type) in purloined clothes belonging to the Master, but, born of coarse country folk in the Midlands, without education or breeding, he was a "base menial—a hound" as Mrs. Grose sniffed.

He had a certain reputation as a ladies' man. Excepting of course, as the clumsy riposte went, Quint's ladies were hardly *ladies*.

Infrequently, on unpredictable weekends, Master came by train to Bly—"To my country retreat"—with a flushed, sullen look of, indeed, a gentleman in retreat. (From amorous mishaps?—gambling debacles? Not even his valet knew.) He paid scant attention to the quivering Miss Jessel, whom, to her chagrin, he persisted in calling by the wrong name; he paid virtually no attention at all to poor little Flora, beaming with hope like an angel and dressed in her prettiest pink frock. He did make it a point to speak with Peter Quint in private, bringing up the unexpected subject of his little nephew Miles, enrolled at Eton—"I want, you know, Quint, this boy of my poor dear fool of a brother to be a boy; and not, you know," here he paused, frowning, "—*not* a boy. D'you see?" Master's face flushed brick-red with discomfort and a sort of choked anger.

Politic Quint murmured a polite, "Yes, sir. Indeed."

"These boys' schools—notorious! All sorts of—" Another pause, a look of distaste. A nervous stroking of his moustache—"Antics. Best not spoken aloud. But you know what I mean."

Quint, who had not had the privilege of attending any public boys' school, let alone the distinguished one in which little Miles was enrolled, was not sure that he did know; but could guess. Still, the gentleman's man hesitated, now stroking his own whiskery chin.

Seeing Quint's hesitation, and interpreting it as a subtle refinement of his own distaste, Master continued, hurriedly, "Let me phrase it thus, Quint: I require that those for whom I am responsible subscribe to decent standards of Christian behavior, that's to say normal standards of human behavior. D'you see? That is not much to ask, but it is everything."

"Certainly, sir."

"A nephew of mine, blood of my blood, bred to inherit my name, the bearer of a great English lineage—he must, he *will*, marry, and sire children to continue the line to—" Another pause, and here a rather ghastly slackening of the mouth, as if the very prospect sickened, "—perpetuity. D'you see?"

Quint mumbled a vague assent.

"Degenerates will be the death of England, if we do not stop them in the cradle."

"In the cradle, sir?"

"For, y'know, Quint, just between us two, man to man: I would rather see the poor little bugger dead, than *unmanly.*"

At this Quint started, and so forgot himself as to look the Master of Bly searchingly in the face; but the gentleman's eyes were red-veined, with a flat, opaque cast that yielded little light.

The interview was over, abruptly. Quint bowed to Master, and took his leave. Thinking, *My God! the upper classes are more savage than I had guessed.*

Yet little Miles, though blood of Master's blood, and bred to the inheritance not merely of a revered English lineage but a good deal of wealth, was a child starved for affection—a sweet-natured, sometimes a bit mischievous, yet always sunnily charming boy; fair-skinned like his sister, but with honey-brown hair and eyes, and, though small-framed, with an inclination toward heart palpitations and breathlessness, indefatigably high-spirited when others were around. (Alone, Miles was apt to be moody and secretive; no doubt he mourned his parents, whom, unlike Flora, he could recall, if confusedly. He had been five at the time of their deaths.) However quick and intelligent he was, Miles did not like school, or, in any case, his more robust classmates at Eton. Yet he rarely complained, and, in Peter Quint's presence, as in the presence of any adult male of authority, it seemed resolute in the child that he *not* complain.

From the start, to Quint's astonishment, Miles attached himself to him with childish affection, hugging and kissing him, even, if he was able, clambering onto Quint's lap. Such unguarded demonstrations of feeling both embarrassed the valet, and flattered him. Quint tried to fend off Miles, laughingly, rather red-faced, protesting, "Your uncle would not approve of such behavior, Miles!—indeed, your uncle would call this 'unmanly.'" But Miles persisted; Miles was adamant; Miles wept if pushed forcibly away. It was a habit of his to rush at Quint if he had not seen him in a while and seize him around the hips, burrowing his flushed little face into the elder man as a kitten or puppy might, blindly seeking its mother's teats. Miles would plead, "But, you know, Quint, Uncle doesn't love me. *I only want to be loved.*" Taking pity on the child, Quint would caress him, awkwardly, bend over to kiss the top or his head, then push him away, in a nervous reflex. "Miles, dear chap, this is really not what we want!" he laughed.

But Miles held tight, laughing too, breathless and defiant, pleading, "Oh, but isn't it, Quint?—*isn't* it?—*isn't it?*"

As Miss Jessel and little Flora were inseparable companions, so too were Peter Quint and little Miles, when Miles was home from school. And, as the children were intensely, one might almost say desperately, attached to each other, the shy, plain-pretty governess from Glyngden and the coarser valet from the Midlands were very often in each other's company.

Damned hard to pride oneself on one's feral good looks when a man is forced to shave with a dull razor in a cracked looking glass, and when his clothes, regardless of how "smart," are covered with a patina of grime; when, drifting into a thin, ragged sleep as the moon seems on windy nights to be sailing through a scrim of cloud, he wakes with a start of terror. *As if,* thinks Quint, *I am not even dead yet: and the worst is yet to come.*

Poor Jessel!—whom *crossing over* has humbled yet more egregiously!

In puddles of dirty water the once-chaste young governess with the lustrous "Scots curl" tries repeatedly, compulsively, to cleanse herself. The brackish mud-muck of Flora's Sea of Azof clings to her underarms, the pit of her belly, the hot dark crevice between her legs with its own brackish odor; a particular sort of spiny iridescent beetle that breeds copiously in the earthy damp of the cellar is attracted to hair, and sticks tight as snarls. Her single good dress, which, out of defiance, she'd worn as she waded into the water, is stiff with filth, and her petticoats, once white, are striated with mud, and not yet fully dry. She rages, she weeps, she claws at her cheeks with her broken nails, she turns against her lover, demanding why, if he'd known she was hysterically inclined, he'd made love to her at all.

Quint protests. Guiltily. A man is a man, a pronged creature destined to impregnate: how, given their attraction to each other, in the romantically sequestered countryside of Bly, could he, lusty Peter Quint, *not* have made love to her? How could he have known she was "hysterically inclined" and would take her own, dear life, in an excess of shame?

Not that Miss Jessel's desperate act was solely a consequence of shame: it was pragmatic, practical. Word had come from Harley Street (fed, of course, by tales told by Mrs. Grose and others) that Miss Jessel was dismissed from Bly, commanded at once to vacate her room, disappear.

Where, then, could she have gone?—back to the Glyngden parsonage?

A ruined woman, a despoiled woman, a humiliated woman, a fallen woman, a woman made incontrovertibly a *woman.*

Jessel says tartly that all virgins of this time and place are "hysterically inclined"—little Presbyterian governesses above all. If, in life, she'd had the luck to have been born a man, she'd have avoided such pathetic creatures like the plague.

Quint laughs irritably. "Yes, but, dear Jessel, you know—*I love you.*"

The statement hovers in the air, forlorn and accusing.

Here is perversity: in this twilit realm to which *crossing over* has brought the accursed lovers, Jessel seems, in Quint's eyes, far more beautiful than she'd been in life; Quint, to Jessel, despite her anger, quite the most attractive man she has ever seen—touching in his vanity even now, in grimy and tattered vests, shirts, and breeches, his rooster's-crest of brick-red hair threaded with gray, his jaws covered in wiry stubble. The most manly of men!—graced now with sobriety and melancholy. Yearning for each other, moaning in frustration, they grasp each other's hands, they slip their arms around each other, they stroke, squeeze, kiss, bite, sighing when their "material beings" turn immaterial as vapor—and Quint's arms shut around mere air, a shadow, and Jessel paws wildly at him, her fingers in his hair, her mouth pressed against his, except, damnably, Quint too is a shadow: an apparition.

"We are not 'real,' then?—any longer?" Jessel asks, panting.

"If we can love, if we can desire—who is more 'real' than we?" Quint demands.

But of course, why mince words, Quint's a man, he's chagrined at *impotence.*

Yet, sometimes, they can make love. Of a kind. If they act swiftly, spontaneously. If they don't articulate, in conscious thought, what they are about to do, they can, almost, with luck, do it.

At other times, by some mysterious law of decomposition, though unpredictably, the molecules that constitute their "bodies" shift in density, and become porous. But not inevitably at the same time: so that Jessel, reaching out to touch Quint with a "real" hand, might recoil in horror as her "real" hand passes through his insubstantial body.... How the lovers yearn for those days, not so very long ago, when they inhabited wholly ordinary "human bodies" they had not understood were miracles of molecular harmony!

Flesh of our flesh, blood of our blood. Dear Flora, dear Miles.

How to leave Bly?—Jessel and Quint cannot give up their little charges, who have no one but them. Their days and nights are passed in drifting, brooding ... how, next, to make contact with the children? Time passes strangely in these catacombs, as a night of intermittent dreams passes for the living, during which hours are pleated, or protracted, or reduced to mere seconds. Sometimes, in a paroxysm of despair, Jessel believes that time, for the dead who are linked to the world by desire, thus insufficiently dead, cannot pass. Suffering is infinite *and will never diminish.* "Quint, the horror of it is: we're frozen forever at a single point of time, the ghastly point of our *crossing over,*" Jessel says, her eyes dilated, all pupil, "—and nothing will, nothing *can,* change for us," and Quint says quickly, "Dear girl, time *does* pass. Of course it does! You went first, remember, and I followed; there were our funerals (swiftly and a bit cursorily performed, indeed); we hear them, upstairs, speak of us less and less frequently, where once the damned prigs spoke of nothing else. Miles has been away at school and will, I think, shortly be home again for Easter recess. Flora's eighth birthday was last week ..."

"And we dared not be with her, but had to watch through the window, like lepers," Jessel says hotly.

"And there is this new governess expected tomorrow, I've heard—your replacement."

Jessel laughs. Harsh, scratchy-throated, brief laughter, without mirth. "*My* replacement! *Never.*"

"Dun-colored, and so plain! Skin the color of curdled milk! And the eyes so squinty and small!—the forehead so *bony*!"

Jessel is incensed. Jessel is quivering with rage. Quint would admonish her, but that would only make things worse.

From the summit of the square tower to the east, that overlooks the drive, the accursed lovers regard the newly hired governess as she steps down, not very gracefully, with a scared smile, from the carriage. Mrs. Grose has little Flora by the hand, urging the child forward to be introduced. How eager she is, fattish Grose!—who'd once been Miss Jessel's friend, and had then so cruelly rejected her. The new governess (as Quint overheard, from Ottery St. Mary, Devonshire—a rural village as obscure and provincial as Glyngden) is a skinny broomstick of a girl, in a gray bonnet that does not flatter her, and a badly wrinkled gray traveling cloak; her small, pale, homely face is lit from within by a hope, a prayer, of "succeeding"—Jessel recoils, recalling such, in herself. Jessel mutters, half-sobbing, "Quint, how could he! Another! To take my place with Flora! *How dare he!*"

Quint assures her, "No one will take your place with Flora, dear girl. You know that."

As the new governess stoops over Flora, all smiles and delight, Jessel sees, with a trip of her heart, how the child glances over her shoulder, stealthily, to ascertain that Miss Jessel is somewhere near.

Yes, dear Flora. Your Jessel is always somewhere near.

So it begins, the bitter contest.

The struggle for little Flora, and little Miles.

"That woman is one of *them,*" Jessel says, her fist jammed against her mouth, "—the very worst of *them.*" Quint, who would like to stay clear of his mistress's fanatic plots, that turn, and turn, and turn upon the hope, to his skeptical mind not very likely, of reuniting the four of them someday, says, with a frown, "The very worst of—?" Jessel replies, her eyes brimming with tears, "A vicious little—Christian! A Puritan! You know the sort: one who hates and fears life in others. Hates and fears joy, passion, love. All that *we've* had."

There is a moment's silence. Quint is thinking of certain slumberous summer afternoons, heat lightning flashing in the sweetly bruised sky, a weeping Miss Jessel cradled in his arms, the smell of tall grasses and the calls of rooks and little Flora and little Miles approaching through the grove of acacia trees calling softly, slyly, happily, *Oh, Miss Jessel! Oh, Mr. Quint! Where are you hiding? May we see?*

Quint shivers, recalling. He understands that Jessel, too, is thinking of those lovely lost afternoons.

Of course, it has also irked Quint that Master has hired a new governess for little Flora, yet, to be reasonable, would there not have to be a new governess, soon? So far as the world knows, Miss Jessel is dead, and has departed to where all the dead go. Master would have hired a new governess within twenty-four hours of the death of the old, had decorum not forbade it.

Yes, and there is a new valet, too: but this gentleman's man, Quint has heard, will live in Harley Street, and will never meet little Miles.

Quint has wondered, *Did Master know?—not just of Jessel and me, but of the children, too?*

Quint asks Jessel, "You see all that, darling? In the poor pinched thing's face?"

"Of course! Can't you?"

Jessel's mad beautiful eyes, her skin gleaming with the ferocity of moonlight. Her mouth is a wound. To gaze upon it, Quint thinks, succumbing, is to be aroused.

Quint appears to the new governess first. He must confess, there is something in the young woman's very bearing, the thin, stiff little body inside the clothes, the nervously high-held head, the quick-darting steely gray eyes, that both repels and attracts him. Unlike Flora, who is capable of staring in a trance of mystic contentment at her Miss Jessel (who will appear to Flora, for instance, across the pond, as the new governess, her back to the pond, chatters to her little charge in complete ignorance), and occasionally at Peter Quint as well (for Quint sometimes appears with Jessel, arms entwined), the new governess reacts with a shock, an astonishment, a naked terror, that is immensely gratifying to a man.

A man of still-youthful vigor and lusts, deprived by this damnable *crossing over* of his manhood.

Quint ascends the square tower to the west, dashing up the spiral stairs to the crenelated top, bodiless, thus weightless, and feeling quite good. The "battlements" of the House of Bly are architectural fancies not unlike manufactured fossils, for they were added to the house in a short-lived romantic-medieval revival of a decade or so ago, touchingly quaint, yet, who can deny it?—wonderfully atmospheric. Quint sees that the governess is approaching below on the path, she is alone, meditative, exciting in her maiden vulnerability, he preens his feathers glancing down the lean length of himself liking what he sees, he *is* a damned fine figure of a man. The vagrant late-afternoon wind dies down; the rooks cease their fretful, ubiquitous cries; there is an unnatural "hush"—and Quint feels with a shudder of delight the governess's shock as she lifts her eyes to the top of the tower, to the machicolated ledge, to *him*. Ah, bliss!

For some dramatic seconds, protracted as minutes, Quint and the governess stare at each other: Quint coolly and severely, with his "piercing" eyes (which few women, inexperienced young virgins or no, would be likely to forget); the governess with an expression of alarm, incredulity, terror. The poor thing takes an involuntary step backward. She presses a tremulous hand to her throat. Quint gives her the full, *full* impact of his gaze—he holds her fast there below on the path, he wills her to stand as if paralyzed. For this performance, Quint has pieced together an attractive costume that does not altogether embarrass him. Trousers still holding their crease, a white silk shirt kept in readiness for just such an occasion, that elegant coat of Master's, and the checked vest—another's things, but put to superior use on Quint's manly body. His beard is freshly trimmed, which gives him a sinister-romantic dash; he's hatless, of course—that virile-red rooster's crest of hair must be displayed.

"The Devil," as Quint remarked to Jessel, "—who is, you know, as you women prefer it, also a Dandy."

So indeed the governess stands rooted to the spot, her

small pale face disguising nothing of the turbulent emotions she feels. With the studied nonchalance of a professional actor, though such a "visitation," so calibrated, is entirely new to him, Quint walks slowly along the ledge, continuing to stare at the governess: *You do not know me, my dear girl, but you can guess who I am. You have been forewarned.*

Cunning Quint, as the governess stares up at him like a transfixed child, strolls to the farther curve of the tower, *disappears.*

Thinking afterward, in the golden-erotic glow of a wholly satisfactory experience, *How otherwise to know what power we wield, except to see it in another's eyes?*

Excitedly, extravagantly, Jessel predicts that her "replacement" will flee Bly immediately—"*I* should do so, under such circumstances!"

"Seeing a ghost, do you mean?" Quint asks, bemused, "—or seeing *me*?"

Yet, to Jessel's surprise, and extreme disappointment, the governess from Ottery St. Mary, Devonshire, does not flee Bly; but seems to be digging in, as for a siege. She is intimidated, surely, but also wary, and alert. She exudes an air of—what? A Puritan's prim, punitive zeal?—a Christian martyr's stubborn resolve? The second time Quint appears to her, the two of them, alone, no more than fifteen feet apart, separated by a pane of glass, the young woman draws herself up to her full height (she lacks Jessel's stature, is no more than five feet two inches tall) and stares unwaveringly at Quint for a long tense moment.

Quint frowns severely. *You know who I am! You have been forewarned!*

The governess is so frightened that the blood drains from her face, turning it a ghastly waxen color; her fists are clenched, white-knuckled, against her flat bosom. Yet, staring at Quint, she seems to challenge him. *Yes, I know who you are. But, no, I will not give in.*

When Quint releases her, she does not run to hide in her room, but, again most unexpectedly, bounds out of the house, and rushes around to the terrace, where, if Quint were a flesh-and-blood man, a "real" man, he would have stood to peer through the window. Of course, no one is there. A scattering of bruised forsythia blossoms on the terrace beneath the window lies undisturbed.

The governess, white-faced, yet arrogant, peers about with the nervous intensity of a small terrier. Clearly, she *is* frightened; yet, it seems, fear alone is not enough to deter her. (Her behavior is the more courageous in that it is Sunday, and most of the household, including the ever-vigilant Mrs. Grose, are at church in the Village of Bly.) Quint has retreated to a hedgerow a short distance away, where, joined by a somber Jessel, he contemplates the governess in her plain, prim, chaste Sunday bonnet and provincial costume: how defiant the gawky little thing is! Jessel gnaws at a thumbnail, murmuring, "How can it be, Quint! A normal woman, thinking she'd seen a ghost—or, indeed, thinking she'd seen, in such circumstances, an actual man—would have run away screaming for help." Quint says, annoyed, "Maybe, love, I'm not so formidable as we think." Jessel says, worriedly, "Or *she* is not a normal woman."

Afterward, Quint recalls the episode with, beyond annoyance and chagrin, a stir of sexual arousal. It excites him that there is a new, young, willful woman at Bly; homely as a pudding, and with a body flat, bosom and buttocks, as a board. Certainly she lacks Jessel's passion, as she lacks Jessel's desperation. Yet she is *alive,* and poor dear Jessel is *dead.*

Quint makes himself snake-slender, incorporeal: yet gifted with a prodigious red-skinned erection: an incubus: insinuating himself into the governess's bedroom, and into her bed, and, despite her faint flailing protests, into her very body.

When he groans aloud, shuddering, Jessel pokes him with a sharp little fist.

"Are you having a nightmare, Quint?" she asks ironically.

And then, an unexpected development: poor little Miles has been expelled from Eton!

Quint and Jessel contrive to overhear the governess and Mrs. Grose as they discuss the subject, and the mystery embedded in it, repeatedly; obsessively. The governess, quite shocked, and puzzled, reads the headmaster's letter of dismissal to Mrs. Grose; together, the women dissect the chill, blunt, insultingly formal sentences, which present the expulsion as a *fait accompli,* about which there can be no negotiations. It seems, simply, that Eton "declines" to keep little Miles as a student. That is all.

Jessel, crouched beside Quint, murmurs in a low, sensuous voice, "Delightful for you, Quint, to have your boy back again, eh? The four of us will be reunited soon!—I know it."

But Quint, who has a notion that he knows why Miles has been expelled, says, gravely, "But, poor Miles! He *must* go to school, after all; he can't hang about here like his sister. His uncle will be furious when he learns. The old bugger wants nothing but that Miles grow up to be a 'manly man' like himself."

"Oh, what do we care for *him*?" Jessel asks. "He is the worst of the enemy, after all."

A day later, Miles appears. He is much the same as Quint recalls, perhaps an inch or so taller, a few pounds heavier; fair-skinned, clear-eyed, with that slightly feverish flush to his cheeks and that air of startled breathlessness that Quint found so appealing—finds appealing still. A sweet, clever, circumspect lad of ten, but far, far older than his years, Miles wins the heart of the new governess at their first meeting; forestalls, by his very innocence, any awkward questions about Eton; and, that night, when he should have been in bed, slips past the door of the governess's room (which little Flora shares) and wanders out into the deep, shifting shadows of the park, seeking—who, or what?

Moonlight cascades over the slated roofs of the great ugly House of Bly. The cries of nocturnal birds sound in a rhythmic, staccato pulse.

Quint observes dear little Miles, in pajamas, barefoot, making his way across the slope of the lawn, and back beyond the stables, to one of their old trysting places: there the child throws himself, with an air of abandon, on the dewy grass, as if to declare *I am here, where are you?* When Quint died, little Miles was said to have been "stony-cold"—not a tear shed. So Quint overheard the servants talking. When Miss Jessel drowned, little Flora was said to have been "heartbroken"—inconsolable for days. Quint approves of Miles's stoicism.

Hidden close by the restive child (Miles is looking impatiently about, pulling at blades of grass), Quint observes him with fond, guilty eyes. In life, Quint's passion was for women; his affection for little Miles was in reaction to little Miles's affection for him, thus not a true passion, perhaps. Quint wonders is it fair to the child, the secret bond between them?—the attachment, of such tender, wordless intimacy, even Quint's abrupt *crossing over* seems not to have weakened it?

In the moonlit silence the child's voice is low, fearful, quavering with hope. "Quint? Damn you, Quint, *are* you here?"

Quint, choked with emotion suddenly, does not reply. He sees the child's beautiful eyes, glittering as with a fever. What a tragedy, to be orphaned at the age of five!—no wonder the child grasped Quint's knee as a drowning person a lifeboat.

It had been Miles's habit, charming, and touching, perhaps a bit pitiful, to seek out the lovers Quint and Miss Jessel in just such trysting places, if he could find them; then, silky hair disheveled and eyes dilated as with an opiate, he would hug, burrow, twist, groan with yearning and delight—who could resist him, who could send him away? And little Flora, too.

"Quint?" Miles whispers, glancing nervously about, his rapt, eager face luminous as a lily, "—I know you're here, you couldn't, could you, *not* be here! It has been so damnably long."

Those happiest of times. Because most unexpected, uncalculated of times.

And what a dreamy infinity of time, at Bly: the Bly of lush rural England: unimaginable, indeed, in the bustle of London and the stern verticality of Harley Street.

Miles continues, more desperate, and demanding, "Quint, damn you! I know you're here—somewhere." Indeed, the boy is staring, with a frown that creases his perfect little forehead like crumpled paper, at Quint—without seeming to see him. "Not 'dead'—" Miles's perfect mouth twists in distaste, "—not you. She has seen you, eh?—the new, the supremely awful governess? 'St. Ottery,' I call her—aren't I clever? Quint? *Has* she seen you? She doesn't let on, of course, she's far too cunning, but Flora has guessed. There's been such a tedious prattle of the 'purity' of childhood, and the need to 'be good, starting with clean *hands.*' " Miles laughs shrilly.

"Quint? They've sacked me, you know—sent me down—as you'd worried—warned. *I'm* to blame, I suppose—what a fool!—telling only two or three boys about it—boys I liked, oh! ever so much—and who liked me, I know—they vowed never to tell, and yet—somehow—it all came out—there was a nasty hue and cry—Quint, how I hate them all!—they are the enemy, and they are so many! Quint? I love only you."

And I love only you, dear Miles.

Quint appears before Miles, a tall, glimmering shape, taller than he had been in life. Miles gapes up at him, astonished; then, on hands and knees he crawls to Quint, now weeping, "Quint! Quint!" groaning in a delirium of joy as he tries to hug the phantom flesh—legs, thighs. The porousness of Quint's being does not deter him, perhaps in his excitement he does not comprehend. "I knew! I knew! I knew!—you would not abandon me, Quint!"

Never, dear boy: you have my word.

Then, horribly, there comes an abrupt call, nasal, reedy, scolding—"Miles? You naughty boy, where are you?"

It is the governess from Ottery St. Mary: a diminutive, stubborn figure, just rounding the corner of the stable some thirty feet away, holding aloft a lighted candle: groping, yet persistent, bravely undaunted by the night and by the feeble, flickering radius of the candle-flame: *her!*

"—Miles? *Miles—?*"

So the tryst ends, rudely interrupted. Quint, swearing, retreats. Miles in his pajamas, so charmingly barefoot, rises, rueful, brushing at himself, composing a face, a child's angelic face, untwisting his mouth, with no recourse but to say, "Here I am."

But who is guiding us, Quint, if not ourselves?—is there Another whose face we cannot see and whose voice we cannot hear, except as it echoes in our own thoughts?

Jessel fairly spits the words, her lovely mouth turned ugly—"I despise her! *She* is the ghoul. If only we could destroy her outright!"

As rarely in the past she'd done, coaxed by the child's urgent need, Jessel appears to little Flora in emboldened daylight, daring to "materialize" on the farther shore of the placid Sea of Azof. A cloudless afternoon in early summer, a vertigo of honeysuckle in the air, and, so suddenly, out of nowhere, there appears, on the grassy bank, a somber yet beautiful figure, hair shockingly undone, darkly lustrous, falling past her shoulders, her face alabaster pale: an heraldic figure, one might think, out of an ancient legend, or a curse. And the child's doll-like figure in the foreground, blond curls, an angel's profile, pinafore brightly yellow as the buttercups that grow in happy profusion in the surrounding grass—is not little Flora in her innocence, as in her need, necessary to the vision?

And, on a stone bench close by the child, busily knitting, yet keeping a watchful and jealous eye on her—"St. Ottery," as Miles has wittily dubbed her.

So like a Fate, indeed!

A common jailer.

Eyes like ditch-water, scanty fair lashes, brows; the small brave chin, sparrow body, skin stretched tight as the skin of a drum. The narrow face is too small for the head, and the head is too small for the body, the body too small for such long, angular feet. The shoulder blades are painfully prominent beneath the dark cotton of her governess's dress, like folded wings.

Flora is playing, quite absorbedly it seems, on the bank of the pond, humming a nonsensical little tune as she cradles her newest doll in her arms, and an exquisitely beautiful, life-like doll it is, from France, Flora's guardian-uncle's gift to her on the occasion of her eighth birthday (which, to Uncle's regret, he could not attend), her head is lowered, yet she is gazing, staring fixedly, through her eyelashes, at beloved Miss Jessel on the other bank. How the child's heart beats, in yearning! *Take me with you, Miss Jessel, oh please! I am so lonely here,* the child mutely begs. *I am so unhappy, dear Miss Jessel, since you went away!* and Jessel's heart too beats in yearning, in love, for Flora *is* her own little girl, the babe cruelly drowned in her womb, hers and Quint's, in this very pond.

Jessel fixes her gaze upon Flora, across the pond: Jessel would comfort the child, as a hypnotist might. *Dear Flora, dear child, you know I love you: you know we will be together soon, and never again apart. My darling—*

But, then, the rude interruption, in a most shrill, reedy voice: "Flora, is something wrong?—what is it?"

The terrier "St. Ottery" leaps to her feet and hurries to Flora, glancing level, myopic eyes narrowed, to the opposite bank—seeing the figure of her predecessor, whom perhaps she recognizes; an apparition of the most sorrowful beauty; yet more frightful, in its very solemnity, than the other, the man. (For the man, in his sexually aggressive, self-conscious posture, might have been interpreted as, simply, a *man*; this creature, "St. Ottery" shrewdly sees, can be nothing but a *ghoul.*)

The governess grips little Flora by the arm, with unconscious force, crying, appalled, "My God, what a—horror! Hide your eyes, child! Shield yourself!"

Flora protests, in tears. Dazed and blinking as if slapped, insists she sees nothing, there *is* nothing. Even as Jessel stares in impotent rage, the governess swiftly, indeed rather brutally, leads the whimpering child away, pulling her by both arms, murmuring words of reproachful comfort: "Don't look at her, Flora! The horrid, obscene thing! You're safe now."

Horrid, obscene thing. When, in life, she'd been so sweetly modest a girl, impeccably groomed in ways spiritual no less than material; yes, and a Christian, of course; and a virgin—of course.

That ticklish scuttling in her hair?—a hard-shelled beetle falls to the ground.

Fanatic Jessel, stung to the core of her being, begins to lose control. Ever more carelessly by day she prowls the House of Bly seeking her darling girl alone, if only for a few snatched moments. "It seems *I* am haunted," Jessel laughs despairingly, "but what's to be done? Flora is my soul." Yet the jealous and vindictive "St. Ottery" hovers over the child every waking hour; she has pulled Flora's pretty little bed up snug beside her own, for safekeeping at night. (Since the upset on the bank of the pond, neither the governess nor her agitated, feverish charge is capable of sleeping for more than a few minutes at a time.)

Flora pleads: *Miss Jessel, help me! Come to me! Hurry!*

And Jessel: *Flora, my darling, I will come. Soon.*

But the vigilant young woman from Ottery St. Mary refuses to allow the shutters in her and Flora's room to be opened! Nor the shutters in the adjoining nursery. In Miss Jessel's reign, when she and the red-bearded Quint were lovers, how these rooms were flooded with sunshine!—yes, and with moonlight, too! The very air pulsed with their love, humid and languorous; the baroque silver sconces on the walls trembled with their love-cries. Now the air is stale and sour, fresh linen laid upon the beds turns soiled within minutes.

Pushing her authority, as there is no one here at Bly to oppose it, "St. Ottery" tries to insist that the windows in poor Miles's bedroom be permanently shuttered as well; but, being a boy, and a most willful boy, whose angelic face belies his precocious soul, little Miles resists. "What are windows for, pray, you silly old thing—" for so Miles has affected a gay, jocose, just slightly taunting flirtatious tone with the terrible woman, "—if not, you know, to look *out* of?"

To which the reply is a grim-jawed, "Miles, I will put that question to *you.*"

As if shutters, of mere wood, can keep at bay love's most violent yearnings.

Poor damned soul: by now, all of the household staff has seen her.

Drifting through the house, now upstairs, now down, now at the French windows opened upon a profusion of sticky-petaled glaring-white clematis . . . that wailing sound is hers, a sigh torn from her . . . woman sighing for her lost child, or her own soul as it nears extinction. How is it "St. Ottery" is always between her and Flora—always! Most recently, the New Testament in her hand.

This morning, Jessel finds herself exhausted at her old desk in the schoolroom. A soft moan escapes her. Her arms slumped on the desk and head heavy with sorrow resting on her arms, her face hidden, eyes brimming hot with tears of hurt, bewilderment, rage, *How am I, who is love, evil?* and a footfall behind her, a sharp intake of breath, rouse her to wakefulness, and she stands, swaying, and turns, to see her enemy confronting her hardly six feet away: "St. Ottery" bent at the waist like a crippled woman, her arms upraised as if to ward off the devil, but the colorless eyes narrowed in loathing, and the certitude of that loathing, the pale, prominent forehead, the thin lips—"Go away, out of here! This is no place for you!—vile, unspeakable horror!"

Where once Jessel would have stood her ground, now, seeing the revulsion in the other's eyes, she is sickened, defenseless. She cannot protest, she feels herself dissolving, surrendering the field to her enemy, who calls after her, in ecstatic triumph, a shrill reedy voice wholly without pity—"And never return! Never, never dare return!"

Now, with more concentrated zeal, the fierce "St. Ottery" interrogates poor Flora, mercilessly. "Flora, dear, is there something you would like to tell me?" and, "Flora, dear, you *can* tell me, you know: I've seen the dreadful thing, I'm aware." And, most cruelly: "My child, you may as well confess! I've spoken with your 'Miss Jessel,' and *she* has told *me.*"

Jessel is a witness, albeit an invisible and powerless witness, when a bubble bursts at last in Flora's brain. Her sobs might be those of countless children, reverberating horribly in the catacombs beneath the great ugly House of Bly. Flora screams, "No no no *no*! I didn't! I don't! I don't know what you mean! I hate you!"

Jessel is powerless to interfere even as she sees the hysterical child caught up in Mrs. Grose's arms.

What more bitter irony, that Jessel should find herself grateful for, of all people, her old enemy Mrs. Grose.

I will be extinct by daylight: it's time. I have been only a memory of night.

The old house rings, down to the very catacombs, with the mad child's howls, her guttural little barks of profanity, obscenity. Mrs. Grose and another woman servant, accompanying Flora on the journey to London, where she will be put under the supervision of a noted child physician, are obliged numerous times to clap their hands over their ears, for shame.

Mrs. Grose asks tearfully, "Where did that angel pick up such *language*?"

* * *

"St. Ottery" remains behind, of course, to care for little Miles. She is shaken—saddened-baffled—infuriated—by the loss of little Flora, but she is determined not to lose Miles.

She, too, the virgin daughter of a country parson, a Methodist. On her knees, praying to Our Father for strength against the Devil. She reads the New Testament for solace, and for a girding of the loins. Did not Our Savior cast out evil demons from the afflicted?—did not He, when He chose, have the power of raising the dead? In such a universe, of fiercely contending spirits, all things are possible.

"Miles, dear! Where are you? Come, it's time for your lessons!"

Far below, in the dank-dripping catacombs, heartsick with mourning his beloved Jessel (Quint was no husband, but feels a husband's loss: half his soul torn from him), Peter Quint hears the governess hurrying from room to room, surprisingly heavy on her heels. Her call is like a rook's, shrill, persistent. "Miles? Miles—"

Quint, with trembling fingers, readies himself for the final confrontation. He perceives himself as a figure in a drama, or it may be an equation, there is Good, there is Evil, there is deception, there must be deception, for otherwise there would be no direction in which to move.... Squinting at his sallow reflection in a shard of mirror, plucking at his graying beard to restore, or to suggest, its old virility; recalling, with a swoon in the loins, poor Miles hugging him about the knees, mashing his heated face against him.

How is it evil, to give, as to receive, love's comforts?

Jessel has vanished. Dissolved, faded: as the morning mist, milkily opaque at dawn, fades in the gathering light. His beloved Jessel!—the girl with the "Scots curl," and the hymen so damnably hard to break! A mere cloud of dispersing molecules, atoms?

For that dispersal is Death. To which *crossing over* is but an overture. It was desire that held them at Bly, the reluctance of love to surrender the beloved. Desire holds Quint here, still. The fact stuns him. Mere molecules, atoms? When we love so passionately? He sees Miles's yearning face, feels Miles's shyly-bold groping caress.

Readying himself for the enemy.

* * *

Panting like a beast, feet damp with dew, Quint peers through the dusty windowpane. Inside, poor Miles has been tracked down at last, discovered by "St. Ottery" hidden away, suspiciously, and cozily, in a wingback chair turned to face a corner in the library—a vault-like room on the first floor of the house, into which no one (including Master on one of his rare visits) has stepped foot for some time. It is a gentleman's place, a mausoleum of a kind, its dark-grained oak panelings hung with portraits of patriarchs long since dissolved to dust, and forgotten; twelve-foot bookshelves rear to the ceiling, crammed with aged and mildewed books, great leather-bound and gilt-etched tomes that look as if they have not been opened in centuries. How incongruous, in such gloom, the fresh-faced ten-year-old Miles with the quick, seemingly carefree smile!

White-lipped "St. Ottery" asks, hands on her hips, why Miles has "crept away" here, why, hidden in a chair, legs drawn up beneath him, so *still*?—"When, you know, I've been calling and *call*ing you?"

Miles glances toward the window, the merest flicker of a glance, even as he says, gaily, "I was just so lost in this, you see—!" showing the governess an absurdly heavy, antique tome on his knees—the *Directorium Inquisitorum*. "St. Ottery" says dryly, "And since when, my boy, do you read Latin for pleasure?" and Miles giggles charmingly, "My dear, I read Latin as everyone does—for *pain*."

"St. Ottery" would remove the *Directorium Inquisitorum* from Miles's knees but, prankishly, the boy spreads them, and the heavy book crashes to the floor in a cloud of dust. Miles murmurs, "Oh! Sorry."

Again, Miles glances toward the window. *Quint, are you here?*

Quint strains forward, hoping to lock eyes with the boy, but the damnable governess moves between them. How he wishes he could strangle her, with his bare hands! She falls to interrogating Miles at once, sternly, yet with an air of pleading. "Tell me, Miles: your sister *did* commune with that ghastly woman, didn't she? My predecessor here? That is why Flora is so terribly, tragically ill, isn't it?" But cunning Miles denies this at once, denies even knowing what "St. Ottery" is talking about. He reverts to the behavior of a much younger child, grimacing and wriggling about, eluding "St. Ottery" as she reaches for him. Again, his eyes snatch at the window. *Quint, damn you, where are you? Help me!*

"St. Ottery," snake-quick, seizes his arm. Her no-color myopic eyes shine with a missionary's good intentions. "Miles, dear, only tell the truth, you know, and don't lie: you will break Jesus's heart, and *my* heart, if you lie. Poor Flora was seduced by 'Miss Jessel,' is that it?—and you, what of you and 'Peter Quint'? There is nothing to fear from him, you know, if you tell *me.*"

Miles's laughter is wild and skittering. He simply denies all, everything: "I don't know a thing of what you say. Flora isn't ill. Flora has gone to visit our uncle in London. I know nothing of Miss Jessel, who died when I was away at school. And Peter Quint—why," his flushed face creasing in distaste, "—the man is *dead.*"

"Dead, yes! But here with us, at Bly, constantly!" the governess cries, with the aggrieved air of a betrayed lover, "—as, Miles, I think, *you* know."

"'Here with us'? 'Constantly'? What do you mean? Where?" The boy's face, struck blank, is so dazzling an image of innocence Quint stares in wonder. "Damn you, *where*?"

In triumph "St. Ottery" turns, and points to the windowpane against which Quint presses his yearning face. Surely, the woman cannot have known Quint is there, yet with fanatic certainty she whirls about, points her accusatory finger, directing Miles's terrified gaze. "There!—as you've known all along, you wicked, wicked boy!"

Yet, it seems, Miles, though staring straight at Quint, cannot see him. "What?" he cries. "'Peter Quint'—where?"

"There, I say—*there*!" In a fury, the governess taps against the glass, as if to break it. Quint shrinks away.

Miles gives an anguished cry. His face has gone dead-white, he appears on the verge of a collapse, yet, when "St. Ottery" tries to secure him in her arms, he shoves her away. "Don't touch me, leave me alone!" he shouts. *"I hate you."*

He runs from the room, leaving "St. Ottery" behind.

Leaving "St. Ottery" and Peter Quint to regard each other through the window, passionless now, spent as lovers who have been tortured to ecstasy in each other's arms.

* * *

We must have imagined that, if Evil could be made to exist, Good might exist as rightfully.

Into the balmy-humid night the child Miles runs, runs for his life, damp hair sticking to his forehead, and his heart, that slithery fish, thumping against his ribs. Though guessing it is futile, for the madwoman was pointing at nothing, Miles cries, in a hopeful, dreading voice, "Quint?—*Quint*?"

The wind in the high trees, a night sky pierced with stars. No answer of course.

Miles hears, with a smile, bullfrogs in the pond. Every year at this time. Those deep guttural urgent rhythmic croaks. Comical, yet with dignity. And so many! The night air is warmly moist as the interior of a lover's mouth. The bullfrogs have appropriated it. Their season has begun.

Kim Paffenroth

(1966–)

Born in Syosset, New York, Kim Paffenroth earned a BA at St. John's College in Annapolis, Maryland, an MTS at Harvard Divinity School (1990), and a PhD in theology at the University of Notre Dame (1995). A professor of religious studies at Iona College in New Rochelle, New York, he has published extensively on Saint Augustine, including *Augustine and Liberal Education* (2000), *A Reader's Companion to Augustine's Confessions* (2003), *Augustine and Literature* (2006), and *Augustine and World Religions* (2008). His fascination with the depiction of zombies is reflected in his editing of an anthology of stories that portray the undead throughout the ages, *History Is Dead* (2007), in *Gospel of the Living Dead: George Romero's Visions of Hell on Earth* (2006), and in his novels, *Dying to Live: A Novel of Life Among the Undead* (2006) and *Dying to Live: Life Sentence* (2008).

Excerpt from
Dying to Live

(2006)

I awoke to find a lone zombie underneath my little hideaway. The tree house I had spent the night in was poorly constructed—the bottom was just a square of plywood, reinforced with a couple boards, with plywood walls on three sides and the fourth one open. It had no roof, but the sky was clear, so no bother. All the pieces were irregular and unpainted, with big gaps between them in many spots, and the walls were only between two and three feet high. But it was higher up than most, a good twelve feet off the ground (the kid's mom must've been one of the ones we always called a "cool mom," to allow such a dangerous playhouse), so I was even more surprised to see my unwanted visitor.

I scanned the surrounding field and trees and saw that the zombie and I were alone; my heart slowed down. In a few moments, my situation had gone from peaceful morning reverie, to possible or near-certain death, to minor inconvenience. In that respect, this was a typical morning.

One reason the zombie and I were alone this morning was that it lacked the ability to make sound. Like so many of its kind, its throat was torn open, leaving its windpipe a ragged hole, and the front of its suit stained brown with blood.

It looked up at me with its listless cloudy eyes, which lacked all expression—not hatred, not evil, not even hunger, just blanks. It was chilling in its own way, like the stare of a snake or an insect. Its look would never change, whether you drove a spike through its head or it sank its yellow teeth into your soft, warm flesh; it lacked all capacity to be afraid or to be satisfied. Its mouth, however, had a great deal more bestial expression to it, for it was wide-open, almost gnawing at the bark of the tree as it clawed upward.

I stood looking down at it for a few moments. It was times like this—and there had been several in the last few months—that I had always wished that I smoked. In a few seconds, I would fight this thing and one or both of us would cease to exist—"die" is obviously the wrong word here—and just to stand here and contemplate that inevitability cried out for some distraction, some mindless and sensual habit like smoking, to make it less horrible. I guess I could've chewed gum, but that would make the whole scene ridiculous, when it was really as serious, overwhelming, and sad as any that had ever occurred to a man.

With nothing to distract me, I just felt the full weight of a terrible and necessary task, and the tediousness and unfairness of it. I had just awakened from a relatively peaceful sleep, and I already felt a crushing weariness coming over me. Again, it was developing into a pretty typical morning.

My zombie this morning looked to have been a middle-aged man in its human life, slightly graying, average build.

Its suit was intact, and other than its throat wound, there were no signs of further fights with humans or other zombies. Decay had taken its toll, and it looked more desiccated than gooey, a brittle husk rather than the dripping bag of pus that some of them became.

At first, I looked it over to size up its threat and plan my attack, but that quickly turned into contemplating its human existence. Maybe his kids had built the tree house, and that's why he'd been hanging around here, almost as if he were protecting it, or waiting for them to come back. Or even worse, maybe his kids had been the ones to tear out his throat, when he had rushed home in the midst of the outbreak, hoping against hope they were still okay. Or, just as bad, maybe he'd been bitten at work or on the way home, only to break in to his own house and kill his kids.

My mind reeled, and I clutched the wall of the tree house. I'd heard of soldiers in other wars having a "thousand-yard stare," a blank look that signaled they were giving in to the hopelessness and horror around them, soon to be dead or insane. As for me, I was suffering the thousand-yard stare of the war with the undead: once you contemplated the zombies as human beings, once you thought of them as having kids and lives and loves and worries and hopes and fears, you might as well just put your gun in your mouth and be done with it right then, because you were losing it—fast. But, God knows, if you never looked at them that way, if they were just meat puppets whose heads exploded in your rifle's sights, then hopefully somebody would put a bullet in your brain, because you had become more monstrous than any zombie ever could be.

I shook myself free of my paralysis. I'm not exactly sure why, but I wasn't ready to give up yet. I tossed my backpack beyond where the zombie stood. It turned to see where it landed, then immediately looked back up at me. Its head lolled from side to side, and I was again glad that it couldn't vocalize, as it was clearly getting worked up and would've been making quite a racket if it could.

You never used a gun if you didn't have to, for its noise brought lots of unwanted attention, so I pulled out a knife, the one I carried with a long, thin blade, like a bayonet, as that would work best. I stood at the edge of the plywood platform. "I'm sorry," I said, looking right in the zombie's eyes. "Maybe somewhere, deep down, you still understand: I'm sorry."

I took a step forward and started to fall. I tried to hit it on the shoulder with my right foot, but its arms were flailing about, and my boot hit its left wrist, sliding along its arm. I sprawled to the right and then rolled away as the zombie was shoved into the tree.

As it turned to face me, I scrambled up, took a step forward, and drove the knife into its left eye. Its hands flailed about, either to attack me or to ward off the blow. The blade was long and thin enough that it went almost to the back of its skull. The whole attack was noiseless, without so much as the sound of a squish or a glitch as the blade slid through its eyeball and brain.

As I drew the blade out, I grabbed the zombie by the hair and shoved it downward to the side, where it fell to the ground and lay motionless.

And that was that. I always used to imagine deadly fights would be much more dramatic. But usually, like this morning, there were just a couple of savage, clumsy blows, and it was over.

I was barely breathing at all, let alone breathing hard, the way I felt someone should when they kill something that was somehow, in some small way, still human. A few months ago, I would've at least felt nauseous, but not anymore. Looking down at the creature from the tree house had been much more traumatic than delivering the killing blow.

I bent down over my would-be killer and cleaned the blade on his suit jacket. I then reached into his pocket. It was a little ritual I still followed when I could, though the horrible exigencies of a zombie-infested world usually made it impossible. I pulled out his wallet and got out his driver's license. Rather than look at the bloody horror at my feet, with its one undead eye and one bloody, vacant socket, I stared at his driver's license picture—smiling, happy, alive, years and decades of life ahead of him. I cleared my throat to speak clearly. "I have killed Daniel Gerard. I hope he's somewhere better now."

I cast the wallet and license on top of his motionless body, scooped up my backpack, and hurried away.

* * *

It had been close to a year since all the worst parts of the Bible started coming true. Armageddon. Apocalypse. The End of Days. God's righteous judgment on a sinful humanity. Whatever the self-righteous jerk who railed at you once a week from a pulpit used to call it. Well, he might have been self-righteous and a jerk, and now he was probably lurching around like most everyone else, drooling on himself with half his face torn off, but it sure seemed as though he had had some inside information that we all wish we'd gotten a little sooner.

Almost one year after the first corpse rose, the world was now ruled by the undead, who wandered about with no discernible goal other than to kill and eat living people. The undead were everywhere, the new dominant species that took the place of the old, extinct one. Places where there had been large human populations were especially thick with the walking dead, though they never took any notice of one another.

The living, meanwhile, as was their wont, almost always congregated in little groups. The government or society or culture had imploded or disintegrated with terrifying speed as the infection spread. Within hours, there had been no telephone service, no police or rescue response to the terrified calls for help. Within days, there was no power or television. And within weeks, the last organized military and government resistance collapsed, at least in the U.S.

But groups of survivors quickly came together into little groups, little communities with a pecking order and rules and authority, but also some of the little perks of being around other people—companionship, conversation, sex, someone to hold your hand when you die, someone to put a bullet in your brain when you went to get back up as a zombie. (And if you've ever seen a zombie—and God love you, I hope you haven't, but if you're reading this, I suspect you have—then you know that last perk is by no means the least important one.) You didn't have to be a damned philosopher to know that we're social animals, and would be till the last zombie bit the last human and dragged us all down to hell, which, judging by the zombies, looked like it was going to be the most unsociable place imaginable.

Yes, humans always build their little communities in order to survive, and in order to make surviving a little more bearable. Except me. I was alone. And it sucked. It was dangerous and it sucked.

By midday, I was moving closer to what looked like a small-sized city. I had thrown my maps away a few days ago when I had failed to find my family. After that, I figured, I didn't have much need for maps: if I didn't have any place to go anymore—and I had decided that I didn't—what difference did it make where I was at the moment? Besides, the end of civilization had wreaked a lot of havoc with the things depicted on maps: I guess the rivers and mountains were still there, but cities were gone, roads were clogged with wrecked cars, bridges and tunnels and dams had been blown up to try to stop the rampaging hordes of the undead. So long as I was out of reach of those things, and had one bullet for myself if it came to that, I was in about the best location I could hope for.

It was a late-spring day, bursting with a sunshine that didn't make it hot, but just made things seem better, brighter, more alive than they were on other days. I still had the instinct to call it beautiful as I looked around and forgot the obvious shortcomings of the day for a moment. One shortcoming I couldn't forget, however, was the gnawing hunger I felt.

From what I'd seen, many cities had burned more or less to the ground, once fire crews were no longer there to put out the inevitable fires. But here, for whatever reason of wind or rain or luck, many buildings were still standing. Some were gutted or damaged by fire, and all had the usual marks of looting, ransacking, and the final, desperate battles between the living and the dead. There were few unbroken windows.

In the street, wrecked or abandoned cars were everywhere. There were a few bodies and pieces of bodies in extremely advanced stages of decay, and paper and dead leaves rustled about on a light breeze.

The sight of the burnt-out remains of a city was almost as overwhelmingly depressing as the human wrecks that wandered everywhere as zombies: this place should have been bustling and alive, and instead it was—quite literally—a graveyard. I checked the remains of a couple stores, barely venturing inside the darkened buildings, for fear of the dead hiding in ambush. The inventories of a clothing store and a jewelry store were barely touched: it was funny how quickly things had been reprioritized in the final, chaotic days of the human race.

I looked at what appeared to be hundreds of thousands of dollars of diamonds, now mixed in with the smashed glass of the cases that had once displayed them: both sparkled in the sun, but their value had been radically and traumatically equalized a few months ago. I imagined that during last winter—the first winter of a world that would now remain more or less dead in every season—the snow too had sparkled just as brightly when it blew in and covered the diamonds that, in better times, would've adorned hundreds of brides.

A quick look into a liquor store revealed much less remaining stock—human nature and appetites being what they are—but there was a bottle of some bad bourbon just a few feet inside the door, so I reached in and grabbed it. I didn't know when I'd be able to drop my guard enough to partake, but since I wasn't carrying that much, it made sense to take it.

I knew I was getting too far into the dead city, but on the next street was a convenience store where there might be food. It was facing perpendicularly from the stores I had examined, so at least it would be brighter inside. The big front windows were still intact, but the glass of the front door had been smashed. Looking up and down the street and still seeing no movement, I went inside the store.

I was looking for snack cakes. When the final crisis of humanity had begun, people had instinctively stocked up on canned food: I guess Spam is forever etched in our collective consciousness as the foodstuff of the apocalypse. People at first had bought up everything canned, and then, within just a couple days, as cash became utterly worthless and stores weren't even open, the stronger smashed and grabbed from the weaker. I had never seen a can of food in a store since I had started foraging: you could only find cans in people's houses, and even then they were getting pretty rare at this point. So, for now, snack cakes were the way to go. What I would do when those finally went bad and the last few cans ran out—that was a question still a few months off, and therefore way beyond any reasonable contingency plans.

I don't know if all the old urban legends that Twinkies and those pink Snow Ball cakes could survive a nuclear explosion were true, but they and their kind definitely had a shelf life well over a year, if the box wasn't opened and you weren't fussy, which I clearly wasn't at this point.

There was a treasure trove of them in the second aisle into the store, and I smiled when I saw there were no chocolate ones: I guessed some priorities remained effective right up till the last gasp of humanity. I made my way quietly to them, tore open the boxes, shoveled a bunch of the wrapped ones into my backpack, and proceeded to gorge myself on what I couldn't carry. I was licking white crème filling off my fingers when I heard the crunch of a shoe stepping on broken glass.

The zombie was about twelve feet away from me, at the end of the Twinkie aisle. It was staggering toward me with the usual slow, stiff motions of the undead. It had been a teenage girl, blond and pretty, as far as I could tell now, wearing her boyfriend's high school letter jacket, way too big for her. Its mouth moved noiselessly, except for the clacking of her bloody, yellow teeth.

The jacket was open, and the lower half of her T-shirt was flayed and soaked with blood, which also had soaked her jeans down past her knees. Her abdomen was torn wide-open in a wound about a foot wide. They'd ripped all her organs out when they killed her. She wasn't moaning now the way zombies usually did, because she didn't have lungs. You could see right through to her ribs and spine, not glistening and drippy the way a wound on a living person would be, but dark and dry and caked, like mummies I'd seen in museums.

It was coming closer, slowly but inexorably, but I couldn't look away from that horrible tribute to mortality and incarnation. You saw all kinds of wounds on the living dead, but some still commanded shock, almost a reverential awe at the miracle of life and the horrible mystery of death. Sometimes you couldn't help the pity that spasmed up from your own gut, putting a lump in your throat, at how awful and degrading and unfair the person's death must have been. People—even young and pretty ones—died in car crashes, or from diseases, or in war, or from horrible crimes, and their young, healthy bodies might even be mutilated and disfigured. But no one was supposed to be gutted like a fish, butchered like an animal, and left to dry out like a damn piece of jerky. You might see shit go down most every day, but if you were going to go on living, you had to know, deep down, that some things were still just plain wrong, and you could still let out a primal scream against them as some kind of evil abomination. And what I was staring at in that convenience store, on a glorious spring day, licking sweet white crème off my fingers, was as wrong as anything ever could be.

There was that damn thousand-yard stare again, closing me off, tunneling my vision and lulling me to just let go.

To my left, something roared, and I turned. Over the shelves, I could see what could only be described as a hairless bear, its arms out in front, Frankenstein-like, lurching toward me. I swear the thing looked like it had been a professional wrestler in its human life—probably 350 pounds, almost a head taller than me, covered in tattoos, though its flesh was now a mottled gray that obscured much of the artwork.

It crashed into the shelves, tipping them over onto me and the other zombie. I was pushed back and pinned against the opposite shelves as the monster scrabbled at my face with its foul nails; the shelving unit kept it from getting closer. The girl zombie wasn't pinned as tightly as I was, so she was still slowly working her way toward me, teeth clacking.

The top shelf pressed into my upper chest and arms, making it hard to breathe, as well as almost impossible to get to a weapon, and even if I did, I wouldn't be able to bring it up to eye level to get a head shot at either of them. I had no leverage to push the shelving unit off me, and I wasn't sure I could do it anyway, as the zombie was so much bigger than me.

I struggled and drew my .357 Magnum from the holster in the small of my back. I shot from the hip, and my ears started ringing from the roar of the Magnum. The window behind the big zombie shattered as the bullet went through his torso. He staggered back just enough for me to push the shelving unit off of me.

The zombie lunged again—I stuck the barrel in its face and fired. Its arms shot up as it spun around and dropped on its face, the back of its head blown off.

I turned as the girl zombie grabbed my shoulder. I grabbed her hair, wrenched myself free from her grip, and shoved the barrel of the gun under her chin. I yanked her head down and to the left so she wasn't looking at me. "I'm sorry," I rasped as I pulled the trigger. Her brains were blasted out in a gray slop all over the ceiling surveillance camera and the cigarette display case above the counter.

I shoved her away from me, and she fell on her back with a cracking sound. I was panting and drenched in sweat. I grabbed my backpack and looked down at her one more time. Thankfully, her long hair covered her face. I pulled the flap of the too-large jacket across her belly. What a world, where that'd be considered an unusually kind gesture, covering up the magnificent corpse I had made out of what had been a ninety-five-pound girl.

As I stood up, I heard the moaning underneath the ringing in my ears, and I suddenly felt icy cold. One zombie was already stepping through the broken window. At least ten were closing in on the shattered storefront, and I knew there were dozens more nearby, and hundreds more behind them.

I made my way to the back exit of the store, holstering the Magnum, shouldering my backpack, and drawing my Glock. The seventeen-round magazine of the 9mm would increase what little chance I had.

I was only a few steps ahead of the growing horde of zombies filling the store. The closest zombie was at the end of the hallway that led to the back door, maybe fifteen feet away from me. Several were right behind it, and more were shuffling in steadily—old women in housecoats, men in suits, young people in shorts, men and women in aprons or uniforms. Most were white, while several were black, Hispanic, or Asian. Normally, they would've staggered around without even noticing one another, but their hunger had united them in a way that would've been quite remarkable in life.

The door was a big, heavy metal one. That was a huge bonus for me, as was the fact that it opened inward, though for the undead, these two facts slightly lessened their chance for lunch that day. Before the first zombie could figure out to push down on the thumb latch and pull the handle toward itself, the others would have pressed up against him and mashed him against the door in a writhing, moaning mass. I squeezed the handle and yanked back on it. I couldn't afford to examine the alley behind the store before I went outside: so long as a bony hand didn't grab me immediately, I was going out that door.

No bony hand.

I stepped through the door and closed it. With my left hand, I drew my knife—not the thin-bladed, eye-poking one this time, but the big Crocodile Dundee–type one, the kind you could use to hack off a grasping hand or to bash in the side of a zombie's head with the pommel. Within seconds, I heard the thumping of the dead assaulting the door from within.

At the end of the alley, several zombies were staggering toward me, and they let out a moan that would surely bring more. I ran the other way until I reached the next cross street. Zombies this time were everywhere, though there were definitely more to the left, closing in on where I had originally fired the shots. I turned right and began running down that street. I dodged between the scattered undead, only once getting close enough to actually fight one off. It was an older woman, and it came around the front of a van that was up on the sidewalk as I ran between the vehicle and the building. The hair was matted to the left side of her head with blood from where her ear had been bitten off.

Her left arm reached out for me, clutching, even though much of the flesh of her forearm had been torn off, so much so that you could see the bones and tendons in her forearm moving back and forth. Her soulless moan sounded the alarm to any other zombies nearby.

"Die, bitch!" I growled as I drove the blade up under her chin until the tip of the blade shattered through the decayed top of her skull. I quickly drew the blade out and let her fall. For the first time that day, I felt exhilarated, and I almost wanted to spit on her body. I shivered at my reaction. I wanted to get out of that town and to somewhere relatively safe before I descended further into that or some other species of madness.

I was making good and uneventful progress, not running too fast, conserving my strength, and not taking any more shots that would draw more zombies. For almost a block, I was able to jump from the top of one wrecked car to another to avoid the grasping dead.

As I came over a rise, the street descended slightly to end in a cross street, beyond which was a park on the banks of a fairly large river. On the other side of the river looked to be a continuation of the park, and then lower buildings, not like the small downtown district I was in at the moment. The bridge across the river was one block to the left. All I had to do was run there, across the bridge, and I would be outside the city proper, on my way to the suburbs.

But as soon as I turned left, something moaned behind me. On the cross street that paralleled the river, at least a hundred zombies were heading my way.

I needed to get way ahead of them before nightfall, but that in itself was not a huge problem. They were slow, and once the mob didn't see you, it would start to disperse. So as terrifying as a crowd of a hundred zombies looks, if you keep moving, it's not nearly as dangerous as a small crowd in an enclosed space, like I had just faced in the convenience store.

I kept running and made it to the bridge. It was a broad, low bridge, with four lanes plus a sidewalk on each side. At my end, a barricade had been built: two Humvees, parked perpendicularly across the roadway, supplemented with some cop cars, sandbags, concrete traffic barriers, and barbed wire. It may well have held, for whatever good it had done, as the vehicles still effectively blocked the bridge. They did not appear to have been moved from their original spot, nor was there any sign of fire or explosion, common at such scenes.

As usual when you came across a battle site, there weren't many bodies lying around, as most had gotten up and walked away, but there were a few scattered before the barricade, most in civilian garb, with a couple in military and police uniforms. There was no smell of decay, beyond the usual in a city of the dead, as the bodies had—unlike zombies—almost completely rotted away.

As was also usual at a battle site—I suppose from any war, but the war with the undead was the only one I knew—it was impossible to guess the details of what had gone on here: how many had fought, or died, or even whether the barricade had been intended to keep the undead on this side of the river, or to keep them from coming over from the other side.

Well, it all seemed pretty moot now. It was just a few vehicles and lifeless bodies, with weeds growing up through the cracks around them. It wasn't like there were going to be any people to make a monument here, like it was some kind of Gettysburg or Normandy. Just one of probably ten thousand places where the human race had just puttered out. In a few years, it'd be like finding the campsite and spearheads of some Neanderthals, the odd and poorly designed remnants of some species that didn't have what it takes to survive.

I looked back as I climbed over the barricade. Although, for the long haul, the dead seemed well suited to survival, at the moment, they were falling behind me. The roadblock would probably slow them down enough that, by the time some of them made it over, I'd be way out of sight, and they'd sit down on the bridge and forget all about me.

I ran across the bridge. The wrecked vehicles made it impossible to see all the way to the other side, but there were no signs of zombies anywhere, and I almost started to relax. I looked down at the water, crystal clear and fast moving from the center of the channel to the far bank, shallower nearer the side I had left. I dodged past a few more vehicles and I was to the opposite side of the bridge. I could no longer see the barricade, but I was sure the dead had not surmounted that yet.

To my right was the park I had seen from the other side of the river, but to my left was a parking lot, beyond which was a high brick wall, brightly painted. It ran from the river, along the parking lot, to where it connected to a large, irregularly-shaped brick building, maybe four stories tall. In the wall facing the parking lot, there was a large metal gate, while along the wall was spray painted "R U DYING 2

LIVE?" I wished I had time to ponder that, as it had been some time since I'd had someone other than myself to pose abstract questions, but there was an obvious impediment to such philosophizing—the crowd of zombies, probably almost two hundred, that was crowded in front of the wall, pressing against it.

They hadn't seen me yet. They were pretty intent on the wall, and they must've been for some time, as they weren't moaning or agitated, but just kind of milling around.

The street on this side was not as clogged with wrecked cars, so I couldn't dodge between them and hope to remain unseen. I would be running along an empty street, less than fifty yards from them. Still, if I just started running, I'd be in no worse situation than I had been with the previous mob: I just had to keep running for long enough that I was out of their sight, then keep going till I was in a safer area. It was either that or jump off the bridge into the river. Although the fall looked survivable, the chance of spraining an ankle, losing all my supplies and equipment, and coming up somewhere downstream was just as bad and made me think that it was not the better option.

I set off at a good sprint, trying to get as far down the street as I could before they started pursuit. Sure enough, after just a few yards, the moan started, and the chase was on. They turned, almost as a group, and begin staggering toward me. I kept running. But then another group emerged from a grove of trees and from behind a building in the park. It was just a dozen or so, nowhere near as big a mob as the zombies at the wall, but with just a few lurching steps, they had effectively cut off the street ahead.

I stopped. Now I either had to turn right, into the park, and hope the trees held no more surprises, or turn back and jump into the river. I didn't like either option.

"You there!" an amplified voice called. The zombies stopped their march toward me, and I looked around. Over the top of the high brick wall, two platforms appeared on either side of the gate, the kinds of platforms on scissor-type lifts that people used to paint tall buildings or clean their windows. On each platform, two men stood, together with the .50 caliber machine guns from the Humvees. On the platform to my right was the guy with the bullhorn. I hadn't seen people in weeks, and these were, obviously, an especially welcome sight.

The zombies were temporarily frozen. It was one of the many disadvantages of almost completely lacking a working intellect—they couldn't handle multiple threats at all, or change from one target to another easily. They looked at their enemies above the wall, then back at me, swaying uncertainly. I, too, was frozen, as I wasn't sure at all what I was supposed to do. There were still about two hundred zombies, fanned out now in a more or less crescent-shaped wall of rotting, grasping flesh, between me and the people.

"Start moving toward the gate," the guy with the bullhorn said. "We're going to get you."

He sounded confident, and their setup indicated a good deal of planning and equipment, like they had done this before, but I still wasn't too enthusiastic about moving toward a mob of mindless cannibals. I took a few slow steps, and again, the zombies moved toward me. But then we all heard the gate rattle as it slid to one side.

Again, the zombies were confused, and many at the back turned toward the gate. I took a few more steps, and then a crowd of about twenty people came rushing out from the gate. Like the guy on the cherry picker, they seemed pretty disciplined and organized, letting out a loud "Arrrrrr!" as they charged the zombies. They looked like the crazy post-apocalyptic bikers and villagers in *The Road Warrior* movie, all decked out with various kinds of impromptu armor—football pads, paintball and fencing masks, pieces of tires cut up and bound to their arms and legs as armor, hubcaps and garbage can lids for shields. They crashed into the zombies, wielding bats, clubs, machetes, axes, shovels—any hand-to-hand weapon that could deal a fatal blow to the head.

The zombies were now completely confused, and they began to fall back before the assault. I was impressed and grateful for the people's bravery, but I didn't see how they stood a chance of clearing a path.

Up on the cherry pickers, the two people who were not on the machine guns were swinging things at the end of a rope, the way you would a sling, but the objects were bigger, so they were using both arms, like in a hammer throw. "Set!" the guy on the bullhorn commanded, and they let go of their projectiles, which flew over the crowd and crashed down slightly in front of me, one to either side. When they hit the ground, I heard loud popping and then splashing sounds. I wasn't sure, but I started to catch on, so I stopped and took a couple steps back.

The people who had thrown the objects were now wielding bows with flaming arrows, and from where I was standing, it looked like they were aimed right at me. I also got a whiff of something I hadn't smelled in years, that smell you always associated with summer evenings, when Dad went out and lit the Kingsford in the backyard. I kept backing up as the zombies again advanced on me.

"Fire!" came the command from the guy on the cherry picker, and the arrows shot into the zombie crowd right in front of me on either side. I ducked down, brought my right arm across my face, and hoped these people knew what they were doing.

When the arrows hit and ignited the lighter fluid, the hair on the back of my hand singed and curled in the heat and blast of the expanding fireball. Unlike the zombies, I needed to breathe, and I staggered back a step to catch my breath as the flames receded slightly after the initial flare-up. The people in the cherry pickers pressed the attack, throwing another pair of fuel bombs, redoubling the flames and driving me another step back.

Just a few feet closer to the centers of the two conflagrations, the zombies were faring much worse than I. With their dried-up flesh and hair, most of them were burning briskly, and their moaning now turned to screams as they flailed about in whatever it was they experienced as pain. It smelled like a cross between a barbecue and the seventh circle of hell.

Though horribly burned, many of them were still capable of motion, with their limbs still moving, even though scorched bones could now be seen through their burned clothes and flesh. But even the more hardy ones were losing their struggle to carry on the fight, as their eyelids had shriveled up in the first blast of flame, and their eyeballs looked like singed marshmallows, with sizzling goo running down their dried, cracked cheeks. They would walk into one another, or collapse to their knees, their burning hands clutching their faces in a slow agony that looked appallingly like a final supplication to the God who had made them, punished them, and was now punishing them again.

Between the edges of the two puddles of burning fuel, there were only a few zombies who had completely escaped the flames. I started walking toward them, as this was the gap in the midst of the two burning mobs that led to the gates. The first zombie to get close to me I shot in the face; then I kicked him in the stomach and sent him crashing into the burning zombies to my right. Unfortunately, another burning one grabbed my gun arm and lunged for it with its mouth. I twisted away as I drove my knife into its mouth. It flailed around, still burning, with the tip of my knife stuck in the back of its throat. I wrestled my right arm out of its grip and stuck the barrel in its left eye. I fired as I pulled my knife out, and the zombie fell back into the burning crowd.

This altercation had slowed me down, and two more were closing in: one from my left and the other right in front of me. The one on my left was horribly cadaverous, even by zombie standards. It had been a very old woman before its death, and from the look of its torso, it had been run over and crushed by some large vehicle since then. It couldn't move its arms. All its bones were crushed, so its two limbs just hung at its sides, swaying randomly as it walked. Its dress was torn, revealing the shriveled, dried flesh underneath, crisscrossed with feathery lines of dried blood and caked with dirt. Its insatiable maw kept coming nevertheless, and would keep on doing so no matter what.

The one in front of me, on the other hand, was a fairly robust male, with just the typical neck wound and blood-stain down his shirt. I leveled the Glock at him and fired, sending him falling back into another zombie behind him. At almost the same time, I slashed the old zombie's throat as hard as I could with the serrated back edge of my knife. The blow spun her around and dropped her, with her neck severed almost all the way to the spine. She landed on her face, but her head bounced up and twisted around so she was looking completely backward, up at me, before the head flopped back down on its side.

Even then, she started to pull her knees up under herself and struggle to rise. She'd be able to get up, doubtless, but not before I got out of there.

There were just a few more zombies between me and the people who had come out from the gates. I kept moving, but the zombie that the robust male had fallen on was getting up, just as another was coming at me from the right. I kicked the rising one in the head as I shot the standing one in the face. I was just a few feet now from rescue, when something grabbed my left wrist.

I turned and raised the Glock, but saw that I was aiming too high. I was held by something less than four feet tall, what had been a little boy of six or seven. Its jugular was torn open on the left side, but there were no other marks on it. It was slowly bending its mouth toward my wrist, ignoring any danger I might pose in its obsession for human flesh, its only remaining goal or desire. I raised my left arm, lifting the child zombie off the ground even as it continued craning its neck, its bared teeth yearning for my arm.

Oddly enough, the color of this zombie's flesh was like that of milk, like all his blood had drained out when he died, but had not been replaced with the horrible putrefaction and discoloration that inevitably accompanied undeath, instead leaving him pristine and undefiled. Here was flesh without blood, but also flesh without decay. It was animal existence at its purest—deadly, unholy, and unstoppable.

I holstered the Glock and grabbed the horrible, beautiful thing by the throat as I wrenched my left arm free of its grip. I sheathed the knife and held the thing with both hands around its neck. It wouldn't have been so bad if I could've throttled it to end its eternally pitiable existence, letting it slip slowly into a merciful death, but zombie physiology wouldn't allow this. It didn't help that this thing in my hands was the same age as my youngest son last year. The only minuscule consolation was that he didn't look at me, but up at the sky, unblinking even though he stared right at the sun, his jaw still working in his hellish, animal hunger.

"Sorry" fell so far short of what was going on here and what I was feeling that I wasn't going to bother with it this time. "Damn you," I whispered instead, and I flung the little thing away from me and back into the flames. Damn who? The zombie? Me? God? The asshole who invented the disease that caused the dead to rise? What the hell? It looked like there was plenty of damnation to go around, so why not just damn us all together, Lord, in one big mass of suffering, with you as the King of it all? Unlike earlier that day, this time I really did feel nauseous.

Two of the people from the gate had reached me by this point. "Come on," one shouted, grabbing me by the shoulder, "let's get inside." I followed them dumbly through the gate as it rattled closed behind us.

Anne Rice

(1941–   )

Named Howard Allen O'Brien at birth, Anne Rice was born in New Orleans, where she and her sister, Alice, spent much of their childhood. Named after her father, Howard, she chose the name Anne when she began to go to school. After the family moved to Texas, she attended two Texas colleges but earned her BA at San Francisco State University when she moved to the San Francisco Bay Area in 1962. Her husband, the poet Stan Rice, would later become a faculty member at the university. Her first novel, *Interview with the Vampire*, was written in 1973 and published in 1976. The novel's enormous success inspired the Vampire Chronicles series, which included *The Vampire Lestat* (1985), *The Queen of the Damned* (1988), *The Vampire Armand* (1998), *Merrick* (2000), *Blackwood Farm* (2002), and *Blood Canticle* (2003). Additional novels include *The Witching Hour* (1990), *Lasher* (1993), *Taltos* (1994), *Exit to Eden* (1985), and *Belinda* (1986), which was published under the pseudonym Anne Rampling.

The Master of Rampling Gate

(1984)

Spring 1888

Rampling Gate. It was so real to us in the old pictures, rising like a fairy-tale castle out of its own dark wood. A wilderness of gables and chimneys between those two immense towers, grey stone walls mantled in ivy, mullioned windows reflecting the drifting clouds.

But why had Father never taken us there? And why, on

his deathbed, had he told my brother that Rampling Gate must be torn down, stone by stone? "I should have done it, Richard," he said. "But I was born in that house, as my father was, and his father before him. You must do it now, Richard. It has no claim on you. Tear it down."

Was it any wonder that not two months after Father's passing, Richard and I were on the noon train headed south for the mysterious mansion that had stood upon the rise above the village of Rampling for four hundred years? Surely Father would have understood. How could we destroy the old place when we had never seen it?

But, as the train moved slowly through the outskirts of London I can't say we were very sure of ourselves, no matter how curious and excited we were.

Richard had just finished four years at Oxford. Two whirlwind social seasons in London had proved me something of a shy success. I still preferred scribbling poems and stories in my room to dancing the night away, but I'd kept that a good secret. And though we had lost our mother when we were little, Father had given us the best of everything. Now the carefree years were ended. We had to be independent and wise.

The evening before, we had pored over all the old pictures of Rampling Gate, recalling in hushed, tentative voices the night Father had taken those pictures down from the walls.

I couldn't have been more than six and Richard eight when it happened, yet we remembered well the strange incident in Victoria Station that had precipitated Father's uncharacteristic rage. We had gone there after supper to say farewell to a school friend of Richard's, and Father had caught a glimpse, quite unexpectedly, of a young man at the lighted window of an incoming train. I could remember the young man's face clearly to this day: remarkably handsome, with a head of lustrous brown hair, his large black eyes regarding Father with the saddest expression as Father drew back. "Unspeakable horror!" Father had whispered. Richard and I had been too amazed to speak a word.

Later that night, Father and Mother quarrelled, and we crept out of our rooms to listen on the stairs.

"That he should dare to come to London!" Father said over and over. "Is it not enough for him to be the undisputed master of Rampling Gate?"

How we puzzled over it as little ones! Who was this stranger, and how could he be master of a house that belonged to our father, a house that had been left in the care of an old, blind housekeeper for years?

But now after looking at the pictures again, it was too dreadful to think of Father's exhortation. And too exhilarating to think of the house itself. I'd packed my manuscripts, for—who knew?—maybe in that melancholy and exquisite setting I'd find exactly the inspiration I needed for the story I'd been writing in my head.

Yet there was something almost illicit about the excitement I felt. I saw in my mind's eye the pale young man again, with his black greatcoat and red woollen cravat. Like bone china, his complexion had been. Strange to remember so vividly. And I realized now that in those few remarkable moments, he had created for me an ideal of masculine beauty that I had never questioned since. But Father had been so angry. I felt an unmistakable pang of guilt.

It was late afternoon when the old trap carried us up the gentle slope from the little railway station and we had our first real look at the house. The sky had paled to a deep rose hue beyond a bank of softly gilded clouds, and the last rays of the sun struck the uppermost panes of the leaded windows and filled them with solid gold.

"Oh, but it's too majestic," I whispered, "too like a great cathedral, and to think that it belongs to us!"

Richard gave me the smallest kiss on the cheek.

I wanted with all my heart to jump down from the trap and draw near on foot, letting those towers slowly grow larger and larger above me, but our old horse was gaining speed.

When we reached the massive front door Richard and I were spirited into the great hall by the tiny figure of the blind housekeeper Mrs. Blessington, our footfalls echoing loudly on the marble tile, and our eyes dazzled by the dusty shafts of light that fell on the long oak table and its heavily carved chairs, on the sombre tapestries that stirred ever so slightly against the soaring walls.

"Richard, it is an enchanted place!" I cried, unable to contain myself.

Mrs. Blessington laughed gaily, her dry hand closing tightly on mine.

We found our bedchambers well aired, with snow-white linen on the beds and fires blazing cosily on the hearths. The small, diamond-paned windows opened on a glorious view of the lake and the oaks that enclosed it and the few scattered lights that marked the village beyond.

That night we laughed like children as we supped at the great oak table, our candles giving only a feeble light. And afterward we had a fierce battle of pocket billiards in the game room and a little too much brandy, I fear.

It was just before I went to bed that I asked Mrs. Blessington if there had been anyone in this house since my father left it, years before.

"No, my dear," she said quickly, fluffing the feather pillows. "When your father went away to Oxford, he never came back."

"There was never a young intruder after that? . . ." I pressed her, though in truth I had little appetite for anything that would disturb the happiness I felt. How I loved the Spartan cleanliness of this bedchamber, the walls bare of paper and ornament, the high lustre of the walnut-panelled bed.

"A young intruder?" With an unerring certainty about her surroundings, she lifted the poker and stirred the fire. "No, dear. Whatever made you think there was?"

"Are there no ghost stories, Mrs. Blessington?" I asked suddenly, startling myself. *Unspeakable horror.* But what was I thinking—that that young man had not been real?

"Oh, no, darling," she said, smiling. "No ghost would ever dare to trouble Rampling Gate."

Nothing, in fact, troubled the serenity of the days that followed—long walks through the overgrown gardens, trips in the little skiff to and fro across the lake, tea under the hot glass of the empty conservatory. Early evening found us reading and writing by the library fire.

All our inquiries in the village met with the same answers: The villagers cherished the house. There was not a single disquieting legend or tale.

How were we going to tell them of Father's edict? How were we going to remind ourselves?

Richard was finding a wealth of classical material on the library shelves and I had the desk in the corner entirely to myself.

Never had I known such quiet. It seemed the atmosphere of Rampling Gate permeated my simplest written descriptions and wove its way richly into the plots and characters I created. The Monday after our arrival I finished my first real short story, and after copying out a fresh draft, I went off to the village on foot to post it boldly to the editors of *Blackwood's* magazine.

It was a warm afternoon, and I took my time as I came back. What had disturbed our father so about this lovely corner of England? What had so darkened his last hours that he laid his curse upon this spot? My heart opened to this unearthly stillness, to an indisputable magnificence that caused me utterly to forget myself. There were times here when I felt I was a disembodied intellect drifting through a fathomless silence, up and down garden paths and stone corridors that had witnessed too much to take cognizance of one small and fragile young woman who in random moments actually talked aloud to the suits of armour around her, to the broken statues in the garden, the fountain cherubs who had had no water to pour from their conches for years and years.

But was there in this loveliness some malignant force that was eluding us still, some untold story? *Unspeakable horror* . . . Even in the flood of brilliant sunlight, those words gave me a chill.

As I came slowly up the slope I saw Richard walking lazily along the uneven shore of the lake. Now and then he glanced up at the distant battlements, his expression dreamy, almost blissfully contented.

Rampling Gate had him. And I understood perfectly because it also had me.

With a new sense of determination I went to him and placed my hand gently on his arm. For a moment he looked at me as if he did not even know me, and then he said softly:

"How will I ever do it, Julie? And one way or the other, it will be on my conscience all my life."

"It's time to seek advice, Richard," I said. "Write to our lawyers in London. Write to Father's clergyman, Dr. Matthews. Explain everything. We cannot do this alone."

* * *

It was three o'clock in the morning when I opened my eyes. But I had been awake for a long time. And I felt not fear, lying there alone, but something else—some vague and relentless agitation, some sense of emptiness and need that caused me finally to rise from my bed. What was this house, really? A place, or merely a state of mind? What was it doing to my soul?

I felt overwhelmed, yet shut out of some great and dazzling secret. Driven by an unbearable restlessness, I pulled on my woollen wrapper and my slippers and went into the hall.

The moonlight fell full on the oak stairway, and the vestibule far below. Maybe I could write of the confusion I suffered now, put on paper the inexplicable longing I felt. Certainly it was worth the effort, and I made my way soundlessly down the steps.

The great hall gaped before me, the moonlight here and there touching upon a pair of crossed swords or a mounted shield. But far beyond, in the alcove just outside the library, I saw the uneven glow of the fire. So Richard was there. A sense of well-being pervaded me and quieted me. At the same time, the distance between us seemed endless and I became desperate to cross it, hurrying past the long supper table and finally into the alcove before the library doors.

The fire blazed beneath the stone mantelpiece and a figure sat in the leather chair before it, bent over a loose collection of pages that he held in his slender hands. He was reading the pages eagerly, and the fire suffused his face with a warm, golden light.

But it was not Richard. It was the same young man I had seen on the train in Victoria Station fifteen years ago. And not a single aspect of that taut young face had changed. There was the very same hair, thick and lustrous and only carelessly combed as it hung to the collar of his black coat, and those dark eyes that looked up suddenly and fixed me with a most curious expression as I almost screamed.

We stared at each other across that shadowy room, I stranded in the doorway, he visibly and undeniably shaken that I had caught him unawares. My heart stopped.

And in a split second he rose and moved toward me,

closing the gap between us, reaching out with those slender white hands.

"Julie!" he whispered, in a voice so low that it seemed my own thoughts were speaking to me. But this was no dream. He was holding me and the scream had broken loose from me, deafening, uncontrollable and echoing from the four walls.

I was alone. Clutching at the doorframe, I staggered forward, and then in a moment of perfect clarity I saw the young stranger again, saw him standing in the open door to the garden, looking back over his shoulder; then he was gone.

I could not stop screaming. I could not stop even as I heard Richard's voice calling me, heard his feet pound down that broad, hollow staircase and through the great hall. I could not stop even as he shook me, pleaded with me, settled me in a chair.

Finally I managed to describe what I had seen.

"But you know who it was!" I said almost hysterically. "It was he—the young man from the train!"

"Now, wait," Richard said. "He had his back to the fire, Julie. And you could not see his face clearly—"

"Richard, it was he! Don't you understand? He touched me. He called me Julie," I whispered. "Good God, Richard, look at the fire. I didn't light it—he did. He was here!"

All but pushing Richard out of the way, I went to the heap of papers that lay strewn on the carpet before the hearth. "My story . . ." I whispered, snatching up the pages. "He's been reading my story, Richard. And—dear God—he's read your letters, the letters to Mr. Partridge and Dr. Matthews, about tearing down the house!"

"Surely you don't believe it was the same man, Julie, after all these years . . . ?"

"But he has not changed, Richard, not in the smallest detail. There is no mistake, I tell you. It was the very same man!"

The next day was the most trying since we had come. Together we commenced a search of the house. Darkness found us only half finished, frustrated everywhere by locked doors we could not open and old staircases that were not safe.

And it was also quite clear by suppertime that Richard

did not believe I had seen anyone in the study at all. As for the fire—well, he had failed to put it out properly before going to bed; and the pages—well, one of us had put them there and forgotten them, of course . . .

But I knew what I had seen.

And what obsessed me more than anything else was the gentle countenance of the mysterious man I had glimpsed, the innocent eyes that had fixed on me for one moment before I screamed.

"You would be wise to do one very important thing before you retire," I said crossly. "Leave out a note to the effect that you do not intend to tear down the house."

"Julie, you have created an impossible dilemma," Richard declared, the colour rising in his face. "You insist we reassure this apparition that the house will not be destroyed, when in fact you verify the existence of the very creature that drove our father to say what he did."

"Oh, I wish I had never come here!" I burst out suddenly.

"Then we should go, and decide this matter at home."

"No—that's just it. I could never go without knowing. I could never go on living with knowing now!"

Anger must be an excellent antidote to fear, for surely something worked to alleviate my natural alarm. I did not undress that night, but rather sat in the darkened bedroom, gazing at the small square of diamond-paned window until I heard the house fall quiet. When the grandfather clock in the great hall chimed the hour of eleven, Rampling Gate was, as usual, fast asleep.

I felt a dark exultation as I imagined myself going out of the room and down the stairs. But I knew I should wait one more hour. I should let the night reach its peak. My heart was beating too fast, and dreamily I recollected the face I had seen, the voice that had said my name.

Why did it seem in retrospect so intimate, that we had known each other before, spoken together a thousand times? Was it because he had read my story, those words that came from my very soul?

"Who are you?" I believe I whispered aloud. "Where are you at this moment?" I uttered the word, "Come."

The door opened without a sound and he was standing

there. He was dressed exactly as he had been the night before and his dark eyes were riveted on me with that same obvious curiosity, his mouth just a little slack, like that of a boy.

I sat forward, and he raised his finger as if to reassure me and gave a little nod.

"Ah, it is you!" I whispered.

"Yes," he said in a soft, unobtrusive voice.

"And you are not a spirit!" I looked at his mud-splattered boots, at the faintest smear of dust on that perfect white cheek.

"A spirit?" he asked almost mournfully. "Would that I were that."

Dazed, I watched him come toward me; the room darkened and I felt his cool, silken hands on my face. I had risen. I was standing before him, and I looked up into his eyes.

I heard my own heartbeat. I heard it as I had the night before, right at the moment I had screamed. Dear God, I was talking to him! He was in my room and I was talking to him! And then suddenly I was in his arms.

"Real, absolutely real!" I whispered, and a low, zinging sensation coursed through me so that I had to steady myself.

He was peering at me as if trying to comprehend something terribly important. His lips had a ruddy look to them, a soft look for all his handsomeness, as if he had never been kissed. A slight dizziness came over me, a slight confusion in which I was not at all sure that he was even there.

"Oh, but I am," he said, as if I had spoken my doubt. I felt his breath against my cheek, and it was almost sweet. "I am here, and I have watched you ever since you came."

"Yes . . ."

My eyes were closing. In a dim flash, as of a match being struck, I saw my father, heard his voice. *No, Julie* . . . But that was surely a dream.

"Only a little kiss," said the voice of the one who was really here. I felt his lips against my neck. "I would never harm you. No harm ever for the children of this house. Just the little kiss, Julie, and the understanding that it imparts, that you cannot destroy Rampling Gate, Julie—that you can never, never drive me away."

The core of my being, that secret place where all desires

and all commandments are nurtured, opened to him without a struggle or a sound. I would have fallen if he had not held me. My arms closed about him, my hands slipping into the soft, silken mass of his hair.

I was floating, and there was, as there had always been at Rampling Gate, an endless peace. It was Rampling Gate I felt enclosing me; it was that timeless and impenetrable secret that had opened itself at last. . . . *A power within me of enormous ken . . . To see as a god sees, and take the depth of things as nimbly as the outward eyes can size and shape pervade* . . . Yes, those very words from Keats, which I had quoted in the pages of my story that he had read.

But in a violent instant he had released me. "Too innocent," he whispered.

I went reeling across the bedroom floor and caught hold of the frame of the window. I rested my forehead against the stone wall. There was a tingling pain in my throat where his lips had touched me that was almost pleasurable, a delicious throbbing that would not stop. I knew what he was!

I turned and saw all the room clearly—the bed, the fireplace, the chair. And he stood still exactly as I'd left him and there was the most appalling anguish in his face.

"Something of menace, unspeakable menace," I whispered, backing away.

"Something ancient, something that defies understanding," he pleaded. "Something that can and will go on." But he was shaken and he would not look into my eyes.

I touched that pulsing pain with the tips of my fingers and, looking down at them, saw the blood. "Vampire!" I gasped. "And yet you suffer so, and it is as if you can love!"

"Love? I have loved you since you came. I loved you when I read your secret thoughts and had not yet seen your face."

He drew me to him ever so gently, and slipping his arm around me, guided me to the door.

I tried for one desperate moment to resist him. And as any gentleman might, he stepped back respectfully and took my hand.

Through the long upstairs corridor we passed, and through a small wooden doorway to a screw stair that I had not seen before. I soon realized we were ascending in the north tower, a ruined portion of the structure that had been sealed off years before.

Through one tiny window after another I saw the gently rolling landscape and the small cluster of dim lights that marked the village of Rampling and the pale streak of white that was the London road.

Up and up we climbed, until we reached the topmost chamber, and this he opened with an iron key. He held back the door for me to enter and I found myself in a spacious room whose high, narrow windows contained no glass. A flood of moonlight revealed the most curious mixture of furnishings and objects—a writing-table, a great shelf of books, soft leather chairs, and scores of maps and framed pictures affixed to the walls. Candles all about had dripped their wax on every surface, and in the very midst of this chaos lay my poems, my old sketches—early writings that I had brought with me and never even unpacked.

I saw a black silk top hat and a walking stick, and a bouquet of withered flowers, dry as straw, and daguerreotypes and tintypes in their little velvet cases, and London newspapers and opened books.

There was no place for sleeping in this room.

And when I thought of that, where he must lie when he went to rest, a shudder passed over me and I felt, quite palpably, his lips touching my throat again, and I had the sudden urge to cry.

But he was holding me in his arms; he was kissing my cheeks and my lips ever so softly.

"My father knew what you were!" I whispered.

"Yes," he answered, "and his father before him. And all of them in an unbroken chain over the years. Out of loneliness or rage, I know not which, I always told them. I always made them acknowledge, accept."

I backed away and he didn't try to stop me. He lighted the candles about us one by one.

I was stunned by the sight of him in the light, the gleam in his large black eyes and the gloss of his hair. Not even in the railway station had I seen him so clearly as I did now, amid the radiance of the candles. He broke my heart.

And yet he looked at me as though I were a feast for his eyes, and he said my name again and I felt the blood rush to my face. But there seemed a great break suddenly in the passage of time. What had I been thinking! *Yes, never tell, never disturb . . . something ancient, something greater than good and evil . . .* But no! I felt dizzy again. I heard Father's voice: *Tear it down, Richard, stone by stone.*

He had drawn me to the window. And as the lights of Rampling were subtracted from the darkness below, a great wood stretched out in all directions, far older and denser than the forest of Rampling Gate. I was afraid suddenly, as if I were slipping into a maelstrom of visions from which I could never, of my own will, return.

There was that sense of our talking together, talking and talking in low, agitated voices, and I was saying that I should not give in.

"Bear witness—that is all I ask of you, Julie."

And there was in me some dim certainty that by these visions alone I would be fatally changed.

But the very room was losing its substance, as if a soundless wind of terrific force were blowing it apart. The vision had already begun. . . .

We were riding horseback through a forest, he and I. And the trees were so high and so thick that scarcely any sun at all broke through to the fragrant, leaf-strewn ground.

Yet we had no time to linger in this magical place. We had come to the fresh-tilled earth that surrounded a village I somehow knew was called Knorwood, with its gabled roofs and its tiny, crooked streets. We saw the monastery of Knorwood and the little church with the bell chiming vespers under the lowering sky. A great, bustling life resided in Knorwood, a thousand voices rising in common prayer.

Far beyond, on the rise above the forest, stood the round tower of a truly ancient castle; and to that ruined castle—no more than a shell of itself anymore—as darkness fell in earnest we rode. Through its empty chambers we roamed, impetuous children, the horses and the road quite forgotten, and to the lord of the castle, a gaunt and white-skinned creature standing before the roaring fire of the roofless hall, we came. He turned and fixed us with his narrow and glittering eyes. A dead thing he was, I understood, but he carried within himself a priceless magic. And my companion, my innocent young man, stepped forward into the lord's arms.

I saw the kiss. I saw the young man grow pale and struggle and turn away, and the lord retreated with the wisest, saddest smile.

I understood. I knew. But the castle was dissolving as surely as anything in this dream might dissolve, and we were in some damp and close place.

The stench was unbearable to me; it was that most terrible of all stenches, the stench of death. And I heard my steps on the cobblestones and I reached out to steady myself against a wall. The tiny marketplace was deserted; the doors and windows gaped open to the vagrant wind. Up one side and down the other of the crooked street I saw the marks on the houses. And I knew what the marks meant. The Black Death had come to the village of Knorwood. The Black Death had laid it waste. And in a moment of suffocating horror I realized that no one, not a single person, was left alive.

But this was not quite true. There was a young man walking in fits and starts up the narrow alleyway. He was staggering, almost falling, as he pushed in one door after another, and at last came to a hot, reeking place where a child screamed on the floor. Mother and father lay dead in the bed. And the sleek fat cat of the household, unharmed, played with the screaming infant, whose eyes bulged in its tiny, sunken face.

"Stop it!" I heard myself gasp. I was holding my head with both hands. "Stop it—stop it, please!" I was screaming, and my screams would surely pierce the vision and this crude little dwelling would collapse around me and I would rouse the household of Rampling Gate, but I did not. The young man turned and stared at me, and in the close, stinking room I could not see his face.

But I knew it was he, my companion, and I could smell his fever and his sickness, and the stink of the dying infant, and see the gleaming body of the cat as it pawed at the child's outstretched hand.

"Stop it, you've lost control of it!" I screamed, surely with all my strength, but the infant screamed louder. "Make it stop."

"I cannot," he whispered. "It goes on forever! It will never stop!"

And with a great shriek I kicked at the cat and sent it

flying out of the filthy room, overturning the milk pail as it went.

Death in all the houses of Knorwood. Death in the cloister, death in the open fields. It seemed the Judgement of God—I was sobbing, begging to be released—it seemed the very end of Creation itself.

But as night came down over the dead village he was alive still, stumbling up the slopes, through the forest, toward that tower where the lord stood at the broken arch of the window, waiting for him to come.

"Don't go!" I begged him. I ran alongside him, crying, but he didn't hear.

The lord turned and smiled with infinite sadness as the young man on his knees begged for salvation, when it was damnation this lord offered, when it was only damnation that the lord would give.

"Yes, damned, then, but living, breathing!" the young man cried, and the lord opened his arms.

The kiss again, the lethal kiss, the blood drawn out of his dying body, and then the lord lifting the heavy head of the young man so the youth could take the blood back again from the body of the lord himself.

I screamed, "Do not—do not drink!" He turned, and his face was now so perfectly the visage of death that I couldn't believe there was animation left in him; yet he asked: "What would you do? Would you go back to Knorwood, would you open those doors one after another, would you ring the bell in the empty church—and if you did, who would hear?"

He didn't wait for my answer. And I had none now to give. He locked his innocent mouth to the vein that pulsed with every semblance of life beneath the lord's cold and translucent flesh. And the blood jetted into the young body, vanquishing in one great burst the fever and the sickness that had wracked it, driving it out along with the mortal life.

He stood now in the hall of the lord alone. Immortality was his, and the blood thirst he would need to sustain it, and that thirst I could feel with my whole soul.

And each and every thing was transfigured in his vision—to the exquisite essence of itself. A wordless voice spoke from the starry veil of heaven; it sang in the wind that rushed through the broken timbers; it sighed in the flames that ate at the sooted stones of the hearth. It was the eternal rhythm of the universe that played beneath every surface as the last living creature in the village—that tiny child—fell silent in the maw of time.

A soft wind sifted and scattered the soil from the newly turned furrows in the empty fields. The rain fell from the black and endless sky.

Years and years passed. And all that had been Knorwood melted into the earth. The forest sent out its silent sentinels, and mighty trunks rose where there had been huts and houses, where there had been monastery walls. And it seemed the horror beyond all horrors that no one should know anymore of those who had lived and died in that small and insignificant village, that not anywhere in the great archives in which all history is recorded should a mention of Knorwood exist.

Yet one remained who knew, one who had witnessed, one who had seen the Ramplings come in the years that followed, seen them raise their house upon the very slope where the ancient castle had once stood, one who saw a new village collect itself slowly upon the unmarked grave of the old.

And all through the walls of Rampling Gate were the stones of that old castle, the stones of the forgotten monastery, the stones of that little church.

We were once again back in the tower.

"It is my shrine," he whispered. "My sanctuary. It is the only thing that endures as I endure. And you love it as I love it, Julie. You have written it . . . You love its grandeur. And its gloom."

"Yes, yes . . . as it's always been . . ." I was crying, though I didn't move my lips.

He had turned to me from the window, and I could feel his endless craving with all my heart.

"What else do you want from me!" I pleaded. "What else can I give?"

A torrent of images answered me. It was beginning again. I was once again relinquishing myself, yet in a great rush of lights and noise I was enlivened and made whole as I had been when we rode together through the forest, but it was into the world of now, this hour, that we passed.

We were flying through the rural darkness along the railway toward London, where the nighttime city burst like an enormous bubble in a shower of laughter and motion and glaring light. He was walking with me under the gas lamps, his face all but shimmering with that same dark innocence, that same irresistible warmth. It seemed we were holding tight to each other in the very midst of a crowd. And the crowd was a living thing, a writhing thing, and everywhere there came a dark, rich aroma from it, the aroma of fresh blood. Women in white fur and gentlemen in opera capes swept through the brightly lighted doors of the theatre; the blare of the music hall inundated us and then faded away. Only a thin soprano voice was left, singing a high, plaintive song. I was in his arms and his lips were covering mine, and there came that dull, zinging sensation again, that great, uncontrollable opening within myself. Thirst, and the promise of satiation measured only by the intensity of that thirst. Up back staircases we fled together, into high-ceilinged bedrooms papered in red damask, where the loveliest women reclined on brass beds, and the aroma was so strong now that I could not bear it and he said: "Drink. They are your victims! They will give you eternity—you must drink." And I felt the warmth filling me, charging me, blurring my vision until we broke free again, light and invisible, it seemed, as we moved over the rooftops and down again through rain-drenched streets. But the rain did not touch us; the falling snow did not chill us; we had within ourselves a great and indissoluble heat. And together in the carriage we talked to each other in low, exuberant rushes of language; we were lovers; we were constant; we were immortal. We were as enduring as Rampling Gate.

Oh, don't let it stop! I felt his arms around me and I knew we were in the tower room together, and the visions had worked their fatal alchemy.

"Do you understand what I am offering you? To your ancestors I revealed myself, yes; I subjugated them. But I would make you my bride, Julie. I would share with you my power. Come with me. I will not take you against your will, but can you turn away?"

Again I heard my own scream. My hands were on his cool white skin, and his lips were gentle yet hungry, his eyes yielding and ever young. Father's angry countenance blazed before me as if I, too, had the power to conjure. *Unspeakable horror*. I covered my face.

He stood against the backdrop of the window, against the distant drift of pale clouds. The candlelight glimmered in his eyes. Immense and sad and wise, they seemed—and oh, yes, innocent, as I have said again and again. "You are their fairest flower, Julie. To them I gave my protection always. To you I give my love. Come to me, dearest, and Rampling Gate will truly be yours, and it will finally, truly be mine."

Nights of argument, but finally Richard had come round. He would sign over Rampling Gate to me and I should absolutely refuse to allow the place to be torn down. There would be nothing he could do then to obey Father's command. I had given him the legal impediment he needed, and of course I told him I would leave the house to his male heirs. It should always be in Rampling hands.

A clever solution, it seemed to me, since Father had not told me to destroy the place. I had no scruples in the matter now at all.

And what remained was for him to take me to the little railway station and see me off for London, and not worry about my going home to Mayfair on my own.

"You stay here as long as you wish and do not worry," I said. I felt more tenderly toward him than I could ever express. "You knew as soon as you set foot in the place that Father was quite wrong."

The great black locomotive was chugging past us, the passenger cars slowing to a stop.

"Must go now, darling—kiss me," I said.

"But what came over you, Julie—what convinced you so quickly . . . ?"

"We've been through all that, Richard," I said. "What matters is that Rampling Gate is safe and we are both happy, my dear."

I waved until I couldn't see him anymore. The flickering lamps of the town were lost in the deep lavender light of the early evening, and the dark hulk of Rampling Gate appeared for one uncertain moment like the ghost of itself on the nearby rise.

I sat back and closed my eyes. Then I opened them slowly, savouring this moment for which I had waited so long.

He was smiling, seated in the far corner of the leather seat opposite, as he had been all along, and now he rose with a swift, almost delicate movement and sat beside me and enfolded me in his arms.

"It's five hours to London," he whispered.

"I can wait," I said, feeling the thirst like a fever as I held tight to him, feeling his lips against my eyelids and my hair. "I want to hunt the London streets tonight," I confessed a little shyly, but I saw only approbation in his eyes.

"Beautiful Julie, my Julie . . ." he whispered.

"You'll love the house in Mayfair," I said.

"Yes . . ." he said.

"And when Richard finally tires of Rampling Gate, we shall go home."

Anne Sexton

(1928–74)

Best known as a brilliant poet, Anne Gray Harvey was born in Newton, Massachusetts, and grew up in Boston. In 1967, she was awarded the Pulitzer Prize for her 1966 poetry volume, *Live or Die*. Among her collections of poems are *To Bedlam and Part Way Back* (1960), *The Starry Night* (1961), *Love Poems* (1969), *Transformations* (1971), and *The Book of Folly* (1972). With Maxine Kumin, she coauthored four children's books, and in 1978, her daughter, Linda Sexton, edited *Words for Dr. Y.: Uncollected Poems with Three Stories*. She was hospitalized on a number of occasions with mental illnesses that have been described as bipolar disorder, hysteria, and depression. Sexton lost her battle against the voices' calls for her death, taking her life at the age of forty-five by carbon monoxide in a locked garage.

The Ghost

(1978)

I was born in Maine, Bath, Maine, Down East, in the United States of America, in the year of 1851. I was one of twelve (though only eight lasted beyond the age of three) and within the confines of that state we lived at various times in our six houses, four of which were scattered on a small island off Boothbay Harbor. They were not called houses on that island for they are summering places and thus entitled cottages. My father, at one time Governor, was actually a frustrated builder and would often say to the carpenters, "another story upwards, please." One house had five stories, and although ugly to look upon, stood almost at the edge of the rocks that the sea locked in and out of.

I was, of course, a Victorian lady, however I among my brothers and sisters was well educated and women were thought, by my father, to be as *interesting* as men, or as capable. My education culminated at Wellesley College, and I was well-versed in languages, both the ancient and unusable as well as the practical, for the years after Wellesley College I spent abroad perfecting the accent and the idiomatic twists. Later I held a job on a newspaper. But it was not entirely fulfilling and made no use of these foreign languages but only of the mother tongue. I was fortunately a maiden lady all my life, and I do say *fortunate* because it allowed me to adopt to maiden heart the nieces and nephews, the grandnieces, the grandnephews. And there was one in particular, my sister's grandchild, who was named after me. And as she wore my name, I wore hers, and at the end of my life she and her mother and an officious practical nurse stood their ground beside me as I went out. Death taking place twice. Once at sixty-four when my ears died and the most ignominious madness overtook me. Next the half-death of sixty shock treatments and then still deaf as a haddock—a half-life until seventy-seven spent in a variety of places called nursing homes. Dying on a hot day in a crib with diapers on. To die like a baby is not desirable and just barely tolerable, for there is fear spooned into you and radios playing in your head. I, the suffragette, I of the violet sachets, I who always changed my dress for dinner and kept my pride, died like a baby with my breasts bared, my corset, my camisole, tucked away, and every other covering that was my custom. I would have preferred the huntsman stalking me like a moose to that drooling away.

There is more to say of my lifetime, but my interest at this point, my main thrust, is to tell you of my life as a ghost. Life? Well, if there is action and a few high kicks, is that not similar to what is called life? At any rate, I *bother* the living, act up a bit, slip like a radio into their brains or a sharp torch-light going on suddenly to blind and then reveal myself. (With no explanation!) I can put a moan into my namesake's dog if I wish to make a point. (I have always liked to make my point!) It is *her* life I linger over, for she is wearing my name and that gives a ghost a certain right that no one knows when they present the newborn with a name. She is somewhat aware—but of course denies it as best she can—that there are any ghosts at all. However, it can be noted that she is unwilling to move into a house that is not newly made, she is unwilling to live within the walls that might whisper and tell stories of other lives. It is her ghost theory. But like many, she has made the perfect mistake; the mistake being that a ghost belongs to a house, a former room, whereas this ghost (and I can only speak for myself for we ghosts are not allowed to converse about how we go about practicing our trade) belongs to my remaining human, to bother her, to enter the human her, who once was given my name. I could surmise that there are ghosts of houses wading through the attics where once they hoarded their hoard, throwing dishes off shelves, but I am not sure of it. I think the English believe it because their castles were passed on from generation to generation. Indeed, perhaps an American ghost does something quite different, because the people of the present are very mobile, the executives are constantly thrown from city to city, dragging their families with them. But I do not know, for I haunt namesake's, and she lives in the suburbs of Boston—despite a few moves from new house to new house. I follow her as a hunting dog follows the scent, and as long as she breathes, I will peer in her window at noon and watch her sip the vodka, and if I so desire, can place one drop of an ailment into it to teach her a little lesson about such indulgence and imperfection. I gave her five years ago a broken hip. I immobilized her flat on the operating table as I peered over his shoulder, the surgeon said as he did a final X-ray before slicing in with his knife, "shattered," and there was namesake, her hip broken like a crystal goblet and later with two four-inch screws in her hip she lay in a pain that had only been an intimation of pain during the birth of two children. A longing for morphine dominated her hours and her conscience rang in her head like a bell tolling for the dead. She had at the time been committing a major sin, and I found it so abhorrent that it was necessary to make my ailment decisive and sharp. When the morphine was working, she was perfectly lucid, but as it wore off, she sipped a hint of madness and that too was an intimation of things to come. Later, I tried lingering fevers that were quite undiagnosable and then when the world became summer and the green leaves whispered, I sat upon leaf by leaf and called out with a voice of my youth and cried, "Come to us, come to us" until she finally pulled down each shade of the house to keep the leaves out of it—as best she could. Then there are the small things that I can do. I can tear the pillow from under her head at night and leave her as flat as I was when I lay dying and thus crawl into her dream and remind her of my death, lest it be her death. I do not in any way consider myself evil but rather a good presence, trying to remind her of the Yankee heritage, back to the Mayflower and William Brewster, or back to kings and queens of the Continent who married and intermarried. She is becoming altogether too modern, and when a man enters her, I am constantly standing at the bedside to observe and call forth a child to be named my name. I do not actually *watch* the copulation because it is an alien act to me, but I know full well what it should mean and have often plucked out a few of her birth control pills in hopes. But I fear it is a vain hope. She is perhaps too old to conceive, or if she should, the result might be imperfect. As I stand there at that bedside while this man enters her, I hum a little song into her head that we made up, she and I, when she was eight and we sang each year thereafter for years. We had kissed thirteen lucky times over the mistletoe that hung under a large chandelier and two doorframes. This mistletoe was *our* custom and *our* act and tied the knot more surely year by year. The song that she sang haunted me in the madness of old age and now I let it enter her ear and at first she feels a strange buzzing as if a fly has been caught in her brain and then the song fills her head and I am at ease.

She senses my presence when she cooks things that are not to my liking, or drives beyond the speed limit, or makes a left turn when it says NO LEFT TURN. For I play in her head the song called "The Stanley Steamer" for Mr. Stanley's wife was my close friend and we took a memorable ride from Boston to Portland and the horses were not happy, but we disobeyed nothing and were cautious—though I must add, a bit dusty and a little worse for wear at the end of the trip.

It is unfortunate that she did not inherit my felicity with the foreign tongue. But not all can be passed on, the genes carry some but not all. As a matter of fact, it is far *more* unfortunate that she did not inherit my gift with the English language. But here I do interfere the most, for I put *my* words onto her page, and when she observes them, she wonders how it came about and calls it "a gift from the muse." Oh how sweet it is! How adorable! How the song of the mistletoe rips through the metal of death and plays on, singing from two mouths, making me a loyal ghost. Loyal though I am I have felt for a long time something missing from her life that she must experience to be whole, to be truly alive. Although one might say it be the work of the devil, I think that it is not (the devil lurks among the living and she must push him out day by day, but first he must enter her as he entered me in my years of deafness and lunacy). Thus I felt it quite proper and fitting to drop such a malady onto a slice of lemon that floated in her tea at 4 P.M. last August. It started immediately and became in the end immoderate. First the teacup became two teacups, then three, then four. Her cigarettes as she lit them in confusion tasted like dung and she stamped them out. Then she turned on the radio and all it would give at every station on the dial were the names and the dates of the dead. She turned it off quickly, but it would not stop playing. The dog chased her tail and then attacked the woodwork, baying at the moon as if their two bodies had gone awry. At that point, she sat very still. She kept telling herself to dial "O" for operator but could not. She shut her eyes, but they kept popping open to see the objects of the kitchen multiply, widen, stretch like rubber and their colors changing and becoming ugly and the lemon floated in the multiplying and dividing teacups like something made of neon.

When her husband returned home, she was as if frozen and could not speak, though I had put many words in her head they were like a game and were mixed and had lost their meaning. He shook her, she wobbled side to side. He spoke, he spoke. For an hour at least he tried for response then dialed the doctor, and she went into Mass. General, half carried, half walking like a drunk, feet numb as erasers, legs melting and stiffening and was given the proper modern physical and neurological exams, EEG, EKG, etc., but the fly in her head still buzzed and the obituaries of the radio played on, and when they took her in an ambulance to a mental hospital, she could not sign her name on the commitment papers but spoke at last, "no name." They could not, those psychiatrists, nurses aides, diagnose exactly and most days she is not able to swallow. The tranquilizers they shot into her, variety after variety, have no power over *this.* I will give her a year of it, an exact to the moment year of it, and during that time, I will be constantly at her side to push the devil from her although there was no one in my time to push him from me. She is at this point enduring a great fear, but I am with her, I am holding her hand and she senses this despite her conviction that each needle is filled with Novocain, for that is the effect on her limbs and parts. Still, the slight pressure of my hand, the sound of the song of the mistletoe must comfort her. Right now they scream to her and fill her with an extraordinary terror. But somehow, I know full well she is indubitably pleased that I have not left. Nor do I plan to.

Bram Stoker

(1847–1912)

Abraham (Bram) Stoker, the third of seven children, was born in Dublin. He was a distant relative of Sir Arthur Conan Doyle and a college friend of Oscar Wilde at Trinity College in Dublin. He began his career as a writer of theater reviews for the *Dublin Evening Mail*. Employed as a civil servant in Dublin, he began to publish stories. In 1878, he made a major career change when he moved to London to become the business manager of the famous actor and theatrical producer Henry Irving. In spite of his heavy workload for Irving, this position, which he held for almost three decades, enabled him to continue publishing his fiction. Among his novels are *The Snake's Pass* (1890), *The Shoulder of Shasta* (1895), *Dracula* (1897), *The Mystery of the Sea* (1902), *The Lady of the Shroud* (1909), and *The Lair of the White Worm* (1911). Many of his stories are collected in three volumes, *Under the Sunset* (1881), *Snowbound: The Record of a Theatrical Touring Party* (1908), and the posthumously published *Dracula's Guest and Other Weird Stories* (1914).

Excerpt from Dracula

(1897)

Despite Professor Van Helsing's efforts, Lucy Westenra (Arthur's fiancée) has become Dracula's victim.

DR. SEWARD'S DIARY

. . . . . .

I duly relieved Van Helsing in his watch over Lucy. We wanted Arthur to go to rest also, but he refused at first. It was only when I told him that we should want him to help us during the day, and that we must not all break down for want of rest, lest Lucy should suffer, that he agreed to go. Van Helsing was very kind to him. "Come, my child," he said, "Come with me. You are sick and weak, and have had much sorrow and much mental pain, as well as that tax on your strength that we know of. You must not be alone; for to be alone is to be full of tears and alarms. Come to the drawing-room, where there is a big fire, and there are two sofas. You shall lie on one, and I on the other, and our sympathy will be comfort to each other, even though we do not speak, and even if we sleep." Arthur went off with him, casting back a longing look on Lucy's face, which lay on her pillow, almost whiter than the lawn. She lay quite still, and I looked around the room to see that all was as it should be. I could see that the Professor had carried out in this room, as in the other, his purpose of using the garlic; the whole of the window-sashes reeked with it, and round Lucy's neck, over the silk handkerchief which Van Helsing made her keep on, was a rough chaplet of the same odorous flowers. Lucy was breathing somewhat stertorously, and her face was at its worst, for the open mouth showed the pale gums. Her teeth, in the dim, uncertain light, seemed longer and sharper than they had been in the morning. In particular, by some trick of the light, the canine teeth looked longer and sharper than the rest. I sat down beside her, and presently she moved uneasily. At the same moment there came a sort of dull flapping or buffeting at the window. I went over to it softly, and peeped out by the corner of the blind. There was a full moonlight, and I could see that the noise was made by a great bat, which wheeled round—doubtless attracted by the light, although so dim—and every now and again struck the window with its wings. When I came back to my seat, I found that Lucy had moved slightly, and had torn away the garlic flowers from her throat. I replaced them as well as I could, and sat watching her.

Presently she woke, and I gave her food, as Van Helsing had prescribed. She took but a little, and that languidly. There did not seem to be with her now the unconscious struggle for life and strength that had hitherto so marked her illness. It struck me as curious that the moment she became conscious she pressed the garlic flowers close to her. It was certainly odd that whenever she got into that lethargic state, with the stertorous breathing, she put the flowers from her; but that when she waked she clutched them close. There was no possibility of making any mistake about this, for in the long hours that followed, she had many spells of sleeping and waking and repeated both actions many times.

At six o'clock Van Helsing came to relieve me. Arthur had then fallen into a doze, and he mercifully let him sleep on. When he saw Lucy's face I could hear the hissing indraw of breath, and he said to me in a sharp whisper: "Draw up the blind; I want light!" Then he bent down, and, with his face almost touching Lucy's, examined her carefully. He removed the flowers and lifted the silk handkerchief from her throat. As he did so he started back and I could hear his ejaculation, "Mein Gott!" as it was smothered in his throat. I bent over and looked too, and as I noticed some queer chill came over me.

The wounds on the throat had absolutely disappeared. For fully five minutes Van Helsing stood looking at her, with his face at its sternest. Then he turned to me and said calmly:—

"She is dying. It will not be long now. It will be much difference, mark me, whether she dies conscious or in her sleep. Wake that poor boy, and let him come and see the last; he trusts us, and we have promised him."

I went to the dining-room and waked him. He was dazed for a moment, but when he saw the sunlight streaming in through the edges of the shutters he thought he was late, and expressed his fear. I assured him that Lucy was still asleep, but told him as gently as I could that both Van Helsing and I feared that the end was near. He covered his face with his hands, and slid down on his knees by the sofa, where he remained, perhaps a minute, with his head buried, praying, whilst his shoulders shook with grief. I took him by the hand and raised him up. "Come," I said, "my dear old fellow, summon all your fortitude; it will be best and easiest for *her*."

When we came into Lucy's room I could see that Van Helsing had, with his usual forethought, been putting matters straight and making everything look as pleasing as possible. He had even brushed Lucy's hair, so that it lay on the pillow in its usual sunny ripples. When we came into the room she opened her eyes, and seeing him, whispered softly:—

"Arthur! Oh, my love, I am so glad you have come!" He was stooping to kiss her, when Van Helsing motioned him back. "No," he whispered, "not yet! Hold her hand; it will comfort her more."

So Arthur took her hand and knelt beside her, and she looked her best, with all the soft lines matching the angelic beauty of her eyes. Then gradually her eyes closed, and she sank to sleep. For a little bit her breast heaved softly, and her breath came and went like a tired child's.

And then insensibly there came the strange change which I had noticed in the night. Her breathing grew stertorous, the mouth opened, and the pale gums, drawn back, made the teeth look longer and sharper than ever. In a sort of sleep-waking, vague, unconscious way she opened her eyes, which were now dull and hard at once, and said in a soft, voluptuous voice, such as I had never heard from her lips:—

"Arthur! Oh, my love, I am so glad you have come! Kiss me!" Arthur bent eagerly over to kiss her; but at that instant Van Helsing, who, like me, had been startled by her voice, swooped upon him, and catching him by the neck with both hands, dragged him back with a fury of strength which I never thought he could have possessed, and actually hurled him almost across the room.

"Not for your life!" he said; "not for your living soul and hers!" And he stood between them like a lion at bay.

Arthur was so taken aback that he did not for a moment know what to do or say; and before any impulse of violence could seize him he realized the place and the occasion, and stood silent, waiting.

I kept my eyes fixed on Lucy, as did Van Helsing, and we saw a spasm as of rage flit like a shadow over her face; the sharp teeth clamped together. Then her eyes closed, and she breathed heavily.

Very shortly after she opened her eyes in all their softness, and putting out her poor, pale, thin hand, took Van Helsing's great brown one; drawing it to her, she kissed it. "My true friend," she said, in a faint voice, but with untellable pathos, "My true friend, and his! Oh, guard him, and give me peace!"

"I swear it!" he said solemnly, kneeling beside her and

holding up his hand, as one who registers an oath. Then he turned to Arthur, and said to him, "Come, my child, take her hand in yours, and kiss her on the forehead, and only once."

Their eyes met instead of their lips; and so they parted.

Lucy's eyes closed; and Van Helsing, who had been watching closely, took Arthur's arm, and drew him away.

And then Lucy's breathing became stertorous again, and all at once it ceased.

"It is all over," said Van Helsing. "She is dead!"

I took Arthur by the arm, and led him away to the drawing-room, where he sat down, and covered his face with his hands, sobbing in a way that nearly broke me down to see.

I went back to the room, and found Van Helsing looking at poor Lucy, and his face was sterner than ever. Some change had come over her body. Death had given back part of her beauty, for her brow and cheeks had recovered some of their flowing lines; even the lips had lost their deadly pallor. It was as if the blood, no longer needed for the working of the heart, had gone to make the harshness of death as little rude as might be.

We thought her dying whilst she slept,
*And sleeping when she died.**

I stood beside Van Helsing, and said:—

"Ah well, poor girl, there is peace for her at last. It is the end!"

He turned to me, and said with grave solemnity:—

"Not so, alas! not so. It is only the beginning!"

* * *

There was a long spell of silence, a big, aching void, and then from the Professor a keen "S-s-s-s!" He pointed; and far down the avenue of yews we saw a white figure advance—a dim white figure, which held something dark at its breast. The figure stopped, and at the moment a ray of moonlight fell between the masses of driving clouds and

*Thomas Hood, "The Death-Bed."

showed in startling prominence a dark-haired woman, dressed in the cerements of the grave. We could not see the face, for it was bent down over what we saw to be a fair-haired child. There was a pause and a sharp little cry, such as a child gives in sleep, or a dog as it lies before the fire and dreams. We were starting forward, but the Professor's warning hand, seen by us as he stood behind a yew-tree, kept us back; and then as we looked the white figure moved forwards again. It was now near enough for us to see clearly, and the moonlight still held. My own heart grew cold as ice, and I could hear the gasp of Arthur, as we recognized the features of Lucy Westenra. Lucy Westenra, but yet how changed. The sweetness was turned to adamantine, heartless cruelty, and the purity to voluptuous wantonness. Van Helsing stepped out, and, obedient to his gesture, we all advanced too; the four of us ranged in a line before the door of the tomb. Van Helsing raised his lantern and drew the slide; by the concentrated light that fell on Lucy's face we could see that the lips were crimson with fresh blood, and that the stream had trickled over her chin and stained the purity of her lawn death-robe.

We shuddered with horror. I could see by the tremulous light that even Van Helsing's iron nerve had failed. Arthur was next to me, and if I had not seized his arm and held him up, he would have fallen.

When Lucy—I call the thing that was before us Lucy because it bore her shape—saw us she drew back with an angry snarl, such as a cat gives when taken unawares; then her eyes ranged over us. Lucy's eyes in form and colour; but Lucy's eyes unclean and full of hell-fire, instead of the pure, gentle orbs we knew. At that moment the remnant of my love passed into hate and loathing; had she then to be killed, I could have done it with savage delight. As she looked, her eyes blazed with unholy light, and the face became wreathed with a voluptuous smile. Oh, God, how it made me shudder to see it! With a careless motion, she flung to the ground, callous as a devil, the child that up to now she had clutched strenuously to her breast, growling over it as a dog growls over a bone. The child gave a sharp cry, and lay there moaning. There was a cold-bloodedness in the act which wrung a groan from Arthur; when she advanced to him with outstretched arms and a wanton smile, he fell back and hid his face in his hands.

She still advanced, however, and with a languorous, voluptuous grace, said:—

"Come to me, Arthur. Leave these others and come to me. My arms are hungry for you. Come, and we can rest together. Come, my husband, come!"

There was something diabolically sweet in her tones—something of the tingling of glass when struck—which rang through the brains even of us who heard the words addressed to another. As for Arthur, he seemed under a spell; moving his hands from his face, he opened wide his arms. She was leaping for them, when Van Helsing sprang forward and held between them his little golden crucifix. She recoiled from it, and, with a suddenly distorted face, full of rage, dashed past him as if to enter the tomb.

When within a foot or two of the door, however, she stopped as if arrested by some irresistible force. Then she turned, and her face was shown in the clear burst of moonlight and by the lamp, which had now no quiver from Van Helsing's iron nerves. Never did I see such baffled malice on a face; and never, I trust, shall such ever be seen again by mortal eyes. The beautiful colour became livid, the eyes seemed to throw out sparks of hell-fire, the brows were wrinkled as though the folds of flesh were the coils of Medusa's snakes, and the lovely, bloodstained mouth grew to an open square, as in the passion masks of the Greeks and Japanese. If ever a face meant death—if looks could kill—we saw it at that moment.

And so for full half a minute, which seemed an eternity, she remained between the lifted crucifix and the sacred closing of her means of entry. Van Helsing broke the silence by asking Arthur:—

"Answer me, oh my friend! Am I to proceed in my work?"

Arthur threw himself on his knees, and hid his face in his hands, as he answered:—

"Do as you will, friend; do as you will. There can be no horror like this ever any more!" and he groaned in spirit. Quincey and I simultaneously moved towards him, and took his arms. We could hear the click of the closing lantern as Van Helsing held it down; coming close to the tomb, he began to remove from the chinks some of the sacred emblem which he had placed there. We all looked on in horrified amazement as we saw, when he stood back, the woman, with a corporeal body as real at that moment as our own, pass in through the interstice where scarce a knife blade could have gone. We all felt a glad sense of relief when we saw the Professor calmly restoring the strings of putty to the edges of the door.

When this was done, he lifted the child and said:—

"Come now, my friends; we can do no more till tomorrow. There is a funeral at noon, so here we shall all come before long after that. The friends of the dead will all be gone by two, and when the sexton locks the gate we shall remain. Then there is more to do; but not like this of tonight. As for this little one, he is not much harm, and by tomorrow night he shall be well. We shall leave him where the police will find him, as on the other night; and then to home." Coming close to Arthur, he said:—

"My friend Arthur, you have had sore trial; but after, when you will look back, you will see how it was necessary. You are now in the bitter waters, my child. By this time tomorrow you will, please God, have passed them, and have drunk of the sweet waters; so do not mourn overmuch. Till then I shall not ask you to forgive me."

Arthur and Quincey came home with me, and we tried to cheer each other on the way. We had left the child in safety, and were tired; so we all slept with more or less reality of sleep.

29 September, night.—A little before twelve o'clock we three—Arthur, Quincey Morris, and myself—called for the Professor. It was odd to notice that by common consent we had all put on black clothes. Of course, Arthur wore black, for he was in deep mourning, but the rest of us wore it by instinct. We got to the churchyard by half-past one, and strolled about, keeping out of official observation, so that when the gravediggers had completed their task and the sexton, under the belief that every one had gone, had locked the gate, we had the place all to ourselves. Van Helsing, instead of his little black bag, had with him a long leather one, something like a cricketing bag; it was manifestly of fair weight.

When we were alone and had heard the last of the footsteps die out up the road, we silently, and as if by ordered intention, followed the Professor to the tomb. He unlocked the door, and we entered, closing it behind us. Then he took from his bag the lantern, which he lit, and also two wax candles, which, when lighted, he stuck, by melting their own ends, on other coffins, so that they might give light sufficient to work by. When he again lifted the lid off Lucy's coffin we all looked—Arthur trembling like an aspen—and saw that the body lay there in all its death-beauty. But there was no love in my own heart, nothing but loathing for the foul Thing which had taken Lucy's shape without her soul. I could see even Arthur's face grow hard as he looked. Presently he said to Van Helsing:—

"Is this really Lucy's body, or only a demon in her shape?"

"It is her body, and yet not it. But wait a while, and you shall see her as she was, and is."

She seemed like a nightmare of Lucy as she lay there; the pointed teeth, the bloodstained, voluptuous mouth—which made one shudder to see—the whole carnal and unspiritual appearance, seeming like a devilish mockery of Lucy's sweet purity. Van Helsing, with his usual methodicalness, began taking the various contents from his bag and placing them ready for use. First he took out a soldering iron and some plumbing solder, and then a small oil-lamp, which gave out, when lit in a corner of the tomb, gas which burned at fierce heat with a blue flame; then his operating knives, which he placed to hand; and last a round wooden stake, some two and a half or three inches thick and about three feet long. One end of it was hardened by charring in the fire, and was sharpened to a fine point. With this stake came a heavy hammer, such as in households is used in the coal-cellar for breaking the lumps. To me, a doctor's preparations for work of any kind are stimulating and bracing, but the effect of these things on both Arthur and Quincey was to cause them a sort of consternation. They both, however, kept their courage, and remained silent and quiet.

When all was ready, Van Helsing said:—

"Before we do anything, let me tell you this; it is out of the lore and experience of the ancients and of all those who have studied the powers of the Un-Dead. When they become such, there comes with the change the curse of immortality; they cannot die, but must go on age after age adding new victims and multiplying the evils of the world; for all that die from the preying of the Un-Dead become themselves Un-Dead, and prey on their kind. And so the circle goes on ever widening, like as the ripples from a stone thrown in the water. Friend Arthur, if you had met that kiss which you know of before poor Lucy die; or again, last night when you open your arms to her, you would in time, when you had died, have become *nosferatu*, as they call it in Eastern Europe, and would for all time make more of those Un-Deads that so have filled us with horror. The career of this so unhappy dear lady is but just begun. Those children whose blood she suck are not as yet so much the worse; but if she live on, Un-Dead, more and more they lose their blood, and by her power over them they come to her; and so she draw their blood with that so wicked mouth. But if she die in truth, then all cease; the tiny wounds of the throats disappear, and they go back to their plays unknowing ever of what has been. But of the most blessed of all, when this now Un-Dead be made to rest as true dead, then the soul of the poor lady whom we love shall again be free. Instead of working wickedness by night and growing more debased in the assimilation of it by day, she shall take her place with the other Angels. So that, my friend, it will be a blessed hand for her that shall strike the blow that sets her free. To this I am willing; but is there none amongst us who has a better right? Will it be no joy to think of hereafter in the silence of the night when sleep is not: 'It was my hand that sent her to the stars; it was the hand of him that loved her best; the hand that of all she would herself have chosen, had it been to her to choose?' Tell me if there be such a one amongst us?"

We all looked at Arthur. He saw, too, what we all did, the infinite kindness which suggested that his should be the hand which would restore Lucy to us as a holy, and not an unholy, memory; he stepped forward and said bravely, though his hand trembled, and his face was as pale as snow:—

"My true friend, from the bottom of my broken heart I

thank you. Tell me what I am to do, and I shall not falter!" Van Helsing laid a hand on his shoulder, and said:—

"Brave lad! A moment's courage, and it is done. This stake must be driven through her. It will be a fearful ordeal—be not deceived in that—but it will be only a short time, and you will then rejoice more than your pain was great; from this grim tomb you will emerge as though you tread on air. But you must not falter when once you have begun. Only think that we, your true friends, are round you, and that we pray for you all the time."

"Go on," said Arthur hoarsely. "Tell me what I am to do."

"Take this stake in your left hand, ready to place the point over the heart, and the hammer in your right. Then when we begin our prayer for the dead—I shall read him, I have here the book, and the others shall follow—strike in God's name, that so all may be well with the dead that we love, and that the Un-Dead pass away."

Arthur took the stake and the hammer, and when once his mind was set on action his hands never trembled nor even quivered. Van Helsing opened his missal and began to read, and Quincey and I followed as well as we could. Arthur placed the point over the heart, and as I looked I could see its dint in the white flesh. Then he struck with all his might.

The Thing in the coffin writhed; and a hideous, blood-curdling screech came from the opened red lips. The body shook and quivered and twisted in wild contortions; the sharp white teeth champed together till the lips were cut, and the mouth was smeared with a crimson foam. But Arthur never faltered. He looked like a figure of Thor as his untrembling arm rose and fell, driving deeper and deeper the mercy-bearing stake, whilst the blood from the pierced heart welled and spurted up around it. His face was set, and high duty seemed to shine through it; the sight of it gave us courage, so that our voices seemed to ring through the little vault.

And then the writhing and quivering of the body became less, and the teeth ceased to champ, and the face to quiver. Finally it lay still. The terrible task was over.

The hammer fell from Arthur's hand. He reeled and would have fallen had we not caught him. The great drops of sweat sprang out on his forehead, and his breath came in broken gasps. It had indeed been an awful strain on him; and had he not been forced to his task by more than human considerations he could never have gone through with it. For a few minutes we were so taken up with him that we did not look towards the coffin. When we did, however, a murmur of startled surprise ran from one to the other of us. We gazed so eagerly that Arthur rose, for he had been seated on the ground, and came and looked too; and then a glad, strange light broke over his face and dispelled altogether the gloom of horror that lay upon it.

There, in the coffin lay no longer the foul Thing that we had so dreaded and grown to hate that the work of her destruction was yielded as a privilege to the one best entitled to it, but Lucy as we had seen her in her life, with her face of unequalled sweetness and purity. True that there were there, as we had seen them in life, the traces of care and pain and waste; but these were all dear to us, for they marked her truth to what we knew. One and all we felt that the holy calm that lay like sunshine over the wasted face and form was only an earthly token and symbol of the calm that was to reign for ever.

Van Helsing came and laid his hand on Arthur's shoulder, and said to him:—

"And now, Arthur, my friend, dear lad, am I not forgiven?"

The reaction of the terrible strain came as he took the old man's hand in his, and raising it to his lips, pressed it, and said:—

"Forgiven! God bless you that you have given my dear one her soul again, and me peace." He put his hands on the Professor's shoulder, and laying his head on his breast, cried for a while silently, whilst we stood unmoving. When he raised his head Van Helsing said to him:—

"And now, my child, you may kiss her. Kiss her dead lips if you will, as she would have you to, if for her to choose. For she is not a grinning devil now—not any more a foul Thing for all eternity. No longer she is the devil's Un-Dead. She is God's true dead, whose soul is with Him!"

Arthur bent and kissed her, and then we sent him and Quincey out of the tomb; the Professor and I sawed the top off the stake, leaving the point of it in the body. Then we cut off the head and filled the mouth with garlic. We soldered up the leaden coffin, screwed on the coffin-lid, and gathering up our belongings, came away. When the Professor locked the door he gave the key to Arthur.

Outside the air was sweet, the sun shone, and the birds sang, and it seemed as if all nature were tuned to a different pitch. There was gladness and mirth and peace everywhere, for we were at rest ourselves on one account, and we were glad, though it was with a tempered joy.

Before we moved away Van Helsing said:—

"Now, my friends, one step of our work is done, one the most harrowing to ourselves. But there remains a greater task: to find out the author of all this our sorrow and to stamp him out. I have clues which we can follow; but it is a long task, and a difficult, and there is danger in it, and pain. Shall you not all help me? We have learned to believe, all of us—is it not so? And since so, do we not see our duty? Yes! And do we not promise to go on to the bitter end?"

Each in turn, we took his hand, and the promise was made. Then said the Professor as we moved off:—

"Two nights hence you shall meet with me and dine together at seven of the clock with friend John. I shall entreat two others, two that you know not as yet; and I shall be ready to all our work and our plans unfold. Friend John, you come with me home, for I have much to consult about, and you can help me. Tonight I leave for Amsterdam, but shall return tomorrow night. And then begins our great quest. But first I shall have much to say, so that you may know what is to do and to dread. Then our promise shall be made to each other anew; for there is a terrible task before us, and once our feet are on the ploughshare we must not draw back."

Whitley Strieber

(1945–)

Born in San Antonio, Texas, Louis Whitley Strieber is a graduate of the University of Texas at Austin and the London School of Film Technique. After a successful career as an advertising executive, he published the first of his horror novels, *The Wolfen*, in 1978. It was followed by the vampire novel *The Hunger* in 1981; both works became Hollywood films. Strieber has written extensively about a 1985 occurrence that defies easy description: his encounter with otherworldly beings who were possibly creations of his imagination. His experiences are the topics of *Communion* (1987), *Transformation* (1988), *Breakthrough* (1995), and *The Secret School* (1996). Among his numerous novels are *Warday* (1984), *The Last Vampire* (2001), *Lilith's Dream* (2002), *The Grays* (2006), *2012: The War for Souls* (2007), *Critical Mass* (2009), and *The Omega Point* (2010). His stories are collected in *Evenings with Demons* (1997).

Excerpt from The Wolfen

(1978)

6

They were hungry, they wanted food. Normally they preferred the darker, desolate sections of the city, but their need to follow their enemies had brought them into its very eye. Here the smell of man lay over everything like a dense fog, and there was not much cover.

But even the brightest places have shadows. They moved in single file behind the wall that separates Central Park from the street. They did not need to look over the wall to know that few of the benches that lined the other side were occupied—they could smell that fact perfectly well. But they also smelled something else, the rich scent of a human being perhaps a quarter of a mile farther on. On one of the benches a man was sleeping, a man whose pores were exuding the smell of alcohol. To them the reek meant food, easily gotten.

As they moved closer they could hear his breathing. It was long and troubled, full of age. They stopped behind him. There was no need to discuss what they would do; each one knew his role.

Three jumped up on the wall, standing there perfectly still, balanced on the sharply angled stone. He was on the bench below them. The one nearest the victim's head inclined her ears back. She would get the throat. The other two would move in only if there was a struggle.

She held her breath a moment to clear her head. Then she examined her victim with her eyes. The flesh was not visible—it was under thick folds of cloth. She would have to jump, plunge her muzzle into the cloth and rip out the throat all at once. If there were more than a few convulsions on the part of the food she would disappoint the pack. She opened her nose, letting the rich smells of the world back in. She listened up and down the street. Only automobile traffic, nobody on foot for at least fifty yards. She cocked her ears toward a man leaning in a chair inside the brightly lit foyer of a building across the street. He was listening to a radio. She watched his head turn. He was glancing into the lobby.

Now. She was down, she was pushing her nose past cloth, slick hot flesh, feeling the vibration of subvocal response in the man, feeling his muscles stiffening as his body reacted to her standing on it, then opening her mouth against the flesh, feeling her teeth scrape back and down, pressing her tongue against the deliciously salty skin and *ripping* with all the strength in her jaws and neck and chest, and jumping back to the wall with the bloody throat in her mouth. The body on the bench barely rustled as its dying blood poured out.

And the man in the doorway returned his glance to the street. Nothing had moved, as far as he was concerned. Ever watchful, she scented him and listened to him. His breathing was steady, his smell bland. Good, he had noticed nothing.

Now her job was over, she dropped back behind the wall and ate her trophy. It was rich and sweet with blood. Around her the pack was very happy as it worked. Three of them lifted the body over the wall and let it drop with a thud. The two others, skilled in just this art, stripped the clothing away. They would carry the material to the other side of the park, shred it and hide it in shrubs before they returned to their meal.

As soon as the corpse was stripped it was pulled open. The organs were sniffed carefully. One lung, the stomach, the colon were put aside because of rot.

Then the pack ate in rank order.

The mother took the brain. The father took a thigh and buttock. The first-mated pair ate the clean organs. When they returned from their duty the second-mated pair took the rest. And then they pulled apart the remains and took them piece by piece and dropped them in the nearby lake. The bones would sink and would not be found at least until spring, if then. The clothing they had shredded and scattered half a mile away. And now they kicked as much new snow as they could over the blood of their feast. When this was done they went to a place they had seen earlier, a great meadow full of the beautiful new snow that had been falling.

They ran and danced in the snow, feeling the pleasure of their bodies, the joy of racing headlong across the wide expanse, and because they knew that no human was in earshot they had a joyous howl full of the pulsing rhythm they liked best after a hunt. The sound rose through the park, echoing off the buildings that surrounded it. Inside those buildings a few wakeful people stirred, made restive by the cold and ancient terror that the sound communicated to man.

Then they went to a tunnel they had slept in these past four nights and settled down. By long-learned habit they slept in the small hours of the morning when men mostly did not stir. During daylight, man's strongest time, they remained awake and alert and rarely broke cover unless they had to. In the evening they hunted.

This traditional order of life went back forever.

Before sleeping the second-mated pair made love, both to entertain the others and to prepare for spring. And afterward, father and mother licked them, and then the pack slept.

7

Carl Ferguson was horrified and excited at the same time by what he was reading. He seemed to drift away, to a quiet and safe place. But he came back. Around him the prosaic realities of the Main Reading Room of the New York Public Library reasserted themselves. Across from him a painfully pretty schoolgirl cracked her gum. Beside him an old man breathed long and slow, paging through an equally old book. All around him there was a subdued clatter, the scuttle of pen on paper, the coughs, the whispers, the drone of clerks calling numbers from the front of the room.

Because you could not enter the stacks and because you could neither enter nor leave this room with a book, its collection had not been stolen and was still among the best in the world. And it was because of the book that he had finally obtained from this superb collection that Carl Ferguson felt such an extremity of fear. What he read, what he saw before him was almost too fantastic and too horrible to believe. And yet the words were there.

"In Normandy," Ferguson read for the third time, "tradition tells of certain fantastic beings known as lupins or lubins. They pass the night chattering together and twattling in an unknown tongue. They take their stand by the walls of country cemeteries and howl dismally at the moon. Timorous and fearful of man they will flee away scared at a footstep or distant voice. In some districts, however, they are fierce and of the werewolf race, since they are said to scratch up graves with their hands and gnaw poor dead bones."

An ancient story, repeated by Montague Summers in his classic *The Werewolf.* Summers assumed that the werewolf tales were folklore, hearsay conjured up to frighten the gullible. But Summers was totally, incredibly wrong. The old legends and tales were true. Only one small element was incorrect—in the past it was assumed that their intelligence and cunning meant that werewolves were men who had assumed the shape of animals. But they weren't. They were not that at all, but rather a completely separate species of intelligent creature. And they had been sharing planet Earth with us all these long eons and we never understood it. What marvellous beings they must be—a virtual alien intelligence right here at home. It was a frightening discovery, but to Ferguson also one of awesome wonder.

Here were legends, stories, tales going back thousands of years, repeating again and again the mythology of the werewolf. And then suddenly, in the latter part of the nineteenth century, silence.

The legends died.

The stories were no longer told.

But why? To Ferguson's mind the answer was simple: the werewolves, tormented for generations by humanity's vigilance and fear, had found a way to hide from man. Their cover was now perfect. They lived among us, fed off our living flesh, but were unknown to all except those who didn't live to tell the tale. They were a race of living ghosts, unseen but very much a part of the world. They understood human society well enough to take only the abandoned, the weak, the isolated. And toward the end of the nineteenth century the human population all over the world had started to explode, poverty and filth had spread. Huge masses of people were ignored and abandoned by the societies in which they lived. And they were fodder for these werewolves, who range through the shadows devouring the beggars, the wanderers, those without name or home.

And no doubt the population of werewolves had exploded right along with the human population. Ferguson pictured hundreds, thousands of them scavenging the great cities of the earth for their human prey, rarely being glimpsed, using their sensitive ears and noses to keep well distant of all but the weak and helpless, taking advantage of man's increasing multitudes and increasing poverty. Their faculties combined with their intelligence must make them fearsome indeed—but what an opportunity they also represented to science—to him—as another intelligence capable of study, even perhaps communication.

But there was something else about Summers' book, something even more disquieting, and that was the continual references to men and werewolves in communication with one another. "Two gentlemen who were crossing a forest glade after dark suddenly came upon an open space where an old woodsman was standing, a man well-known to them, who was making passes in the air, weaving strange signs and signals. The two friends concealed themselves behind a tree, whence they saw thirteen wolves come trotting along. The leader was a huge grey wolf who went up to the old man fawning upon him and being caressed. Presently the forester uttered a sing-song chant and plunged into the wood followed by the wolves."

Just a story, but tremendously interesting in the context of the information that the two detectives had brought him. Obviously the references to signs and a "sing-song" chant referred to human attempts to mimic the language of the werewolves, to communicate. Why did men once run with the werewolves?

Summers said that vampires were often connected to werewolves. Vampires—the eaters of blood. In other words, cannibals. To a less knowledgeable person such an idea might have seemed fantastic, but Ferguson knew enough about old Europe to understand the probable truth behind the legend. Men did indeed run with werewolves, and those men were called vampires because they fed off human flesh like the wolves themselves. Cannibalism must have been common in the Europe of the Dark Ages, when grinding poverty was the fate of all except a tiny minority. When men were the weakest and most numerous creatures around it must have tempted the hungry . . . to go out and find the werewolves, somehow build up a rapport, and then hunt with them living like a scavenger off the pickings.

So much for the image of the vampire as a count with a castle and a silk dinner jacket. The truth was more like Summers' description—a filthy old forester scrabbling along with a pack of werewolves to glean the leavings of their monstrous feasts.

Man the scavenger, in the same role among werewolves that dogs play among men! And the human prey, unsuspecting now, but in those days it knew. People approached the night with terror crackling in their hearts. And when darkness fell only the desperate and the mad remained out of doors.

What, then, was the role of the human scavenger, the vampire, that ran with the werewolves? Why did they tolerate him? Simple enough, to coax people out of their houses, to lure them into the shadows where they would be ripped apart. It was ugly but it also meant that there had been communication of a sort between man and werewolf in the past, and could be again. And how immeasurably richer communication between this extraordinary species and modern science might be. There could be no comparison between the promise of the future and the sordid mistakes of the distant past.

It had gotten much easier for the werewolves in recent centuries. No longer were the human vampires needed. Nowadays the werewolves could do it on their own. Just take up residence in any big city, live in abandoned buildings among the city's million byways, and prey on the human strays.

Man and wolf. It had been an age-old animosity. The image of the wolf baying at the moon on a winter's night still calls primitive terrors to the heart of man.

And with good reason, except that the innocent timber wolf with his loud howling and once conspicuous presence was not the enemy. Lurking back there in the shadows, perhaps along the path to the well, was the real enemy, unnoticed, patient, lethal beyond imagining. The wolf-being with its long finger-like paws, the werewolf, the other intelligent species that shared this planet.

We killed off the innocent timber wolf and never even discovered the real danger. While the timber wolf bayed to the oblivious moon the real enemy crept up the basement steps and used one of those clever paws to throw the bolt on the door.

Ferguson ran his fingers through his hair, his mind trying to accept the fearful truth he had uncovered. That damn detective—Wilson was his name—had an absolutely uncanny intuition about this whole matter. It was Detective Wilson who had first said the word werewolf, the word that had gotten Ferguson really thinking about that strange paw. And Wilson had claimed that the werewolves were hunting him and the woman down. With good reason! Once their secret was out the life of the werewolf would be made immeasurably harder, like it was in the old days in Europe when humanity bolted its doors and locked its windows, or in the Americas where the Indian used his knowledge of the forest to play a deadly game of hide and seek, a game commemorated to this day in the traditional dances of many tribes. The werewolf undoubtedly followed man to this continent across the Bering land bridge eons ago. But always and everywhere he kept himself as well hidden as he could. And it made good sense. You wouldn't find beggars sleeping on sidewalks if the werewolf was common knowledge. A wave of terror would sweep the city and the world unlike anything known since the Middle Ages. Unspeakable things would be done in the name of human safety. Man would declare all-out war on his adversary.

And at last he would have a fair fight on his hands. With all our technology, we have never faced an alien intelligence before, have never faced a species with its own built-in technology far superior to our own. Ferguson could not imagine what the mind behind the nose and ears of the werewolf must be like. The sheer quantity of information pouring in must literally be millions of times greater than that reaching a man through his eyes. The mind that gave meaning to all that information must be a miracle indeed. Maybe even greater than the mind of man. And man must, this time, react responsibly. If there was intelligence there it could be reasoned with, and eventually the two enemy species could learn to live together in peace. If Carl Ferguson had any part in this at all it was as the missionary of reason and understanding. Man could either declare war on this species or try to come to an understanding. Carl Ferguson raised his head, closed his eyes and hoped with every fiber of his being that reason would for once prevail.

He was surprised to notice somebody was standing beside him.

"You've got to take this call slip to the rare books department. We don't have this book in the reading room. All of our stuff is post-1825 and this book was written in 1597." The call clerk dropped the card on the table in front of Ferguson and went away. Ferguson got up and headed for the rare books collection, card clutched in his hand.

He moved through the empty, echoing halls of the great library, finally arriving at the rare books collection. A middle-aged woman sat at a desk working on a catalogue under a green-shaded lamp. The only sound in the room was the faint clatter of the steam pipes and the snow-muted mutter of the city beyond the windows.

"I'm Carl Ferguson of the Museum of Natural History. I'd like to take a look at this book." He handed her the card.

"Do we have this?"

"It's catalogued."

She got up and disappeared behind a wire-covered doorway. Ferguson waited standing expectantly for a few moments, then found a chair. There was no sound from the direction the woman had gone. He was alone in the room. The place smelled of books. And he was impatient for her to return. It was urgent that she produce the book he needed. It was by Beauvoys de Chauvincourt, a man considered an authority on werewolves in his day, and more interestingly, a familiar of them. The manner of his death was what had excited Ferguson—it indicated that the man may indeed have known the creatures firsthand. Beauvoys de Chauvincourt had gone out one night in search of his friends the werewolves and had simply disappeared. The dark suspicions of the time notwithstanding, Ferguson felt that he almost certainly had met his end observing the ancestors of the very creatures whose work the two cops had uncovered.

"Do you know books, Mr. Ferguson?"

"It's Doctor. Y-yes, I do. I can handle antique books."

"That's exactly what shouldn't be done with them." She eyed him. "I'll turn for you," she said firmly. "Let's go over there." She placed the book before him at a table and turned on one of the green shaded lights.

"Discours de la Lycanthropie, ou de la transformation des hommes en loups," read the title page.

"Turn."

She opened the book, turning the stiff pages to the frontispiece. And Ferguson felt sweat trickling down his temples. What he was seeing was so extraordinary that it was almost too much to bear without crying out. For there on the frontispiece of the ancient book was engraved a most amazing picture.

In this ancient engraving a sparse plain was shown lit by a full moon. And walking through the plain was a man surrounded by things that looked somewhat like wolves but were not wolves. The man appeared at ease, strolling along playing a bagpipe that was slung over his shoulder. And the werewolves walked with him. The artist had rendered his subjects faithfully, Ferguson guessed. The heads with their high, wide brain cases and large eyes, the delicate and sinister paws, the voracious, knowing faces—it all fit the image Ferguson had created in his own mind of what the creatures must look like. And the man with them—incredible. In those days there must certainly have been communication between humans—some humans—and werewolves. De Chauvincourt himself must have . . . known them. And in the end they destroyed him.

"Turn."

Ferguson cursed his French. Here were lists of names—no, they were invocations of demons. Nothing to be learned here. "Turn."

More invocations.

"Keep turning."

The pages rolled past until something caught Ferguson's eye. "The Language They Assume."

Here followed a description of a complex language composed of tail movements, ear movements, growls, changes in facial expression, movements of the tongue and even clicks of the nails. It was as if human language had consisted not only of words but also of myriad gestures to augment those words.

And Ferguson knew something he hadn't known before. The creatures had vocal cords inadequate to the needs of true verbal language. How fast their brain must have evolved! Perhaps it took only fifty or a hundred thousand years and there they were, strange intelligent beings roaming the world in pursuit of man, engaged in the age-long hunt that occupied them to this day.

"Turn."

Here the book had another engraving—hand movements. "Can I get a Xerox of this page?"

"We can't copy this book."

He had brought paper and pencil and made rough sketches of the positions shown, noting the meaning of each: stop, run, kill, attack, flee.

Stop—the tips of the fingers drawn down to the edge of the palm.

Run—the hands held straight out before the face.

Kill—the fists clenched, held against the throat.

Attack—the hands clutching the stomach like claws.

Flee—the palms against the forehead.

But these were human signals. Obviously the werewolves did not use such gestures among themselves because they were four-legged. There must have been a mutual language composed of signals like these between the werewolves and—

"Les vampires." The book said it. And there was the source of another legend, the vampires again. This must be the language they used to communicate with the werewolves. The vampires, those who followed the wolves and scavenged the remains. And the wolves needed them to induce people to come out of their locked houses.

What a different world it had been then! Werewolves and vampires stalking the night, the vampires luring people from their homes to be devoured. No wonder the Middle Ages were such a dark and cruel time. The terrors of the night were not imaginary at all, but stark realities faced from birth by everybody. Only as the sheer numbers of mankind had increased had the threat seemed to disappear. Man grew so numerous that the work of the werewolves was no longer noticed. In the days of de Chauvincourt the human helpers must already have been unnecessary in most places . . . and so as soon as the vampire weakened with age the werewolves turned on him. The librarian turned the page.

Ferguson jumped up. He tried to stop himself, but took an involuntary step backward and knocked over the chair.

"Sir!"

"I-I'm sorry!" He grabbed the chair, righted it. Now he felt like a fool. But the engraving that covered both of the pages facing was so terrible that he almost could not look at it.

He was seeing the werewolf close-up, face-to-face. This would be a reliable rendition of the features. Even in this three-hundred-and-eighty-year-old engraving he could see the savagery, the sheer voraciousness of the creature. The eyes stared out at him like something from a nightmare.

And they *were* from a nightmare. His mind was racing now as he remembered, an incident that had occurred when he was no more than six or seven. They were in the Catskills, spending the summer near New Paltz in upstate New York. He was asleep in his ground-floor bedroom. Something awakened him. Moonlight was streaming in the open window. And a monstrous animal was leaning in, poking its muzzle toward him, the face clear in the moonlight.

He had screamed and the thing had disappeared in a flash. Nightmare, they said. And here it was staring at him again, the face of the werewolf.

The librarian closed the book. "That will be enough," she said. "I think you're upset."

Oscar Wilde

(1854–1900)

Born in Dublin, Oscar Fingal O'Flahertie Wills Wilde was the son of a mother who was a poet and a father who was a noted surgeon. After attending Trinity College in Dublin, where he won a scholarship, he went on to complete his education at Oxford's Magdalen College, where he distinguished himself as a student of the classics. He settled in London, where he began to publish poetry and fiction, but he is best known as a witty, comic dramatist who brilliantly satirized Victorian values and institutions. His works include the novel *The Picture of Dorian Gray* (1891) and the highly successful plays *Lady Windermere's Fan* (1892), *A Woman of No Importance* (1893), *An Ideal Husband* (1895), and *The Importance of Being Earnest* (1895). Wilde was convicted of engaging in homosexual acts in 1895 and served a prison sentence of two years at hard labor. After his release from prison, he lived in France in poor health for the remaining three years of his life.

The Canterville Ghost
A Hylo-Idealistic Romance

(1887)

I

When Mr. Hiram B. Otis, the American Minister, bought Canterville Chase, everyone told him he was doing a very foolish thing, as there was no doubt at all that the place was haunted. Indeed, Lord Canterville himself, who was a man of the most punctilious honour, had felt it his duty to mention the fact to Mr. Otis, when they came to discuss terms.

"We have not cared to live in the place ourselves," said Lord Canterville, "since my grand-aunt, the Dowager Duchess of Bolton, was frightened into a fit, from which she never really recovered, by two skeleton hands being placed on her shoulders as she was dressing for dinner, and I feel bound to tell you, Mr. Otis, that the ghost has been seen by several living members of my family, as well as by the rector of the parish, the Rev. Augustus Dampier, who is a fellow of King's College, Cambridge. After the unfortunate accident to the Duchess, none of our younger servants would stay with us, and Lady Canterville often got very little sleep at night, in consequence of the mysterious noises that came from the corridor and the library."

"My Lord," answered the Minister, "I will take the furniture and the ghost at a valuation. I come from a modern country, where we have everything that money can buy; and with all our spry young fellows painting the Old World red, and carrying off your best actresses and prima donnas, I reckon that if there were such a thing as a ghost in Europe, we'd have it at home in a very short time in one of our public museums, or on the road as a show."

"I fear that the ghost exists," said Lord Canterville, smiling, "though it may have resisted the overtures of your enterprising impresarios. It has been well known for three centuries, since 1584 in fact, and always makes its appearance before the death of any member of our family."

"Well, so does the family doctor for that matter, Lord Canterville. But there is no such thing, sir, as a ghost, and I guess the laws of nature are not going to be suspended for the British aristocracy."

"You are certainly very natural in America," answered Lord Canterville, who did not quite understand Mr. Otis's last observation, "and if you don't mind a ghost in the house, it is all right. Only you must remember I warned you."

A few weeks after this, the purchase was completed, and at the close of the season the Minister and his family went to Canterville Chase. Mrs. Otis, who, as Miss Lucretia R. Tappan, of West 53rd Street, had been a celebrated New York belle, was now a very handsome middle-aged woman, with fine eyes, and a superb profile. Many American ladies on leaving their native land adopt an appearance of chronic ill health, under the impression that it is a form of European refinement, but Mrs. Otis had never fallen into this error. She had a magnificent constitution, and a really wonderful amount of animal spirits. Indeed, in many respects, she was quite English, and was an excellent example of the fact that we have really everything in common with America nowadays, except, of course, language. Her eldest son, christened Washington by his parents in a moment of patriotism, which he never ceased to regret, was a fair-haired, rather good-looking young man, who had qualified himself for American diplomacy by leading the German in the Newport Casino for three successive seasons, and even in London was well-known as an excellent dancer. Gardenias and the peerage were his only weaknesses. Otherwise he was extremely sensible. Miss Virginia E. Otis was a little girl of fifteen, lithe and lovely as a fawn, and with a fine freedom in her large blue eyes. She was a wonderful amazon, and had once raced old Lord Bilton on her pony twice round the park, winning by a length and a half, just in front of Achilles statue, to the huge delight of the young Duke of Cheshire, who proposed for her on the spot, and was sent back to Eton that very night by his guardians, in floods of tears. After Virginia came the twins, who were usually called "The Stars and Stripes" as they were always getting swished. They were delightful boys, and with the exception of the worthy Minister the only true republicans of the family.

As Canterville Chase is seven miles from Ascot, the nearest railway station, Mr. Otis had telegraphed for a waggonette to meet them, and they started on their drive in high spirits. It was a lovely July evening, and the air was delicate with the scent of the pine woods. Now and then they heard a wood pigeon brooding over its own sweet voice, or saw, deep in the rustling fern, the burnished breast of the pheasant. Little squirrels peered at them from the beech trees as they went by, and the rabbits scudded away through the brushwood and over the mossy knolls, with their white tails in the air. As they entered the avenue of Canterville Chase, however, the sky became suddenly overcast with clouds, a curious stillness seemed to hold the atmosphere, a great flight of rooks passed silently over their heads, and, before they reached the house, some big drops of rain had fallen.

Standing on the steps to receive them was an old woman, neatly dressed in black silk, with a white cap and apron. This was Mrs. Umney, the housekeeper, whom Mrs. Otis, at Lady Canterville's earnest request, had consented to keep on in her former position. She made them each a low curtsey as they alighted, and said in a quaint, old fashioned manner, "I bid you welcome to Canterville Chase." Following her, they passed through the fine Tudor hall into the library, a long, low room, panelled in black oak, at the end of which was a large stained-glass window. Here they found tea laid out for them, and, after taking off their wraps they sat down and began to look round, while Mrs. Umney waited on them.

Suddenly Mrs. Otis caught sight of a dull red stain on the floor just by the fireplace and, quite unconscious of what it really signified, said to Mrs. Umney, "I am afraid something has been spilt there."

"Yes, madam," replied the old housekeeper in a low voice, "blood has been spilt on that spot."

"How horrid," cried Mrs. Otis; "I don't at all care for bloodstains in a sitting-room. It must be removed at once."

The old woman smiled, and answered in the same low, mysterious voice, "It is the blood of Lady Eleanor de Canterville, who was murdered on that very spot by her own husband, Sir Simon de Canterville, in 1575. Sir Simon survived her nine years, and disappeared suddenly under very mysterious circumstances. His body has never been discovered, but his guilty spirit still haunts the Chase. The bloodstain has been much admired by tourists and others, and cannot be removed."

"That is all nonsense," cried Washington Otis; "Pinkerton's Champion Stain Remover and Paragon Detergent will clean it up in no time," and before the terrified housekeeper could interfere he had fallen upon his knees, and was rapidly scouring the floor with a small stick of what looked like a black cosmetic. In a few moments no trace of the bloodstain could be seen.

"I knew Pinkerton would do it," he exclaimed triumphantly, as he looked round at his admiring family, but no sooner had he said these words than a terrible flash of lightning lit up the sombre room, a fearful peal of thunder made them all start to their feet, and Mrs. Umney fainted.

"What a monstrous climate!" said the American Minister calmly, as he lit a long cheroot. "I guess the old country is so overpopulated that they have not enough decent weather for everyone. I have always been of opinion that emigration is the only thing for England."

"My dear Hiram," cried Mrs. Otis, "what can we do with a woman who faints?"

"Charge it to her like breakages," answered the Minister; "she won't faint after that"; and in a few moments Mrs. Umney certainly came to. There was no doubt, however, that she was extremely upset, and she sternly warned Mr. Otis to beware of some trouble coming to the house.

"I have seen things with my own eyes, sir," she said, "that would make any Christian's hair stand on end, and many and many a night I have not closed my eyes in sleep for the awful things that are done here." Mr. Otis, however, and his wife warmly assured the honest soul that they were not afraid of ghosts, and, after invoking the blessing of Providence on her new master and mistress, and making arrangements for an increase of salary, the old housekeeper tottered off to her own room.

II

The storm raged fiercely all that night, but nothing of particular note occurred. The next morning, however, when they came down to breakfast, they found the terrible stain of blood once again on the floor.

"I don't think it can be the fault of the Paragon Detergent," said Washington, "for I have tried it with everything. It must be the ghost."

He accordingly rubbed out the stain a second time, but the second morning it appeared again. The third morning also it was there, though the library had been locked up at night by Mr. Otis himself, and the key carried upstairs. The whole family were now quite interested; Mr. Otis began to suspect that he had been too dogmatic in his denial of the existence of ghosts, Mrs. Otis expressed her intention of joining the Psychical Society, and Washington prepared a long letter to Messrs. Myers and Podmore on the subject of the Permanence of Sanguineous Stains when connected with crime. That night all doubts about the objective existence of phantasmata were removed for ever.

The day had been warm and sunny; and, in the cool of the evening, the whole family went out for a drive. They did not return home till nine o'clock, when they had a light supper. The conversation in no way turned upon ghosts, so there were not even those primary conditions of receptive expectation which so often precede the presentation of psychical phenomena. The subjects discussed, as I have since learned from Mr. Otis, were merely such as form the ordinary conversation of cultured Americans of the better class, such as the immense superiority of Miss Fanny Davenport over Sarah Bernhardt as an actress; the difficulty of obtaining green corn, buckwheat cakes, and hominy, even in the best English houses; the importance of Boston in the development of the world-soul; the advantages of the baggage check system in railway travelling; and the sweetness of the New York accent as compared to the London drawl. No mention at all was made of the supernatural, nor was Sir Simon de Canterville alluded to in any way. At eleven o'clock the family retired, and by half-past all the lights were out. Some time after, Mr. Otis was awakened by a curious noise in the corridor, outside his room. It sounded like the clank of metal, and seemed to be coming nearer every moment. He got up at once, struck a match and looked at the time. It was exactly one o'clock. He was quite calm, and felt his pulse, which was not at all feverish. The strange noise still continued, and with it he heard distinctly the sound of footsteps. He put on his slippers, took a small oblong phial out of his dressing-case, and opened the door. Right in front of him he saw, in the wan moonlight, an old man of terrible aspect. His eyes were as red as burning coals; long grey hair fell over his shoulders in matted coils; his garments, which were of antique cut, were soiled and ragged, and from his wrists and ankles hung heavy manacles and rusty gyves.

"My dear sir," said Mr. Otis, "I really must insist on your oiling those chains, and have brought you for that purpose a small bottle of the Tammany Rising Sun Lubricator. It is said to be completely efficacious upon one application, and there are several testimonials to that effect on the wrapper from some of our most eminent native divines. I shall leave it here for you by the bedroom candles, and will be happy to supply you with more should you require it." With these words the United States Minister laid the bottle down on a marble table, and, closing his door, retired to rest.

For a moment the Canterville ghost stood quite motionless in natural indignation; then, dashing the bottle violently upon the polished floor, he fled down the corridor, uttering hollow groans, and emitting a ghastly green light. Just, however, as he reached the top of the great oak staircase, a door was flung open, two little white-robed figures appeared, and a large pillow whizzed past his head! There was evidently no time to be lost, so, hastily adopting the Fourth Dimension of Space as a means of escape, he vanished through the wainscoting, and the house became quite quiet.

On reaching the small secret chamber in the left wing, he leaned up against a moonbeam to recover his breath and began to try and realize his position. Never, in a brilliant and uninterrupted career of three hundred years, had he been so grossly insulted. He thought of the Dowager Duchess, whom he had frightened into a fit as she stood before the glass in her lace and diamonds; of the four housemaids, who had gone off into hysterics when he merely grinned at them through the curtains of one of the spare bedrooms; of the rector of the parish, whose candle he had blown out as he was coming late one night from the library, and who had been under the care of Sir William Gull ever since, a perfect martyr to nervous disorders; and of old Madame de Tremouillac, who, having wakened up one morning early and seen a skeleton seated in an armchair by the fire reading her diary, had been confined to her bed for six weeks with an attack of brain fever, and, on her recovery, had become reconciled to the Church, and had broken off her connection with that notorious sceptic Monsieur de Voltaire. He remembered the terrible night when the wicked Lord Canterville was found choking in his dressing-room, with the knave of diamonds half-way down his throat, and confessed, just before he died, that he had cheated Charles James Fox out of £50,000 at Crockford's by means of that very card, and swore that the ghost had made him swallow it. All his great achievements came back to him again, from the butler who had shot himself in the pantry because he had seen a green hand tapping at the window pane, to the beautiful Lady Stutfield, who was always obliged to wear a black velvet band round her throat to hide the mark of five fingers burnt upon her white skin, and who drowned herself at last in the carp pond at the end of the King's Walk. With the enthusiastic egotism of the true artist he went over his most celebrated performances, and smiled bitterly to himself as he recalled to mind his last appearance as "Red Ruben, or the Strangled Babe," his debut as "Gaunt Gibeon, the Bloodsucker of Bexley Moor," and the furore he had excited one lovely June evening by merely playing ninepins with his own bones upon the lawn-tennis ground. And after all this, some wretched modern Americans were to come and offer him the Rising Sun Lubricator, and throw pillows at his head! It was quite unbearable. Besides, no ghosts in history had ever been treated in this manner. Accordingly, he determined to have vengeance, and remained till daylight in an attitude of deep thought.

III

The next morning when the Otis family met at breakfast, they discussed the ghost at some length. The United States Minister was naturally a little annoyed to find that his present had not been accepted.

"I have no wish," he said, "to do the ghost any personal injury, and I must say that, considering the length of time he has been in the house, I don't think it is at all polite to throw pillows at him"—a very just remark, at which, I am sorry to say, the twins burst into shouts of laughter. "Upon the other hand," he continued, "if he really declines to use the Rising Sun Lubricator, we shall have to take his chains from him. It would be quite impossible to sleep, with such a noise going on outside the bedrooms."

For the rest of the week, however, they were undisturbed, the only thing that excited any attention being the continual renewal of the bloodstain on the library floor. This certainly was very strange, as the door was always locked at night by Mr. Otis, and the windows kept closely barred. The chameleon-like colour, also, of the stain excited a good deal of comment. Some mornings it was a dull (almost Indian) red, then it would be vermilion, then a rich purple, and once when they came down for family prayers, according to the simple rites of the Free American Reformed Episcopalian Church, they found it a bright emerald green. These kaleidoscopic changes naturally amused the party very much, and bets on the subject were freely made every evening. The only person who did not enter into the joke was little Virginia, who, for some unexplained reason, was always a good deal distressed at the sight of the bloodstain, and very nearly cried the morning it was emerald green.

The second appearance of the ghost was on Sunday night. Shortly after they had gone to bed they were suddenly alarmed by a fearful crash in the hall. Rushing downstairs, they found that a large suit of old armour had become detached from its stand, and had fallen on the stone floor, while, seated in a high-backed chair, was the Canterville ghost, rubbing his knees with an expression of acute agony on his face. The twins, having brought their peashooters with them, at once discharged two pellets on him, with that accuracy of aim which can only be attained by long and careful practice on a writing master, while the United States Minister covered him with his revolver, and called him, in accordance with Californian etiquette, to hold up his hands! The ghost started up with a wild shriek of rage, and swept through them like a mist, extinguishing Washington Otis's candle as he passed, and so leaving them all in total darkness. On reaching the top of the staircase he recovered himself, and determined to give his celebrated peal of demoniac laughter. This he had on more than one occasion found extremely useful. It was said to have turned Lord Raker's wig grey in a single night, and had certainly made three of Lady Canterville's French governesses give warning before their month was up. He accordingly laughed his most horrible laugh, till the old vaulted roof rang and rang again, but hardly had the fearful echo died away when a door opened, and Mrs. Otis came out in a light blue dressing gown.

"I am afraid you are far from well," she said, "and have brought you a bottle of Dr. Dobell's tincture. If it is indigestion, you will find it a most excellent remedy."

The ghost glared at her in fury, and began at once to make preparations for turning himself into a large black dog, an accomplishment for which he was justly renowned, and to which the family doctor always attributed the permanent idiocy of Lord Canterville's uncle, the Hon. Thomas Morton. The sound of approaching footsteps, however, made him hesitate in his fell purpose, so he contented himself with becoming faintly phosphorescent, and vanished with a deep churchyard groan, just as the twins had come up to him.

On reaching his room he entirely broke down, and became prey to the most violent agitation. The vulgarity of the twins, and the gross materialism of Mrs. Otis, were naturally extremely annoying, but what really distressed him most was that he had been unable to wear the suit of mail. He had hoped that even modern Americans would be thrilled by the sight of a Spectre In Armour, if for no more practical reason, at least out of respect for the national poet Longfellow, over whose graceful and attractive poetry he himself had whiled away many a weary hour when the Cantervilles were up in town. Besides, it was his own suit. He had worn it with success at the Kenilworth tournament, and had been highly complimented on it by no less a person than the Virgin Queen herself. Yet when he had put it on, he had been completely overpowered by the weight of the huge breastplate and steel casque, and had fallen heavily on the stone pavement, barking both his knees severely, and bruising the knuckles of his right hand.

For some days after this he was extremely ill, and hardly stirred out of his room at all, except to keep the bloodstain in proper repair. However, by taking great care of himself, he recovered, and resolved to make a third attempt to frighten the United States Minister and his family. He selected Friday, 17th August, for his appearance, and spent most of that day in looking over his wardrobe, ultimately deciding in favour of a large slouched hat with a red feather, a winding sheet frilled at the wrists and neck, and a rusty dagger. Towards evening a violent storm of rain came on, and the wind was so high that all the windows and doors in the old house shook and rattled. In fact, it was just such weather as he loved. His plan of action was this. He was to make his way quietly to Washington Otis's room, gibber at him from the foot of the bed, and stab himself three times in the throat to the sound of slow music. He bore Washington a special grudge, being quite aware that it was he who was in the habit of removing the famous Canterville bloodstain, by means of Pinkerton's Paragon Detergent. Having reduced the reckless and foolhardy youth to a condition of abject terror, he was then to proceed to the room occupied by the United States Minister and his wife, and there to place a clammy hand on Mrs. Otis's forehead, while he hissed into her trembling husband's ear the awful secrets of the charnel-house. With regard to little Virginia, he had not quite made up his mind. She had never insulted him in any way, and was pretty and gentle. A few hollow groans from the wardrobe, he thought, would be more than sufficient, or, if that failed to wake her, he might grabble at the counterpane with palsy-twitching fingers. As for the twins, he was quite determined to teach them a lesson. The first thing to be done was, of course, to sit upon their chests, so as to produce the stifling sensation of nightmare. Then, as their beds were quite close to each other, to stand between them in the form of a green, icy-cold corpse, till they became paralysed with fear, and finally, to throw off the winding-sheet, and crawl round the room, with white bleached bones and one rolling eyeball, in the character of "Dumb Daniel, or the Suicide's Skeleton," a role in which he had on more than one occasion produced a great effect, and which he considered quite equal to his famous part of "Martin the Maniac, or the Masked Mystery."

At half-past ten he heard the family going to bed. For some time he was disturbed by wild shrieks of laughter from the twins, who, with the light-hearted gaiety of schoolboys, were evidently amusing themselves before they retired to rest, but at a quarter past eleven all was still, and, as midnight sounded, he sallied forth. The owl beat against the window panes, the raven croaked from the old yew tree, and the wind wandered moaning round the house like a lost soul; but the Otis family slept unconscious of their doom, and high above the rain and storm he could hear the steady snoring of the Minister for the United States. He stepped stealthily out of the wainscoting, with an evil smile on his cruel, wrinkled mouth, and the moon hid her face in a cloud as he stole past the great oriel window, where his own arms and those of his murdered wife were blazoned in azure and gold. On and on he glided, like an evil shadow, the very darkness seeming to loathe him as he passed. Once he thought he heard something call, and stopped; but it was only the baying of a dog from the Red Farm, and he went on, muttering strange sixteenth-century curses, and ever and anon brandishing the rusty dagger in the midnight air. Finally he reached the corner of the passage that led to luckless Washington's room. For a moment he paused there, the wind blowing his long grey locks about his head, and twisting into grotesque and fantastic folds the nameless horror of the dead man's shroud. Then the clock struck the quarter, and he felt the time was come. He chuckled to himself, and turned the corner; but no sooner had he done so, than, with a piteous wail of terror, he fell back, and hid his blanched face in his long, bony hands. Right in front of him was standing a horrible spectre, motionless as a carven image, and monstrous as a madman's dream! Its head was bald and burnished; its face round, and fat, and white; and hideous laughter seemed to have writhed its features into an eternal grin. From the eyes streamed rays of scarlet light, the mouth was a wide well of fire, and a hideous garment, like to his own, swathed with its silent snows the Titan form. On its breast was a placard with strange writing in antique characters, some scroll of shame it seemed, some record of wild sins, some awful calendar of crime, and, with its right hand, it bore aloft a falchion of gleaming steel.

Never having seen a ghost before, he naturally was terribly frightened, and, after a second hasty glance at the awful phantom, he fled back to his room, tripping up in his long winding-sheet as he sped down the corridor, and finally dropping the rusty dagger into the Minister's jackboots, where it was found in the morning by the butler. Once in the privacy of his own apartment, he flung himself down on a small pallet bed, and hid his face under the clothes. After a time, however, the brave old Canterville spirit asserted itself, and he determined to go and speak to the other ghost as soon as it was daylight. Accordingly, just as the dawn was touching the hills with silver, he returned towards the spot where he had first laid eyes on the grisly phantom, feeling that, after all, two ghosts were better than one, and that, by the aid of his new friend, he might safely grapple with the twins. On reaching the spot, however, a terrible sight met his gaze. Something had evidently happened to the spectre, for the light had entirely faded from its hollow eyes, the gleaming falchion had fallen from its hand, and it was leaning up against the wall in a strained and uncomfortable attitude. He rushed forward and seized it in his arms, when, to his horror, the head slipped off and rolled on the floor, the body assuming a recumbent posture, and he found himself clasping a white dimity bedcurtain, with a sweeping brush, a kitchen cleaver, and a hollow turnip lying at his feet! Unable to understand this curious transformation, he clutched the placard with feverish haste, and there, in the grey morning light, he read these fearful words:—

YE OTIS GHOSTE.
Ye Onlie True and Originale Spook.
Beware of Ye Imitationes.
All Others are Counterfeite.

The whole thing flashed across him. He had been tricked, foiled, and outwitted! The old Canterville look came into his eyes; he ground his toothless gums together; and, raising his withered hands high above his head, swore, according to the picturesque phraseology of the antique school, that when Chanticleer had sounded twice his merry horn, deeds of blood would be wrought, and Murder walk abroad with silent feet.

Hardly had he finished this awful oath when, from the red-tiled roof of a distant homestead, a cock crew. He laughed a long, low, bitter laugh, and waited. Hour after hour he waited, but the cock, for some strange reason, did not crow again. Finally, at half-past seven, the arrival of the housemaids made him give up his fearful vigil, and he stalked back to his room, thinking of his vain hope and baffled purpose. There he consulted several books of ancient chivalry, of which he was exceedingly fond, and found that, on every occasion on which his oath had been used, Chanticleer had always crowed a second time.

"Perdition seize the naughty fowl!" he muttered. "I have seen the day when, with my stout spear, I would have run him through the gorge, and made him crow for me an 'twere in death!"

He then retired to a comfortable lead coffin, and stayed there till evening.

IV

The next day the ghost was very weak and tired. The terrible excitement of the last four weeks was beginning to have its effect. His nerves were completely shattered, and he started at the slightest noise. For five days he kept his room, and at last made up his mind to give up the point of the bloodstain on the library floor. If the Otis family did not want it, they clearly did not deserve it. They were evidently people on a low material plane of existence, and quite incapable of appreciating the symbolic value of sensuous phenomena. The question of phantasmic apparitions, and the development of astral bodies, was of course quite a different matter, and really not under his control. It was his solemn duty to appear in the corridor once a week, and to gibber from the large oriel window on the first and third Wednesday in every month, and he did not see how he could honourably escape from his obligations. It is quite true that his life had been very evil, but, upon the other hand, he was most conscientious in all things connected with the supernatural. For the next three Saturdays, accordingly, he traversed the corridor as usual between midnight and three o'clock, taking every possible precaution against being either heard or seen. He removed his boots, trod as lightly as possible on the old worm-eaten boards, wore a large black velvet cloak, and was careful to use the Rising Sun Lubricator for oiling his chains. I am bound to acknowledge that it was with a good deal of difficulty that he brought himself to adopt this last mode of protection. However, one night, while the family were at dinner, he slipped into Mr. Otis's bedroom and carried off the bottle. He felt a little humiliated at first, but afterwards was sensible enough to see that there was a great deal to be said for the invention, and, to a certain degree, it served its purpose. Still, in spite of everything, he was not left unmolested. Strings were continually being stretched across the corridor, over which he tripped in the dark, and on one occasion, while dressed for the part of "Black Isaac, or the Huntsman of Hogley Woods," he met with a severe fall, through treading on a butter-slide, which the twins had constructed from the entrance of the Tapestry Chamber to the top of the oak staircase. This last insult so enraged him that he resolved to make one final effort to assert his dignity and social position, and determined to visit the insolent young Etonians the next night in his celebrated character of "Reckless Rupert, or the Headless Earl."

He had not appeared in this disguise for more than seventy years; in fact, not since he had so frightened pretty Lady Barbara Modish by means of it that she suddenly broke off her engagement with the present Lord Canterville's grandfather, and ran away to Gretna Green with handsome Jack Castleton, declaring that nothing in this world would induce her to marry into a family that allowed such a horrible phantom to walk up and down the terrace at twilight. Poor Jack was afterwards shot in a duel by Lord Canterville on Wandsworth Common, and Lady Barbara died of a broken heart at Tunbridge Wells before the year was out, so, in every way, it had been a great success. It was, however, an extremely difficult make-up, if I may use such a theatrical expression in connection with one of the greatest mysteries of the supernatural, or, to employ a more scientific term, the higher-natural world, and it took him fully three hours to make his preparations. At last everything was ready, and he was very pleased with his appearance. The big leather riding-boots that went with the dress were just a little too large for him, and he could only find one of the two horse pistols, but, on the whole, he was quite satisfied, and at a quarter past one he glided out of the wainscoting and crept down the corridor. On reaching the room occupied by the twins, which I should mention was called the Blue Bed Chamber, on account of the colour of its hangings, he found the door just ajar. Wishing to make an effective entrance, he flung it wide open, when a heavy jug of water fell right down on him, wetting him to the skin, and just missing his left shoulder by a couple of inches. At the same moment he heard stifled shrieks of laughter proceeding from the four-post bed. The shock to his nervous system was so great that he fled back to his room as hard as he could go, and the next day he was laid up with a severe cold. The only thing that at all consoled him in the whole affair was the fact that he had not brought his head with him, for, had he done so, the consequences might have been very serious.

He now gave up all hope of ever frightening this rude American family, and contented himself, as a rule, with creeping about the passages in list slippers, with a thick red muffler round his throat for fear of draughts, and a small arquebuse, in case he should be attacked by the twins. The final blow he received occurred on 19th September. He had gone downstairs to the great entrance hall, feeling sure that there, at any rate, he would be quite unmolested, and was amusing himself by making satirical remarks on the large Saroni photographs of the United States Minister and his wife, which had now taken the place of the Canterville family pictures. He was simply but neatly clad in a long shroud, spotted with churchyard mould, had tied up his jaw with a strip of yellow linen, and carried a small lantern and a sexton's spade. In fact he was dressed for the character of "Jonas the Graveless, or the Corpse-Snatcher of Chertsey Barn," one of his most remarkable impersonations, and one which the Cantervilles had every reason to remember, as it was the real origin of their quarrel with their neighbour, Lord Rufford. It was about a quarter past two o'clock in the morning, and, as far as he could ascertain, no one was stirring. As he was strolling towards the library, however, to see if there were any traces left of the bloodstain, suddenly there leaped out on him from a dark corner two figures, who waved their arms wildly above their heads, and shrieked out "BOO!" in his ear.

Seized with a panic, which, under the circumstances, was only natural, he rushed for the staircase, but found Washington Otis waiting for him there with the big garden syringe; and being thus hemmed in by his enemies on every side, and driven almost to bay, he vanished into the great iron stove, which, fortunately for him, was not lit, and had to make his way home through the flues and chimneys, arriving at his own room in a terrible state of dirt, disorder and dispair.

After this he was not seen again on any nocturnal expedition. The twins lay in wait for him on several occasions, and strewed the passages with nutshells every night to the great annoyance of their parents and the servants, but to no avail. It was quite evident that his feelings were so wounded that he would not appear. Mr. Otis consequently resumed his great work on the history of the Democratic Party, on which he had been engaged for some years; Mrs. Otis organized a wonderful clambake, which amazed the whole country; the boys took to lacrosse, euchre, poker, and other American national games; and Virginia rode about the lanes on her pony, accompanied by the young Duke of Cheshire, who had come to spend the last week of his holidays at Canterville Chase. It was generally assumed that the ghost had gone away, and, in fact, Mr. Otis wrote a letter to that effect to Lord Canterville, who, in reply, expressed his great pleasure at the news, and sent his best congratulations to the Minister's worthy wife.

The Otises, however, were deceived, for the ghost was still in the house, and though now almost an invalid, was by no means ready to let matters rest, particularly as he heard that among the guests was the young Duke of Cheshire, whose grand-uncle, Lord Francis Stilton, had once bet a hundred guineas with Colonel Carbury that he would play dice with the Canterville ghost, and was found the next morning lying on the floor of the card-room in such a helpless paralytic state that though he lived on to a great age, he was never able to say anything again but "Double Sixes." The story was well known at the time, though, of course, out of respect to the feelings of the two noble families, every attempt was made to hush it up; and a full account of all the circumstances connected with it will be found in the third volume of Lord Tattle's *Recollections of the Prince Regent and His Friends.* The ghost, then, was naturally very anxious to show that he had not lost his influence over the Stiltons, with whom, indeed, he was distantly connected, his own first cousin having been married *en secondes noces* to the Sieur de Bulkeley, from whom, as everyone knows, the Dukes of Cheshire are lineally descended. Accordingly, he made arrangements for appearing to Virginia's little lover in his celebrated impersonation of "The Vampire Monk, or, the Bloodless Benedictine," a performance so horrible that when old Lady Startup saw it, which she did on one fatal New Year's Eve, in the year 1764, she went off into the most piercing shrieks, which culminated in violent apoplexy, and died in three days, after disinheriting the Cantervilles, who were her nearest relations, and leaving all her money to her

London apothecary. At the last moment, however, his terror of the twins prevented his leaving his room, and the little Duke slept in peace under the great feathered canopy in the Royal Bedchamber, and dreamed of Virginia.

V

A few days after this, Virginia and her curly-haired cavalier went out riding on Brockley meadows, where she tore her habit so badly in getting through a hedge that, on her return home, she made up her mind to go up by the back staircase so as not to be seen. As she was running past the Tapestry Chamber, the door of which happened to be open, she fancied she saw someone inside, and thinking it was her mother's maid, who sometimes used to bring her work there, looked in to ask her to mend her habit. To her immense surprise, however, it was the Canterville Ghost himself! He was sitting by the window, watching the ruined gold of the yellow trees fly through the air, and the red leaves dancing madly down the long avenue. His head was leaning on his hand, and his whole attitude was one of extreme depression. Indeed, so forlorn, and so much out of repair did he look, that little Virginia, whose first idea had been to run away and lock herself in her room, was filled with pity, and determined to try and comfort him. So light was her footfall, and so deep his melancholy, that he was not aware of her presence till she spoke to him.

"I am so sorry for you," she said, "but my brothers are going back to Eton tomorrow, and then, if you behave yourself, no one will annoy you."

"It is absurd asking me to behave myself," he answered, looking round in astonishment at the pretty little girl who had ventured to address him, "quite absurd. I must rattle my chains, and groan through keyholes, and walk about at night, if that is what you mean. It is my only reason for existing."

"It is no reason at all for existing, and you know you have been very wicked. Mrs. Umney told us, the first day we arrived here, that you had killed your wife."

"Well, I quite admit it," said the Ghost petulantly, "but it was a purely family matter, and concerned no one else."

"It is very wrong to kill anyone," said Virginia, who at

times had a sweet Puritan gravity, caught from some old New England ancestor.

"Oh, I hate the cheap severity of abstract ethics! My wife was very plain, never had my ruffs properly starched, and knew nothing about cookery. Why, there was a buck I had shot in Hogley Woods, a magnificent pricket, and do you know how she had it sent up to table? However, it is no matter now, for it is all over, and I don't think it was very nice of her brothers to starve me to death, though I did kill her."

"Starve you to death? Oh Mr. Ghost, I mean Sir Simon, are you hungry? I have a sandwich in my case. Would you like it?"

"No, thank you, I never eat anything now; but it is very kind of you, all the same, and you are much nicer than the rest of your horrid, rude, vulgar, dishonest family."

"Stop!" cried Virginia, stamping her foot. "It is you who are rude, and horrid, and vulgar; and as for dishonesty, you know you stole the paints out of my box to try and furbish up that ridiculous bloodstain in the library. First you took all my reds, including the vermilion, and I couldn't do any more sunsets, then you took the emerald green and the chrome yellow, and finally I had nothing left but indigo and Chinese white, and could only do moonlight scenes, which are always depressing to look at, and not at all easy to paint. I never told on you, though I was very much annoyed, and it was most ridiculous, the whole thing; for who ever heard of emerald green blood?"

"Well, really," said the Ghost, rather meekly, "what was I to do? It is a very difficult thing to get real blood nowadays, and, as your brother began it all with his Paragon Detergent, I certainly saw no reason why I should not have your paints. As for colour, that is always a matter of taste: the Cantervilles have blue blood, for instance, the very bluest in England; but I know you Americans don't care for things of this kind."

"You know nothing about it, and the best thing you can do is to emigrate and improve your mind. My father will be only too happy to give you a free passage, and though there is a heavy duty on spirits of every kind, there will be no difficulty about the Custom House, as the officers are all Democrats. Once in New York, you are sure to be a great success. I know lots of people there who would give a hundred thousand dollars to have a grandfather, and much more than that to have a family Ghost."

"I don't think I should like America."

"I suppose because we have no ruins and no curiosities," said Virginia satirically.

"No ruins! No curiosities!" answered the Ghost; "you have your navy and your manners."

"Good evening; I will go and ask Papa to get the twins an extra week's holiday."

"Please don't go, Miss Virginia," he cried; "I am so lonely and so unhappy, and I really don't know what to do. I want to go to sleep and I cannot."

"That's quite absurd. You have merely to go to bed and blow out the candle. It is very difficult sometimes to keep awake, especially at church, but there is no difficulty at all about sleeping. Why, even babies know how to do that, and they are not very clever."

"I have not slept for three hundred years," he said sadly, and Virginia's beautiful blue eyes opened in wonder. "For three hundred years I have not slept, and I am so tired."

Virginia grew quite grave, and her little lips trembled like rose leaves. She came towards him, and kneeling down at his side, looking up into his old withered face.

"Poor, poor Ghost," she murmured; "have you no place where you can sleep?"

"Far away beyond the pine woods," he answered, in a low dreamy voice, "there is a little garden. There the grass grows long and deep, there are the great white stars of the hemlock flower, there the nightingale sings all night long. All night long he sings, and the cold, crystal moon looks down, and the yew tree spreads out its giant arms over the sleepers."

Virginia's eyes grew dim with tears, and hid her face in her hands.

"You mean the Garden of Death," she whispered.

"Yes, Death. Death must be so beautiful. To lie in the soft brown earth, with the grasses waving above one's head, and listen to silence. To have no yesterday, and no tomorrow. To forget time, to forgive life, to be at peace. You can help me. You can open for me the portals of Death's house, for Love is always with you, and Love is stronger than Death is."

Virginia trembled, a cold shudder ran through her, and for a few moments there was silence. She felt as if she was in a terrible dream.

Then the Ghost spoke again, and his voice sounded like the sighing of the wind.

"Have you ever read the old prophecy on the library window?"

"Oh often," cried the little girl, looking up; "I know it quite well. It is painted in curious black letters, and it is difficult to read. There are only six lines:

When a golden girl can win
Prayer from out the lips of sin,
When the barren almond bears,
And a little child gives away its tears,
Then shall all the house be still
And peace come to Canterville.

But I don't know what they mean."

"They mean," he said sadly, "that you must weep for me for my sins, because I have no tears, and pray with me for my soul, because I have no faith, and then, if you have always been sweet, and good, and gentle, the Angel of Death will have mercy on me. You will see fearful shapes in darkness, and wicked voices will whisper in your ear, but they will not harm you, for against the purity of a little child the powers of Hell cannot prevail."

Virginia made no answer, and the Ghost wrung his hands in wild despair as he looked down at her bowed golden head. Suddenly she stood up, very pale, and with a strange light in her eyes. "I am not afraid," she said firmly, "and I will ask the Angel to have mercy on you."

He rose from his seat with a faint cry of joy, and taking her hand bent over it with old-fashioned grace and kissed it. His fingers were as cold as ice, and his lips burned like fire, but Virginia did not falter, as he led her across the dusty room. On the faded green tapestry were broidered little huntsmen. They blew their tasselled horns and with their tiny hands waved to her to go back. "Go back, little Virginia," they cried, "go back!" but the Ghost clutched her hand more tightly, and she shut her eyes against them. Horrible animals with lizard tails, and goggle eyes, blinked at her from the carven chimney piece, and murmured, "Beware, little Virginia, beware! We may never see you again," but the Ghost glided on more swiftly, and Virginia did not listen. When they reached the end of the room he stopped, and muttered some words she could not understand. She opened her eyes, and saw the wall slowly fading away like a mist, and a great black cavern in front of her. A bitter cold wind swept round them, and she felt something pulling at her dress.

"Quick, quick," cried the Ghost, "or it will be too late," and, in a moment, the wainscoting had closed behind them, and the Tapestry Chamber was empty.

VI

About ten minutes later, the bell rang for tea, and, as Virginia did not come down, Mrs. Otis sent up one of the footmen to tell her. After a little time he returned and said that he could not find Miss Virginia anywhere. As she was in the habit of going out to the garden every evening to get flowers for the dinner table, Mrs. Otis was not at all alarmed at first, but when six o'clock struck, and Virginia did not appear, she became really agitated, and sent the boys out to look for her, while she herself and Mr. Otis searched every room in the house. At half-past six the boys came back and said that they could find no trace of their sister anywhere. They were all now in the greatest state of excitement, and did not know what to do, when Mr. Otis suddenly remembered that, some few days before, he had given a band of gypsies permission to camp in the park. He accordingly at once set off for Blackfell Hollow, where he knew they were, accompanied by his eldest son and two of the farm servants. The little Duke of Cheshire, who was perfectly frantic with anxiety, begged hard to be allowed to go too, but Mr. Otis would not allow him, as he was afraid there might be a scuffle. On arriving at the spot, however, he found that the gypsies had gone, and it was evident that their departure had been rather sudden, as the fire was still burning, and some plates were lying on the grass. Having sent off Washington and the two men to scour the district, he ran home, and dispatched telegrams to all the police inspectors in the county, telling them to look out for a little girl who had been kidnapped by tramps or gypsies. He then ordered his horse to be brought round, and, after insisting on his wife and the three boys sitting down to dinner, rode off down the Ascot Road with a groom. He had hardly, however, gone a couple of miles when he heard somebody galloping after him, and, looking round, saw the little Duke coming up on his pony, with his face very flushed and no hat.

"I'm awfully sorry, Mr. Otis," gasped out the boy, "but I can't eat any dinner as long as Virginia is lost. Please, don't be angry with me; if you had let us be engaged last year, there would never have been all this trouble. You won't send me back, will you? I can't go! I won't go!"

The Minister could not help smiling at the handsome young scapegrace, and was a good deal touched at his devotion to Virginia, so leaning down from his horse, he patted him kindly on the shoulders, and said, "Well, Cecil, if you won't go back I suppose you must come with me, but I must get you a hat at Ascot."

"Oh, bother my hat! I want Virginia!" cried the little Duke, laughing, and they galloped on to the railway station. There Mr. Otis inquired of the station master if anyone answering the description of Virginia had been seen on the platform, but could get no news of her. The station master, however, wired up and down the line, and assured him that a strict watch would be kept for her, and, after having bought a hat for the little Duke from a linen-draper, who was just putting up his shutters, Mr. Otis rode off to Bexley, a village about four miles away, which he was told was a well-known haunt of the gypsies, as there was a large common next to it. Here they roused up the rural policeman, but could get no information from him, and, after riding all over the common, they turned the horses' heads homewards, and reached the Chase about eleven o'clock, dead-tired and almost heart broken. They found Washington and the twins waiting for them at the gatehouse with lanterns, as the avenue was very dark. Not the slightest trace of Virginia had been discovered. The gypsies had been caught on Broxley meadows, but she was not with them, and they had explained their sudden departure by saying that they had mistaken the date of Chorton Fair, and had gone off in a hurry for fear they might be late. Indeed, they had been quite distressed at hearing of Virginia's disappearance as they were very grateful to Mr. Otis for having allowed them to camp in his park, and four of their number had stayed behind to help in the search. The carp pond had been dragged, and the whole Chase thoroughly gone over, but without any result. It was evident that, for the night at any rate, Virginia was lost to them; and it was in a state of the deepest depression that Mr. Otis and the boys walked up to the house, the groom following behind with the two horses and the pony. In the hall they found a group of frightened servants, and lying on a sofa in the library was poor Mrs. Otis, almost out of her mind with terror and anxiety, and having her forehead bathed with eau-de-Cologne by the old housekeeper. Mr. Otis at once insisted on her having something to eat, and ordered up supper for the whole party. It was a melancholy meal, as hardly anyone spoke, and even the twins were awestruck and subdued, as they were very fond of their sister. When they had finished, Mr. Otis, in spite of the entreaties of the little Duke, ordered them all to bed, saying that nothing more could be done that night, and that he would telegraph in the morning to Scotland Yard for some detectives to be sent down immediately. Just as they were passing out of the dining room, midnight began to boom from the clock tower, and when the last stroke sounded they heard a crash and a sudden shrill cry; a dreadful peal of thunder shook the house, a strain of unearthly music floated through the air, a panel at the top of the staircase flew back with a loud noise, and out on the landing, looking very pale and white, with a little casket in her hand, stepped Virginia. In a moment they had all rushed up to her. Mrs. Otis clasped her passionately in her arms, the Duke smothered her with violent kisses, and the twins executed a wild wardance round the group.

"Good heavens, child, where have you been?" said Mr. Otis, rather angrily, thinking that she had been playing some foolish trick on them. "Cecil and I have been riding all over the country looking for you, and your mother has been frightened to death. You must never play these practical jokes any more."

"Except on the Ghost! Except on the Ghost!" shrieked the twins, as they capered about.

"My own darling, thank God you are found; you must never leave my side again," murmured Mrs. Otis, as she kissed the trembling child, and smoothed the tangled gold of her hair.

"Papa," said Virginia quietly, "I have been with the Ghost. He is dead, and you must come and see him. He had been very wicked, but he was really sorry for all that he had done, and he gave me this box of beautiful jewels before he died."

The whole family gazed at her in mute amazement, but she was quite grave and serious; and, turning round, she led them through the opening in the wainscoting down a narrow secret corridor, Washington following with a lighted candle, which he had caught up from the table. Finally, they came to a great oak door, studded with rusty nails. When Virginia touched it, it swung back on its heavy hinges, and they found themselves in a little low room, with a vaulted ceiling, and one tiny grated window. Imbedded in the wall was a huge iron ring, and chained to it was a gaunt skeleton, that was stretched out at full length on the stone floor, and seemed to be trying to grasp with its long fleshless fingers an old-fashioned trencher and ewer, that were placed just out of its reach. The jug had evidently been once filled with water, as it was covered inside with green mould. There was nothing on the trencher but a pile of dust. Virginia knelt down beside the skeleton, and, folding her little hands together, began to pray silently, while the rest of the party looked on in wonder at the terrible tragedy whose secret was now disclosed to them.

"Hallo!" suddenly exclaimed one of the twins, who had been looking out of the window to try and discover in what wing of the house the room was situated. "Hallo! The old withered almond tree has blossomed. I can see the flowers quite plainly in the moonlight."

"God has forgiven him," said Virginia gravely, as she rose to her feet, and a beautiful light seemed to illumine her face.

"What an angel you are!" cried the young Duke, and he put his arm round her neck and kissed her.

VII

Four days after these curious incidents a funeral started from Canterville Chase at about eleven o'clock at night.

The hearse was drawn by eight black horses, each of which carried on its head a great tuft of nodding ostrich plumes, and the leaden coffin was covered by a rich purple pall, on which was embroidered in gold the Canterville coat of arms. By the side of the hearse and the coaches walked the servants with lighted torches, and the whole procession was wonderfully impressive. Lord Canterville was the chief mourner, having come up specially from Wales to attend the funeral, and sat in the first carriage along with little Virginia. Then came the United States Minister and his wife, then Washington and the two boys, and in the last carriage was Mrs. Umney. It was generally felt that, as she had been frightened by the ghost for more than fifty years of her life, she had a right to see the last of him. A deep grave had been dug in the corner of the churchyard, just under the old yew tree, and the service was read in the most impressive manner by the Rev. Augustus Dampier. When the ceremony was over, the servants, according to an old custom observed in the Canterville family, extinguished their torches, and, as the coffin was being lowered into the grave, Virginia stepped forward and laid on it a large cross made of white and pink almond blossoms. As she did so, the moon came out from behind a cloud, and flooded with its silent silver the little churchyard, and from a distant copse a nightingale began to sing. She thought of the ghost's description of the Garden of Death, her eyes became dim with tears and she hardly spoke a word during the drive home.

The next morning, before Lord Canterville went up to town, Mr. Otis had an interview with him on the subject of the jewels the ghost had given to Virginia. They were perfectly magnificent, especially a certain ruby necklace with old Venetian setting, which was really a superb specimen of sixteenth-century work, and their value was so great that Mr. Otis felt considerable scruples about allowing his daughter to accept them.

"My Lord," he said, "I know that in this country mortmain is held to apply to trinkets as well as to land, and it is quite clear to me that these jewels are, or should be, heirlooms in your family. I must beg you, accordingly, to take them to London with you, and to regard them simply as a portion of your property which has been restored to you under certain strange conditions. As for my daughter, she is merely a child, and has as yet, I am glad to say, but little interest in such appurtenances of idle luxury. I am also informed by Mrs. Otis, who, I may say, is no mean authority upon Art—having had the privilege of spending several winters in Boston when she was a girl—that these gems are of great monetary worth, and if offered for sale would fetch a tall price. Under these circumstances, Lord Canterville, I feel sure that you will recognize how impossible it would be for me to allow them to remain in the possession of any member of my family; and, indeed, all such vain gauds and toys, however suitable or necessary to the dignity of the British aristocracy, would be completely out of place among those who have been brought up on the severe, and I believe immortal, principles of republican simplicity. Perhaps I should mention that Virginia is very anxious that you should allow her to retain the box as a memento of your unfortunate but misguided ancestor. As it is extremely old, and consequently a good deal out of repair, you may perhaps think fit to comply with her request. For my own part, I confess I am a good deal surprised to find a child of mine expressing sympathy with medievalism in any form, and can only account for it by the fact that Virginia was born in one of your London suburbs shortly after Mrs. Otis had returned from a trip to Athens."

Lord Canterville listened very gravely to the worthy Minister's speech, pulling his grey moustache now and then to hide an involuntary smile, and when Mr. Otis had ended, he shook him cordially by the hand, and said, "My dear sir, your charming little daughter rendered my unlucky ancestor, Sir Simon, a very important service, and I and my family are much indebted to her for her marvellous courage and pluck. The jewels are clearly hers, and, egad, I believe that if I were heartless enough to take them from her, the wicked old fellow would be out of his grave in a fortnight, leading me the devil of a life. As for their being heirlooms, nothing is an heirloom that is not so mentioned in a will or legal document, and the existence of these jewels has been quite unknown. I assure you I have no more claim on them than your butler, and when Miss Virginia grows up I dare say she will be pleased to have pretty things to wear. Besides, you forget, Mr. Otis, that you took the furniture and the ghost at a valuation, and anything that belonged to the ghost passed at once into your possession, as, whatever activity Sir Simon may have shown in the corridor at night, in point of law he was really dead, and you acquired his property by purchase."

Mr. Otis was a good deal distressed at Lord Canterville's refusal, and begged him to reconsider his decision, but the good-natured peer was quite firm, and finally induced the Minister to allow his daughter to retain the present the ghost had given her, and when in the spring of 1890, the young Duchess of Cheshire was presented at the Queen's first drawing-room on the occasion of her marriage, her jewels were the universal theme of admiration. For Virginia received the coronet, which is the reward of all good little American girls, and was married to her boy-lover as soon as he came of age. They were both so charming, and they loved each other so much, that everyone was delighted at the match, except the old Marchioness of Dumbleton, who had tried to catch the Duke for one of her seven unmarried daughters, and had given no less than three expensive dinner parties for that purpose, and, strange to say, Mr. Otis himself. Mr. Otis was extremely fond of the young Duke personally, but, theoretically, he objected to titles, and, to use his own words, "was not without apprehension lest, amid the enervating influences of a pleasure-loving aristocracy, the true principles of republican simplicity should be forgotten." His objections, however, were completely overruled, and I believe that when he walked up the aisle of St. George's, Hanover Square, with his daughter leaning on his arm, there was not a prouder man in the whole length and breadth of England.

The Duke and Duchess, after the honeymoon was over, went down to Canterville Chase, and on the day after their arrival they walked over in the afternoon to the lonely churchyard by the pine woods. There had been a great deal of difficulty at first about the inscription on Sir Simon's tombstone, but finally it had been decided to engrave on it simply the initials of the old gentleman's name, and the verse from the library window. The Duchess had brought with her some lovely roses, which she strewed upon the grave, and after they had stood by it for some time they strolled into the ruined chancel of the old abbey. There the Duchess sat down on a fallen pillar, while her husband lay at her feet smoking a cigarette and looking up at her beautiful eyes. Suddenly he threw his cigarette away, took hold of her hand, and said to her, "Virginia, a wife should have no secrets from her husband."

"Dear Cecil! I have no secrets from you."

"Yes, you have," he answered, smiling, "you have never told me what happened to you when you were locked up with the ghost."

"I have never told anyone, Cecil," said Virginia gravely.

"I know that, but you might tell me."

"Please don't ask me, Cecil, I cannot tell you. Poor Sir Simon! I owe him a great deal. Yes, don't laugh, Cecil, I really do. He made me see what Life is, and what Death signifies, and why Love is stronger than both."

The Duke rose and kissed his wife lovingly.

"You can have your secret as long as I have your heart," he murmured.

"You have always had that, Cecil."

"And you will tell our children some day, won't you?" Virginia blushed.

Chelsea Quinn Yarbro

(1942–)

Born in Berkeley, California, Chelsea Quinn Yarbro, whose mother taught at the University of California, studied at San Francisco University. She has worked as a demographic cartographer and from time to time as a professional reader of tarot cards and palms in San Francisco. Music is a major interest of hers, and she has studied numerous instruments, music theory and composition, and voice. Among Yarbro's honors are the titles of Grand Master at the World Horror Convention and Living Legend from the International Horror Guild, and she is a recipient of the Bram Stoker Lifetime Achievement Award and the Fine Foundation Award for Literary Achievement. Her popular series of novels depicting the vampire Count Saint-Germain include *Hotel Transylvania* (1978), *Blood Games* (1980), *Tempting Fate* (1982), *Darker Jewels* (1993), *Mansions of Darkness* (1996), *States of Grace* (2005), *A Dangerous Climate* (2008), and *Burning Shadows* (2009). *The Saint-Germain Chronicles* (1983) and *Saint-Germain: Memoirs* (2007) are story collections about the Count.

Disturb Not My Slumbering Fair

(1978)

It was already Thursday when Diedre left her grave. The rain had made the soil soft and the loam clung to her cerements like a distracted lover. It was so late, the night so sodden, that there was no one to see her as she left the manicured lawns and chaste marble stones behind her for the enticing litter of the city.

"Pardon me, miss." The night watchman was old, white-haired under his battered hat. He held the flashlight aimed at her face, seeing only a disheveled young woman with mud in her hair, a wild look about her eyes, a livid cast to her face like a bruise. He wondered if she had been attacked; there was so much of that happening these days. "You all right, miss?"

Diedre chuckled, but she had not done it for some time and it came out badly. The watchman went pale and his mouth tightened. Whatever happened to her must have been very bad. "Don't you worry, miss. I'll call the cops. They'll catch the guy. You stay calm. He can't get you while I'm around."

"Cops?" she asked, managing the sounds better now. "It's not necessary."

"You look here, miss," said the night watchman, beginning to enjoy himself, to feel important once more. "You can't let him get away with it. You lean on me: I'll get you inside where it's warm. I'll take care of everything."

Diedre studied the old man, weighing up the risk. She was hungry and tired. The old man was alone. Making a mental shrug she sighed as she went to the old man, noting with amusement that he drew back as he got a whiff of her. She could almost see him recoil. "It was in the graveyard," she said.

"Christ, miss." The night watchman was shocked.

"Yes," she went on, warming to her subject. "There was a new grave . . . the earth hadn't settled yet . . . And the smell . . ." *was delicious,* she thought.

He was very upset, chafing her hand as he led her into the little building at the factory entrance. "Never you mind," he muttered. "I'll take care of you. Fine thing, when a man can . . . can . . . and in a graveyard, too . . ."

"Yes," she agreed, her tongue showing pink between her teeth.

He opened the door for her, standing aside with old-fashioned gallantry until the last of her train had slithered through before coming into the room himself. "Now, you sit down here." He pointed to an ancient armchair that sagged on bowed legs. "I'm going to call the cops."

Diedre wasn't quite ready for that. "Oh," she said faintly,

"will you wait a bit? You've been so kind . . . and understanding. But sometimes the police think . . ." She left the sentence hanging as she huddled into the chair.

The night watchman frowned. Obviously the poor girl didn't know what she looked like. There could be no doubt about her case. "You won't get trouble from them," he promised her.

She shivered picturesquely. "Perhaps you're right. But wait a while, please. Let me collect myself a little more."

The night watchman was touched. He could see that she was close to breaking down, that only her courage was keeping her from collapsing. "Sure, miss. I'll hold off a bit. You don't want to wait too long, though. The cops are funny about that." He reached over to give her a reassuring pat but drew away from her when he saw the look in her eyes. Poor soul was scared to death, he could tell.

"Uh, sir," Diedre said after a moment, realizing that she didn't know his name. "I was wondering . . . I don't want you to get into trouble, after you've been so kind, but . . ."

He looked at her eagerly. "But what, miss?"

She contrived to look confused. "I just realized . . . I seem to have lost my ring." She held up both hands to show him. "It was valuable. An heirloom. My mother . . ." Her averted eyes were full of mischief.

"Oh, dear," said the night watchman solicitously. "Do you think you lost it back there?" He looked worried.

She nodded slowly. "Back at the grave," she whispered.

"Well, miss, as soon as the cops get here, we'll tell them and they'll get it for you." He paused awkwardly. "Thing is, miss. It might not still be there. Could have been taken, you know." He wanted to be gentle with her, to reassure her.

"Taken?" She stared at him through widened eyes. "My ring? Why?" Slowly she allowed comprehension to show in her face. "Oh! You think that he . . . that when he . . . that he took it?"

The night watchman looked away, mumbling, "He could have, miss. That's a fact. A man who'd do a thing like this, he'd steal. That's certain."

Diedre leaped up, distraction showing in every line of her sinuous body. "Then I've got to check! Now!" She rushed to the door and pulled on the knob. "It can't be gone. Oh, you've got to help me find it!" Pulling the door wide she ran into the night and listened with satisfaction as the old man came after her.

"Miss! Miss! Don't go back there! What if he hasn't gone? Let me call the cops, miss!" His breath grew short as he stumbled after her.

"Oh, no. No. I've got to be sure. If it's gone, I don't know what I'll do." She let herself stumble so that the old man could catch up with her; if he fell too far behind, Diedre knew she would lose him. This way it was so easy to lead him where she wanted him. Ahead she saw the cemetery gates gleaming faintly in the wan light.

"You don't want to go back in there, miss," said the night watchman between jagged breaths. His face was slippery with cold sweat that Diedre saw with a secret, predatory smile. "Oh, I can't . . ." It was the right sound, the right moment. He automatically put out his arm. Pretending to lean against him, she felt for his heart and was delighted at the panic-stricken way it battered at his ribs.

"But I've got to find it. I've got to." She broke away from him once more and ran toward the grave she had so recently left. "Over here," she cried, and watched as he staggered toward her, trying to speak.

Then his legs gave way and he fell against the feet of a marble angel. His skull made a pulpy noise when it cracked.

With a shriek of delight Diedre was upon him, her eager teeth sinking into the flesh greedily, although the body was still unpleasantly warm. Blood oozed down her chin and after a while she wiped it away.

Toward the end of the night she made a halfhearted attempt to bury the litter from her meal. It was useless; she knew that the body would be discovered in a little while, and there would be speculation on the state of it: the gnawed bones and the torn flesh. As an afterthought, she broke one of the gnawed arms against a pristinely white vault, just to confuse the issue. Then she gathered up a thigh and left, walking back into the city, filled, satisfied.

By the time the last of the night watchman was discovered, Diedre was miles away, sleeping off her feast in the cool damp of a dockside warehouse. Her face, if anyone had seen it, was soft and faintly smiling, the cyanose pallor of the grave fading away to be replaced with a rosy blush. She didn't look like a ghoul at all.

That night, when she left the warehouse, she saw the first headlines:

NIGHT WATCHMAN FOUND DEAD IN GRAVEYARD
GRISLY SLAYING AT CEMETERY

Diedre giggled as she read the reports. Apparently there was some hot dispute in the police department about the teeth marks. There was also a plan to open the grave where the old man had been killed. This made Diedre frown. If the grave were opened, they would find it empty, and there would be more questions asked. She bit her lip as she thought. And when the solution came to her, she laughed almost merrily.

It was close to midnight when she spotted her quarry, a young woman about her own height and build. Diedre followed her away from the theater and into the many-tiered parking lot.

When the woman had opened the car door and was sliding into the seat, Diedre came up beside her. "Excuse me," she said, knowing that the old jacket and workmen's trousers she had found in the warehouse made her look suspicious. "I saw you come up, and maybe you can help me?"

The woman looked at her, her nose wrinkling as she looked Diedre over. "What is the matter?" There was obvious condemnation in her words. Diedre had not made a good impression.

"It's my car," Diedre explained, pointing to a respectable Toyota. "I've been trying to get it open, but the key doesn't work. I've tried everything." She made a helpless gesture with her hands, then added a deprecating smile.

"I don't think I can help you," said the woman stiffly. She was seated now and had her hand on the door.

"Well, look," said Diedre quickly, holding the door open by force. "If you'd give me a ride down, maybe there's a mechanic still on duty. Or maybe I could phone the Auto Club . . ."

The woman in the car gave her another disapproving

look, then sighed and opened the door opposite her. "All right. Get in."

"Gee, thank you," Diedre said and slipped around the car, slid into the seat, and closed the door. "This is really awfully good of you. You don't know how much I appreciate it."

The woman turned the key with an annoyed snap and the car surged forward. "That's quite all right." The tone was glacial.

She was even more upset when they reached the ground level. The attendant who took her money told the woman that there was no mechanic on duty after ten and that it would take over an hour for the Auto Club to get there, and the locksmith would have to make a new key, and that would take time as well. Diedre couldn't have painted a more depressing picture of her plight if she tried.

"I guess I'll have to wait," she said wistfully, looking out at the attendant.

"Well," the man answered, "there's a problem. We close up at two, and there's no way you'll be out of here by then. Why don't you come back in the morning?"

This was better than Diedre had hoped. "Well, if that's all I can do . . ." She shrugged. "Where can I catch a bus around here?"

"The nearest is six blocks down. What part of town you going to, lady?" the attendant asked Diedre.

"Serra Heights," she said, choosing a neighborhood near the cemetery, middle income, city-suburban. Altogether a safe address.

Reluctantly the woman driving the car said, "That's on my way. I'll drop you if you like." Each of the words came out of her like pulled teeth.

Diedre turned grateful eyes on her. "Oh, would you? Really? Oh, thanks. I don't mean to be a bother, but . . . well, you know." She added, as the inspiration struck her, "Jamie was so worried. This'll help. Really."

The woman's face softened a little. "I'll be glad to drive you." She turned to the attendant. "Perhaps you'll be good enough to leave a note for the mechanic so that there'll be no delay in the morning?" She was making up for her previously frosty behavior and gave Diedre a wide smile.

"Oh, thanks a lot for telling him that," Diedre said as the

car sped out into the night. "I wouldn't have thought of it. I guess I'm more upset than I thought."

The conversation was occasional as they drove, Diedre keeping her mind on the imaginary Jamie, building the other woman a picture of two struggling young people, trying to establish themselves in the world. The woman listened, wearing a curious half-smile. "You know," she said as she swung off the freeway toward the Serra Valley district, "I've often thought things would be better with Grant and me if we'd had to work a little harder. It was too easy, always too easy."

"Oh," said Diedre at her most ingenuous, "did I say something wrong?"

"No," the woman sighed. "You didn't say anything wrong." She shook her head, as if shaking clouds away and glanced around. "Which way?"

"Umm. Left onto Harrison and then up Camino Alto." Camino Alto was the last street in the district, and it followed the boundary of the cemetery.

"Do you live on Camino Alto?" the woman asked.

"No. In Ponce de Leon Place. Up at the top of the hill." Behind that hill was open country, covered in brush. By the time the woman's body was found, the police would stop wondering about the missing one from Diedre's grave.

The car swung onto Harrison. "Doesn't it bother you, having that gruesome murder so close to home?"

Diedre smiled. "A little. You never know what might happen next."

They drove up the hill in silence, the woman glancing toward the thick shrubs that masked the cemetery. There was concern in her face and a lack of animation in her eyes. Diedre knew she would freeze when frightened.

"This is where I get out," she said at last, looking at the woman covertly. As the car came to a halt, Diedre reached over and grabbed the keys. "Thanks for the lift," she grinned.

"My keys . . ." the woman began.

Diedre shook her head. "Don't worry about them. I'll take care of them. Now, if you'll step out with me."

"Where are we going?" the woman quavered. "Not in there?"

"No," Diedre assured her. "Get out."

In the end she had to club the woman and drag her unconscious body from the car. It was awkward managing her limp form, but eventually she wrestled the woman from the car and into the brush. Branches tore at her and blackberry vines left claw marks on her arms and legs as she plunged farther down the hill. The woman moaned and then was silent.

It was almost an hour later when Diedre climbed up the hill again, scratched, bruised, and happy. Tied to her belt by the hair, the woman's head banged on her legs with every step she took.

Taking the car, Diedre drove to the coast and down the old treacherous stretch of highway that twisted along the cliffs. Gunning the motor at the most dangerous curve, she rode the car down to its flaming destruction on the rocks where breakers hissed over it, steaming from the flames that licked upward as the gas tank exploded.

It was a nuisance, climbing up the cliff with a broken arm: the ulna had snapped, a greenstick fracture making the hand below it useless. Here and there Diedre's skin was scorched off, leaving black patches. But the job was done. The police would find the head in the wreck, along with one of the night watchman's leg bones, and would assume that the rest of the body had been washed out to sea: the headless woman back on the hillside would not be connected with this wreck, and she was clear.

But she was hungry. The night watchman was used up and she hadn't been able to use any part of the woman. Now Diedre knew she would have to be careful, for the police were checking cemeteries for vandals. And in her present condition the only place she wouldn't attract attention was the morgue.

The morgue!

Her broken arm was firmly splinted under her heavy sweater, her face carefully and unobviously made up as Diedre walked into the cold tile office outside the room where the bodies lay. The burned patches on her face had taken on the look of old acne and she used her lithe body with deliberate awkwardness.

"I'm Watson, the one who called?" she announced uncertainly to the colorless man at the desk.

He looked up at her and grunted. "Watson?"

Mentally she ground her teeth. What if this man had changed his mind; where would she go for food then? "Yes," she said, shuffling from one foot to the other. "I'm going to be a pathologist, and I thought . . . It's expensive, sir. Medical school is very expensive." Her eyes pleaded with him.

"I remember," he said measuredly. "Nothing like a little practical experience." He handed her a form. "I'll need your name and address and the usual information. Just fill this out and hand it in. I'll show you the place when you're done."

She took the form and started to work. The Social Security number stumped her and then she decided to use her old one. By the time it could be checked, she'd be long gone.

"No phone?" he asked as she handed the form back.

"Well, I'm at school so much . . . and it's kind of a luxury . . ."

"You'll make up for it when you get into practice," he said flatly. He knew doctors well.

As he filed her card away, Diedre glared at his back, wishing she could indulge herself long enough to make a meal of him. It would be so good to sip the marrow from his bones, to nibble the butter-soft convolutions of his brain.

"Okay, Watson. Come with me. If you get sick, out you go." He opened the door to the cold room and pointed out the silent drawers that waited for their cargo. "That's where we keep 'em. If they aren't identified, the county takes 'em over. We do autopsies on some of 'em, if it's ordered. Some of these stiffs are pretty messed up, some of 'em are real neat. Depends on how they go. Poison now," he said, warming to the topic, "poison can leave the outsides as neat as a pin and only part of the insides are ruined. Cars, well, cars make 'em pretty awful. Guns—that depends on what and where. Had a guy in here once, he'd put a shotgun in his mouth and fired both barrels. Well, I can tell you, he didn't look good." As he talked he strolled to one of the drawers and pulled it out. "Take this one," he went on.

Diedre ran her tongue over her lips and made a coughing noise. "What happened?"

"This one," said the man, "had a run-in with some gasoline. We had to get identification from his teeth, and even part of his jaw was wrecked. Explosions do that." He glanced at her to see how she was taking it.

"I'm fine," she assured him.

"Huh." He closed the drawer and went on to the next. "This one's drowned. In the water a long time." He wrinkled his nose. "Had to get the shrimps off him. Water really wrecks the tissues."

Five drawers later Diedre found what she had been looking for.

"This one," the man was saying, "well, it's murder, of course, and we haven't found all of him yet, but there's enough here to make some kind of identification, so he's our job."

"When did it happen?" Diedre asked.

"A week or so ago, I guess. Found him out in the Serra Heights cemetery. A big number in the papers about it."

Diedre stared at the bits of the night watchman. Something had shared her feast; she'd left more than this behind. It would be simple to take a bit more of him, here and there. No one would notice. But it paid to be careful. "Can I study this?" she said, doing her best to sound timorous.

"Why?" asked the man.

"To get used to it," she replied.

"If you help me out with ID, you can." He closed the night watchman away into his cold file cabinet. "In fact, you can do a workup on the one we just got in. Get blood type and all those things. This one hasn't got a head, so it's gonna be fun, running her kin to earth."

"Hasn't got a head?" Diedre echoed, remembering the woman left on the hillside. "What happened?"

"Found her out by the cemetery where they got the other. Probably connected. The grave she was found on was new and it was empty. Could be she's the missing one."

"Oh," said Diedre, to fill in the silence that followed before the man closed the drawer. She stared at the body, watching it critically. She hadn't done too bad a job with it.

"Any of this getting to you?" the man asked as he showed her the last of the corpses. Only about half of the shelves were filled, and Diedre wondered at this. "I'm okay," she said, then added, as if it had just occurred to her, "Why are there so many shelves?"

"Right now things are a little slow. But if we get a good fire or quake or a six-car pile-up, we'll be filled up, all right." He gave her a shadowed, cynical smile. In the harsh light his skin had a dead-white cast to it, as if he had taken on the color of his charges.

Nodding, Diedre asked, "What do you want me to do first? Where do I work?"

The man showed her and she began.

It was hard getting food at first, but then she caught on and found that if she took a finger or two from a burn victim or some of the pulpy flesh from a waterlogged drowner it was easy. Accident victims were best because, by the time the metal and fire were through with them, it was too hard to get all of a body together and a few unaccounted-for bits were never missed.

She was lipping just such an accident case one night when the door to her workroom shot open.

"Tisk, tisk, tisk, Watson," said the man she worked with.

Diedre froze, her mouth half-open and her face shocked.

The man strolled into the room. "You're an amateur, my girl. I've been keeping an eye on you. I know." He walked over to her and looked down. "First of all, don't eat where you work. It's too easy to get caught. Bring a couple of plastic bags with you and take the stuff home."

She decided to bluff. "I don't know what you're talking about."

He gave a harsh laugh. "Do you think you're the only ghoul in this morgue? I'm not interested in competition, and that's final. One of us has to go." He glared at her, fingering her scalpel.

It was quiet in the room for a moment, then Diedre put far more panic than she was feeling. "What are you going to do to me? What is going to happen?"

The man sniggered. "Oh, no. Not that way, Watson. You're going to have to wait until I've got everything ready. There's going to be another accident victim here, and there won't be any questions asked." He spun away from her and rushed to the door. "It won't be long; a day or two, perhaps. . . . Then it will be over and done with, Watson." He closed the door and in a moment she heard the lock click.

For some time she sat quietly, nibbling at the carrion in her hands. Her rosy face betrayed no fear, her slender fingers did not shake. And when she was through with her meal, she had a plan.

The telephone was easy to get to, and the number she

wanted was on it. Quickly she dialed, then said in a breathless voice, "Police? This is Watson at the morgue. Something's wrong. The guy in charge here? He's trying to kill me." She waited while the officer on the other end expressed polite disbelief. "No. You don't understand. He's crazy. He thinks I'm a ghoul. He says he's going to beat me into a pulp and then hide me in drawer forty-seven until he can get rid of me. I'm scared. I'm so scared. He's locked me in. I can't get out. And he's coming back. . . ." She let her tone rise to a shriek and then hung up. So much for that.

When she unwrapped her broken arm, she saw that the ulna was still shattered and she twisted it to bring the shards out through the skin again. Next she banged her head into a cabinet, not hard enough to break the skull, but enough to bring a dark bruise to her temples. And finally she tore her clothes and dislocated her jaw before going into the file room and slipping herself into number forty-seven. It was all she could do to keep from smiling.

Somewhat later she heard the door open and the sound of voices reached her. The man she worked with was protesting to the police that there was nothing wrong here, and that his assistant seemed to be out for the night. The officer didn't believe him.

"But number forty-seven is empty," she heard the man protest as the voices came nearer.

"Be a sport and open it anyway," said the officer.

"I don't understand. This is all ridiculous." Amid his protests, he pulled the drawer back.

Diedre lay there, serene and ivory chill.

The man stopped talking and slammed the door shut. The officer opened it again. "Looks like you worked her over pretty good," he remarked, pulling the cloth away from her arm and touching the bruises on her face.

"But I didn't. . . ." Then he changed his voice. "Officer, you don't understand. She's a ghoul. She lives on the dead. That's why she was working here, so she could eat the dead. . . ."

"She said you were crazy," the officer said wearily. "Look at her, man," he went on in a choked tone. "That's a girl—a girl; not a ghoul. You've been working here too long, mister. Things get to a guy after a while." He turned to the men with him. "We'll need some pix of this. Get to work."

As the flashes glared, the officer asked for Diedre's work card, and when he saw it, "No relatives. Too bad. It'll have to be a county grave then."

But the man who ran the morgue cried out. "No! She's got to be buried in stone. In a vault with a lock on the door. Otherwise she'll get out. She'll get out and she'll be after people again. Don't you understand?" He rushed at the drawer Diedre lay in. "This isn't real. It doesn't matter if ghouls break bones or get burned. They're not like people! The only thing you can do is starve them. . . . You have to bury them in stone, locked in stone. . . ."

It was then that the police took the man away.

Diedre lay back and waited.

And this time, it was a full ten days before she left her grave.

Jane Yolen

(1939–)

One of two children of a psychiatric social worker and a journalist and Hollywood film publicist, Jane Hyatt Yolen was born in New York City and earned a BA from Smith College and an MA from the University of Massachusetts. At the age of twenty-two, she sold her first work, a children's book titled *Pirates and Petticoats*. A poet and the author of numerous award-winning children's books and of adult fiction, Yolen is also the editor of various story collections, and she has served as President of Science Fiction Writers of America. Among her works are *Children of the Wolf* (1984), *Dragonfield* (1985), *White Jenna* (1990), *Briar Rose* (1992), *The One-Armed Queen* (1998), and the Pit Dragon volumes: *Dragon's Blood* (1982), *Heart's Blood* (1984), *A Sending of Dragons* (1987), and *Dragon's Heart* (2009).

Green Messiah

(1988)

"It's quite simple, really," Professor Magister was saying. "With the world's population of wild carnivores falling rapidly, the predator-to-prey ratio is way out of balance. A world so out of balance is a world that may die. It's our only hope, really."

Lupe stopped listening. The press conference went on and on and on, but she simply turned her attention inward. She already knew the entire speech Magister would give the reporters. He'd been practicing it on all his coworkers and volunteers. He'd remind them how the conservation movement of the seventies and eighties, Greenpeace and all the rest, had failed. How out of that dismal failure had grown a new movement, connecting all the old fragmented groups: Green Messiah. How Green Messiah had dedicated itself to repopulating the wild kingdoms by means of genetic experimentation developed at the Asimov Institute. How she, Lupe de Diega, had been one of the Chosen Ones, the volunteers, the Green Messengers, because genetically she'd matched the old legends. Dark-haired, long-fingered, yellow-eyed, with a slash of the single eyebrow across her forehead, that was Lupe. All those things that had caused her to be teased and hated for years were now her passport to fame. She would be in all the history books, not for what she was—but for what she would become. Lupe de Diega, the first girl to be genetically changed into wolf.

"Legends," the professor was stating in his deep, resonant voice, "are merely signposts to long-forgotten facts. Our ancestors were leaving us messages, but we did not—*could not*—read them. The Ages of Reason and Cynicism did not allow us to believe that the past could so inform the future."

The reporters in the audience stirred uneasily. Though word of the experiments had already leaked out, they were there for facts, not speeches. Sensing that, Dr. Magister seemed to shake himself all over and begin again.

"Green Messiah looked behind the legends to the facts," he said.

Lupe saw that the reporters were concentrating again.

"Just as we now understand that herbalists knew things long before modern medicine re-proved them acceptable, like belladonna and penicillin, so too the old folktales carried biologic history within the body of the story. Green Messiah followed those tracks. Werewolves, the old stories warned, were people who had fingers of a single length, who had eyebrows that met in the middle, who had hair growing in their palms. We saw the possibility that this was a real genetic link with humanity's past."

Lupe's eyes narrowed. She could feel her breathing deepen. She opened her mouth and panted shallowly. Then, realizing that some of the reporters were staring at her, she forced herself to close her mouth and listen to Magister again.

"Those stories of the *loup-garou,* the werewolf, were left

over from thousands of years of human memory. Our forebears remembered something we did not—that not all humans are descended from apes. Some, it seems, are descended from *Canis lupus,* the wolf. Not even Darwin suspected that! We at Green Messiah are breeding the race backward, but in days, not in decades."

He smiled over at Lupe. She did not smile back. A wolf smile means something entirely different, and she had had enough treatments already to be uncomfortable with the lifting of lips that in humans was used to signify happiness. She shrugged her shoulders in response, restraining the impulse to wag her as yet nonexistent tail.

Magister looked back at the audience. He was a good speaker. He knew how to play the crowd. "And so, my friends of the press, may I present to you the young woman with whom our first hopes lie, Ms. Lupe de Diega, a resident of Brooklyn whose ancestors came from Spain but one generation past. In a matter of a few months, she will become a full-grown werewolf, capable of changing from human to wolf and back again, capable of bringing to the dying breed new life."

Hands went up all over the auditorium and Lupe sat back against her chair. A raised hand seemed threatening these days. Then she stopped herself and stared around. Her nostrils flared slightly. She caught a faint scent in the air, but it was neither anger nor fear. It was, perhaps, curiosity. Then she chided herself mentally. Surely *curiosity* had no smell.

The professor allowed questions, singling out a man halfway toward the back. The man stood so his question might be better heard.

"Will she change on—um—the full moon?"

"Don't be absurd," said Magister, but with a laugh so as not to affront the man. "The notion of a werewolf changing on the full moon is simply"—he smiled, letting them all in on the joke—"moonshine and malarkey. That's a good example of the folk mind at work, disguising, making metaphoric. Do what we of Green Messiah trained ourselves to do, Mr. uh—"

"Hyatt, sir, of UPI."

"Mr. Hyatt. Read *behind* the legends. Ask yourself: What does the full moon represent?"

Lupe thought of the moon, round and beckoning. It represented freedom. *She* knew that, even if Magister did not. For a professor he was very stupid. Very stupid indeed.

"How about magic and mystery?" called out a man from the back.

"The pull of the tides?" shouted another.

"Get your minds away from mysticism," said Magister. "Think of facts."

A reporter from *Ms.* magazine raised her hand and stood. "Do you mean that the female's monthly or moon cycle is linked to this change?"

"Bingo!" Magister said. "That was our best guess."

"What about males?" called out a man behind a television camera.

"We aren't quite sure yet," Magister admitted. "That is why we're starting with Ms. de Diega. We expect she'll bring us back information that will help us figure out what links the male werewolf to his change. If, indeed, there *are* male werewolves. There is one theory that werewolves are only female."

There was an enormous explosion of sounds from the reporters and this time Lupe did smile.

"How does *she* feel about it?" the UPI reporter, Hyatt, called out.

"Why don't you ask *her* directly?" Magister responded. He came over to Lupe murmuring, "Steady Lupe, steady girl. Just come to the microphone. I'll be right by your side. It's going very well. Nothing to be afraid of."

She stood in a single graceful motion and followed at his heels.

"Speak, Lupe," he instructed.

The microphone had a cold, metal scent. She spoke into it, her voice deep and steady. "I wait. I hope. I am ready." The echo coming back to her from the corners of the auditorium made her tremble.

Magister's hand on the small of her back, through the thin cotton dress, calmed her. She had nothing more to say.

"Good girl," he whispered, giving her a little push. She returned to her chair.

The rest of the conference went as planned. Magister brought out maps and charts, and the graduate students handed out photocopied material to the audience so that they could follow along and print accurately what Green Messiah was doing. But Lupe's attention was drawn to a small bird that had, somehow, gotten trapped in the room and was frantically beating against a window. She felt her body straining toward it. It took all her concentration not to whine.

The bird finally swooped toward the back and out through an open door, losing itself somewhere in the maze of halls outside. Lupe lost interest once it had disappeared and turned her head toward Magister. He was just finishing.

"And so, this summer, we will take Ms. de Diega up to an undisclosed taiga or coniferous forest region in northern Canada where moose, elk, and a number of species of deer are abundant, as well as squirrels, marmots, chipmunks, rats, mice, moles, shrews, and hares. But where, alas, the wolf population is now minimal.

"There we shall give her a collar that will allow us to track her movements. We'll help her remove her clothes, and give her the last of the series of injections of the Green Messiah serum to facilitate her change.

"We expect the change to be complete within hours and then Ms. de Diega—Lupe—will be off to find her dwindling pack. With her human mind, she will easily become dominant wolf and guide her fellow canines to a richer and more fruitful heritage than they could otherwise have known."

A single hand was raised in the auditorium.

"Can you be sure?" the reporter asked.

Magister smiled. "Nothing in life is *sure*. However, we have looked at this from all the angles, and Ms. de Diega will report back once a month to us with her findings. And we shall, of course, keep you all apprised of her progress." With a nod to Will Sheddery, his top graduate student, Magister closed the conference and escorted Lupe off the stage.

Lupe was surprised at how quickly the spring months went by. Her sense of time had become peculiar, tied less to the clock and more to the rising and setting of the sun. She found it harder and harder to get up in the morning and do her regular calisthenics with Emma, her trainer. She seemed to need more sleep, but in shorter snatches.

Magister visited her daily to chart her bodily functions and to ask her questions. Her temperature had risen, her senses of smell and hearing had heightened, her ability to pay attention to his nonsense had grown less and less. Often he had to call her name two or three times to get her attention, and when she turned her head toward him slowly, she would narrow her eyes to signal she was listening. More and more often, she hated to talk.

"Lupe," his deep voice called her.

She couldn't be bothered responding.

"Lupe!"

This time the sharp tone caused her to look up.

"You *must* pay attention. We are less than a week away from your last shot and the Change. We *must* go over things. We understand that your responses are less human now. But you *must* retain a part of your humanity. Otherwise you can do us no good."

She let her head flop back down on her hands. She couldn't understand why Magister wanted to bother her now. Now was naptime. Later would be better.

Someone yanked her head up. It was Will. She lifted her lip at him, trying to snarl. The sound was too human and not nearly threatening enough. It was all she could manage.

"Look at her, sir!" Will was saying. "She's as bad as the Duane girl was. You thought that was because Duane was subnormal to begin with. But Lupe tested normal, even in the 120 range, very bright indeed."

Magister made a snorting sound. "Hmmmph. I don't think it's lack of intelligence, Will. Just a different intelligence. It's time we started thinking of her as a canine, and not as a human." He turned his head. "Emma—bring me that can. The red one. That's right." He held out his hand and the dark-haired trainer placed the can in it.

Opening the top, Magister took out a twisted piece of dried meat. "Lupe!" he said, dangling the strip by her nose.

Lupe sat up. It had taken him long enough! she thought. This time she listened, nodding her head at the appropriate pauses, and chewing with what she hoped was a thoughtful expression on her face.

It was one of those brilliant summer days that only the Canadian taiga south of the tundra seemed to produce, the sky beyond the forest a solid blue edging off to a bleached muslin color at the horizon. Snow-capped mountains thrust angrily upward and nearby an aggressive stream tumbled noisily over its rocks.

Lupe's hand went to the collar around her neck. She had told them over and over it was too tight, but no one had listened. Will had smugly informed her that it would fit the wolf just fine. She had bitten back the reply that *she* was the wolf.

Standing barefooted, the light cotton robe wrapped firmly around her, Lupe lifted her face to the slight breeze. She could smell an old scent of weasel and, overlaying it, wolverine. She wrinkled her nose, touched the collar once more, nervously waiting.

Magister came over to her. He smiled, not expecting any return on it. "Well, Lupe, this is the day. Our day."

"*My* day," she growled.

"Your success belongs to all of us. Green Messiah lives as you live," he said, his voice smooth and without affect. She knew he would not use the scolding voice now. Too much was on the line.

She nodded. It took great effort. Too much was on the line for her, too.

"We will withdraw now, to beyond that stand of pines. When you are ready, my dear, cast aside the robe and let the Change take you. You will know when it begins." He reached out and patted her hand awkwardly. She was in between now and she knew he was uncomfortable with her. Inside she was more wolf than woman, outside more woman than wolf. What she needed was integration. He was right. She would know when it began.

Magister signaled to the twelve graduate students and the two Green Messiah doctors with an almost imperceptible hand movement. They finished packing the equipment and loaded it onto the trucks.

Each of them, in turn, came to shake hands with Lupe. Only Emma gave her a hug. Will Sheddery barely touched her.

Magister was last. He held both her hands in his. "Go well, Lupe. Hunt the wind," he whispered. "And don't worry. We will track you with the collar. If there's any trouble, we'll be there for you at once."

Then he got into the last of the trucks and they rumbled across the stone-strewn field.

Lupe could hardly wait for them to leave. She had been ready for over an hour, her thighs wet with blood. Even before the last of the trucks was out of sight, she had ripped off the robe. Standing in the warmth of the sun, she raised her arms up, threw her head back, and began to sing.

Magister had not known, but *she* had known. There was more to the old tales than he suspected. She had memorized the spell from a book she'd found in his library, one of the fairy tales he'd dismissed. The words had settled comfortably in her mouth the very first time she'd spoken them. For she was not any old werewolf, she was *lobombre,* a Spanish werewolf. Like the one in the Goya print that her grandmother had on her kitchen wall.

Lobombre.
Sing wolf. Howl.
The mouth knows the morning,
The teeth the afternoon,
But the heart knows midnight,
And all the predations of the moon.
Sing wolf. Howl.

She sang it first in Spanish, then in English, and then, when the full Change came over her, in Wolf. Her eyes narrowed and she could see the wind. Her ears, now long, could hear the grass grow. She felt her hands tighten, the nails lengthen. Before they were completely paws, she reached up and ripped the collar from her throat, throwing it away from her.

When she could wave her plumed tail from side to side, she put her head back and howled. Then she raced off to the copse of trees, far away from the place where Magister and his students waited, to follow the bright steady scent of the pack.

P.O. 0003692439